This Is the Life

This
Is the Life

by Helen Chappell White

DOUBLEDAY & COMPANY, INC.

GARDEN CITY, NEW YORK

LIBRARY OF CONGRESS CATALOG CARD NUMBER: 54-9834

Contents

Preface

You will not find Middleburg on any map. Nor can you even know, should you reach the signboard which tells you that you are now entering its main streets, in what state you may be; for the legend written thereon reads only "MIDDLEBURG, U.S.A." It follows, therefore, that the Fishers, who live in Middleburg, appear in no telephone book or city directory, and nowhere are registered as voters.

And yet Middleburg and the Fishers are real, and known to thousands of us intimately, in the way we know our own homes, towns, and our own neighbors. They are real because they truthfully represent something that is real—and uniquely American. So from the first time we meet them on our TV screens we recognize them, and we understand their problems and enter into their pleasures, for the reason that these problems and these pleasures also belong to our towns and to us.

They are neither rich nor poor, these Fishers, neither "highbrow" nor ignorant. They are average, middle-class citizens; honest, industrious, intelligent, committed to the peculiarly American belief that education is for the masses and not merely for the few, devoted to their children, their church, their community, their country. We all know them, for there are many millions like them.

And yet, the Fishers are also different. They are different because, while living fully in this world, they yet dwell constantly in the light that shines from an unseen one. They are different because they are Christians who consciously and deliberately bring their faith into every hour of their lives, and every decision, large or small, which they make. And they are different because, in a fearful age, the Source of their strength and their serenity is so sure that they are entirely secure and unafraid.

This, then, is why so many thousands of us eagerly turn our dials to the stations on which the Fishers appear each week; this mingling of utter humanity and utter dedication. They are not saints or seers, to command our awed admiration but perhaps to daunt and discourage us a bit by the conviction that we ourselves could never attain such heights; they are simple, decent, kindly individuals doing quite ordinary jobs, and living rather uneventful lives in rather unremarkable circumstances—but making of those lives a joyous adventure, and achieving a certain grandeur, because of the absorbing interest of a great purpose and the illumination of a shining faith, which expresses itself in outgoing love.

The ten stories in this book are an attempt to retell, in story form, some of the dramas thousands have watched. They do not follow the scripts implicitly, but they are based on them. And the chief hope of the writer who has thus adapted them is just that the reader will recognize his old friends in this different medium; and will find in them here the same qualitites for which he has known them best and loved them most on the screen.

Helen Chappell White.

This Is the Life

1. THE BOOK OF THE FISHERS

*S*TANLEY FISHER had driven all night and was tired. Perhaps, he thought, it was this fatigue which had made him more vulnerable. At any rate, he was hardly prepared for the sharpness and the poignancy with which a flood of memories assailed him as his car entered the city limits of Middleburg. Quite clearly he saw himself five years ago, driving this same road but in the opposite direction; actually, for an instant, it was almost as if a ghostly car, furiously propelled by a white-faced young man, had passed him, this later Stanley, and disappeared into the distance of time.

Well, let it go! He'd been terrifically upset, thought the Stanley of today, his lips quirking in a half-rueful smile, that young man who was rushing away from Middleburg in such a hurry! He'd caught his girl having dates with another man—after she was wearing his ring—and it was as if the world had come to an end.

But it hadn't, of course. On the contrary, after an interval for readjustment it had jogged along very nicely. Stanley doubted if he'd thought of Ruth Harkness for at least a year, even fleetingly. Probably she didn't even live here now. She'd been a pretty kid—it was likely that she'd married and moved away. And Middleburg, which once had meant Ruth for him overwhelmingly, now meant only his cousins, the Carl Fishers and their three children, and his uncle, "Grampa" Fisher, whom he was looking forward to seeing once more, since business would keep him here for ten days.

As he turned into the residence section, he told himself that he had forgotten how pretty the town was in springtime. Nearly everybody here seemed to go in for gardening—he supposed they didn't rush around quite so strenuously doing other things as in some of the larger places. Tulips and jonquils made splashes of bright, bold color in the brilliantly green grass, and when he reached the block where Carl lived, there were so many blossoming trees that the place looked like a bridal bower. Carl had three in his own yard; and on the other side of his driveway, past a narrow strip of green, there was a border of gay spring flowers growing beside a shining white picket fence which evidently belonged to Carl's neighbor.

Stanley had written Anna that he would get there for breakfast if possible, and he judged that he must just about have made it. He honked vigorously to let them know he had arrived, and evidently the signal was heard and understood, for as he turned into the driveway a black-haired boy burst through the door and raced across the lawn. Freddie! And couldn't a kid grow clear out of recognition in five years! He'd been a baby, practically, when Stanley had seen him last, and now——

A split second later he was realizing ruefully that the time for "My-how-you-have-grown" type of musing was definitely not when a man was manipulating a car into a rather narrow drive. He found himself suddenly involved in a medley of violent sounds—the crash of splintering wood, the shriek of the brakes he involuntarily applied, the furious barking of a dog, and Freddie's shouts. He also found, as these sounds diminished slightly, that his car had left the driveway, smashed one end of the flower border, and all but demolished a section of the picket fence. Moreover, an excited dog, an unusually large collie who had evidently been behind the fence, was plunging toward Freddie, whom he doubtless, seeing no one else around at the moment, held responsible for this invasion of his domain.

Stanley wrenched the door open, leaped from the car, and administered a forcible kick in the collie's ribs. The animal, with an outraged howl, promptly washed its paws of the whole affair and streaked off down the street as Stanley bent over Freddie, who was sobbing, "Duke bit me!" and clutching a bloody leg.

At this point the entire Fisher family seemed to Stanley to materialize suddenly from thin air; there they were, at any rate, all around him, greeting him and exclaiming over what had happened all at once. Anna was on her knees in an instant, examining Freddie's bare brown leg.

"Doesn't look bad," she remarked, glancing up. "Just broke the skin. But I'd better clean it up. Don't cry, Freddie—it's nothing for a big boy like you to cry about!"

"It's n-not the b-bite!" wept Freddie. "It's just—I'm so disappointed—in *him*. I went out to see him 'fore breakfast—and he wagged his tail and licked my hand through the fence—I thought we was friends!"

"Well, Stanley, when you do make an arrival after five years, you come with a bang, don't you?" observed Grampa genially. He looked, Stanley noted, hardly a day older. "I wouldn't get my feelings hurt with Duke if I were you, Freddie. After all, he'd just met you—and if a strange car came smashing through the wall into *your* bedroom, *you* might jump on the first person you saw too. Well, here comes our neighbor!"

A worried-looking gentleman in his thirties had arrived on the scene, calling, "Hey, what goes on here?"

Carl, under conditions of some difficulty, managed a sketchy introduction—"Stanley, this is our new neighbor, Mr. Earl Miller —our cousin, Stan Fisher, Mr. Miller. Awfully sorry about this, Mr. Miller—Stan's had a little accident and injured your fence——"

"I don't care about my fence," said Mr. Miller, too agitated to acknowledge the introduction, breaking into the middle of Stanley's "Sorry—glad-to-meet-you" speech. "It's my dog—where's my dog? Duke—here, Duke!"

Stanley stared at him a second, frowning. Nice sort of neighbor his cousins had acquired! No manners, no manners at all. "The dog," he remarked deliberately, "got away after I kicked him in the ribs."

"You kicked *Duke?*"

"Naturally. If you'll look at Freddie's leg, Mr.—er—Miller, you'll see that your dog bit the boy severely."

Anna had straightened up, one arm around her son's shoulders. "Don't worry about it, Mr. Miller—it isn't a bad bite—a sharp nip, that's all. Come on, Freddie, I'll fix it up."

Mr. Miller wasn't worrying about it, Stanley thought indignantly, and that injunction on Anna's part was quite a needless one. Why, the chap barely spared a hasty, "I'm extremely sorry Duke did that—it's not surprising under the circumstances—but I'm *very* sorry, and relieved it's not bad," before turning to Stanley with a sharp, "You didn't need to kick him, Mr. Fisher! Just a word would have been enough—he's very friendly. . . . He was naturally frightened and excited. Which way did he go?"

"That way." Stanley gestured. "Of course, I'll have your fence fixed. And I'm sure the dog will come home."

"I'm not," said the dog's owner distractedly. "Ordinarily—yes. But his first day in a new place—getting scared—and *kicked*——"

Stanley broke into something Carl was trying to say. "Okay." There was an edge to his voice. "I'll get you another dog, too."

"Get me——" The offer appeared, for an instant, to strike Duke's master quite speechless. He merely stared at Stanley, outraged. "As if," thought that gentleman, wavering between amusement and exasperation, "I'd offered to get him another wife!" Carl intervened quickly.

"Duke's a very valuable dog, Stanley," he explained. "Got a lot of ribbons—and expected to walk off with a championship at the next dog show. He'll probably come back, Mr. Miller."

"You'll have to excuse me," said Stanley suavely, "if I'm rather more concerned about Freddie than about Duke—blue ribbons and all."

The blood mounted to the cheeks of Carl's neighbor. He turned his shoulder squarely on Stanley and spoke directly to the others.

"As I said before, I'm very sorry the boy was bitten. Since I had Duke behind a fence, I don't feel responsible. But I'm sorry. And now, if you'll excuse me, please, I'll get my car out and try to find my dog." He strode away—but paused after a few steps to toss curtly over his shoulder, "Of course, get a doctor to look at the bite. And send the bill to me. The animal's been inoculated, naturally."

"Well," Stanley remarked, looking after him, "I'm glad he admit's Duke *is* an animal. He acts like he thinks he's a person. Also like he believes I knocked down his fence and lost his dog on purpose. Disagreeable customer. That's one you'll have trouble with, Carl, if you don't put him in his place at the very start."

"Oh, I don't think so. He's just worried—they wouldn't even bring the dog here till they got that fence up—just got him from the kennel last night. And to tell the truth, Stan"—Carl's friendly grin took the sting from the words—"you rather put his back up, you know. Come on in now—let's get some breakfast. We were just sitting down when the excitement began."

Freddie was downstairs by the time they got in, rather proud of the bandage on his leg, and fully prepared to accept the attitude that Duke had made a natural error and that a small bite was nothing between friends.

"Just the same," said Anna, "I think I'd better take you by Dr. Bergen's on the way to school, Freddie, and let him glance at the place. I'll telephone Ruth that you'll be a little late."

Stanley, who was chatting with Emily, broke off involuntarily in the midst of a sentence, turning a startled face toward Anna. Almost in the next split second, he was irritated with himself. There were, of course, dozens of people named Ruth! But before he could resume his conversation, Anna, her blue eyes fixed on him with a slightly disconcerting steadiness, answered the question he had not asked. "Ruth Harkness. She's Freddie's teacher. He's lucky. She's one of our best. And a lovely girl."

"Never did understand, Stanley," rumbled Grampa amiably, "why you let that girl get away from you!"

No, he hadn't understood. Nobody had; except perhaps Anna. She had known most of the story. But she had known it from Ruth, and she had made it clear at the time that all her sympathy was with Ruth. This visit, Stanley thought wryly, was getting off on the wrong foot!

"Raking over old coals is a dismal occupation, Grampa," he said with a laugh—though his throat was dry. "And so many gals have gotten away since Ruth escaped, anyway! By the way—soon's I've had a shower and a little rest, I'll drop by the drugstore. I've got some business engagements—but I want to see that new soda fountain you've been writing Dad about!"

The household dispersed quickly after breakfast, to school and jobs, and Stanley, his shower over, found himself unable to doze. He tried to fix his mind on the business which had brought him

here, and to make plans—for he expected to place some large or-
ders for his wholesale firm with the local stores—but his thoughts
kept skipping around in an undisciplined way that annoyed him;
now they were back in the past, in that last violent scene with
Ruth, now they were jumping to the very recent encounter with
Carl's neighbor which had left such a bad taste in his mouth.
There was no possible connection between the two episodes: they
were widely separated in time and in importance; he could only
suppose that the link was that both had happened in Middleburg.
. . . But, wait! Didn't they, after all, in spite of radical differences,
have a little something in common besides just their locale? Ruth
had tried to put him in the wrong, hadn't she? And wasn't that
just what Mr. Miller also had been doing this morning? Why,
surely! Ruth had thought she could walk all over him—and so had
Mr. Miller. Well, Ruth had discovered that he wasn't that sort of
person; he hoped that there would be an opportunity to show Mr.
Miller the same fact.

He got up and began to dress, his thoughts running on busily.
It was important, he told himself, to be certain that one was a
positive personality, on whom nobody—*nobody*—could put anything over. One got nowhere in this world by being a door mat.
Door mats were made to be stepped on, and that's what always
happened to them. But it went even further than that, as a matter
of fact; it was in the nature of things that one portion of humanity
would invariably come out on top in relationships with people,
and in the dominating of situations—and the other portion simply
wouldn't. Stanley knew to which class he intended to belong. He
had always known.

As if he had reaffirmed a cardinal principle and gained confidence by so doing, he felt the vague, uneasy uncertainty which
had more or less haunted him from that first, unexpectedly vivid
memory of Ruth when his car had entered Middleburg, blowing
away like a mist. He smiled at his darkly handsome, boldly etched
features in the mirror, as he knotted his scarlet tie; and when he
strode across the lawn to get in his car—which Pete had backed
into the driveway after the accident—he was actually rather
pleased, in his regained self-assurance, to see the dejected figure

of Mr. Earl Miller getting out of *his* car, for he felt quite capable of handling him now.

"Well—did you find your dog?" he called with a slightly mocking cheerfulness.

Mr. Miller bristled and surveyed him with a distinctly unfriendly look. "Do I," he demanded acidly, "appear to have a large collie concealed about my person?"

"Oh well—as for that"—Stanley's voice was smooth—"I thought probably you wouldn't dare bring him back till the fence was fixed—a vicious, dangerous animal like that."

Mr. Miller's temper, plainly none of the best to begin with, flared. "I wouldn't bring him back till the fence was fixed, true, but for his own protection, not for anybody else's! The dog hasn't a vicious bone in his entire body!"

"Now, Mr. Miller! Tell somebody else that, not me! I was the one who saw him lunging at poor little Freddie with bared teeth, remember? If I hadn't scared him off, there's no telling what he'd have done."

Mr. Miller stared at him with a purpling face. "He'd have done nothing but what he did do—nipped the boy once out of sheer nervousness and excitement! Your entirely needless brutality is what has lost me a valuable dog—as if smashing my fence by your inexcusably careless driving was not enough——"

"I'm glad you mentioned my driving—brings up something I wanted to say to you." Stanley's pleasant feeling of confidence was growing. He reflected with satisfaction that the fellow who lost his control was always at a disadvantage; he, Stanley, was in perfect command of himself, and Miller obviously was not. "I'm not a careless driver—quite the contrary. And the more I think about it all, the more I feel sure that what startled me and made me leave the driveway as I did was that your animal suddenly rushed up to the fence and began making a fuss. I probably jumped—it would startle anybody—and that's when it all happened."

"Duke did *not* bark until after the crash!"

"You could swear to that, could you?" asked Stanley pleasantly.

Mr. Miller was looking now as if he had turned over a stone and something disagreeable had crawled out, but this time he did not shout or turn purple, as he had a minute before. He simply remarked in a tone that had gone curiously flat, "So that's the sort you are, is it?" and without another word turned and walked in the house.

Stanley drove off smarting and with a sensation of active resentment which increased with each block.

Grampa and Carl greeted him cordially and showed the improvements and expansions in their drugstore with evident pride. Grampa had just offered to make him a concoction which he declared was known as the "Grampa Fisher Special" and which was, he boasted, in great demand, when Anna telephoned. Carl put the instrument back in place looking thoughtful.

"It's about Freddie," he explained. "The bite's nothing much, just like we thought. But what concerns the doctor is that the dog is lost. You see, those rabies inoculations they give the dogs are not one hundred per cent effective. Ninety per cent, maybe—but not one hundred. And as Dr. Bergen says, any chance at all, even a remote one, of letting a child get anything as terrible as rabies is too much to take. So if Duke hasn't turned up by tomorrow he wants to give Freddie the Pasteur treatment."

"But why wait till tomorrow?" asked Stanley, concerned. "Why not just go on and give him the hypo today?"

"Because it isn't just a hypo, Stan. It's a whole series of hypos—lasts from two to three weeks—and it's put in the hip or stomach with a big needle. Children usually hate it. It's rather an ordeal, really."

Stan had an instant of acute discomfort. If Freddie had to take such a long and uncomfortable treatment, would it be *his* responsibility? The idea was so unpleasant that he quickly repelled it. He said indignantly, "People have absolutely no right to keep dogs that bite!"

There was an instant's silence. It was Carl who replied, slowly, and with a slight constraint, "I doubt if Duke bites—as a rule. It's in the blood of those collies to protect their owners' property. In any event, as Miller himself pointed out, the dog was behind a fence."

"Are you trying to say it was my fault?" demanded Stanley sharply.

"Of course I'm not. Merely defending Duke." And this time Carl accompanied the words by that warm, disarming smile of his.

"You're defending that whole Miller menage too much, to my way of thinking," said Stanley bluntly. He added reluctantly, "I suppose I'd really better do something or other about the fence this afternoon. I'll look it over and see what's needed."

"In the meantime," suggested Grampa with a grin, "how about that Grampa Special?"

Stanley tried to put aside his smoldering irritation. The trouble with these relatives of his was that they were too easygoing.

He reached home after a day of only fairly successful contacts (a fact which he laid on his discomposure over Miller's behavior) about half an hour before the rest of the family. No one but Anna was at home.

"Hello!" she said brightly. "A good day?"

"Not too good. All that business this morning—couldn't throw myself into it. Has the dog been found?"

Anna shook her blond head. "Mr. Miller telephoned a few minutes ago. He said he was putting an advertisement in the newspaper. I didn't tell him Freddie might have to take the Pasteur treatment—he was already so upset." She looked somewhat perturbed. "He seemed so—well, so stiff and offended. I didn't quite understand."

"He's that kind of fellow," Stanley answered shortly, dismissing a memory of a certain encounter that morning which might have provided another reason.

"He hasn't seemed to be—before. We've liked them so much. Maybe it's just because he's so worried—you see, he told me that the dog is their little girl's pride and joy. And they're fond of him too. So I guess he and his wife do feel bad about it."

"In other words," said Stanley angrily, "*you* won't even tell *him* that your child who was bitten by his flea-ridden mongrel may have to take a long, painful treatment—but *he* tries to make *you* feel just as bad as he possibly can!"

Anna giggled suddenly. "Flea-ridden mongrel! Heavens! I'm really glad they didn't hear you say *that*—we *would* be in trouble sure enough! Duke's got a pedigree long as your arm—and I assure you a flea would never be permitted more than two minutes' lodging on his aristocratic hide, the way they take care of him!"

Stanley snorted. "Don't get me more wrought up than I already am! Some prize neighbor you drew this time! Well, I certainly don't enjoy the prospect of fixing his fence after the way he's acted. But I guess I must. I'm going out and look it over."

One by one the other members of the family drifted in; from play, from baseball practice, from work. Each of them asked the same question first of all: "Any news of the dog?"

Stanley, back from his inspection of the fence and occupied apparently with the newspaper in the living room, listened with a little smile tugging at the corners of his mouth. He had some highly gratifying news to give them, but he was waiting for Carl —and Carl, today, came in last.

Like the others, he immediately received the news that there was as yet no word of Duke. "Well," he said with a sigh, "that's two things we must put on tomorrow's list—fixing the fence and starting Freddie's treatment. Where is the kid, by the way?"

"Upstairs," Anna answered. "He's not worried about the treat-ment—he'd fallen violently in love with Duke, and that's what's bothering him."

It was then that Stanley got to his feet, smiling.

"Well, I've got some news for all of you," he announced. "It doesn't help the situation about Freddie—and *that's* really what burns me up the worst. But it does give us an advantage."

Did those last few words bring a flash of misgiving to the five startled faces turned toward him? As if they were saying, "Now what is he up to this time?" The idea was a fleeting one, and so extremely disagreeable that he promptly discarded it.

"A few minutes ago," he said confidently, "I went out to look over the fence and decide what would be needed to put it in shape. Well, naturally the car had plowed up the ground a bit on either side—and guess what I uncovered! The survey stake for your property! I lined it up with the back one, which I found without much trouble, and here's the news! Miller's fence is built at least three inches over his line and on *your* property!"

Had they understood? They all looked curiously blank.

"But—I always thought the line was right along the flower bed," Carl said after a bewildered second. "The border has always marked the line—at least we've taken it for granted—we and the neighbors we had before the Millers."

"Well, either you or the stakes must be wrong. I don't think it's the stakes. I'll show you if you like—but I took surveying in college and I know I'm right."

"I imagine you are, Son." Grampa surveyed him pleasantly. "But what I don't get—why is that such great news?"

None of them got it. He saw, with a flash of impatience, that they didn't. What babes in the woods they were!

"I can't see what earthly difference it makes," Carl supplemented his father.

Stanley gave a mock-despairing shrug. "You can't? Then let me spell it out! You've got the law on your side now—if Miller gets tough, you can threaten to sue him."

Carl looked completely astounded. "Me sue Miller? What on earth for?"

"Why, Cousin Stanley—we wouldn't do that for *any*thing!" cried Emily. Pete and Anna merely stared at him.

Stanley spread his hands in a gesture of irritated frustration. "I simply meant that if Miller takes a notion to sue for the loss of his dog and the smashing of his fence you've got ammunition to fight back with."

"But I'm sure he wouldn't do that, Stanley!" cried Anna, puzzled. "I'm certain it's never occurred to him! And anyway, as far as the fence is concerned, it's going to be fixed."

"Not by me." Stanley's mouth set in a hard line. "Nor by you, if I've got any influence. If he'd been decent about it—shown a little concern for Freddie—been even halfway polite—why, it would all have been different. Under the circumstances—since he's behaved as he has—and knowing as I now do that I didn't knock his fence down at all, I knocked *yours* down, I won't put back one single picket." He looked around the circle and had the queer feeling that all the faces, young and old, had slightly withdrawn from him. It gave him again that sensation of uncertainty which he had found so disagreeable, and even painful, earlier in

the day. He could not bear being put in the wrong like this. He
cried, "Can't you see that you've got Miller right where you want
him now?"

"But the question is, Stanley," said Grampa gently, "are you
sure you know just where we *do* want Miller?"

"On top, apparently! Lording it over you all, stepping all over
you, having things all his own way——"

He stopped, slightly shocked at the anger in his own voice. And
Anna rushed into the breach, her blue eyes darkened with distress.

"Oh, let's don't talk about it any more for a while! My dinner's
practically ready—gracious, we'll all get indigestion arguing like
this before we eat! Carl honey, will you see that Freddie washes
his hands and comes on down?"

Stanley forced his face to relax. "Is that what you call a woman's
tact? We don't seem to see the redoubtable Mr. Miller alike, but
never mind that just now. I very well remember Anna's cooking,
and I admit it's a pleasanter subject."

Nobody mentioned the Millers or their dog again that evening.
Nor did anybody forget them. But one other small incident, not
related directly to the Millers, flicked Stanley on the raw. They
were playing one of the games the Fishers enjoyed, and at a certain contested point Stanley remarked, "Well, that's how I thought
it was spelled, but I suppose I *could* be wrong."

"Why, yes, Stanley—I think that's possible," answered Anna.

The voice was entirely quiet and pleasant. But—did he fancy it,
or was there an undercurrent in it? At any rate, it brought back
quite vividly an unwelcome memory. It was five years ago; he
and Anna were in this very room, and Anna was saying to him,
"Oh, Stan, you're dead-wrong! I know Ruth so well—I've known
her since she was a child—and she's friendly and impulsive and
gets into odd-looking situations sometimes just out of sheer kind-
heartedness, but she's utterly honest and utterly loyal!" He'd replied bitterly, "Loyal? I violently disagree!" And she'd said, a little
sadly, "But you might be wrong, you know—you might be wrong,
Stan, for once!"

"Your play, Stanley," said Grampa—and Stanley came back to

the present with the sudden, vehement wish that he had never set foot in Middleburg.

It was the next morning that he had another encounter with Mr. Miller. He had spent an hour in his room after breakfast, going over some papers before starting on his assignments for the day. Only Anna was in the house when he left, and he called good-by to her as he opened the front door. He had just reached the bottom of the steps when the Miller door opened and Earl Miller came out. There was something so purposeful in the manner in which he strode across the lawn toward Stanley that the latter knew at once that he had seen him come out and was now on the way to meet him.

"May I have one moment, please, Mr. Fisher?" he asked frigidly when he was within speaking distance. "I have no wish to repeat our discussion of yesterday. I merely want to ask you whether you are going to start getting my fence fixed today. Of course, I do not have a dog to put behind it at present—but I have not entirely given up hope of finding Duke, and I do not want to be at the expense of keeping him at a kennel if he is found."

Stanley thought, "He rehearsed that speech very carefully!" Aloud he said smoothly, "Well, Mr. Miller, that brings up some other points. In the first place, you will *have* to keep your dog at the vet's for a while, fence or no fence, for observation. Freddie is starting on the Pasteur treatment this afternoon."

He was pleased to see the other look surprised and taken aback. "But why?" he asked uneasily. "I told you Duke had been in-oculated."

"That's not one hundred per cent protection. In the absence of the dog, Dr. Bergen says he can't take any risk."

"I'm sorry for that—very sorry." For an instant the neighbor's voice lost all resentment and expressed only genuine regret. "My little girl took it once—it's tough and tedious. I'm fond of *Freddie*" —there was an emphasis on the name, Stanley noted—"and I hate for him to be put through all that." Then face and voice hardened again. "I still do not feel that it is my responsibility. And in any event, I repeat my question—when are you going to repair my fence?"

"That also takes a little discussion," said Stanley, and now he did not try to keep the triumph from his face. "It isn't a matter of repairing a section—it's a matter of moving the entire fence. I certainly do not think that's up to me. As the thing stands now, I didn't injure your fence, I injured my cousin Carl's."

"Now what in the universe are you trying to pull this time?" asked the other slowly.

"I'm not trying to pull anything. I'm simply explaining to you that you built your fence on my cousin Carl's property. Are you sure you didn't know it and take advantage of his ignorance of it to increase the area of your own property?"

"Oh, this is too much!" cried Mr. Miller, who was obviously by now practically at the hair-clutching stage. "In the name of reason, will you tell me what you're talking about?"

"I'll do better. I'll show you. When I came out yesterday to look over the damage and assess it, I found the original survey stake, and it's well over on *your* side of the fence. Here it is—you can see for yourself." Stanley strode to the place and pointed it out. "There's your line of demarcation—I lined it up with the back one, too, and there's no manner of doubt. So, Mr. Miller, instead of badgering me about repairing this one section, I suggest that *you* get busy and move the entire fence off Carl's property—and in a hurry!"

Yesterday, in his anger, the blood had mounted hotly to Miller's cheeks; this morning it drained away completely. He was white with fury.

"So that's the game! When Carl Fisher himself showed me where that line was——"

"Really? Are you certain he did? Can you prove it?" asked Stanley interestedly.

"No." Miller was looking at him again in that distasteful way. "I can't prove it. I didn't know then that I was dealing with crooks and would need proof——"

"Hold on, hold on!" Stanley felt his own temper slipping. "There are libel laws, you know! And anyway, our whole attitude might have been different if *you'd* been halfway decent——"

"If *I'd* been halfway decent—what a laugh from you!"

"Stanley—please, please!" cried a distressed voice. Stanley

whirled and saw Anna running across the lawn. She'd evidently overheard something—how much, he did not know. "Mr. Miller —please wait till Carl gets home, he'll explain all this——" she stammered.

But Earl Miller was past listening now. "I'm done talking to any of you! Your Carl and his cousin can do their talking to my lawyer from here on out."

She tried to say "Oh, you don't understand!" to his retreating back, but it did not pause or turn, that stiffly outraged back. It went straight on and the Miller door slammed on it. When Anna turned back to Stanley, he saw that she was very pale and that her blue eyes had darkened. "We've never, never had trouble like that with a neighbor before in all our lives!" she said slowly.

Something queer was happening inside Stanley's stomach. The uncertainty had come back; it was almost like fright—except, of course, that this was such an absurd idea. He tried to speak lightly.

"Well, honey, maybe you've never had a neighbor like this before!"

"No! No!" she cried. "It's that we've never had a guest like this before! I tried to make peace last night—and I shouldn't have, I was a coward. It all should've been talked out right then——" Suddenly she broke into tears and fled.

Stanley stared after her, and the uncertainty within had become at once an ache and an emptiness. There was nothing left in Middleburg now. Long ago he had lost Ruth, and now he had lost the Fishers. The only thing left was to pack and get to a hotel, finish up this business in this cursed town, around which (he realized at this moment) so much sentiment had clung for him for so long, and shake the dust of it forever from his feet.

He had started back up the stairs when Anna called him. She was standing at the foot, her face upturned pleadingly.

"Stanley—forgive me, please. It's just—I can't bear quarrels——"

"I think it's me you can't bear," he said harshly. "I just came back to pack and leave."

"Oh no! Oh, please, no!" There was no mistaking her distress for anything but genuine. It was written all over her expressive face. "I'd feel perfectly awful—all of us would! Why, you're our family and we love you! I only meant—oh, Stan, don't you see?

They're our neighbors and you should have let Carl handle it! Because we don't see it like you do—not a bit. But don't go off hurt with us—as if you'd been turned out! That would break my heart."

According to his own standards, he was being weak. "I'm afraid it's too late," he should have said, and gone ahead. But there was this treacherous softness within him, this surprising longing to stay on as one of them, and not to accept estrangement. He stood irresolute. "Please," she said again, and then he nodded.

"I know it's peace at any price for all of you," he said. "I'm not that sort—it makes it hard for us to understand each other. But— I'd like for us to stay friends."

"Oh, we must!" she cried earnestly. "Anything else is just—out of the question."

The ache was less now. He said, with some of his former confidence coming back, "You see, I don't happen to believe in turning the other cheek."

She stood there with one hand on the newel post, her face still upturned.

"Don't you?" she asked gently. "Don't you, Stanley? And do you happen to remember who said that?" As a matter of fact, he did not. "It was the same One who said 'Love thy neighbor,'" she said.

She smiled at him; she added as she turned to leave, "You'll be home for dinner, of course—have a good day." And he stood there, clutching the banister; stood until he heard her singing softly about her work somewhere in the back of the house. Then, slowly, he came downstairs again and went out to his car.

Freddie was in bed when he got home late that afternoon. He had had a slight reaction to his first shot and was a little bit feverish. Stanley, who had been nursing all day a growing feeling of wrong, a feeling that he had been rather cruelly misunderstood by this family for whom he had been trying to stand up, into whom he had been eager to inject more backbone, felt obscurely justified by the sight of the child's flushed cheeks and overbright eyes. Miller's dog had done this—and Miller acted as if *he* were the abused person! Yes—he, Stanley, was right to try to make these relatives of his, to whom he was truly and unselfishly devoted, see that people had to cultivate a little independence and

firmness in their dealings with others! Even if they resented it—
he was right. "Love thy neighbor" was a fine theory; in practice it
simply wouldn't always work.

He did not know how much Anna had told Grampa and Carl of
the scene that morning; in fact, he shrank a little from speculating.
But before supper Carl went to the Millers and returned in five
minutes, shaking his head in answer to Anna's questioning, anxious look.

"He wasn't at home. His wife—well, she really didn't give me
any chance to come in. She'd been crying. She said she was very
sorry about Freddie, but when I began to tell her that I felt this
matter had gone far enough and wanted to talk to her husband,
she must've misinterpreted me. She said it certainly had—and
that Earl was talking to his lawyer right then and would have a
report by now from a surveyor he'd had there earlier in the afternoon. Then she said good-by and shut the door."

"Oh *dear*," groaned Anna.

Stanley rose. "I'll go upstairs till supper is ready—chat with
Freddie awhile. But I'll just say this—if that doesn't prove that
I'm right when I say it doesn't pay to let people walk on you then
I don't know what would! There you go, leaving Freddie in bed
with fever, a doctor's bill piling up for you, bearing an olive
branch, all placating and apologetic—and for your pains you get
almost insulted and have the door practically slammed in your
face!"

They looked at him seriously, but neither of them answered
and he left the room in a dead silence.

After the evening meal was over and the dishes done, Grampa
went upstairs, taking his latest stamp album—an enthusiasm he
and Freddie shared—to entertain his grandson; Pete and Emily
departed on dates; and Stanley and Anna and Carl had just settled down in the living room and turned on TV when the doorbell
rang.

"It might be Mr. Miller," said Anna with a quick, rather nervous look at her husband. "Shall Stan and I leave?"

Carl shook his head. "Like to have you both stay."

It was indeed their neighbor; very stiff, very formal, very icy,
and obviously slightly startled by the hearty warmth of Carl's

greeting as he flung open the door. But if his face softened ever so little under its influence, it congealed again as he caught sight of Stanley.

"I wanted to talk to you about the fence," he said curtly to Carl, "and also to tell you about the dog. He's turned up. He couldn't find his way back here—he hadn't spent but one night here—so finally he went to the vet's, where we'd kept him while the fence was going up." A flash of pride in his pet's shrewdness appeared for an instant on his face like a fugitive gleam of sunlight, and was almost immediately lost once more in gathering clouds. "The vet telephoned me immediately, of course. He thinks the dog is in splendid condition and that there isn't one chance in a thousand that he could possibly have rabies. But he says he can't prove it without a few days of watching, so if you think Freddie had better continue the treatment a little longer—well, maybe we'd all feel safer." He hesitated. "We've been—quite distressed about the boy."

"We've never really worried about Freddie," said Carl pleasantly. "And *he's* been concerned about nothing but Duke. We're extremely glad the dog's found. As for the fence——"

Stanley interrupted. "I hear," he remarked briskly, "that you've had the property surveyed and hired a lawyer."

Mr. Miller looked at him coldly. "You heard correctly," he said.

"Stan——" Carl began.

Rebellion rose up in Stanley. Couldn't they understand that something important was involved for him? He broke in, his voice rising a little in spite of himself.

"You may all be interested to know that this afternoon I also consulted a lawyer! And from what he told me, it's you who are in trouble, Mr. Miller, not we!"

"If you think, sir," began the neighbor fiercely, "that you can threaten me——"

"I'm not threatening you—I'm telling you! And you're bluffing because you know you haven't got a chance in——"

"Stanley," said Carl sternly, "I must ask you to keep still and let me handle this in my own way!"

"But Carl——"

"But nothing! Sit down—and keep quiet!"

Smarting with humiliation, Stanley began, "You have no right——"

"This," Carl broke in pointedly, face grim, "happens to be my home. You will not be permitted to dictate my attitudes toward my neighbors." He turned his shoulder to Stanley and looked at Mr. Miller. "Mr. Miller, I've never had the slightest idea of bringing a lawyer or a surveyor into this, or of doing anything whatsoever except rebuilding your fence in the same place as promptly as possible."

"But you——" The other was staring at him. "But your cousin——"

"I know how my cousin feels. I couldn't agree with him less."

Mr. Miller was looking almost foolish with surprise. "I don't understand—this changed attitude of yours——"

"I'm trying to tell you," Carl explained patiently, "that my attitude hasn't changed. I simply haven't been give a chance to express it. And every member of my family feels the same way. We do not hold you in the least degree responsible for what happened to Freddie, we know you built that fence in perfectly good faith, those three inches matter not the least to us, and we are sorry for the hours of anxiety about your dog. And that's that."

There was a second's silence. "I don't know what to say," said Miller feebly. "The survey showed my fence *is* on your property——"

"My dear fellow, I tell you we don't *care!*"

Mr. Miller drew a long breath and seemed to struggle with a lump in his throat. "Well," he said a little huskily, "this is what I'd thought you were like—you Fishers—until——"

"Until I came?" asked Stanley suddenly, in a level, expressionless tone that made Anna shoot him a quick glance of troubled sympathy.

"That's right." But Miller's voice held no hostility now, even for Stanley. He spoke again to Carl. "I should have known better—even living beside you the short time I have, I should have known better."

Carl smiled. "We got off to a bad start on the whole thing—and it piled up. But we can forget it all now."

"I mustn't forget it," said his neighbor with a sort of rueful honesty, "till I've learned a few lessons from it. And I'm just as glad to say before your cousin, too, that I'm not at all proud of myself." He looked at Stanley. "You and I—we've been a couple of belligerent fools, young man!"

The turmoil in Stanley was so great that he could not respond to save his life. He stayed resentfully silent, head a little bent, drawn back in on himself. Miller shrugged and turned back to Carl. "At least you'll let me pay for Freddie's hypos, won't you?"

It was Anna who answered. "Carl gets a professional discount! Besides, we don't think Freddie will have many more. In a week he'll be romping with Duke."

"Well, thank goodness I agree with that last," said Duke's master heartily. "But in that case, you must let me fix the fence."

"We'll all fix it," suggested Carl. "Have a get-together Saturday afternoon and repair the fence and have supper together afterward."

"At *our* house!" Mr. Miller did not look like the same person, Stanley realized dully—so relaxed now, so friendly! "Beats me how I could have been such an idiot as to think you folks—— Well, no use talking any more about that! I'll get home and tell Rita now. And—oh yes—fire my lawyer!"

They all laughed. Good will seemed to fill the whole room—like warmth, like light, like fragrance, changing all the atmosphere. Mr. Miller glanced again at Stanley, who alone remained apart.

"Mr. Fisher—if I reacted disagreeably at first, I'm very sorry. Good-by, Mrs. Fisher—Rita'll be over to see you tomorrow, I know. Carl—you don't mind if we drop the 'Misters' now, do you? I'll be seeing you."

At the door he turned for an instant, smiling. "And I don't mind telling you the world looks just about one hundred per cent rosier to me right now than it did this time last night!"

When the door had closed behind him, Carl turned to Stanley, who had risen and stood leaning against the mantelpiece, face somber.

"Stan," he said sincerely, "I didn't enjoy speaking to you like that. I hope you'll try to understand. Miller was taking it for granted that your attitude represented ours. And I couldn't, I really couldn't, old man, let **you** go on speaking for me."

Stanley remembered his accusation against his cousins of "peace at any price." But Carl had been firm enough with *him*. He said slowly, "You spoke to me before a man who was almost my enemy as if I'd been a naughty four-year-old!"

"Yes," Carl agreed regretfully. "But you didn't give me much choice. A principle was involved."

Stanley made a quick movement. "But don't you see," he cried almost passionately, "a principle was involved for me, too? All my life I've believed that a man had to stand up for his own rights—otherwise he wasn't quite a man."

"Are you sure that's the principle at stake?" asked Carl quietly. "Because in this case the rights were so clearly on Miller's side. He built his fence where *I* told him to build it—and he kept his dog up till *you* smashed that fence."

It seemed to Stanley now as if his confusion were almost an audible thing; so many voices were crying, some one thing and some another, inside of him. Over their tumult he made one of the greatest efforts of his life to think honestly.

"Then let me put it this way. I've felt that a strong man ought to come out on top of things and people—ought to get the best of them—ought not to back down and cringe and admit he was wrong! And that's why I tried to fix it up so that you and I would get the best of Miller in this argument, show him we were the strongest. And after I talked to that lawyer, I said to myself, 'Now we can throw the book at him!'"

There was a little silence while Anna looked anxiously from one to the other. Then Carl said gravely, "I don't think we use the same book, Stanley. There's nothing in *my* Book about coming out on top or getting the best of anyone. Mine talks very differently. It tells me to love my fellow man. It goes further than that—it says I'm to do good to those who do wrong to me, and it says that the meek are blessed and shall inherit the earth."

"I never—" and now Stanley's tone held a hint of desperation, as if he saw something on which he had built his life crumbling —"never believed that would work!"

"It's the only thing on God's earth that will work, Stan!" With a dull wonder, Stanley saw the intense conviction that shone on his cousin's face. "Listen! Suppose I'd overplayed Freddie's in-

jury and forced a few dollars out of Miller—suppose I'd been able
to compel him, by law, to move his fence back those few inches!
He'd have built a new fence—and probably added several feet to
it for spite—and I'd have had a lifelong enemy living next door to
me, a man who wouldn't speak to me, whose wife wouldn't speak
to Anna. Is that a happy situation? What sort of 'working' would
you call that? The only thing this getting the best of the other
fellow 'works,' is bitterness and quarreling and hate!"

Stanley began, "But——" and stopped. But what? There must
be an answer—only just now he could not find it.

"There isn't any 'But.'" There was the barest hint of sternness
in the words. "The Golden Rule is the one that works, Stan."

Stanley summoned a last defiance. "Oh, all these rules——"

"It's a lot more than rules." The quiet voice was vibrant with its
earnestness. "It's a faith—a faith in God as a loving Father, and
in His Son, Jesus Christ, as the Savior of the world. It's a way of
life. God's way, the way He's taught us through Jesus." He half
turned, as if to leave, but suddenly turned back. "Don't think,"
he said, "that we're claiming—we Fishers—that we always live up
to our faith, our Book, Stanley! I've never thanked God that I was
not as other men, and there's hardly a day that I don't need to
say, 'Be merciful to me, a sinner.' But because Jesus died for my
sins, I always know I'll get forgiveness—and more, a brand-new
chance to start clean all over again and do better."

This time when Stanley tried to speak, no words at all came.

"Well," said Carl after a moment, "I'll go upstairs and tell
Grampa and Freddie the good news about Duke. And Stan——"
He broke suddenly into a smile; a smile which lent to his dark,
rather heavy features an almost singular sweetness. And on his
face and in his eyes there was such an utter, uncritical kindness
that for an instant it seemed to Stanley to flow out and wrap his
shivering, bruised, humiliated spirit like a warm, comforting garment. "We've been looking forward to this visit for a long time.
We think a lot of you, you know. I hope we can make the rest of
the time pleasanter."

They stood where he had left them, Anna and Stanley, till they
heard Freddie's joyous shout: "Duke come back? Oh boy, oh boy!"

And then Anna moved to where Stanley still stood by the mantelpiece and laid her hand on his arm.

"Stanley"—she spoke almost falteringly, her blue eyes troubled and uncertain—"I'm half afraid to say this. Please don't be angry! It's something I came to know about you five years ago, when Ruth confided in me——"

She felt the hand beneath her arm stiffen, realized that he had jerked his head up and was looking at her almost fiercely. And she hurried on, speaking fast, as if she feared her courage would give out.

"I found out that you admire strength and you want awfully to feel strong. But—forgive me, Stanley—I think you've got the wrong idea of what being strong means. That time, for instance, when you were so angry with Ruth—— Oh, please, don't jerk away, let me tell you just this once! It wasn't really that you believed, deep down, that Ruth had been untrue to you—nobody *could* believe that about Ruth! It was that other people teased you and you felt she'd made you look foolish—and your pride was hurt—and you had to show how strong you were by making her get down and beg your forgiveness for something she hadn't done. . . . Stanley, wait just a minute! Well, she couldn't do that—she's too honest. And you wouldn't let her get the upper hand—remember telling me that? That was what you said—the 'upper hand.' Only Ruth never wanted the upper hand. She just loved you and wanted you to love and trust her."

She stopped, her eyes searching his face anxiously. And he asked, in a hard, level voice, "Are you through, Anna?"

"No!" Just for an instant a little sharpness flared in her tone. "You called that being strong and being positive and standing up for your own rights! Can't you see that by *that* standard Hitler was strong and Jesus, willingly dying on the Cross, was weak? Oh, Stanley!" The voice had softened again, become almost pleading. "You're paying so high, so terribly high, for this wrong idea of strength! You've lost five years when you and Ruth might have been happy—and goodness knows how many other things, like sweet and pleasant friendships for example, you've lost, too! I can't bear it! If only you'd take Carl's Book—our Book—for yours and learn——"

She was not, as Stanley knew well, an aggressive woman. Only
the most urgent interest and concern, the most urgent sense of the
great importance of what she'd tried to say could have driven her
thus uninvited into his private life, made her uncover for his own
view his mistakes and weaknesses. And now, suddenly, the feeling of her own presumptuousness was too much for her; she broke
down and, putting her face into her hands, began to sob.

For half a minute then, those sobs were the only sound in the
room. Then Stanley took the shielding hands down and gently
wiped her eyes.

"Don't!" he said. "Don't!"

She looked up at him uncertainly. "You're not angry?"

He shook his head. He could not tell her. Not angry. Just, suddenly, in the flood of realization, heartbroken. But then—maybe!—
didn't the Fishers' Book say something about a broken and a con-
trite heart . . . ?

In the silence Freddie's little voice rose, chattering excitedly
above them: ". . . and why don't we fix *us* a fence and get a
puppy, Pop, why don't we?"

"Anna . . ." said Stanley, and stopped and swallowed painfully,
and began again, the words coming slowly, with difficulty, "Carl
was talking about forgiveness—and a fresh start. But—seeing your
sins and getting clean of them, wonderful feeling as it must be—
even *that* can't undo their consequences, can it? I mean—if you've
smashed something you've smashed it. And if you've thrown it
away—why, it's gone. What I'm saying is—even when we're sorry
and know ourselves forgiven and begin all over again we still have
to live with the consequences of our old mistakes and sins, don't
we?"

Her eyes were steady and grave on his. "Sometimes we do,
Stanley. Though even that's different, because we start to build
again. But other times—smashed things can be repaired and things
we've thrown away can be found again."

This time he literally could not speak. Trembling, afraid to trust
the half promise of hope that her words seemed to hold, his eyes
clung to hers with a silent, anguished questioning. And she said,
hesitating a little, "I saw Ruth this morning. I told her you were
visiting us."

The words came now, but in a husky croak, not like his voice. "What—did—she—say?"

Anna's eyes had sharpened on his face in a long, keen, searching glance; he looked back helplessly, not trying to keep any emotion from showing, all his defenses broken, all his artificial barriers down. And whatever she read in his face, it seemed to give her the assurance she was seeking from him, for her own face brightened almost into radiance of a sudden.

"Why—nothing!" But her voice was singing. "Nothing at all, Stan. She's so controlled, you know—and all these years she's been so wonderful, going ahead with her job in such a grand way, always cheerful, keeping her chin up and helping so many folks! But today I took her by surprise—coming out with it so suddenly like that! And she couldn't answer, she couldn't say a word. Because she was crying so hard—— Why, Stan! Why, Stan dear!"

Stanley was crying too, for the first time since he had been a small boy. But it was all right. They were not tears of despair, but tears of hope; not tears of weakness, but of the promise of new strength. And clearly, through their mist, he saw gleaming in rainbow colors the road of that fresh start, that different beginning again, that shining other chance, which would surely unfold itself before him when the Fishers' Book should have become truly *his* Book.

2. A BIRTHDAY WISH FROM JENNIE

*I*T WAS late in the afternoon, and that atmosphere of mingled relaxation and anticipation which marks the end of a day of work and the beginning of an evening when one can blessedly do as one pleases was spreading over the Baxter Metal Works. Roy Baxter, its owner and president, usually the last to leave, was the first to close his desk today, and as he strolled out of the building, his heart warmed to the genuine friendliness of the faces that looked up to call cheery good-bys to him.

Now what was it, he thought, that that psychology chap who'd lectured at the Civic Club last month had said? Something about the spirit of the head of any organization spreading right on down through the whole business, so that a grim, sour executive who had no personal interest in the people working for him managed to make everybody, even those who didn't come into direct contact with him, discontented. And vice versa, of course. Something almost mystic about it, the fellow had declared. Roy felt, with humility and a deep sense of satisfaction, that his folks, thank God, were happy in their jobs, loyal to him and to the Works. And a wonderful feeling it gave a man, too.

The street, as he stepped into it, was lit by the apricot-gold glow of an unusually beautiful sunset; and to Roy this evening, with that glow reflected in his own heart, it seemed to irradiate even the faces of the people hurrying by on their several ways home—faces many of which he knew, faces smiling a greeting at him—and to lend them a peculiarly mellow benignity.

He was not an unusually expressive man; his thoughts, as far as he put them into words, were just, "Finest town, finest people on earth!" But as he walked on toward Fisher's Drugstore, he was experiencing one of those rare moments of soul-deep contentment and fulfillment which come to a man occasionally, when everything seems to converge in harmony.

Carl Fisher, stepping forward to meet him when he came into the store, with that smile which always made you feel he was very especially glad to see you, was a part of the mood, blending with it and strengthening it. So was Grampa Fisher, working at the back, who looked up to wave at him. There was something, Roy thought wonderingly, some unique quality, which made the Fishers a little different even in as fine a town as Middleburg. All of them had it—even little Freddie . . . But what was it? Hard to say because the queer part was that they were exactly like everybody else, in a way—the most easygoing, comfortable, everyday sort of folks imaginable. But there it was—in some fashion all their own they were special, and Middleburg wouldn't be Middleburg for dozens of people without them.

He told Carl, in answer to inquiries, that sure he was fine, and yes, business was fine too, and so were Nina and Jennie, and how about reaching back on that shelf and getting him some bunion plasters for Jennie?

Carl laughed. "What's Jennie want with bunion plasters when she won't wear shoes? For Sundays, I guess."

" 'Fraid even her old house slippers are rubbing now," Roy answered, and added soberly, "When feet have been used as long as Jennie's, and always in the service of other folks, I guess they've got a right to hurt. She'll be seventy next week, you know."

Carl looked surprised. "I might have known—if I'd stopped to figure out. But the years have got a way of slipping up on a fellow —Jennie seems about the same age to me now that she seemed when she used to feed us cookies and lemonade under the big oak tree in your yard."

Roy grinned. "Well—Jennie was thirty-three when we were six. To a six-year-old that's ancient. I wasn't but three when she came to my mother—forty years ago. But except for her feet she's just about as lively now as she was then."

Wrapping the plasters, Carl nodded. "I know all about that. One of the most energetic workers in our church."

Roy frowned slightly. "She overdoes that church-work business. But Nina tells me I'd better keep quiet—that both of us are going to have to get into Heaven holding on to Jennie's apron strings! No use talking anyway. The church is half her life."

"And you're the other half," Carl said with a smile.

"Well, she's a pretty big slice of mine," Roy admitted, and a little embarrassed by his own display of sentiment, added a slightly hurried good-by and gave way to another customer.

Nina and Jennie were in the kitchen when he reached home. Nina had evidently just come through the basement door, for it still stood open, and she was bearing two jars of preserves. She put them down and ran toward him, her face lighted by the look that was always especially for him, just for him, and this too became on the instant very deeply a part of the golden contentment that was still flooding him. So did Jennie, smiling at him from the stove, where she stood, the warmth of a devotion she had never once expressed, but of which he was sure as he had been of his mother's, glowing behind the quiet eyes. Built on heroic lines was Jennie, wide of shoulder and hip, with a broad, craggy face. All her beauty was on the inside; the only part that could be discerned from the outside was what glowed through. But for those who had the eyes to see that was enough; in her own way Jennie was beautiful.

Roy kissed his wife and handed Jennie the small package from the drugstore. "Present for you," he explained. "Noticed you were limping even in your slippers this morning."

Jennie tore the wrappings off and Nina, peering at its contents, protested.

"For mercy's sake—do you call bunion plasters a *present?*"

"Why, that's a right nice present—thinking of a body's comfort," said Jennie serenely. "Besides, I don't know as I ever *was* much of a one to get romantic presents from the gentlemen!"

"This ain't no gentleman, this is my husband, and I still think he's a heel to make you believe he'd brought you a *gift* and pro- duce bunion plasters!" Nina gave her husband a shove toward the door, laughing. "Now let's get out of Jennie's way while she finishes dinner. Jennie, there's the preserves on the table."

But the preserves had reminded her of something, and in the living room she turned to Roy.

"Roy! Those basement steps! I was really scared to touch that shaky railing as I came up. I keep telling you——"

"You do indeed," Roy agreed. "And I keep going out to play golf Saturday afternoons, don't I? That's what I'm doing this Saturday, too. Now hold on—don't say it! I didn't forget, I've fixed it all up. Jake's coming to do it—that's the solution."

"Brilliant—must've taken you hours to work that one out," scoffed Nina. "Bother—there's the phone."

"I'll answer." Roy was still smiling as he picked up the receiver, but as the brief conversation proceeded the smile faded. When it was over, he looked distinctly rueful.

"Something on hand at the plant—can't imagine what it is, I've just left. But Doug seems to have the wind up and says he'd better talk to me about it right away. Be back as soon as I can—sorry, honey."

And he was sorry; sorrier, really, than the small incident and the postponed dinner warranted. Because the perfect mood had been clouded by the worry in Doug's voice. He found himself wishing that, whatever it was, his conscientious assistant had let it wait till morning.

Doug was waiting for him when he reached the office, his pleasant, rather serious face wearing a look of concern.

"Hated to bother you," he apologized. "But—well, I thought you ought to know right away. A representative from Lawson Brothers came just after you left—about that big batch of angle irons we sold them last week."

"What about them?" Roy asked sharply.

"Complaints from their customers. The irons are just breaking on the job. They sent one back by the messenger—look!"

Roy sat down at his desk and studied the two broken pieces incredulously. "Broken squarely in two! But I don't understand——"

"Well, I've been thinking—that metal we bought in the bankrupt auction. Suppose it might have been faulty?"

A line came between Roy's brows. "I don't know. I just never thought to test. Mistake, I guess. Well, what do Lawson Brothers want us to do about it?"

"Replace the entire stock with another shipment which we absolutely guarantee to be okay," said Doug ruefully.

"Ouch! All right—nothing else to do, I guess. Fix it up first thing in the morning, will you? Sorry—but there it is." He was rising as he spoke. "I'll be getting back to dinner."

"But Mr. Baxter——" Doug began, and stopped.

Roy turned and looked at him, surprised at the urgency in his voice. He asked impatiently, "Well, what?"

"You—you can't just leave it like that, can you? I—I mean"— Doug was stammering a little in his earnestness—"Won't we have to call in all the other shipments, too?"

"All the other—— Great grief, Doug, are you crazy? Have you any idea what that would cost us?"

"A very good idea. It's just—just that I don't see what else we can do. Because if that auction metal *was* faulty and we mixed it with the regular stock, there's just not going to be any way of telling which angle irons are substandard."

Roy had picked up his hat; he threw it down again almost violently. The last trace of his lovely sense of well-being had vanished now and he resented it. Why in the world did a mess like this have to happen to a man who had bought in good faith and paid a fair price?

"I see what you mean." He tried to keep his tone level and reasonable. "But after all, there's a very good chance that all the bad ones are in that Lawson batch. It doesn't seem good sense to pull all the rest in, too. Besides, it would undermine confidence in the Works."

"It's not up to me to tell you what to do." Doug spoke with a certain slow stubbornness. "I realize that. And of course Lawson Brothers might be the only kickback. But then again—they might not. It's—it's a chance I don't see how we can afford to take."

In the silence of the office Roy's fingers beat a nervous tattoo on the desk. After a moment he said irritably, "It's just too big a loss." He thought of the new car he had promised Nina. He thought of the trip they had planned for the summer. He wished Doug would say, "Well, on second thought, I guess you're right." But Doug, his honest, troubled eyes on his chief's face, was silent.

Roy drew a long breath and made up his mind.

"I can't do it, Doug. I'm sorry if you disapprove, but I simply don't think such drastic measures are necessary. We'll handle each complaint when—or if—it comes up. That's my considered decision."

This time Doug's eyes swerved from his. He got slowly to his feet. "Well, Mr. Baxter," he said heavily, "you're the boss." He was moving toward the door that led to his own office, but with his hand on the knob he turned back. "Sorry to have called you away from your dinner, sir. And—and I sure hope you're right."

Driving home, Roy felt thoroughly disgruntled and irritated. Doug ought to be able to see that there was a difference between honesty and quixotism.

"I could go into the bank tomorrow and borrow ten thousand dollars just on my signature," he said silently and angrily. And then, strangely, it seemed to him all of a sudden as if the unseen opponent with whom he was arguing was not Doug any longer but Carl Fisher. Or maybe Grampa. Or both. They looked at him with eyes that were serious and sorry, and Roy gave the wheel a vicious twist.

"Now look here, Fellows," he cried, though without making a sound, "you're druggists. I don't tell you how to manage your drug business, do I? Then don't you go telling me how to manage my metal business!"

And then, since nobody but himself was telling him anything, he had to laugh—a bit ruefully. Just showed how he'd let Doug upset him. Maybe he'd better not tell Nina any of it. You never could, he thought uneasily, predict exactly what reaction you'd get on business matters from a woman.

As it happened, Nina accepted his halting explanation casually; her mind was on something else. She wanted to talk about Jennie's birthday.

"She's been so wonderful to us, Roy," she explained, eyes bright. "Like a mother, really. All my community work—in the Club and the League of Women Voters and the rest—why, I'd never have been able to do it without Jennie here at home! And she's such a

grand person, so heavenly unselfish. Let's show her this once that
we appreciate her. Let's make it a marvelous birthday."

"A Jennie's Day?" Roy suggested, smiling. "Well, why not? We
have a Mother's Day and a Father's Day—why not a Jennie's Day?"

"Fine!" said Nina, face glowing. "And I won't let her do one lick
of work that day—I'll do it all, every single thing!"

"Maybe you'll get by with that. I'm not sure that Jennie will
like sitting on a cushion and sewing a fine seam!"

"Well, she might try it for just one day in her whole life and
find out!" retorted Nina.

So it was settled. Jennie would "take it easy" that day. In the
afternoon Roy would take her for a nice long drive while Nina got
the dinner. And the big moment, the real celebration, would be in
the evening. They'd ask Carl and Anna to dinner, and they'd
have all the dishes Jennie loved best, and finally they'd bring in
the big pink and white birthday cake all gleaming with candles—
and Jennie, of course, must blow them out and make a wish. Last
of all they'd go in the living room and open the presents.

"And you can give her something useful if you like," Nina said to
Roy. "But *I'm* giving her something glamorous."

"I think my present will look glamorous to Jennie—if not to anybody else. I took her old slippers to an orthopedist, and I'm having
a pair of health shoes made. They'll cost fifty dollars and they'll be
worth every penny of it if they help Jennie walk with comfort,"
Roy answered.

The next day they announced the program to the honoree, who
protested against being exiled from her kitchen but could not keep
from going dewy-eyed with touched excitement. And while she
continued to protest when the day arrived, there was no doubt but
that she was enjoying being made, for a little while, the center of
things by her beloved "children." Still insisting that there "was no
sense to Nina doin' all that work," she was carried off, beaming,
by Roy for the ride. The Fishers were just arriving as they came
home. And so, in due time, the climax of all the planning was
reached and Jennie was ushered, flushed, a little embarrassed, and
very happy, into the flower-decked dining room and seated with
a flourish at the head of the table.

"My job, Jennie," said blond Anna, smiling at her, "is to sit right here beside you while Nina waits on the table—and pull you firmly back every time you try to get up and do it yourself!"

"I wouldn't want the job of bossing Jennie, myself," grinned Carl. "I'm so used to being bossed *by* her at the church I probably couldn't control her here!"

"Go 'long—nobody bosses anybody at our church," said Jennie serenely. "We all work together."

"True." Carl looked at Roy. His mouth was smiling but his eyes were suddenly serious. "Why don't you and Nina come with her sometime, Roy, and see for yourselves?"

"I'm always meaning to," said Nina penitently.

Roy shrugged. "I like my Sundays at home. Anyway—we don't have any children—we don't have to be Examples to the Young like you and Anna."

"Jennie doesn't have any children either," Anna observed quietly.

"Maybe Jennie's trying to be an Example to us," Nina suggested, but Jennie cried "Oh no!" so earnestly that they all laughed.

They managed to keep her in her seat during dinner, and she even sat fairly quiet, fidgeting only a little, while Nina changed the plates for dessert. But when the big cake was set in front of her and they all sang "Happy Birthday" in traditional style, ending "God bless you, dear Jennie, Happy Birthday to you!" the scene threatened for a moment to become emotional. Jennie frankly choked, and made no secret of mopping the tears away.

Roy came to the rescue with a reminder that she must blow out the candles and make a wish; and Jennie, smiling and blinking the mist from her lashes, drew in her breath, then let it out in a mighty puff and extinguished every one.

"Well," cried Nina when the clapping and laughter had ended, "what is your wish?"

"Oh, I can't tell that," Jennie answered, twinkling mysteriously. "It wouldn't come true if I did."

Carl smiled at her. "Bet I know!" he said, and Jennie blushed and put one finger to her lips.

In the living room they seated her in an armchair beside a table covered with brightly wrapped packages. Roy even got an ottoman for her feet, and she hoisted them up, with a somewhat rueful smile for her old slippers.

"I oughta keep 'em under the chair—they're nothing to show off," said she.

Roy patted her hand. "Who cares? Now this is from Nina!"

Nina had bought her three gifts in all, each one carefully frivolous. There was a bottle of cologne in a graceful flask, and Jennie held it up to the light and exclaimed at the way its clear amber gleamed; then she took the top off, sniffed it, and passed it gravely around for the others to smell. There was a bunch of artificial violets which she sat turning over, saying delightedly, "I declare they look just like real!" And there was a necklace of blue-green stones which obviously entranced her. Anna had made her two gay blue-and-red-checked aprons, and Carl had brought a box of candy.

"I declare you folks must've thought I was a debutante or something!" she said with shining eyes.

Last of all, Roy handed her his present.

"It's awful big!" she remarked wonderingly.

But when she had removed the bright paper and ribbon and seen what was inside, she was all but struck speechless. She knew what shoes like that cost; she had once priced them.

"Let's try them on!" cried Roy boyishly, and he knelt in front of her, pulling off her old slippers and helping her adjust the new shoes. And when they were on, Jennie stood up and began walking around the room, a bit gingerly at first, then with increasing confidence and an ever growing brightness on her face. "Why, it feels like walking in my bare feet!" she cried. "I don't want to sit down—I just want to keep walking, it feels so good!"

Her eyes came to Roy's with such glowing, inarticulate gratitude and affection that he felt his throat tighten a little. He'd done so little to get a look like that, he thought humbly. And suddenly then, for no especial reason, he thought about the substandard angle irons and felt a twinge of deep discomfort.

"And now," Jennie's sweet old voice was saying, a bit shyly, "I've got presents for all of *you*. They're in the basement—I'll go and get them."

"Tell me what they are and I'll get them," said Roy.

"You'd never find them. I meant it to be a surprise, but——"
She paused. "I made some cinnamon-stick preserves!" she said
triumphantly, unable to keep the secret. "Even Nina didn't know.
And there's a big jar for each of you!"

She waved away the enthusiastic chorus of thank yous, trying
to be nonchalant, but immensely pleased; and waved away, also,
their renewed insistence that one of them could surely find the
jars.

"I want to try my new shoes on the stairs!" she said, and walked
out of the room with a step almost springy.

"I haven't tasted any of that cinnamon-stick preserve for years,"
remarked Carl.

"And you won't for years to come after this is gone—unless
Jennie makes us some more," said his wife. "*I* can't make it for
you."

"Isn't it aggravating?" Nina agreed with a little gurgle of
laughter. "I follow her exact recipe and it doesn't turn out even
remotely like——"

The scream cut into the pleasant, ordinary words with shocking
suddenness. And even as they sprang to their feet, the crash and
the terrible soft thud that followed it cut off the scream as
quickly as the scream had cut off Nina's sentence. They raced to
the kitchen, Roy in the lead shouting "Jennie!"—and terror went
with them.

The door to the basement stood wide open. The basement
light was on. And they saw the sagging, broken rail on which
Jennie had rested her heavy weight as she went down the steps,
and they saw Jennie on the cement floor at the bottom, very still
and queerly twisted.

It was Roy who reached her first and knelt beside her, feeling
for her pulse.

"She's alive!" The words came on a sob. "Thank God—she's
alive!" His voice sharpened. "We mustn't move her! Carl—quick!
Phone the hospital—get an ambulance—get the doctor!" He bent
his head till his lips just touched her hair. "Oh—*Jennie!*"

They seemed to have waited hours there in the hospital waiting-
room. Nina looked mechanically at the bright upholstery and

drapes, which she, as a member of the Ladies Hospital Auxiliary, had helped plan and raise money to get. She had thought at the time that perhaps the colorful patterns would lend a little cheer to anxious hearts—but now she did not even see them.

"I don't understand it!" she burst out. "I just don't! Jake's such a good workman—and he fixed that railing only last Saturday. Roy inspected it and said it was a fine job!"

Roy had sat, for most of that interminable hour, forehead leaning on hand, not speaking. Now he raised his gray face. It wore an expression that made Nina say to herself, half frightened, "Oh, Roy is taking this terribly hard—*too* hard!" His voice, when he spoke, was flat and harsh.

"The sooner I explain about that the better. I've got to put Jake in the clear—with everybody. His work was all right. I went back and looked—after the ambulance had taken Jennie. It was the angle iron—it broke in half. I telephoned Jake while you were upstairs getting your wrap, Nina, just before we came to the hospital. He said he got the iron at the Sunset Hardware Store. The Sunset people are customers of *mine*."

They were all looking at him, puzzled and troubled by something dark and anguished beneath the words.

"That doesn't make you to blame, Roy," Carl said gently. "You mustn't let yourself feel like that. You didn't know the iron was defective."

Roy's lip twitched.

"It's not quite like that. I knew the whole lot were likely to be defective. I knew a week ago. Doug wanted to call in the entire stock then. Remember the night I went back, Nina? But I wouldn't. I said we'd take a chance. I didn't want to lose the money." He repeated the words bitterly, "I didn't want to lose the *money*."

"Oh, Roy! Oh, darling!" cried Nina, and her hands went out to him.

But Roy moved his own hands from under hers.

"Save your sympathy for Jennie—she's the wronged one," he said in a hard, tight voice.

Carl spoke quickly as Nina shrank back, hurt. "There's the doctor, folks."

They all sprang to their feet to meet him, and Dr. Bergen thought a little sadly how often he had seen people like this, their shoulders braced for whatever news he might be bringing, that expression of mingled hope and dread on tense faces turned toward him. It was Nina, swallowing, who asked the question.

"How—how is she?"

"She's got a pretty good chance. But——"

Roy tried to ask "but what?" and found that his throat had closed. The doctor thought, "Why, he loves her!" and wished for the thousandth time that he knew some good way to break bad news. He sighed and gave it to them straight. "She won't walk again. Her back is broken."

He watched with helpless sympathy the stunned silence in which they received the words and waited patiently for the arguments which years of experience had taught him would come next. "But there must be something——" "Are you certain, Doctor?" . . . "Maybe an operation——" . . . "We'll do anything—take her anywhere—spend any——"

He broke in quietly but firmly.

"Get another opinion if you like. All you want. But I'll guarantee they'll all be the same. At her age—with that sort of break—there isn't a chance."

"Oh, Roy!" Nina turned to her husband, burying her face in his shoulder. He stood stiffly; he seemed hardly aware of her.

"You know something, Doctor?" It was a queer, flat voice, not like Roy's. "You know something funny? Tonight was her birthday. And I gave her a pair of shoes. It *is* funny, isn't it? On the very night when I was going to cripple her for life I gave her——"

The doctor interrupted; this was another thing with which he was thoroughly familiar, that tendency people had to blame themselves and get guilt complexes when disaster struck someone they loved. So he said firmly, "I'm writing you a prescription for a sedative, Mr. Baxter. Carl, fill it for him on the way home, please, and see that he takes it tonight."

Carl nodded. But thinking with a sick pity of what Roy had just told them, he was saying to himself, "I wish I could give him the only prescription that's really going to help him!" He'd fill Dr. Bergen's prescription and refill it often, he was certain, in the weeks to come; and all it would do would be to give Roy a few uneasy hours of unsatisfactory rest. While all the time, just at hand, was a different sort of prescription that would bring him real peace. Well, thought Carl, maybe Jennie herself could help him find it, for it was one that Jennie knew how to compound. However—his fancy ran a little further with the symbolism—you could compound a prescription, you could even give it to the patient, but you couldn't make him take it.

They brought Jennie home from the hospital five weeks later. Roy had lost flesh in those five weeks, and Nina was beginning to watch him anxiously and to look tired and drained herself. Beyond calling in all the angle irons, he had hardly concerned himself about his business at all. Doug had run it, and he had spent the time trudging back and forth from the hospital, sitting on a chair inside Jennie's room, or waiting on another just outside her door. And now she was home with a practical nurse who stayed all day to look after her; home with her serenity undimmed, insisting that she was going to enjoy lying abed and being lazy. Once she said gently, her troubled old eyes on Roy's haunted, haggard face, "I won't be idle, Roy. It gives me lots of chance to pray. Maybe the world needs folks with more time to pray." Roy had answered drearily, "Maybe so, Jennie," but his blank eyes told her how little meaning the words held for him.

The nurse always left after giving Jennie her supper, and Nina had bought a little bell for her to ring in the night if she needed attention. It was two o'clock of the fourth night since she'd returned that Roy slipped quietly from his wife's side and went out to the kitchen. The doctor had said he must cut down on the sedative—and he'd lain there so long, it seemed, staring hot-eyed into the darkness, trying not to disturb Nina, that it had occurred to him that it might help if he heated some milk. He wanted desperately to sleep—but whenever he closed his eyes he kept seeing Jennie's face as it had looked when they'd carried her, four days ago, through her beloved kitchen to the bedroom on the other side, the bedroom she'd used so long. She hadn't said a word, she hadn't wept—but he had seen her eyes going from spotless stove to gleaming refrigerator and sink, taking a silent farewell of each of these tools of a trade which, however humble, she had loved

and made beautiful by a spirit of service. And he had heard the
one involuntary little choked sob that tore its way up through her
throat as they took her through the door and past the sight of it all
and laid her down on the bed which must hereafter be her home.

Before he turned on the kitchen light he tiptoed over to close
her door. But as his hand touched the knob her voice spoke.

"Nina—Roy—who is it?"

"It's me, Jennie," he said quickly. "Sorry I waked you."

"I wasn't asleep. Roy, please come in."

Roy came in and turned on the pink-shaded lamp. "Can I get
you something?" he asked anxiously. "Why didn't you ring?"

"I don't need anything." Her face was thinner now, but her
eyes were the same and they smiled up at him with the same
steady affection. "I only want to talk to you a minute. Roy—I wish
you'd stop being so unhappy about me."

Roy sat rigid. To save his life he could not speak. And she said
quietly, "You know me, Roy. You know I can take this. Or anything else, with the Lord's help. And that won't fail me. And you
know if I've got anything to forgive you for I do forgive it gladly
—only you never meant any harm to me, and really there isn't anything. So what is it that's making you pace up and down night
after night and get all thin and peaked?"

Once more Roy could only look at her in a sort of dumb misery.
And gently she answered her own question.

"I know. You feel guilty. It's one of the worst feelings a body
can ever have—that awful sense of sin. I've had it too—sakes alive,
who hasn't? But I knew where to go——"

She reached out a hand, whiter and slimmer than Jennie's
hands had ever been before, and picked up the Bible that lay on
her bedside table; her fingers gently caressed its worn leather.

"Roy, won't you try it? Listen!" The fingers turned the pages
eagerly. "It says, 'The blood of Jesus Christ his Son cleanseth us
from all sin.' *All* sin. Don't you see? If you believed that, you
wouldn't need to worry and fret and torment your poor self—it
would all be *gone*, you'd be clean!"

Her eyes were shining; he saw with a dull despair that held,
perhaps, a trace of envy, that it was a truth so real, so vivid, so
intensely practical and workable to her that she could hardly im-

agine that he would fail to see it and respond. She said, a little shyly, "I used to remember that word 'cleanseth' sometimes when I was washing clothes. In a way it was sort of wonderful to see them go in all dirty and spotted and come out so shining-white and sweet-smelling. And I'd think to myself, 'That's the way it is with my sins—when I bring them to Him——' "

Suddenly she stopped. Her eyes were searching his face, and slowly the light faded from her own. Wretchedly Roy bestirred himself, wanting to bring the glow back, miserably conscious of having failed her.

"I know, Jennie. That—that was a nice thought. I know——"
She closed the Book and laid it very quietly back.

"No," she said. There was pity and tenderness and regret in her voice. "You don't know. Not yet. But I'm going to keep praying you will know—someday. Run along to bed now."

He got up slowly and stood, hesitant and unhappy. Suddenly he wanted to fall on his knees and put his head on her shoulder and sob his heart out . . . He wanted to tell her, passionately, that he'd spend all the rest of his life trying to make up to her—all his money, all his time . . . He wanted to say that nothing was too much to do for her, nothing, nothing. . . . But this wasn't what Jennie wanted from him. And what she did want—some strange assurance about being "washed clean"—he could not give her. She wanted him, he thought, to be comforted by something he did not accept, to wholeheartedly believe something he could not even understand! He bent over and kissed her broad, compassionate forehead and turned heavily away.

It was just one week later that she took the cold which, all of a sudden, with startling abruptness, turned out to be pneumonia.

"She ought to be back in the hospital," Dr. Bergen fretted. "I don't dare move her, so I've ordered an oxygen tent. And of course, we'll try all the new drugs. But at her age—and in her condition—well, we'll do all we can to save her."

Roy looked at him with a face so white and desperate that Nina found herself thinking almost with terror, "If she dies, he'll smash up—he'll think he killed her and he'll smash up!"

"You've got to save her, Doctor," he said fiercely. "You've got to!"

But the doctor could not save her. Twenty-four hours later Jennie's last breath fluttered from her body.

Her beloved Pastor Martin, who had visited her faithfully almost every day since the accident, was with her. It was he who brought her Bible to Roy standing blankly in the middle of the living room with clenched fists while Nina sobbed on the davenport. And Pastor Martin's face, Roy noted with a dull resentment, wore a strange brightness; almost as if he had just witnessed something wonderful and triumphant instead of something black and tragic.

"Just last week," said the Pastor quietly, "she told me to be sure to give this to you if—she had to leave you. Do you understand, Mr. Baxter? It's her bequest to you."

Roy took it and held it a moment, the book that had been so dear to Jennie. Then with a sudden violent movement he put it down on the table and left the room abruptly. Behind him he heard Nina's tear-drenched voice stammering, "It's just that he feels so awful about everything right now," and the Pastor's quiet tones replying, "I know. But he won't refuse Jennie's last gift. He'll come back to it, you'll see."

After the funeral Roy and Nina went on a two-week trip. It had been Nina's idea—Roy had consented apathetically, and she admitted to Anna when they came back that it hadn't worked very well.

"I suppose it couldn't have," she said with a sigh. "Because after all, he took himself with him."

Roy himself came in to the Fisher drugstore a few days after his return. Grampa was in charge and he came from behind the counter to give him a warm handshake and a hearty "Glad you're back."

"Thanks," said Roy dully. "Carl around?"

"Out just now. Anything I can do?"

"Well—I've decided to sell my house. I'll put it in the hands of a real-estate man, of course, but for the neighbors' sakes I'd like for the right man to buy it. If you or Carl hear of anyone——"

"We'll let you know, sure." A little pause. "Dead-certain you want to sell, Roy?"

Roy sat down abruptly on a stool at the soda fountain. Grampa saw that he had reached that stage where, although he didn't want to talk about what had happened, he wasn't going to be able to help it. It had become an obsession, a pretty near unbearable one, thought Grampa.

"Frankly—I can't live in that house any more!" he burst out. "Everything reminds me of Jennie—of what I did to her——"

Grampa pretended not to see how he was shaking. His tone was almost casual as he asked, "And you think gettin' away from the house will wipe out all these things that are in your mind?"

"Yes—no—nothing will do that, ever. But anyway, I won't have to look at the kitchen where she worked—or her room—or that basement door—— He broke off. "I can't take these constant reminders!" he said violently. "Even Nina doesn't understand—but I *can't!*"

"I see. Well, excuse me askin' so many questions"—Grampa's voice was mild—"but are you disposin' of Jennie's Bible she left you, too? I'd think that would be the biggest reminder of all."

He saw the question stab home, saw Roy quiver under it.

"Naturally I'll keep that—knowing what it meant to her."

Suddenly then, Grampa dropped his casual tone; he leaned across the counter, his sensitive, intelligent old face deeply serious. "She didn't leave it just as a pleasin' memento, Son—she left it hopin' you'd *read* it."

The glance Roy sent him was full of a bewildered appeal. "I know. But I can't. I can't—even bear to touch it."

Grampa straightened up. "Now ain't it the queerest thing about human nature," he observed reflectively, "the way it just keeps pushin' off the help it needs and wants so much? Here you are, breakin' your heart feelin' guilty. And likely as not, the cure for it is right in that little book Jennie left you. But you won't even give it a trial. Think that makes good sense, Son?"

"I don't know," Roy mumbled in unhappy confusion. "I just don't know, Grampa——" and broke off, relieved at the entrance of a group of youngsters.

That night Nina spoke to him again about the house. She had been crying, he saw, and the knowledge made him feel at once guilty and irritable. "Do we—do we *have* to give up the house, Roy?"

He had been trying listlessly to do some figuring. He put down his pencil and she saw a little nerve twitching in his cheek.

"Nina, if you can't bear to leave, I could go to the hotel——"

"You mean—leave me? *Separate?*" She was staring at him with such shock and horror that he tried to pull himself together.

"I'm—sorry," he said with an effort. "Naturally I didn't mean that. Just temporarily, until——" He stopped. "Nina, do you mind if we don't discuss it tonight? I'm terribly tired—I——"

One of Nina's clenched fists went to her trembling lips; above it her big eyes stared at him, lost and desolate. "Oh," she cried suddenly, her voice breaking, "I don't know what to *do.*"

He looked after her bleakly as she fled. He ought to follow her, he thought dully—but what good would it do? He had nothing to say that could comfort her.

He bent over the figures again, but it was no use; he couldn't think straight. And he found himself remembering that on that afternoon which seemed now so long, so long ago, that afternoon just before he took a wrong turning, when life had appeared so peculiarly sweet, he had been thinking that the spirit of the head of an organization seemed to spread, somehow, down through the whole personnel. Maybe that was why nothing seemed to go quite right at the Baxter Works any more.

He brushed a hand wearily across his face, stood up with an unhappy sigh, and pushed the papers aside. And it was at that moment that his eyes fell on Jennie's Bible, lying on the living-room table. Queer! He had left it on Jennie's own table, in her little closed room. Nina, he thought suddenly—she had put it there hoping it would catch his eye. Nina, too. "You won't even give it a trial," he heard Grampa saying. Both of them——

Even while he was muttering "Why don't they leave me alone?" he was moving slowly, reluctantly toward the table; and almost, it seemed to him, against his will his hand had reached out, picked up the little book, and opened it. Then he nearly cried out; from the flyleaf, in Jennie's shaky, labored handwriting, his own name looked up at him. "*Darling Roy,*" the unsteady letters said, "*please read I John 1:7. Read it over and over. Please, with love from Jennie.*"

His fingers were shaking so that he could hardly turn the leaves.

But even before he found the place he knew what it would be; the verse Jennie had read to him that night in her room, of course. "But if we walk in the light, as he is in the light, we have fellowship one with another, and the blood of Jesus Christ, his Son cleanseth us from all sin."

What strange magic had the words had for Jennie? He remembered the soft light on her face, heard her saying, "I used to remember that word 'cleanseth' sometimes when I was washing clothes. It was sort of wonderful to see them go in all dirty and spotted and come out so shining-white. And I'd think to myself, 'That's the way it is with my sins—when I bring them to Him——'"

And suddenly then a longing so passionate swept him to experience that cleansing, to be free from torturing remorse, and whole and unstained again that a great sob broke from him, and within him some stubborn, irrational resistance went down. Stumbling a little in his haste, he went to the telephone and dialed Pastor Martin's number—Pastor Martin, whom Jennie had loved. Heart pounding, holding on to the receiver as if it were supporting him, he waited for the familiar voice, and when it answered and the Pastor replied to his inquiry with a warm "You can come right away if you like," such a wave of relief came over him that he could hardly find his voice to stammer thank you.

The light was out in his and Nina's room as he paused at the door. He stood there irresolutely, not sure whether she was asleep; and then, his eyes growing accustomed to the half-light that came into the room from the hall, he saw that she was kneeling beside the bed, her face buried on the spread. Even as he looked, some sense made her aware of his presence and she stumbled to her feet.

"You're—praying," he said huskily. "For me, Nina?"

Her answer was so low it barely reached him. "For us."

He was able, after an instant, to speak over the lump in his chest and the dryness in his throat. "I wanted to tell you—I've just phoned Pastor Martin. I'm going to see him. Now."

He heard her breath catch . . . Was she weeping? "Oh, Roy," she said, "Oh, Roy! I'm—glad. I'm—so—glad."

The memory of her voice, charged with sudden, painful hope, went with him as he left.

He had taken Jennie's Bible; he was still clinging tightly to it ten minutes later as he sat down in Pastor Martin's study.

"I—I guess you're wondering, sir, why I called you at this time of night. But after I found *this*"—he opened the Bible—"I felt I couldn't wait. It's a note to me—from Jennie——"

"I know," said the Pastor in his quiet, pleasant voice. "She showed it to me herself. The day after she wrote it."

"Oh!" Roy stared at him, taken aback. He swallowed and said with difficulty, "Then—then maybe she also told you *why* she wrote it——"

"Well, that was hardly necessary, was it? It was quite obvious."

"Not to me!" cried Roy. "I—beg your pardon, sir. I didn't mean to shout——"

"It's all right," the Pastor said gravely. His deep-set eyes were compassionate on the other's tormented face. "But if you really don't know, I'll have to speak plainly. Jennie could see what she knew I could see—what, indeed, Mrs. Baxter, all your friends can see by now—that you were, and are, wrecking your life, and of course your wife's along with it, by remorse. She longed to lift that remorse from you. If not before she left you, then afterward. So she wrote that note."

"I—see." Roy hardened his voice to keep it from trembling. "At least—I see what you mean. But I'm afraid I don't see just how this verse is supposed to make me forget that"—he had to wait a moment before he could finish—"that I did a dirty, low, dishonest thing and it cost Jennie her life."

"It isn't quite a matter of forgetting. If we totally forgot all our sins and mistakes, then we might also forget what we've learned from them. That wasn't just what Jennie had in mind——"

"I've learned nothing," Roy interrupted harshly, "except that I am a much worse man than I ever dreamed I was."

"But that's a very valuable thing to learn!" said the Pastor calmly. "No man can ever hope to put his sin behind him until he's faced it squarely, letting all his careful self-justifications go and not dodging one ugly aspect!"

"In that case," Roy answered grimly, "I should be well on the way to putting mine behind me! For there is not one hour of the day when I'm not facing it. But it certainly doesn't seem to have worked any such magic spell for me."

"Well, of course," the Pastor answered mildly, "if you stop right there then it's no more than futile, unavailing remorse. And nothing wrecks a man's personality more thoroughly, nothing is more devastating. Jennie, who was a wise woman and a great Christian, was trying to persuade you not to stop there—she was trying to persuade you to go further."

"I don't see——" Roy began, and stopped. "I don't mean to be seeming to argue with you," he said humbly. "That's not why I'm here. If you could explain—clearly—what you mean, what Jennie meant——" He added, almost to himself, "It's my last chance."

"I'll try," the Pastor answered simply. He was leaning forward a little now, and his eyes held Roy's. "When Jesus died on the Cross, He died for you and me. No, don't look disappointed yet! I know you've heard it before—so often, perhaps, that it's lost meaning for you. Or maybe you never thought about its meaning. Think about it now! Because it isn't just a religious phrase—it's a great and living truth, and it holds the answer to all your painful problems."

He stopped an instant; Roy, watching with wonder the glow on his face, had the feeling that during the tiny pause he was silently praying. He went on:

"You see, in dying He literally took our sins on His shoulders. Do you understand what I mean? *He* paid the penalty for them. *He* paid your debt—and mine. That is God's glorious gift to mankind—through Jesus, He offers every man a brand-new start, a sinless beginning again. And the tragedy is that man so often does not accept that offered gift!"

"But I don't know how to accept! Do you think," Roy said unsteadily, "do you think I wouldn't if I knew? Do you think—excuse me, but I must say it!—a man *enjoys* living in Hell?"

"Why, to tell the truth," said the Pastor with a rueful little smile, "sometimes, my dear sir, I find myself wondering about that very point! Occasionally, I confess, it seems to me that nothing else could account for the persistence with which man closes his eyes and shuts his ears. There now, don't take that too seriously! But look at yourself, for instance—you live in a Christian community, you've probably got half a dozen Bibles in your home, you've lived right in the very house for forty years with one of the grandest Christians I've ever known. And there you sit and tell me that you're not even aware of all these ways in which God has, for so many years, been trying to speak to you, and that you don't know how to accept His gift! Don't know how to acknowledge Him as your Father, and Christ as your Savior, and in sincere repentance get down on your knees and ask for forgiveness!"

"You mean, sir, that if I can do this sincerely—you mean that after that—that then—that I——" Roy stammered, and stopped. All his life he had been what he himself called a "hardheaded businessman," had Roy Baxter. And now, quite suddenly, he seemed to catch a flashing glimpse of splendid spiritual vistas, of a landscape so much broader and brighter, of pastures so infinitely more abundant than any he had ever known before that the vision left him a little shaken and dazed. . . . The Pastor smiled.

"I mean you're clear, you're free, your sin is wiped out—expiated by Christ. And that is only the very start of it—because you'll begin from then on to walk a new path, and I promise you that life will be so much richer for you, so much fuller, will hold such a glow——" He shook his head. "There aren't words for the difference! But after all, you should be able to understand—you watched it change Jennie's humble, perhaps limited, life into a happy adventure!"

Roy remembered how even washing clothes had held a joyous meaning for Jennie. He said it aloud, " 'They go in dirty and spotted, and come out shining-white.' Excuse me, sir. She said that to me one night—she did so much laundry, you know——"

The Pastor seemed to understand the confused explanation perfectly. He nodded.

"It's hard to understand," Roy said wonderingly. "I mean—that it could be like you say, that I could do so little and get so much! How can it be?"

"Ah, that I do not know. No man can understand the boundless mercy of God," the Pastor answered gravely. "I only know it is true."

Roy sat silent, still holding the little Bible tightly. And the

Pastor said, his eyes steady and kind on Roy's face, "Jennie loved you, you know. If Jennie's death turns you in another direction, if through it you find her God and learn to know and love and follow her Savior—believe me, Jennie herself would never have counted dying too high a price to pay for that!"

Roy had come to his feet with a startled movement. He took a few blind steps away, and stood with his back turned and his head bent. And the Pastor had a moment's fear that his words had been too powerful a stab.

But when, after another instant, Roy turned again, he saw with relief and the purest delight that there was no shock in his face. He was even smiling a little, an unsteady smile, but probably, the Pastor thought thankfully, the most genuine that anyone had seen on his lips for many weeks.

"I'm glad you said that, sir." The voice had lost its tense and tortured quality; it was deeply moved, but almost calm now. "I know it's true. The night she fell—it was her birthday, you know. And she made a birthday wish on her cake. She wouldn't tell us what it was, but even then I knew—I knew!—in my heart. Because we'd been talking about how interested she was in her church work—and I'd known for a long time, really, how every Sunday she hoped that this time I'd go with her, and so when Carl said something about it—and then Jennie made her wish——"

He brushed one hand across his eyes. "Well, *that's* what she wished—it was a wish for me——" He could not quite finish the sentence. He stood, swallowing hard, fingers tightening on the little Bible. And after a moment he could look up, could smile again, faintly.

"I guess I must be going now, sir. Nina will be waiting for me. And—and I wish I knew how to thank you."

"Why, you do!" replied the Pastor cheerfully. "You know exactly how!"

"Oh!" He was silent again an instant. Then he said humbly, "I guess I know what you mean. But I'm only barely starting to see it, you know. I'll need a lot of help—to thank you that way."

"You know that all the help I've got to give is yours." The Pastor's voice was quiet and sure. "But there's something much better than that for you—all the strength and help and power anybody could ever need is right there, in that little book you're holding, in your Savior's words."

Roy shifted the Book to his left hand. He did not know that as he looked down at it his face had softened to tenderness. "That's where Jennie found it, all right," he said slowly. He held out his right hand. "Well, good-by, Pastor. We'll be at church Sunday morning in Jennie's pew. We'll be there *every* Sunday morning."

The two hands met in a firm clasp. Roy, half turned to go, suddenly turned back. "Do you think, sir"—his eyes were suspiciously bright—"do you think that maybe Jennie knows?"

"Oh, as to that"—the Pastor's tone as he answered the wistful little question was very warm—"as to that, I don't think we need to worry one bit! We can safely leave all that to God. The one thing you be sure of about Jennie now is that she's fine. And if she doesn't know quite yet—why, she surely will someday. And time must be passing very quickly for *her* these days! There's only one way to feel about Jennie—and that is happy and glad."

He heard the other draw a long breath, the deep sigh of relief of a heart which feels with certainty, at last, that a painful, almost intolerable burden is easing, is beginning to leave. He said, "Thank you, Pastor. And—good night again." And the Pastor answered, smiling, "Good night. And God bless you!"

As Roy Baxter turned away, the last shadow of torment was lifting from his face and something of Jennie's own peace was taking its place.

3. NO TEARS FOR BILL

*W*HEN Emily Fisher dropped into her father's drugstore for lunch that June day, she discovered her young friend and
fervent adorer, Susan Randall, sitting quite alone in the last booth
and poking dejectedly at a piece of pie.

"Hi, Sue!" she called amiably. "If you aren't hiding out away
back there—wanting to meditate or something—I'll eat lunch with
you."

Susan looked up, with a somewhat wan smile momentarily light-
ing her pretty face—which thereafter almost immediately clouded
again.

"I wish you would," she sighed.

Emily sank into the seat opposite; she was practically twenty
and practically engaged, so the air with which she now surveyed
sixteen-year-old Susan was definitely maternal.

"Well, whatever you're doing, you're not eating," said she.
"something wrong with the pie or something wrong with you?"

"I guess it's me." Susan's voice was deeply doleful. "It's somebody else, too, but I'm worried about the somebody else, and that
makes it me."

Emily seemed to find this clear.

"You can tell me about it while I eat lunch if you like," she
offered, with the kindness of one of adult status toward one not
yet arrived at that distinction. "I don't have to get back to the
library for forty minutes." At this moment, seeing her father ap-
proaching, she rapped on the table sharply. "A little service

around here, my good man! Am I to wait all day? A chicken sandwich and a glass of milk, and step lively about it!"

Carl tossed the order back over his shoulder to the boy on duty
at the soda fount. "And see that she gives you a whopping tip
—she's rich and stingy," he advised. He bestowed a smile as of
two people who understand each other on Susan. "She's been like
this," he confided, "ever since she got David so completely under
her thumb. It's gone to her head, I guess."

With which, having made his daughter blush, he retired, apparently satisfied that the honors of the encounter were his. Susan's eyes followed him a little wistfully, then dropped again to
her pie, in which she methodically punched another hole.

"Are you by any chance in love?" asked Emily, watching her.

"Me? I'm not even going steady."

"Well, there're at least half a dozen after you to go steady. I
thought maybe one of them had scored——"

Susan dismissed them all with a wave of the hand, a slightly
contemptuous wave, which declared that she was not interested.

Emily waited a minute. "We won't talk about what's worrying
you if you'd rather not," she said. "I just meant—tell me if it
helps——"

"Maybe it would." Susan lifted troubled dark eyes to her friend.
"Emily—I want to ask you a funny question . . . Do you ever
think about death?"

Emily jumped slightly. She was, as a matter of fact, thinking
very absorbedly about life these days. She took a moment to adjust to the idea, and answered cautiously, "Why—everybody with
any sense thinks about it sometimes, don't they?"

"I mean—how do you *feel* about it?"

Emily frowned a little, rather at a loss. "Well—I believe in life
everlasting . . . I think it's just bodies that die, not people——"
She broke off. "I'm not sure I understand what you're getting at,
Sue."

Susan bit her red underlip nervously. "I'm not sure I do myself.
I guess maybe it's how much we ought to keep thinking about the
folks who aren't on earth any more——"

"Oh!" said Emily blankly, and waited for further enlighten-
ment.

Susan pushed her plate away with a sudden jerky gesture. "I'm worried about Mother. Emily—do you remember my dad at all?"

"Oh yes! I guess I was about eight, when he came back on his last leave." She smiled. "He looked wonderful in his uniform—I was breathless with admiration!"

"I can't remember much—I was only four. But Mother's let me read a lot of his letters. And of course there are his pictures. He started a letter to me the night before he was killed—just one page —he never got to finish it. I know it all by heart. 'Darling Su-Su, This is just for you because I love you and miss you. I wish you could see all the doggies that hang around this place. Dogs love soldiers, you know. I guess it's because we feed them and pet them. They even ride with us on the truck when we go to the air field and I guess they'd get on the bombers with us, too, if they were allowed. There's one funny little black Scottie who always looks as if he's smoking a pipe—he's so little and fat that he can't get on the truck by himself, so he just stands and cries till someone lifts him on.' And that was all——"

She stopped abruptly; and Emily, puzzled, thought, "What's it all about? I don't get it."

Susan's eyes met her friend's puzzled ones, and read the thought.

"I know I sound crazy—it's hard to explain," she said helplessly. "I've always felt like he must've been a sort of wonderful guy, my dad—I've always felt like I—well, wanted to live up to him! But the way Mother's been *acting* lately——" Her teeth came down on her lip again, this time to steady it. "—honest, it seems like it might've been better if she'd torn up his letters and stuck his pictures in the attic and we'd both just forgotten all about him——"

The sandwich and the milk arrived. Emily forgot to banter about the tip. She gave the boy an absent-minded smile as he placed them before her and turned back to Susan.

"I don't see why in the world you'd want to do a thing like that," she said a trifle indignantly.

"Well, I told you. It's the way Mother's doing. I can't make heads or tails of it, but it seems like it started 'cause of Bob."

"Oh!" Emily began, at last, to see a faint glimmer of light. "Bob Hanson?" Susan nodded. "He's in love with her, isn't he?" Another nod. "Well, what's the trouble? Last time I saw them together I had a hunch she was feeling the same way about him."

"She was—she *is*. That's what makes it all so wacky!" Susan was almost in tears. "It seemed like it was all settled—and I was just tickled to death. I'm terribly fond of Bob—he was Daddy's best friend, you know. What could've been nicer, I ask you?" She choked a little. "And now the whole thing has just blown up with a loud bang!"

"Why?" asked Emily puzzled.

"You tell me! It doesn't make sense. It's *fantastic,* simply fantastic. It began to happen right after—well, it was about three weeks ago. I came home from a party and Mother and Bob were in the living room, and a baby," said Susan with the air of a woman of wide experience, "absolutely a *baby* would've known what was up. There was Mother, red and flustered, and there was Bob, redder and with a kind of silly beam, and I just took one look at them and burst out laughing and said, 'Bless you, my children!' "

She paused, and Emily begged, "Don't stop, for pity's sake— I'm dying of suspense! Did they admit it?"

"I'll say! Bob jumped up and hugged me—we had a real old-fashioned sentimental scene." She suddenly abandoned the attempt to sound sophisticated. Her chin began to tremble. "It—it was swell," she said in a low, unsteady tone.

"I'll bet," Emily agreed, deeply sympathetic. "Well, when did it begin to be different?"

"The very next morning," Susan answered drearily. "Mother looked peaked at the breakfast table—as if she hadn't slept. And when I began to talk about it—I was pretty full of it, naturally —and to ask when the wedding would be, and all that, she cut me off very short. She said nothing had been settled yet and please not to give anybody a hint. She said she was certainly past the blushing-bride stage and it would embarrass her very much to have it gossiped about. So of course I said I wouldn't tell. But I told her I did think she ought not to wait long. Because naturally time is sort of running out on anybody who's thirty-eight years old."

Emily, not quite twenty, did not find this last statement—which would have amused Carl immensely had he been listening in—strange; she nodded a serious assent.

"Well, that was just the beginning. Everything got wronger and wronger from then on. Mother began making all sorts of excuses not to see Bob. And she'd send him home early when he did come, or try to keep me hanging round. I could see he was bothered and upset—and I was too. Once I came in just in time to hear her say in a sort of hysterical way, 'Bob, you simply must *not* rush me!' and Bob was answering, sounding kind of desperate, 'But I don't get it! What on earth are we waiting for, Mary?'"

Susan leaned her head on her hand. "Bob and I were both *miserable*. We didn't say anything to each other, of course—but after three weeks of it Bob looked really *haggard*. So last night I just took my nerve in both hands and tackled Mother. I told her she was the last person I'd ever have expected to be fickle and I simply didn't understand her. Well, first she got mad and said if I'd kindly mind my own business she'd appreciate it, thank you! Then she started crying and begged my pardon, and said that of course she could see how it all looked to me but there were things she couldn't explain, and that she was afraid she couldn't possibly marry Bob and hoped I'd just accept that and not make her feel bad about what she couldn't help."

"Funny!" commented Emily wonderingly.

"I s'pose you mean funny-peculiar—it certainly isn't funny-ha-ha," Susan replied grimly. "Anyway, I blew my top. I told her she sounded just *insane*. I told her she was talking like a Woman with a Past in a mystery thriller and I couldn't possibly imagine any reason for not marrying Bob after she'd promised him she would. So finally she told me why."

Here Susan came to a dead stop.

"Well?" Emily prompted.

Susan threw her a glance full of unhappy appeal.

"I hate to tell you. Because you're going to think she's nuts. But she isn't. It's just that she's kind of brooded until—— Oh well, I might as well come out with it! She's gotten the notion that if she marries Bob it will hurt Daddy's feelings."

"Hurt——" Emily's mouth came open and stayed that way for a full second. "Did you say hurt your *father's* feelings?"

Susan winced and gulped. "I know how wild it sounds! But that's what she says. Hurt and offended—those were her very words."

The two girls stared at each other solemnly, and Emily shook her head. "I just don't get it. Whatever in the world put such an idea in her head in the first place? I mean—how did she possibly work it up?"

"It was a dream. I guess getting engaged to Bob made her think of when she was engaged to Daddy. So she had this dream about him that night and in it she thought he was looking at her sadly and saying something about her deserting and forgetting him."

"But she knows that was just a *dream*, doesn't she? I mean— she can't possibly think it really *was* your father, can she?"

"I'm scared that's just what she does think," said Susan nervously. "She says it was his way of reminding her that she had promised to love him forever. I told her I thought it was 'till death do us part' and she said, oh, that was just the ceremony, she was talking about what they'd promised each other privately, not about being married, but about *loving*."

"But who's keeping her from loving him?" asked Emily impatiently. "Not Bob, I'm sure. Bob loves him too. The way I look at it, you don't stop loving people just because they're gone, but you have to learn to love them in a different way. If my mother died tomorrow and I lived to be eighty, don't you s'pose I'd still love her? But I wouldn't grieve for her all that time because I'd have learned to love her *differently*——" She stopped. "I know what I mean, but I don't know how to say it! I just can't see why she couldn't remember and love your father, and yet love Bob, too. And anyway," she added, "it's just plain *absurd* to think that if your father *could* come back in a dream he'd want to look sad and talk about her deserting him. You know *they*—the people in Heaven—couldn't possibly feel like that!"

"In a way that's one thing that bothers me." Susan brushed one hand across her eyes. "I keep thinking—did she have that dream because Daddy was that sort of man? You know—jealous, and all that. It—it kind of upsets my idea of him."

"Well, now *you're* being crazy," said Emily frankly. "Because

I'm dead-certain he wasn't. It was something your mother worked up herself—goodness knows why!"

"I hope so. Anyway—I didn't mean to tell you that part. I was going to tell you what happened just now—and see if you don't agree it was just the last *straw!* No, wait a minute—first I've got to tell you about the way Mother's taken to disappearing all day and won't say where she's been. She's done it twice lately, and today she's at it again. You know I'm going to summer school—and this morning she told me to drop by here for lunch because she'd be gone all day. And I said, 'For the love of Mike, Mother, where are you going on these weird, mysterious expeditions?' and she said, 'Susan, I ask you again to please let me manage my own affairs,' so I still don't know what she's up to. But anyway, I'd left the school and was walking here when Bob came by in his car and picked me up. And he said, 'How's the boy friend, Sue?' And of course I thought he was kidding, and I laughed and said, 'Which one?' And then *he* said, 'Now, sugar, don't try to fool your old man! I've got it on good authority—your mother tells me the case is *very* serious.' Then he got all solemn and said he guessed it was a little early in the game for him to be making a noise like a parent, but it seemed to him I was pretty young to be really engaged and he'd like to meet the boy. I was simply *petrified*—"

Susan choked a little at this point and dabbed, half angrily, at her long lashes. "Oh well, to make a long story short—Emily, Mother had actually told him that the wedding was off indefinitely because *I* was in love and she didn't think it would be fair to me for her to marry 'under those circumstances.' It all came out in our talk, Bob's and mine, 'cause I was so—so *flabbergasted* I kept asking him questions. So in a way he gave Mother away to me and I gave her away to him. She told him a *lie*—a plain *lie*." She added drearily, "I guess her real reason was so crazy she didn't have the nerve to give it to him."

"How did Bob take it?" asked Emily, shocked and sympathetic.

"He's just quitting. He said if it had got to the place where she was telling lies to get rid of him he'd better get out. And he told me to tell her he wouldn't bother her any more. And I know," finished Susan, her voice beginning to tremble, "I know Mother *does* love him, not a wild romance but like a woman her age would, and there's just n-not any s-sense to any of it——"

Emily patted her and gave her an extra Kleenex, and in a moment Susan raised her head and sent her friend a watery small smile. "Sorry. I guess I'd better go. Aren't you due back at the library? Thank you for listening to my long sob story——"

"No, wait—I'm thinking!" Emily pondered a second, brows drawn. "I've got a kind of an idea—it mightn't work, but we can't just do *nothing*, and it wouldn't hurt to try. Why don't you telephone Bob from that booth there and tell him what you've just told me? I mean the part about knowing your mother does love him?"

"You think that would help?" Susan asked doubtfully.

"Well—maybe you'd have to say more. Maybe you'd have to tell him she needs him, really needs him, and that if he just walks out now without even finding out why she's behaving like this it will spoil the rest of her life. Why couldn't you say that she's gotten some awfully queer notions you can't tell him about? And that you're going to feel pretty frantic about her if he doesn't make her talk to *him* about them and straighten her out?"

Emily was leaning forward now, flushed and eager, quite sold on her own idea, and Susan began to catch her spark. She wriggled out of the booth.

"I'll phone now! Can you wait till I come back?"

"I'll wait if they dock me!" Emily assured her cheerfully.

It was seven or eight minutes before Susan returned. Her eyes were bright, and as she slid into her seat again she drew a long, excited breath. "Emily! Oh, I knew you'd think of something constructive! He thanked me—and he said he'd come just as soon as he got away from his office, that he wouldn't telephone or anything, he'd just *arrive*, and if she wasn't there he'd wait till she came!"

"Oh, grand! Then why don't you come and have supper with us? David'll be there—and afterward you and Peter and he and I can go to a movie. *That* ought to get you out from under their feet long enough."

Carl, who had been wondering a little what the long and obviously emotional conversation was about, happened to glance in their direction at this moment, and was pleased to note that little Susan looked less upset. He also thought they looked as if they were hatching some conspiracy.

Emily had risen and was standing by the table.

"Since you seem to feel a little better," she suggested with a grin, "maybe you can drink your milk and eat that poor old pie you've punched all full of holes! And Susan——"

She was suddenly serious. Susan, looking up at her adoringly, thought how lovely her fair hair looked with the light on it, and that nobody was as sweet and pretty and all-round nice as Emily. The frank worship of a younger girl for an older one was written so clearly in her wide eyes and candid face that Emily, seeing it, had a quick sensation both of humility and responsibility; and the little timidity that made her hesitate was gone.

She said gently, "I was only thinking—you and I ought both to be doing some pretty hard praying the rest of the day. . . . 'Bye now. See you tonight."

A few blocks away Bob Hanson, like Susan, was experiencing a lightening of the spirit. The girl was a levelheaded youngster, and very close to her mother, he was thinking. If she said so positively that Mary still loved him, she might just possibly be right. And if she was right—well, he'd get out of Mary whatever it was that was separating them if it took him all summer and all fall and all winter, too!

So he was sitting on the steps when she got home at dusk that night. And he did not allow himself to feel too much discouraged that his reception was decidedly unpromising, for this was what he had expected.

"Oh—hello!" she said, surprised and plainly not pleased to see him. She looked tired and worn, and her voice was weary, too, as she added, "Where's Susan?"

He gestured toward the door. "There's a note there, with 'MOTHER' on the envelope."

"I see. Well—since you're here, come in."

It was not a very gracious invitation, but he accepted it. She snapped on the living-room light and opened Susan's letter. "She's taking supper with the Fishers and they're going to a movie. Bob —I'm sorry to seem rude but I've had a rather hard day—and since

Susan's taken care of and I'm not a bit hungry, I think I'll go right to bed. If you'll excuse me, please——"

For a moment he wavered; she did indeed seem exhausted. Then he shook his head. "Unless you're really sick, I think I'm going to insist this time, Mary. The things I've got to say to you just won't wait."

With a slight shrug, she capitulated; almost, he thought, as if she were too fatigued to argue the point. "Just give me ten minutes, then—to freshen up a little."

When she came downstairs again, he was just putting a tray on the living-room table.

"I know you said you weren't hungry, but I rather suspect you haven't eaten today," he explained, speaking a good deal more cheerfully than he felt. "So I made two egg shakes and sliced some of your nut bread. Sit down, darling."

Her lip quivered a little; perhaps at his concern for her, perhaps at the endearment. Either way, it encouraged him. She sat down and began, slowly, to sip her drink. He chatted idly, paying no attention to her lack of response, until she had finished the glass and eaten half her slice of bread. Then she pushed the other half away, seemed to brace herself, raised her eyes to his, and said, "Well?"

He set down his own glass and moved his chair close to hers. His eyes held her wavering ones steadily.

"Do you need to ask, really? I saw Susan today. Mary, why did you tell me that lie about her being in love and likely to marry early? Why did you give me the idea she didn't want you to marry —till after her own marriage?"

Two bright red spots flared in her cheeks; the stain of humiliation. She sent him one look of anguished shame; her head drooped, and she was silent.

He leaned toward her but did not touch her. He said gently, "If you'd decided you didn't care about me, after all—wouldn't it have been fairer and more honest just to have told me so?"

He could see the painful effort with which she gathered her forces to answer. Her voice was low and husky.

"I know how it looks. But you don't understand. It wasn't that —exactly."

His heart leaped. Then Susan was right, bless her! He schooled his voice to quietness. His beloved was in no mood for ardor, he knew.

"Then—what was—what *is*—it, Mary?"

"You'll never understand! I don't even know how to explain. I thought maybe this was the easiest way——"

She buried her face in her hands, and he saw her shoulders shaking. He wanted badly to take her in his arms, but he held himself rigidly still and waited. And finally she raised her face; it was very white, and her eyes were dark with trouble.

"It's a question of which loyalty is stronger, Bob. Today I went to Royaltown—it was the second time."

He could make no sense of this. He said, "Loyalty? Royaltown?"

"That was my girlhood home. I spent this day—like the other one when I was there—with Bill."

"I don't understand, Mary. Bill who?"

There was a queer defiance in her voice when she answered. "Bill Randall. My husband."

In his shocked amazement the only explanation that occurred to Bob was that Mary, incredibly, had fallen for some "medium" who, for two dollars, had brought her "messages" or perhaps even produced an ectoplasmic Bill.

"Oh no!" he said under his breath. "Oh *no!*"

At that she flamed into a sudden, defensive, half-frightened anger. "What do you mean by that? I suppose you don't believe in immortal life! I suppose you don't believe Bill is still living!"

"I don't," said Bob grimly, "believe he's living in Royaltown!"

She made a hopeless gesture. "I told you you wouldn't understand! I'm trying to tell you that Bill lives on—in Royaltown, and here, too—oh, so vividly!—in my memory. It was in Royaltown that we did our courting. And I've spent these two days going back to all the places that meant so much to us, living it all over again. The park bench where we'd sit and talk and talk, and where he first kissed me—the church where we were married——"

No ectoplasm, at least, thought Bob, relieved. He said, watching her, "It doesn't seem to have been a very happy pilgrimage—judging by the way you looked when you got home!"

She was not listening. She hurried on, voice trembling.

"We were awfully in love. And—and that's why—well, today was to be a kind of test. And it convinced me. It isn't that I'm not fond of you. But we loved each other too much, Bill and I. I just —just can't push him out of my life——"

"But, Mary," he interrupted, puzzled, "I've never asked you to push Bill out of your life! I've never pushed him out of my own, for that matter." She shook her head.

"You still don't understand," she said dully. "It's—you're not going to believe this—but——"

She came to a stop; the glance she sent him was full of appeal. "Bob, try to understand! It's the way I know *Bill* feels about it! It's that *he* would be hurt—and—and—upset—and offended—if I married again."

His first thought was that perhaps even an ectoplasmic Bill would have been better than this! His second feeling was a queer stirring of anger on Bill's behalf. As if Bill were like that!

"He—he walked beside me today," she went on tremulously. "And—and—I could *feel* the message he was sending me. 'How can you desert me, Mary? How can you betray our love by marrying someone else?'"

She drew a long breath. "I knew you wouldn't believe! You're angry—if you could see your face right now——"

The face Bob was seeing was neither his own nor Mary's; it hovered behind his eyeballs, that other face, and for an instant it seemed clearer than the white, troubled one opposite him.

"You're betraying him, all right," he said harshly. "But not the way you're thinking. I must have known a very different Bill from the one you knew. Or else I knew the real one a whole lot better."

"You knew——" Words all but failed her as she stared at him, outraged. "How dare you say you knew Bill better than I did? I was his *wife!* I knew him so well that he was able to get over to me what he was feeling. The very night after you and I got engaged he came to me, I tell you! In a dream. And he looked at me sadly. He felt hurt. So there's no use talking—I can't marry anybody else, ever. I—I'm sorry I told a lie—and ashamed—and I'm glad to tell you the real truth now. Bill doesn't want me to marry anybody else and I never will!"

Bob resolutely put down an instant's appalled doubt of her

sanity. She had got badly off the track, poor girl, that was all. He said, as quietly and calmly as he could:

"Bill didn't come to you in a dream. I only wish he could! Because there wouldn't be any of that sad-look business, I'm dead-sure of that. He'd tell you how happy he is now and that he is glad about you and me. Think straight, Mary! Can't you see how crazy it is for you to think that dream was *Bill?*"

"I don't want to talk about it any more!" she cried hysterically.

"Well then, you don't need to—just listen to me instead. I've got a story to tell you, honey—a story about Bill."

"About . . ." Her voice trailed off; she stared at him.

"About Bill," he repeated. "*My* Bill. Maybe I ought to've told you before—the first time I came to see you, after I got back from overseas. But it went pretty deep with me—that last talk I had with him—and I didn't know you very well then. Anyway, I guess I thought of it as something that belonged just to me. Now I see I was wrong. It belongs to you, too."

"I don't understand," she said faintly. "You did tell me how you both walked over to the village that last evening and Bill played the piano in the Service Club there and the boys all gathered round and sang . . . I remember every word you said."

"Yes," he assented gravely. "And I told you how we walked home, with the stars all bright and the planes flying overhead— and that Bill was laughing about the letter he'd started that day to Susan, with the description of the dogs—and saying he didn't know how they were ever going to adjust to their old homes and their old masters after the war was over, because they seemed to have developed a great loathing of civilians and tried to bite everybody who wasn't in uniform! And then I told you that he'd said all of a sudden that he had a hunch his crew was going to be alerted at dawn—and if this time he shouldn't get back would I please beat it over to his bunk and get that letter and a few other personal things and send them to you—so they wouldn't be delayed by getting mixed up with his effects. But that's all I told you, isn't it?"

She said, almost in a whisper, "Yes. That's all. Was there more?"

"Yes, there was more. That's the story I want to tell you." He paused. "I think I can give it to you just the way it happened.

Because after Bill's ship didn't come back I wrote it all down. I was afraid I might forget some of it. And I didn't want to. It meant too much to me. So I've got the record—and I've read it a hundred times since then, I guess. You see, it changed everything for me."

Mary's hands were clasped so tightly that the knuckles showed white. Her big eyes clung to his face, half—it seemed to him—in painful eagerness and half in a strange fear. She did not speak. He was very aware of her feelings in that moment; of her suspense, of how her emotions were strung to a pitch of nearly intolerable intensity. But as he talked on he almost forgot that he was speaking to anyone else. He was not so much telling a story as reliving a scene.

"The way I felt about dying in those days—well, it's hard to explain. A combat soldier has to take a matter-of-fact attitude toward it—or else he cracks up. I was never anywhere near cracking up. At the same time I still thought of it as the worst thing that could happen to a man and the end of everything.

"So now I said to Bill, 'Why, of course I'll do anything you want me to—but don't start expecting trouble, old chap.'

"And he laughed. 'Oh, I don't expect to die,' he said.

"'Right! You're too tough—they can't kill *you*,' I grinned.

"And he answered me in a perfectly cheerful, everyday voice, 'Can't go along with you there. I know they can kill me—I mean I just don't believe I'm going to *die*.'

"I stared at him. 'You never drink,' I told him. 'So it can't be that.'

"'No, it's not that,' he said, speaking seriously this time. 'Remember that chaplain who was moved last week, and what a lot of time I spent talking with him? We weren't discussing the weather. We were talking about life—and death—and God—and Jesus Christ. Since then the whole business looks different to me.'

"Well, I'd noticed that Bill had been reading his New Testament a lot. And I had such crazy notions in those days—I'd thought to myself that I hoped old Bill wasn't going off too far on the subject of religion.

"'Looks different, eh?' I said, sort of cautiously. 'Well—how does dying, for instance, look so different?'

"'It doesn't look like dying at all,' he answered me promptly.

'It just looks like the doorway to a bigger, more splendid life.'

"I wasn't ready to buy that. 'Bill,' I asked him rather dryly, 'do you *want* to die?'

"I heard him give an amused little chuckle. 'Trying to catch me out, Bob? Of course, I don't want to die. The Lord didn't make us that way. He created us with a tremendous will and passion to survive—physically survive. And it's easy to see,' he went on, somewhat as if he were thinking out loud, 'why it *had* to be like that, why everything that has life, even animals and insects and plants, *must* fight to the last gasp to keep on living. Because otherwise all life would have disappeared from this planet and the human race would have died off ages ago. And now that I've given you this nice little lecture free of charge,' he ended, 'I'll just repeat that I'm a normal, healthy, physical creature at present, and so I want to live and I'll try to live and I think that's what the Lord intended me to feel and do. But all the same—since I'm also a good deal more than a physical creature I know it's going to be all right if I *do* die.'

"I was listening hard, and it struck me he'd given me a very reasonable answer.

"'Well,' I said after a minute, 'could be that you feel a little more sure than I do about how things are going to work out for you in that other world. Maybe you've got less on your conscience than I have.'

"He shook his head. 'No, I've got plenty. You don't imagine I wouldn't be scared plenty if I had to face God tomorrow just on my own record, do you?'

"'Well, what else is there to face Him on?' I asked.

"He stopped short in the middle of the road. 'Funny. I asked the Chaplain pretty near that same question once. I'll try to give you what he gave me.' He thought a minute, and then went on. 'On your faith in God as a great, good, loving Father. On your belief that He sent His Son, Jesus Christ, to be your only Savior and to show you the way to live and finally to die for you. On your penitence, and on your prayers for forgiveness, and on your complete assurance that through Christ and His atoning death your sins are all washed clean.'

"We walked on. I was trying to understand. Finally I mumbled, 'Well, I wish I'd got what you've got.'

"'You can get it, Bob,' he said, real quick. 'After all, it took a war to jolt me awake, to make me hear God calling. Sure, you can get it,' he repeated. 'Just take what's been offered, that's all. Read your New Testament—it's all there. *I* can't explain, but it does. And what I really mean is—*God* does, through Jesus' own words and life.'

"I didn't say anything. I was wondering how long it had been since I'd opened a Bible. And after a little Bill spoke again, sort of slow. He said, 'It's made life over for me. It's made it just what Jesus said He came to make it—more abundant. Happier—lots fuller and richer. That's the way it is now, and that's the way I know it will be, only more, if I go on to another kind of living, and'—here he hesitated, and that's when he mentioned *your* name, Mary—'and that's just the way I want it to be for Mary if I don't come back. I want her to live *abundantly*.'

"Afterwhile I said, kind of awkwardly, 'It'll be tough for Mary if that happens—don't kid yourself it won't.'

"'I don't,' he answered me back very quietly. 'I know the adjustment will be hard. But I'm pretty sure of Mary. She always had a lot more religion than I had. She knows where to go for help. Anyway, she's not the sort to let grief get morbid. And she'll know that wherever I am, that's the last thing I'm wanting her to do.'

"Then I had to ask him a question; not because, of course, I had any personal interest at all then—but because, in a way, it was a sort of test. Even if it was nervy of me, I had to ask it.

"'Bill—do you mean that if you should get killed you hope Mary will marry again? Will put some other fellow in your place?'

"I sure wish I could tell you how cheerful and calm his voice sounded!

"'Nobody can take anybody else's place, exactly,' he said. 'What I've had from Mary in these years—it'll always be mine. As to whether she'd marry again—that's not for me to say, is it? If that's what's right for her and happiest for her, then sure, that's what I hope she'll do. But I'm not trying to work out the details of her life for her if I'm not around. I'm just saying I want her to live fully and happily. Is that an answer, Bob?'"

" 'Yes,' I told him. 'Yes—it certainly is.' "

His voice stopped. He had thrown every bit of himself into the telling of the story, and suddenly he felt drained and tired. The little room seemed very still. And Mary had buried her face in her hands so he could not see her expression. He came slowly to his feet.

"Well," he said, "that's all. That's my Bill, Mary. That's the Bill I knew. So you can see why this jealous, selfish ghost of yours couldn't ever be Bill to me. You can see why I just don't believe in him—in *it*."

He could not read the face she raised to his—save that it was twisted by some strong emotion.

"Why didn't Bill tell *me*? I never knew he felt like that! Why didn't he share it with me, too?"

He answered sincerely, "I'm sure he meant to. But it probably came easier to say it than to write it. And I expect he was waiting for a chance to write a long letter. Maybe, too, he thought if he didn't find that chance and didn't come back to talk about it to you that I'd tell you. I wish I had—but somehow I never realized till tonight that you didn't know."

She had buried her face in her hands again, and he stood looking down rather helplessly at the dark bent head. "It's like he said —you've got the right to decide your own life. But if you *don't* marry me—don't let it be for the reasons you've been giving me tonight. Because you're a Christian, honey, and those aren't Christian."

She sobbed once; and then her voice came, muffled by those shielding hands, indistinct.

"Then—if it wasn't Bill—what was it? What made me dream it? There must've been a reason why I did——"

He tried, as he had almost never tried before, to marshal his thoughts to clearness.

"Maybe—maybe that's where most Christians fall down, Mary —in the way they feel about death. Maybe they don't quite really believe what they say they believe. Because to me it looks like without knowing it you might've felt the way I used to feel, that dying ends things. And so you felt sorry for Bill because everything had ended for him, and sort of guilty that *you* could be happy when Bill had to be dead and done for, poor fellow!"

He waited for her to lift her face again, but she kept it hidden. He said, half in hope and half in fear, "But now that you know nothing's ended for him and he isn't done for, and that you don't need to feel guilty——"

And still she did not move or show him her face.

When he spoke again, his voice had gone flat and tired. "Or it might have been that you don't love me, after all, and don't want to marry me. The dream might have been an excuse."

The room was very still. He sighed.

"Well—I'll be going now. If there's anything you want to say, you know where to find me."

He had reached the door, his hand was on the knob, he had even opened the door a little way. And then he heard her. "Bob!"

He turned quickly. She was on her feet—ah, no, with a rush she was in his arms!

"No, no! It wasn't that I didn't love you! It was the other! Oh, Bob, I've been such a silly, *wicked* little idiot——"

The face upturned to his was wet with tears, and bright with such a radiance as he had never seen on it before. She drew away after a little, smiling at him. She said, "'He, being dead, yet speaketh.' Oh, Bob, oh, darling! Know who's going to be the next happiest person in the world to us when I tell her? Susan!"

4. FREDDIE AND THE TANGLED WEB

*A*NNA FISHER was spring-cleaning.

That simple statement covers the complete dislocation of a household for three or four days. Emily and Peter were the lucky ones, Carl Fisher had several times announced plaintively, for since the annual rite coincided with their spring holidays they were away on visits to friends. Carl, Grampa, and ten-year-old Freddie, having no such escape, had to stay and take it with what philosophy they could muster.

"Well," observed Grampa mildly, at that stage of the process where practically everything in the house seemed to be turned upside down or hind side before, "all I got to say is clean everything in sight, includin' Carl and the dog, just so's you don't get the idea of shinin' up my stamp cabinet."

"I wouldn't dare even dust the outside of it," his daughter-in-law assured him. "I'm much too smart a gal for that. I know better."

They all knew better, everybody in the family. Nobody but Grampa touched Grampa's stamps. That was a rule. And the Fishers had never subscribed to the theory that rules were made to be broken. They did not believe there should be too many of them, nor that they should exist arbitrarily without good reasons; but once established for those aforesaid good reasons, it was their simple conviction that rules should be kept.

Moreover, they considered Grampa's rule entirely reasonable. His stamp collection was his pride and joy, and they were proud

for and with him. It was also valuable. Valuable as a matter of
sentiment, for some of the stamps had been in the family for a
hundred years, but valuable in dollars and cents as well. Just a
few days before the era of spring cleaning had dawned again for
the Fishers, the Middleburg newspaper had carried a long article
about Grampa's collection; a full-page Sunday feature with photo-
graphs of him and some of his best stamps, and a personal interview as to how he had acquired them—an interview which, it may
be said, he had granted with no show of coy reluctance; rather, in
fact, with a zest which had required some deft cutting on the
reporter's part later. Grampa's stamps were famous—around
Middleburg, at any rate; and stamps are tiny things, easily torn,
easily lost, fragile and delicate. So, though Grampa never locked
his cabinet, it was fully understood that no one but him opened it.

Probably Freddie was the only one to whom it represented any
temptation. The rest of the family were merely gratified specta-
tors as far as stamp collecting went, pleased with Grampa's
achievements. They had no ambitions at all on their own accounts.
But Freddie was made of different material. In his veins, to
Grampa's immense delight, flowed the blood of a true philatelist.
Already he had, with Grampa's help, made a creditable start toward a collection of his own; and when Grampa chose to work,
evenings, over the larger collection, it was equally difficult either
to get Freddie to do his homework or to go to bed—he remained
glued to Grampa's side at the long table, listening and watching,
fascinated.

Spring cleaning was nearing its end, and things had just begun
to look a little bit normal again on the afternoon when Freddie
elected to educate his friend Greg in some of the worth-while
things of life. Both boys were sprawled on the floor, and Freddie
had, for the past fifteen minutes, been displaying and thoroughly
explaining his stamp album to his guest. As small boys go, Greg
was rather a polite one; but at this point both his courtesy and
his friendship began to show the first signs of cracking under the
strain imposed on them. So when Freddie started importantly,
"Now this one's English—a King George—and I've got a new
Queen 'Lizbeth, too——" Greg interrupted.

"Ole English stamps!" said he scornfully. "I'd ruther have a good

American one any day. George Washington, or somebody like that."

"Well, I've just started, but my grampa, he's got loads like that," said Freddie quickly, eager to regain his audience. "Why, he's got one block of stamps with George Washington's picture that's more'n a hundred years old, and awful valuable. It's a black stamp, a twelve-center."

"I don't call twelve cents so awful valuable," said Greg.

Freddie laughed. "You sure are ign'rant about stamps, Greg. The latest catalogue price on that stamp was three hunderd and fifty *dollars,* that's what. It was a twelve-cent stamp—like some stamps are three-centers and some two and some eight—and all that. Say, didn't you read that article in the newspaper last week about Grampa's stamp collection?"

Greg, beginning to feel at a disadvantage, shook his head.

"You deliver papers and don't read 'em. Well, it told specially about his commen"—Freddie bogged down momentarily and took a fresh start—"commenorative stamps!" he finished triumphantly.

"What are *they?*" asked Greg, speaking quite respectfully now.

"Oh—they menorate something in history—or somebody who's done something famous. Grampa's got a lot like that. They're awful interesting."

Freddie's eyes were so bright that Greg, still hazy as to what commemorative stamps were exactly, felt curiosity swelling within him. "Whyn't you show me some of *those?*" he asked eagerly. "They're the ones I'd like to see."

Freddie's face fell. "I'll have to ask Grampa to do it sometime. I'm not s'posed to touch 'em. Nobody is. Not even Mom when she spring-cleans."

This was all that was needed to whet Greg's curiosity. "I don't see why," he began argumentatively. "We wouldn't hurt 'em——" And broke off suddenly to say, "Oh, hello, Mr. Jake!"

Jake, all-round handy man and, Anna was wont to declare, the neighborhood's most valuable asset, was coming down the stairs, overall-clad, and managing somehow to carry all at once a mop, cleaning rags, and a big pasteboard carton filled with trash and papers. His seamed face broke into a smile when he saw the boys.

"How you doin', boys? Studyin' your stamps?" He set the big box down by the table. "This trash box worry you here for a while? I'm goin' to take it home with me, but I got another little job first —'fore your mama gets back from the store."

Freddie nodded an absent-minded "Okay," hardly hearing, as Jake set down the box and left. He was wishing with all his heart that just once *he*, all by himself, could have the fun of showing Grampa's stamps.

"Where does he keep 'em, Freddie?" asked Greg.

"Grampa, you mean? His stamps? In that cabinet over there."

Greg scrambled up and went to the cabinet; and Freddie followed, with a queer sort of scared excitement stirring in him.

"I can't see a thing—they're in boxes and books and things," Greg complained. "Freddie, *why* won't your grampa let you touch 'em?"

"Well—he puts 'em away just like he wants 'em is one thing."

"Couldn't you put 'em back the same way?" Greg inquired reasonably, and suddenly reached out his hand and turned the knob of the cabinet door. Immediately it swung open.

"Why, it's not even locked!" he cried. "He can't mind their being touched much, your grampa can't, or he'd lock the door, wouldn't he?"

The answer to that one was right on the tip of Freddie's tongue: "Crazy, what would he lock it for when he trusts us?" But somehow it did not get said. Instead, Freddie heard himself remarking in a weak, small voice, "Does kinda look that way, I guess."

And after that he was not even much surprised to find himself lifting out one of the boxes and adding, "I reckon it won't hurt if we just look at this one."

"Oh boy!" said Greg exultantly. "Shall we spread 'em on the floor?"

"No, no—not these, these are *valuable*, you got to re'lize! I'll lay 'em out real careful on the table, and we'll just stand up here and I'll show you—— No, don't you touch 'em, Greg, just me! Grampa, he uses tweezers and things to pick 'em up. Now look at that one —with the ship—ain't it a beauty?"

"What's those that look like a battle?"

"Oh, they're new—but here's one you oughta see . . ."

The stamps were spread all over the table now while Freddie hunted feverishly for this or that special one. But, he assured himself over a slight qualm in his stomach, he knew how they ought to go back, he could get them in right.

And perhaps he did know, almost as well as he thought he did, and perhaps he could have replaced them very nearly as he found them; but he was not to be given a chance to prove it. For he had just found the block of Washington stamps when a voice that he knew well—and was usually glad to hear—came floating through the open window. And to Freddie, just then, it sounded like the trump of doom itself.

"Hello, Jake!" boomed Grampa pleasantly from somewhere outside. "How's the world treatin' you?"

"Seldom, sir, seldom," Jake's voice came back in answer, and both of them laughed uproariously at the feeble little pun. But inside the house Freddie, frozen with terror, was in no mood to appreciate a form of wit which was generally just his dish.

Since fear is infectious, Greg, looking at his friend's dismayed face, suddenly became almost as frightened himself.

"I'll help you," he gasped. "Quick, let's get 'em back——"

"You'll mess 'em all up!" Freddie spoke in an anguished wail. "No—this goes here and that goes there and——"

"You can't wait for all that 'this goes here' stuff! Just get 'em in any old way," Greg panted.

No, he couldn't wait; Freddie knew it all too well. Much as the necessity wrenched his heart, there was nothing to do but to dump the precious stamps back in the box helter-skelter. Even so, there was barely time to close the cabinet door and dive to the floor, pretending to be absorbed in Freddie's album, before Grampa came in and greeted them heartily, clearly pleased at their occupation. "Freddie tryin' to make a convert of you, Greg? I'll have to show you my collection sometime."

Greg, who felt just then that he never wanted to see another stamp, shot an uneasy glance at Freddie, and after a mumbled "Thank you, sir," remarked hastily that he'd better be getting home, and took his departure forthwith. At this point Jake ambled in, explaining that he had come for the carton.

"Don't go without tellin' me how your wife's doin' now, Jake,"

Grampa said concernedly, and in the ensuing conversation Freddie made his own escape. If just Grampa wouldn't want to look at his stamps for two or three days! If just there'd come another time when none of them were around so Freddie could have a chance to straighten the box up! He started to say "Please let it be like that, Jesus," and stopped with the unhappy feeling that perhaps asking the Lord to get you out of the results of your own wrongdoing just wasn't going to work very well.

He managed to forget about it all for a little while at dinner—Grampa and Pop had some unusually funny stories to tell about things that had happened at the drugstore that day—but afterward, while he was lying on the floor in the living room looking at the comic page, Grampa remarked, "Well, guess I'll work over my collection a little while." And instantly Freddie felt as if he were in an airplane that had taken a sudden, violent, downward swoop. He fastened his eyes to the comic page, although he did not see a single picture, every bit of him tensed and waiting; and sure enough, after a moment, Grampa's puzzled voice sounded behind him. "That's funny!"

"What's funny?" asked Freddie's father.

"My cabinet. It don't look the way I left it. Different, somehow. Oh, I know—it's this big box. Turned hind side before. I'm sure I didn't put it in like that——"

Freddie did not raise his eyes; his head sank even lower over the comic page. But just as well as if he had been staring hard, he knew how Grampa's perplexed frown looked, knew that he was taking the box out and placing it on the table.

"Why, it's all mixed up!" Grampa's tone was genuinely bewildered now. "Stamps just flung in—— Freddie!"

Freddie had to raise his head this time, but he managed to look blank, as if his whole mind were still on the comics. "Yessir?"

"Were you boys by any chance looking at my collection today?"

Afterward it seemed to Freddie that if he'd had time to think he might have answered differently. But the words just said themselves—or so it appeared to him. "No, Grampa, 'course not." And then it was too late.

"Why, Grampa!" cried Freddie's mother, a trifle indignantly. "You know Freddie wouldn't touch your stamps!"

"Well, sure, I know it now, since he told me," said Grampa. "And I thought I knew it before. I was just askin', Anna."

Freddie suddenly felt as if he might be getting the flu, like he'd done in the winter. It was almost exactly the same; stomach griping, cheeks hot, hands cold.

"I guess," he said unhappily, "I guess it's about time for me to be gettin' to bed," a remark which produced a mild sensation in his audience of three, since this was a decision he usually arrived at only under considerable pressure.

But at ten years old even a troublesome conscience does not often keep one lying awake nights, when the young body is healthfully tired. So Freddie woke the next morning, after a deep sleep, to the sound of his mother's voice from the doorway advising him to get up; to the sight of spring sunshine streaming over his red bedspread; and to the feeling that the events of yesterday belonged to some dim and faraway period, too long past to worry about any more. In this happy mood he came into the living room with his father, both laughing at a small joke Carl had just told him—and stopped, surprised, at the sight of Grampa sitting at the table with his stamp collection spread around him; an occupation generally assigned only to the evening hours.

"Say, didn't you go to bed at all last night?" asked Carl with a grin. "You're just where I left you!"

But there was no answering smile on Grampa's face. Freddie had not often seen him look bothered, but he looked bothered now.

"Carl," he said solemnly, "I hate to tell you—but somebody has been tampering with my stamps."

And suddenly all Freddie's nice morning spirits were gone and what had happened wasn't in the dim past at all, but right here and now in a dark and forbidding present. Carl was looking incredulous.

"Oh, Dad, you must be mistaken!"

Grampa shook his head wearily. "Wish I were, Son. It's not just the mess. It's worse than that. I've checked everything very carefully and there's a packet of stamps missin'."

If his father's arm hadn't been still around his shoulders, Freddie might have turned tail and run, out of sheer panic. How could

a packet be missing? He and Greg had put them all back. He was
certain. But if anybody found out now, they'd sure be
blamed. . . .

His mother had come in by this time, asking what the trouble
was, and they were all talking. The packet held some of his best
stamps, Grampa was saying; particularly one block. How much
were they worth? Well, probably, all put together, about eight
hundred dollars. To Freddie the sum was astronomical. It might
almost as well have been eight million. He could not have felt
more stricken and guilty.

"But, Grampa," his mother kept protesting, "it just isn't possible
for anybody to have taken your stamps!" till finally Grampa answered, "Well, Anna, I don't know as you can say a thing is impossible if it's happened, can you?"

"No—of course not." They were all looking worried now. "But
it's so *peculiar*. Outside of Freddie and Greg, there was no one
here yesterday but Jake."

As soon as she had spoken, she looked startled; as if some idea
which she didn't like at all had suddenly occurred to her. Moreover, the other two grownups were looking the same way. The
room was heavy with a special quality of silence; the silence that
comes when people are thinking something they don't want to
say.

"Freddie," asked Grampa gravely, "did you see Jake anywhere
near that cabinet yesterday?"

"Jake?" echoed Freddie, startled. "No, sir."

"Oh, Grampa!" cried Anna, almost as if she felt remorseful.
"Jake *wouldn't*——"

"Anna's right," said Carl quickly. "Jake's not the kind of man
who'd take anything."

Grampa was pacing up and down now. "Sure, I've always felt
that way about him. But he was here alone for a while before
Freddie came home from school." He paused, looking quite miserable. "And Jake's wife's been sick—sometimes under a strain like
that——"

"I don't think we ought to consider that as a possibility without
a lot more evidence," said Carl positively.

Grampa stopped pacing, and his face cleared. "You're right, Son.

Sorry I suggested it. Come to think of it—I haven't had the collection out since just before the article about it was published. Maybe the packet wasn't taken yesterday at all—might have been a few days ago. You s'pose Emily or Peter——"

"But why in the world would they?" asked Anna. "Anyway—don't you remember? You worked over the whole collection three hours *after* they left. Well, in the meantime—breakfast is getting cold!"

As they all moved toward the dining room, Grampa said, "Still, I hope you folks'll feel that I ought to go and see Jake about it—just to find out if he can shed any light on it. If, for instance, he saw anything—or anybody——"

"Oh yes," Carl agreed. "I don't think we ought to leave any stone unturned."

They were all at the table now. The sunshine lay in patterns of gold on the blue-and-white-checked cloth.

"Freddie!" said his mother.

Freddie fairly leaped in his seat, turning on her a pair of startled brown eyes. "Had you gone to sleep again?" She was laughing at him. "I just wanted you to say grace for us."

"Oh!" breathed Freddie, and bowed his head and mumbled one of the blessings he'd been taught.

His life had been short, and until now uncomplicated. He had never had occasion to learn that the guilty flee when no man pursueth, and probably would not have understood the meaning of the text. But he did know that for an instant just the sudden calling of his name had frightened him; and he felt that for a fellow to get scared as quick and easy as *that* was a most uncomfortable way to be.

This time, moreover, he could not shake the discomfort off. It kept on nagging at him all through school hours; and finally he told Greg about it as they walked home together afterward, seeking at least the relief of sharing his unease.

"*You* didn't take that missin' block, did you?" he asked suddenly at the end of the story, sending Greg a searching glance.

"*Me?* Me steal your Grampa's stamps?" Greg snorted. "I oughta bust you in the nose for that!"

"Go on, try!" said Freddie threateningly, and such was his mood by now that he would almost have welcomed violence and was half sorry when Greg backed down with a hasty "Oh well, I reckon you're too worried to know what you're sayin'."

He cut through the back yard as usual when he got home, coming in by way of the kitchen, and was faintly cheered by the sight of his mother baking cookies. One plate was already done, hot and fragrant, and the gesture with which he reached for it was as automatic as was hers when she caught his arm midway.

"No, darling, not now. They're for dessert tonight. Besides—Grampa wants to see you in the front room."

"Oh!" said Freddie blankly, all his interest in the cookies gone. "Okay—I'll go see what he wants."

But in the archway leading to the living room he stopped short. The police—Grampa had called the police! It was no less a person than Chief of Police Baldwin himself who stood before the cabinet beside Grampa, their backs to Freddie.

"Now, Mr. Fisher," the Chief was saying, "just one more question—are you dead-sure the kids didn't take those stamps?"

"Freddie told me positively that they hadn't touched them, Chief. The boy don't lie. Besides, Freddie would never have left the stamps in a mess like that—he knows how they go." He looked at the Chief over his glasses. "I don't expect you to feel as sure of this as I do," he said quietly. "But even if you think Freddie might've been playing with the stamps and deceived us all about it, it's just out of the question to suppose he'd steal any of 'em. There wouldn't be any reason—it wouldn't make sense—and—well, he just didn't, that's all. Forget that angle."

"I'm inclined to think you're right," said the Chief unexpectedly. "I know the boy—he's in the same Sunday school class with my little daughter——"

Just then he turned and saw Freddie, standing hesitant and white-faced, in the doorway.

"Why, hello, Freddie!" He made a special effort to be cordial, uncertain how much the child had heard. "Come in, Sonny. I only wanted to ask you a question or two. What time did you and Greg get home yesterday?"

"I—I think about three-thirty," stammered Freddie.

"And you didn't see Jake in the living room here except when he carried out the box of trash?"

"Why—he came in once. Just passing through. He spoke to Greg and me—we was lookin' at my stamps—and went on."

"It's all right, Freddie," Grampa said quickly, thinking that the boy looked frightened. "You're not doin' Jake any harm. Chief Baldwin's just checkin' up everywhere—tryin' to unravel our mystery. He thinks somebody who read that article about my collection might've slipped in and taken some stamps."

"But then—why didn't they take the whole collection 'stead of just one packet?" Freddie asked.

"A smart question," said the Chief approvingly. "But I think I know the answer, Freddie. The thief could've been smart too. He might've figured that one packet wouldn't be missed so soon, and would stand considerably better chance of being peddled without his getting caught. Well, Mr. Fisher, I guess I've got all the facts now, and I'll be checking up every angle I can."

"Just one more thing," said Grampa. "I did want to tell you, Chief, that when I talked to Jake this morning it was him urged me to put the matter into the hands of the police. He said he knew there'd be some talk about him after it got out that the stamps had been stolen, as it'd be bound to do. He said he made his living doin' odd jobs around people's houses and he'd be ruined if folks didn't trust him. So he's mighty anxious to have the guilty party found."

The Chief nodded, somewhat noncommittally, promised to do his best, and left. Freddie watched him go with mingled worry and relief.

That night for the first time he was sorry when Grampa got out his stamp collection and invited him to "sit in—so's I can explain a few fine points to you." Stamps were a subject he would have been happier to be allowed to forget just now. But he came—dutifully—though with slightly dragging steps.

Grampa lifted one stamp delicately with a pair of tweezers. "Now this one, Freddie—how do you like it?"

"It's pretty," said Freddie. "Bright colors—nice picture."

Grampa nodded. "Yes, it's pretty, and that's *all* it is. Not worth a nickel."

Freddie looked more closely. "But why?" he asked, puzzled.

"Because it's a counterfeit. An imitation of the real one, not the real one itself. No more good than a five-dollar bill a man would run off on his own printing press."

"Oh!" Freddie studied it with growing interest. "Then what made you buy it?"

Grampa grinned. "Got fooled. 'Course I'd a lot rather be the fellow that gets cheated than the one that does the cheating, but I don't aim for you to be either. That's what I mean by the fine points. If I'd been noticing like I ought, there's two tiny things about this would have warned me. And I want you to learn by my experience. Look here——"

They were deep in it now, and Freddie had grown thoroughly interested in spite of himself when Anna called time on them.

"Your bedtime, Freddie. And by the way, Jake left his screwdriver here the other day. I'm going to slip it in your lunch basket tomorrow, and you stop by his house on the way home and give it to him."

"Yes'm," said Freddie reluctantly. He felt a curious shrinking from seeing Jake, as if Jake were another subject he'd like very much to forget. But he had no excuse handy.

He found Jake, the next afternoon, in his workshed at the back, busy sorting out junk and papers.

"Well, thank you, Freddie," he said. "I must be gettin' old—leavin' things around like this. Any news of the stamps?"

Freddie shook his head. "What you doin', Mr. Jake?" he asked hastily. "I mean with all that stuff you're goin' over."

"Why, I always sort out the trash people give me to carry away," Jake explained. "Sometimes I find things I can repair and use. The papers and magazines I bale up and sell. Got a big box of papers your mother had me carry off back in there—I'll get around to baling 'em pretty soon. And by the way, look on that shelf behind me. There's a baseball mitt somebody throwed away the other day—see it? That's the one—it's perfectly good, if somebody'd just take the trouble to mend that one little rip."

"Sure is," Freddie agreed, examining it eagerly.

"Well, if you can use it take it along."

"Oh!" A lump seemed to have come up strangely in Freddie's throat. "Why—why, thank you, Mr. Jake—lots."

He swallowed the lump almost angrily. What was the matter with him, anyway? Why did he have to keep feeling like he'd done something bad to Mr. Jake? He hadn't, he'd never done anything bad to Mr. Jake in all his life. All the same, the glove, as he walked toward home carrying it, seemed to make him feel worse and worse.

Halfway home he met Greg, just starting out to deliver his afternoon papers. Greg wasn't, however, delivering them at the moment; he wasn't on his bicycle, even. He was leaning against a fence and reading one of the papers. And when he saw Freddie he called to him excitedly.

"Hey—come here! Look! Right on the front page!"

Freddie suddenly felt a profound disinclination to look. It was going to be something about the stamps—every time anybody wanted to see him about anything lately, he thought moodily, it was the stamps, and it would be this time, too. He was right. It was.

"See here!" Greg began to read aloud. "It says—the headlines say—in big letters—'"IT DOESN'T PAY TO ADVERTISE," SAYS GRAMPA FISHER.' And down underneath: 'We know he's only kidding——'"

"I can read," said Freddie crossly, and snatched the paper away.

"We know he's only kidding," stated the article, "but the thieves who stole some of his stamps after reading about his stamp collection in this paper recently *weren't* kidding. Chief Baldwin is making every effort to apprehend the burglars. He says he has a lead, but refused to disclose it . . ."

Freddie handed the newspaper back silently. He had seen all and more than he wanted to see.

"I didn't know about your grampa calling in the police," said Greg. He was looking a little frightened. "Say, Freddie, you didn't tell anybody about us lookin' at the stamps, did you?"

"No, I didn't," said Freddie slowly. "But I think I ought to've."

"You can't!" Greg's voice had gone up a note with alarm. "If you tell now, they'll think we took the missin' stamps!"

"They wouldn't, either—they know me better."

"Your folks might. But the police'll be sure of it."

Freddie remembered the conversation he had overheard between Grampa and the Chief, and turned white under his healthy tan.

"Greg—could we possibly have dropped one packet?"

"We could've, I guess. But then it would've been right on the floor and your grampa or somebody'd have seen it and picked it up."

"I guess that's so. I guess somebody did steal one. But it's just funny—it bein' missin' right after we——"

"Well, it happened," said Greg edgily. "And you keep still about it or we might have to go to jail for sumpin' we didn't do."

Freddie couldn't eat his dinner that night, and his mother inquired if he "felt bad." He shook his head; he was "just not hungry," he said. Anna, who believed that children needed attention and love but also quite a good deal of being let alone, did not press him. She thought, however, that he did not look like himself—his color was not quite right and his mouth drooped a little, and she felt a twinge of anxiety. She and Carl were going out to a party immediately after dinner. When she came downstairs, dressed in the new blue that was so becoming to her blond hair, she was relieved to find him engaged in a lively game of quoits with Grampa. One ring narrowly missed hitting her, and as she dodged it expertly, protesting that she was being subjected to "assault and battery in my own house," Freddie whooped with laughter in a manner that was quite reassuring as to any lurking illness. It was just then that the doorbell rang and Jake was ushered in.

At the very first sight of him Freddie, who had briefly forgotten his troubles, felt them all swooping down on him again like so many black buzzards. Jake could only be coming at this hour because something else had happened about the stamps—and every new development about those stamps thus far had been a new cause for worry.

"Evening, folks," said Jake's voice, and suddenly they all realized that it was trembling with a queer excitement or agitation.

"Mr. Fisher, sir, I sure got good news for you. Look here! I found your stamps for you!"

"What?" cried Grampa incredulously, just as Anna said, "Not really!" and Carl exclaimed amazedly, "Where on earth?"

Jake smiled at them all proudly. "Here they are, sir. Look 'em over for yourself!"

Grampa's hands were positively shaking. "They're all there," he declared, scanning them eagerly. "It's too good to be true!"

"I got to thinkin' about it," said Jake, beaming, "and all of a sudden I remembered about that big carton of papers I ain't got round to baling yet that I took away for Mrs. Fisher. And I said to myself, 'Maybe I'd better look over them things before I cart 'em off!' So I went over every bit of it—and sure enough, there they was!"

"Wonderful!" Grampa exclaimed. "Wonderful!" But he looked puzzled as well as happy. "Only—how in the world did they *get* there?"

Grampa had asked the question quite naturally and innocently, but it was one for which nobody had an answer. And in the tiny silence that followed, a queer sort of strain crept into the atmosphere. Jake glanced quickly from one perplexed face to another —and slowly the brightness faded from his own.

"I never thought how funny it might look," he said heavily. "I was just so glad to find 'em—but I guess I ain't quite in the clear, after all. I guess some folks'll think I *did* take 'em—and got scared after the hullabaloo and only pretended to find 'em——"

"Oh, Jake, we don't think that!" cried Anna, almost in tears. Carl echoed her quickly, "You know we don't!" Grampa, looking distressed, made a suggestion. "Tell you what, we'll just give out that the stamps got found in some of our trash, Jake—we won't say it was trash *you'd* taken home or that *you* found 'em."

But Jake shook his head. "It's too late for that, Mr. Fisher. Like I said, I never thought about its lookin' funny. I told my daughter right off to telephone Chief Baldwin and tell him all about it while I was on the way over here—didn't want to wait to do it myself, I was so anxious to bring 'em on. I thought——"

He choked a little, and just at that instant the telephone rang.

Grampa reached it first; they had all guessed who it would be, and they waited, not trying to talk or pretending that they were not listening to Grampa's end of the conversation.

"Why, yes, Chief," said the pleasant old voice. "Jake's just brought 'em." . . . "All of 'em—yes." . . . "Yes, he got to thinkin' and wondered if they mightn't be in the trash he'd carried away and sure enough they were—smart of him, we think." . . . "No—no—we haven't figured out how they got there—guess that don't matter now, the important thing is they're back . . ." He frowned suddenly. "No, sir," he said sharply, "we don't want you to talk to him. Let's just drop the whole matter." . . . "What?" He stiffened. "Yes, that's just exactly the way we feel about it! We want the whole thing dropped and forgotten." Another pause, and his voice grew cordial again. "Well, thanks for all your efforts, Chief. Good-by."

He put the receiver down and faced them. "Now, Jake," he said heartily, "you know where we stand, and we'll see to it that everybody else knows too—you just do what I told the Chief to do—drop the whole business and forget it."

Anna and Carl seconded him, quickly and warmly, and Jake thanked them and tried to smile. But Grampa's replies to the Chief had left him in no doubt that the latter's reaction to the news had been one of suspicion; and as he shook hands and told them good-by, there was hurt and bewilderment on his lined face and his big body was sagging.

"I feel terrible about this!" Anna burst out as soon as the door had closed behind him.

The two men looked as if they agreed with her. "I don't like it," Grampa said, shaking his head. "I don't like it at all. I'm afraid some people *are* going to suspect Jake."

Carl nodded soberly. "We'll do the best we can about it—after all, we've got some influence in this town. Well, Anna, if we're going to this party at all we'd better be off."

Anna was looking at Freddie; she thought, "Now he looks all white and sick again!" And as she bent to kiss him good night she whispered, "Are you sick, dear? If you are, I won't go."

"I'm all right," mumbled Freddie.

Anna hesitated, but Carl's voice came again, a little impatiently,

"Really, honey, we're going to be late," and she kissed her son's cheek lightly and straightened up.

"Well, good night, both of you!" she said cheerfully. But even after the door had closed between them and she and Carl were on their way, she was still troubled by the feeling that something was wrong with Freddie—in which she was more right than she knew. For never before had things been so blackly wrong with Freddie.

"Guess we'll have to finish our game tomorrow night," Grampa remarked. "Bedtime for you. You call me when you're all ready. I'll be working over my stamps, but I'll come up and tell you good night after you're in bed."

Freddie nodded dully, without the customary protest, and went with unwonted slowness upstairs. Mechanically he took his shower and got into his pajamas. Then he sat on the edge of his bed awhile, staring miserably at nothing. Prayers came next, and tonight Freddie felt quite unequal to prayers. Since, however, he had never in his life gone to sleep without them, he slid at last to his knees and began. "Dear Jesus, please forgive——"

Abruptly he stopped. "It's not a bit of use!" he thought despairingly. For suddenly it was very plain to him that if he kept quiet about what had happened to those stamps it was exactly the same as continuing to lie about it. And what was the good of asking Jesus to forgive you for lying if you were only planning to go right straight ahead lying as hard as ever? It wasn't as if he didn't know now exactly how the packet had gotten into that trash. The whole picture had come clear to him in a flash from the first moment Jake had told about the find. So there wasn't but one thing to do. And Freddie didn't in the least want to do it. . . . With a deep sigh he got slowly to his feet and went reluctantly down the stairs.

Grampa was seated at a table, poring happily over his returned packet, his back to the door, and he did not see or hear when the little boy came in on bare feet, silently. Freddie stood watching him; and twice his courage failed and he turned and took a few steps toward the staircase, and twice he came back. The third time he managed to get as far as Grampa's elbow and to say weakly, "Grampa?"

Grampa looked up, startled. "Huh? Why, you came in like a mouse! I told you I'd come up if you called."

"I know, but——" He stood twisting his hands and fighting back tears. "I got somethin' to tell you."

Grampa's old eyes were suddenly keen on the terrified little face. "The boy's in trouble," he thought. He put his arm around the trembling shoulders. "What is it, Freddie?" he asked gently.

"It's just that——" He swallowed twice, and then it came with a rush. "I can't let anybody think Mr. Jake took those stamps, 'cause —I got it all figgered out now what happened, and it's all my fault——"

"*What?*" asked Grampa, amazed. "What do you mean?"

Freddie knew he had to say it fast and get it over with, else he'd break down and cry like a sissy.

"I—I'd been showing Greg your stamps that day. He wanted to see 'em—and first I said you'd have to show 'em, but then *I* wanted to be the one to do it, myself—so I did, and all of a sudden we heard you comin'—and I was scared of gettin' caught—so we had to put 'em back quick. *That's* why they was so messed up, and one of the packets must've dropped in that trash box, 'cause I remember it was standing right there by the table where we was standing too. So Mr. Jake didn't have nothing to do with any of it——"

But at this point, in spite of himself, he began to sob.

Grampa, his arm still around him, led him to the davenport and pushed him gently down, sitting beside him. "Sit down, Freddie. This'll take a little talkin' over. Stop cryin' now and tell me—did you lie because you were too scared to tell me the truth? What did you think I'd do to you, boy?"

His voice was so mild and steady that the child himself was unconsciously steadied by it. He wiped his eyes with the big handkerchief Grampa had pressed into his hand. His chest was still heaving, but he could speak, chokily.

"It—it wasn't like that. I wasn't scared of what you'd *do* to me. I—I just didn't want you to know I'd broke the rule——"

"Yes," said Grampa. "I see. Well, when you're older you'll study the writings of a great man, Freddie, who said, 'Conscience does make cowards of us all.' It was a bad conscience made a coward of you, wasn't it? 'Cause it didn't make much sense to try to get out of one wrong deed by committin' another that was wronger, did it? Handlin' the stamps when it was forbidden was wrong, but lyin' was worse and you knew it was worse. Funny how often folks'll do just that—try to get loose from a smaller sin by doin' a bigger one. I've done it myself. Till I found out it didn't work, that it just got me in worse trouble."

"That's what it did for me, too," gulped Freddie. "But—but I didn't know it was goin' to hurt anybody—Mr. Jake—or anybody——"

"Well, it mightn't have involved Jake—if you hadn't happened to drop that packet," said Grampa reasonably. "But of course lyin' is wrong whether it hurts anybody or not. Anyway, there's always two it hurts—it hurts you and it hurts God."

He was glad to see that the boy was able to look at him by now. The young eyes were still clouded with distress, but they could meet his own squarely.

And if just at this point Grampa hesitated an instant, it was not because he shared the horror of some modern parents, lest they might be considered to be "preaching" to their children. Grampa never lectured in any pompous way, and he believed with all his heart that tenderness and understanding were the first requisites in dealing with children. But he had no prejudice against the right sort of preaching, and in fact, held a good sermon to be a desirable thing. His hesitation, therefore, sprang from his anxiety to find exactly the most helpful thing to say to Freddie. For he did not minimize what Freddie had done; he knew that a child's first serious and deliberate lie may prove a turning point for good or for ill. So he did an instant's hard praying before he spoke again.

"There's another thing about lies, Freddie. It so often happens, just like it did this time for you, that what started out to be just one little lie grows and grows, and means doin' a lot more deceivin', and finally drags in a lot of other people, too. I guess it's that way with all our sins—they don't seem big when they start, but they grow like weeds, and that's why it's important to root 'em up as soon's they begin."

"Have mine just beginned?" asked Freddie hopefully.

"Why, sure," Grampa told him comfortingly. "And you've learned a lot, too, I think. There was another poet—I seem to be quotin' poetry tonight—who said, 'Oh, what a tangled web we weave, When first we practise to deceive.' You can understand that if you try, because you've been doin' some weavin' yourself. And it's got worse and worse tangled up, hasn't it?" He added cheerfully, "And now we got to think how to unweave it and put things straight again. That's what you want, to put 'em straight. That's why you came to me, isn't it?"

Freddie nodded soberly.

"All right then. What's the first thing to do?"

Freddie answered this quite simply and directly, with no pose or self-consciousness. "Ask Jesus to forgive me."

"And you don't have any doubts about the answer to that, do you?" asked Grampa matter-of-factly.

"Not now," said Freddie. "It wouldn't work upstairs a little while ago, though."

"But you think it will now?"

"Why, yes, sir." Freddie looked slightly surprised at the question. "It's different now." Then his face clouded. "The only thing is——" He cleared his throat; his voice had begun to tremble a little. "The only thing——"

Grampa waited.

"I—I was thinkin' the next thing to do—you got to get it published in the newspapers. I mean what really happened. About me takin' the stamps and droppin' 'em—and then keepin' still. I guess that's the only way to get it right for Mr. Jake, ain't it?"

Grampa noted, with a surge of pride, that though he looked frightened the boy also looked resolute.

"Well, now," said Grandpa carefully, "we *would* do that, of course, if it was necessary. And we ought to tell Chief Baldwin the whole tale, seems to me. But for the newspaper story—we'll get that girl reporter, Emily's friend, to write it for us. And we'll say—let's see . . ."

Freddie hung on the next words a little breathlessly.

"We'll just say," Grampa decided, "that it turned out that a member of the family had dropped the packet in the trash box while handlin' the stamps. We'll say that when Jake brought the packet back this person realized right off what had happened because he could remember plain as could be that the trash box had been standing right by his side while he was gathering the stamps up to replace 'em in the cabinet. Now that's all true, isn't it? And we'll put in something about how fine and smart it was of Jake to figure the things *might* be in the trash box and find 'em for us. Tell you what! We'll make it sorta funny—put in something about spring-cleaning being to blame."

"I know what!" Freddie's eyes were shining with relief. "We'll have a headline: NOT THIEVES BUT SPRING-CLEANING!"

They laughed together at this none too subtle humor, and then Freddie's face sobered again.

"But I guess you're right about tellin' Chief Baldwin. And—" his voice faltered ever so slightly—"Mom and Pop . . . I don't know how they'll feel about it—awful bad, I guess."

"Why, yes," said Grampa gently. "They'll be sorry. Naturally. Sorry you disobeyed and broke the rule, and sorry you told the lies, and sorry about the hard time you've been having. But glad you came and told about it, and glad you're ready and willin' to do anything to make it right, and gladdest that you know just where to go to get forgiven and washed clean inside and straightened out." He paused. "Yes—for that last I think they'll be specially *mighty* glad."

There was no shadow left on Freddie's face now; it was relaxed and happy.

"By the way, Grampa," he asked, "what was in that lost packet, anyway?"

"Well, the most valuable ones were the Washington stamps— the black twelve-centers." Grampa's smile shared a special coincidence with him. "The fellow who couldn't tell a lie!"

"Oh, you mean about the cherry tree?" Freddie was only very slightly condescending. "I had a teacher said that prob'ly didn't really happen, Grampa—she said it was prob'ly only a legend."

"As to that, I don't actually know," Grampa admitted. "I can't prove it's not just a kind of legend, like she said. But I'll tell you one thing—when legends like that grow up around a man it seems to me it's a pretty good sign that they got started because everybody knew how truthful he was."

"I reckon that's so," Freddie agreed thoughtfully.

He stooped and picked up a quoit ring from the floor. "Here's a ring you missed when you was puttin' away the quoit game, Grampa."

"So it is. Now you better be off to bed, Freddie."

"Maybe I had, at that." But at the door he turned. "Beat you real bad at quoits tomorrow night, Grampa!"

"Better wait till you've done it to crow!" advised Grampa. "Good night, Son."

"Good night," said Freddie.

Grampa watched him to the top of the stairs; and when he turned to go back into the living room, he was still smiling.

5. THE MUSIC BOX

*A*FTERWARD, when she looked back, Dorothy knew that the explosion of an emotional bomb, so to speak, with all the resultant din and fireworks, seldom occurs as suddenly as might appear to an onlooker. Her own bomb, for example, as she could clearly see in retrospect, had been planted a long time ago; and for as long a time had been ticking away toward its devastating climax of eruption—a climax only she could have prevented—by disconnecting and smashing the dangerous thing.

But Paul, her husband, had only recently begun to be aware, in a troubled and puzzled fashion, of certain ominous signs by that day in Fisher's Drugstore when he bought the music box. And to him it always seemed that the whole shattering experience began and ended with the small, bright box and its melody.

On that midafternoon he and Harvey Dixon had run in from their office building just down the street for a coffee break. It was something of a habit with Middleburg people to drop in often at Fisher's for coffee, or perhaps a snack of milk and crackers; and probably neither the Fishers nor their customers quite realized that they came for more than material refreshment. Without formulating it, the Fishers' friends and acquaintances knew that they simply "felt better" and problems seemed easier after these brief visits—and they did not bother to ask how much was due to food and drink and relaxation, and how much to the special atmosphere Grampa and Carl managed to disseminate; an atmosphere as cheerful and friendly and wholesome as sunshine—and one which, like sunshine, warmed and lighted.

It was Carl who was serving the two on this particular day. Grampa was on the other side of the store arranging a display of music boxes. Carl, who believed that human nature presented the most fascinating study on earth, and on the whole held a high opinion of it, was thinking as he drew the coffee that these young men, both working in the same office and close friends, were an interesting contrast. Paul was quiet and gentle; his mouth was sensitive, his quick smile a little shy, and dreams hid deep in his eyes. Harvey, alert, capable, kindly, was much more expressive and aggressive, and he radiated self-confidence. But there, Carl thought, putting the cups down before them and pushing the sugar across to them, you mustn't try to put people into pigeon-holes! None of them ever exactly fitted into *one* classification. Paul, for instance, was no shrinking violet but a competent businessman, for all the tincture of poet in his composition, and Harvey, on the other hand, had certainly nothing of the loud, over-hearty, too persistent salesman in his manner or make-up. Thoroughly nice fellows, both of them; and probably a fine office team because they complemented each other. Carl only wished he could get them and their wives a little more interested in his own beloved church, which they attended semioccasionally, Christmas and Easter, mostly. Well, someday they'd find they needed more than they had. It happened to everybody, sooner or later, Carl held—and broke off his thoughts to listen to what they were saying.

"Well, Carl"—it was Harvey, his wide grin showing that his words were not to be taken seriously—"I may be hunting another job next week!"

"So? How come?" asked Carl.

Harvey gestured toward Paul. "On account of this old so-and-so might be my boss. Promotion coming up at the office—new sales manager. Looks like it's between me and him. He'll probably fire me first thing he does."

"Look who's talking!" Paul scoffed good-naturedly. "All hooey, I promise you, Carl. He knows very well that all the chances are in favor of *me* working for *him*. Myself, I plan to stick around doing my nice quiet little job and watching him grow ulcers."

"Sales manager sounds like an important place." Carl found himself wondering, as he spoke, whether they both wanted it very much, and feeling sorry that friends had to be forced into the position of rivals.

"It is." Harvey was suddenly sober. "Next step, vice-president. And if I should turn out to be the lucky guy—well, Paul here had better stick around or I sure *will* get ulcers."

Paul shook his head. "Not you. You're not the ulcer variety. That's more like me. And that's one of the reasons why you ought to get it."

"Well—I won't pretend I don't want it," Harvey said honestly. "They won't have to beg me." Then he added suddenly, his voice changing a little, slightly husky with embarrassed sincerity, "All the same—I'll be happy for you, sure enough happy, if you're the one——" He broke off, and laughed. "Ain't I noble?"

"What's he trying to get out of me?" Paul demanded of Carl.

But Carl had seen the look that passed between the two, the quiet confidence and inarticulate affection it held, and his heart was warm. Whichever one got it, there wasn't going to be any cloud on that friendship, he thought. Immediately on the heels of this he found himself wondering with somewhat less assurance whether their wives would be able to take the same attitude. He knew Dorothy Fuller and Lucille Dixon well; nice girls, both of them—well, not girls exactly, about the age of his own Anna—but nice, and rather pretty. . . . It was only that wives were sometimes more sensitive for their husbands than——

"By the way, Harvey"—Paul's voice broke in on his thoughts—"you've certainly gotten me in trouble, getting Lucille a car of her own. Now Dot wants one too."

"*Me?* You think I bought Lucille that car? She bought it for herself. With that legacy from her aunt. Fat chance I could buy her a separate car. My salary only supplies the bread and butter—not the cake."

"Well, with a rich wife you can pay for both the coffees," Paul offered generously. "Matter of fact, I'm glad you married money.

Now Lucille takes Dot shopping in her car and I get to use ours. Carl, about time we three couples were getting together again for dinner, isn't it?"

Carl nodded. "And it's our turn. Anna'll call Lucille and Dorothy and set it up."

It was just at this moment that Grampa started playing one of the music boxes. The thin, sweet tones tinkled out, filling the store, and Paul turned with a sudden startled attention.

"Why, that's the 'Angel's Serenade,' isn't it?" he cried. "Grampa, I want that box!"

"Makes me pay for his coffee and then buys whatever strikes his fancy without even asking the price!" grumbled Harvey.

"It's two-eighty," said Grampa matter-of-factly.

"If you'd been smart you'd have asked him five," bantered Harvey. "I think I heard Dorothy say once that song is connected with their engagement. Here's a fellow who's still courting his wife— after twenty years!"

"I wonder!" Paul muttered surprisingly. "Courting—or—appeasing?"

Into the puzzled pause that followed Harvey flung a light "Don't we all? Appease, I mean." And the slightly awkward silence ended with laughter and the brisk order from Paul to "wrap it fancy."

When he reached his home a few hours later, bearing his gift, he found Lucille with Dorothy. They had evidently just come in, for they had not removed their wraps. Once Paul would not have noticed how much better in cut and material Lucille's coat was than his wife's; nor how softly luxurious were the silver fox furs she wore. Today he did notice; he noticed because Dorothy herself had been assiduously pointing out things like this to him of late, and drawing the contrast. Once, too, he might not have seen that Dorothy's smile was set and strained—back in the days when he was so sure that she was happy that he hadn't felt the need to watch.

"Hello, dear!" she called. Her tone was a bright, brittle one that recently he had been learning to recognize—and dread.

He kissed her lightly and shook hands with Lucille, and she explained that they'd been shopping.

"At least Lucille has—I've trailed along, admiring."

Paul's discomfort deepened. Hastily he said the first thing that came into his mind—a comment on the beauty of Lucille's new car, parked outside; and immediately, seeing the cloud on Dorothy's face deepen, wished he had chosen any other subject.

Lucille seemed to be unaware of the atmosphere. She flashed him a pleased smile as she said good-by, promised to call for Dorothy and take her to the Women's Club next day, and was gone, leaving behind her the faint, sweet fragrance of Chanel 5.

"Where's Judy?" asked Paul.

Dorothy, her back to him, her head bent, answered curtly, "At the Garmers'—she'll be home in a minute." He wondered when she would notice his gaily wrapped package.

"What'd you buy today?"

He was trying to make conversation, and again, he realized, he'd hit on the wrong theme. Dorothy's voice dripped with self-pity as she answered him. "Oh, a couple of *very* cheap things."

He essayed a feeble joke, dismayed and half angry to realize that his voice held a distinctly placating note—a nice thing when a man had to come home and coax his wife into a decent humor!

"Letting me off easy, eh?"

"What else can I do? We're too poor——" She broke off. "It certainly must be wonderful to have a car of one's own!"

"Oh, come now, Dot!" His tone sharpened. "You know perfectly well they bought that car with money from Lucille's legacy."

She whirled around, facing him.

"Well, it isn't just Lucille! *All* our friends are getting ahead of us! And now there's this promotion coming up. Paul"—her hands had doubled into fists, her voice had risen to passion—"I'll die if you don't get that! I simply can't stand it. If Harvey has to be your boss, I—I—I tell you I can't *take* it!"

Paul put his ignored package on the table; a slow anger was stirring in him.

"There might be some things I can't take, either—and one of them could be this sort of talk. Harvey's my best friend and a better bet, if you want the truth, for that particular job than I am. Besides, I like what I'm doing now—it suits me, I'm happy in it——"

"And that is exactly one trouble!" He hardly knew that shrill, tense voice scolding at him. "You're not ambitious enough! You just sit back and let other people advance!"

"Okay," he said, "okay," and turned to leave the room. But before he had reached the door she was after him with a rush.

"No—wait, Paul!" Her tone had changed. She was a little frightened now. "You think I'm just jealous. Try to understand me—you might do that much——"

Paul shook off her hand, which was clutching his arm.

"All I know is that lately whenever any of our friends get a lucky break you seem to resent it."

"But don't you see? It's only because every time it just makes me realize how far *we're* slipping behind!" She bit hard on her lip; she was struggling for self-control. "Yesterday we could live on dreams and hopes and count on tomorrow. But now we're forty —tomorrow is *here*—and where are we?"

Paul stepped back. There was a white line around his lips.

"Once I thought I knew the answer to that one. I thought we were just where we wanted to be—with a nice home, reasonable financial security, a wonderful kid, and a pretty wonderful love. But now the only thing that doesn't look different is Judy. You're not satisfied with anything we've got—most of all you're not satisfied with me. You think I'm a failure——"

"No, no, don't say that!" She was pressing close to him, her eyes wide and alarmed. "I know how smart and wonderful you are— why, that's one reason I want to see you rewarded."

The front door opened and slammed shut; a young voice shouted, "Hey! Mommy, Daddy, where are you?" And Judy was with them, like a fresh breeze in the room. Instantly her eyes fell on the package which her mother still had not noticed. "What's that?" she cried interestedly. "A present? It's gift-wrapped. Who's it for?"

"It's something I brought your mother—haven't had time to give it to her. Unwrap it, Dot."

Dorothy sent him a glance, half pleading, half ashamed. Her fingers shook a little as she untied the ribbon.

"Oh, what a cute little box. What's in it?" Judy asked excitedly.

"Something you don't usually find in boxes. Lift the lid, Dot," Paul said.

" 'Angel's Serenade!' It's—it's beautiful. Oh, Paul!"

She had come into his arms and raised her face to his. The lashes that brushed his cheek were wet. Paul gave only a very small sigh before he kissed her. One more time the storm had blown over.

The music box completely fascinated Judy. When Paul came home the next afternoon she was sitting on the floor listening to it again, entranced. He stooped and kissed the smooth cheek.

"Hi, Cricket! You seem to like that tune."

"I love it," said Judy solemnly. "It sorta reminds me of the song I sang in my play. You know. The one I played in at Sunday school."

"Mm-hm," he agreed absent-mindedly, straightening. "Where's Mommy?"

"In the kitchen." A small hand caught at his coat. "And, Daddy —I'm going to be in another play next month."

"Sure enough? That's fine." He was moving on, but the slim fingers tightened on his coattail.

"I want you to come to see me in *this* one," said his daughter.

"Oh!" Paul looked down at the upturned face a little guiltily. She was so crazy about that Sunday school—he really ought to show more interest. "I promise, honey," he said, and carried with him, as he went toward the kitchen, the warmth of a radiantly pleased smile.

But there was nothing radiant about the face that lifted itself to his dutifully for his evening kiss when he reached the kitchen. Dorothy was at the stove, and she turned instantly back to it, bending over something she was manipulating there.

"Smells good—what is it?" he asked, throwing a cheeriness he was far from feeling into his voice. Honestly, these moods of hers were getting pretty monotonous!

"Lamb chops," Dorothy answered dully. She still did not look at him. "We can't afford them—but I have to get *some*thing."

Over a mounting irritation Paul tried again.

"What have you been doing today?"

Angry life sprang into her voice.

"I thought you knew I went to the Club! Lucille took me. Anna and I worked addressing envelopes—a lot of notices to be sent out. *We* were back in the office. Lucille spent her time out front—sashaying around the reception room and library and dining room—having whispered conferences—lobbying!"

"Lobbying?" He was completely at a loss.

"Of course!" Her tone snapped and crackled. "The nominating committee'll be meeting soon. I'm certain Lucille is campaigning for the presidency. What's more—I think she'll get it."

This time he did not try to keep the weary irritation from his voice. "Well, what's wrong with that?"

Her head jerked up.

"Oh, nothing at all! She'll be terrific! It carries a lot of prestige, you know. All the stores give the new president things—clothes and jewelry and silver. And a charge account with the taxi company—she won't need that, she has a car of her own, but I suppose the allocated fifteen a month will go for its upkeep—and there's always a big fall reception to honor the new president—all the florists send flowers——"

She had turned back to the stove and was stirring the contents of a saucepan with furious energy; and Paul found that his irritation had evaporated in a sudden pity. Why, the poor kid—he hadn't guessed. He said gently, "I didn't know you wanted it, Dot."

"I suppose you didn't!" Her head was bent, her voice came muffled; he knew that she was crying. "Since you haven't got any ambition, I guess you don't see why anybody else should have any. I ought to have it—I've worked hard enough for it——"

He answered quietly, "I didn't realize that was what you were working for—I thought it was for the Club and what it does for the community. You'll probably get the presidency someday—if you'll be patient——"

"Patient!" She turned, and with a sudden, shockingly violent gesture she flung the spoon with which she had been stirring into the far corner of the room. She was breathing hard and two red spots had come just below her eyes. "Patient! And while I'm being

patient Lucille gets the presidency, and while you're being patient
Harvey gets the promotion——"

"*Dorothy!*"

He had her by the shoulders, his fingers biting deep.

"You've got to stop this—do you hear? You act like a crazy person! You've got to quit talking this way!"

She twisted under his hands, close to hysteria.

"I won't quit! That's the way I feel and that's the way I'll talk!"

"Daddy—Mommy!" Paul's hands dropped as Judy came burst-
ing excitedly through the swinging door. She was carrying the
music box, and her eyes were shining. "There's another tune on
it—see, you twist this little knob, and then 'stead of the angel's
it plays 'Annie Laurie.' Listen!"

She was far too thrilled to notice anything amiss. "Hear?" she
cried. "I like the angel's, better, but this is nice, isn't it?"

"Judy! Turn—that—thing—off!"

It was a voice Judy had never heard her mother use before. It
was a voice, indeed, in which, up to now, nobody had ever spoken
to Judy. Startled and bewildered by its mysterious violence and
anger, she did not obey; she only stood staring in blank amazement while the music tinkled on.

Dorothy stamped her foot. "I said—*turn it off!*"

Judy, eyes big with shock, merely backed off a step, clutching
the box, still valiantly playing "Annie Laurie," to her breast; and
suddenly Dorothy stooped and lunged for it. Involuntarily Judy's
fingers stiffened on it; there was a brief, slight struggle—and then
the box clattered to the floor and abruptly stopped playing.

For an instant the little group remained curiously frozen, all
three staring at it. Then as Paul turned on his wife a look almost of
disbelief, Judy burst into the hysterical sobs of a frightened child.

Paul put his arm around her, but she jerked loose and picked
up the box, shutting, then opening the lid. The box was silent.

"It's broked! Mommy broked it! Why did she break it? Oh——"

"Don't cry so, darling!" Paul was kneeling beside her now, holding her in his arms. "It was just an accident—Mommy didn't mean
to break it. She has a headache and didn't want to hear it——"

Over the golden head his eyes met Dorothy's; never had they
looked at her like that before—bright with anger, a brightness as

chill as ice when the sun is shining on it, and as hard as ice, too. He got to his feet and lifted Judy in his arms. "Now Daddy'll take you in and watch TV with you awhile." He rubbed her cheek against his own. "Will you stop crying if I do?" he asked, and got a watery, uncertain smile in return. But she did not look at Dorothy as he carried her off.

When he came back, nearly fifteen minutes later, dinner had not progressed. Dorothy was sitting in a chair staring at the broken music box on the kitchen table with a white, strained face. The eyes she raised to his were as shocked as Judy's had been a few moments before.

"Paul . . ." she whispered.

Paul, with a grim face, picked up the music box and turned to leave the room.

"Paul—please . . . I'm sorry . . ."

She had been sorry last night, too, but it hadn't kept her from making this disgraceful scene tonight.

"I said—I said I was *sorry*, Paul . . ."

He lifted his shoulders slightly. "All right." His voice was expressionless, his face mask-like. Dorothy waited; then seeing that he was going to say nothing more, she moved slowly toward the door. "I guess," she said drearily, "I'd better go and try to make my peace with Judy."

The dinner party at the Fishers' had been set for Friday night. In the two days between this date and the breaking of the music box neither Dorothy nor Paul mentioned that scene or any of the issues involved. When Judy was there they kept up a pretense of comradely cheer; alone, they were polite as strangers are polite. All the affectionate spontaneity, all the gay naturalness had left their relationship as thoroughly as the melodies had deserted the little box.

It would not come back, that lost delight, Paul thought bleakly, till Dorothy really felt differently, till she had what his mother had used to call a "change of heart."

And it would not come back, Dorothy thought passionately, till Paul tried at least a little to understand and sympathize. Granted she'd been hateful, if he knew how many times she'd bit her tongue and kept still . . . ! And couldn't he see now that she was at the breaking point, that if Harvey got this promotion and Lucille got the Club presidency she'd *die?*

Anna's dinner, Friday night, was delicious, as her meals always were, and in Paul's opinion there wasn't any better company than the Fishers. But he found it hard to enter in; he could not keep his gaze from going anxiously, again and again, to Dorothy, and what he saw did not reassure him. It was a pretty good front, but it was only a front. And to Paul, who knew her so well, the overbright eyes, the slightly too loud laughter indicated that it was also a front which was in danger of cracking. Once, when the coming promotion was laughingly mentioned, she turned almost alarmingly white; and again, as Harvey asked about the Women's Club election, Paul saw her intercept a smiling, perhaps a meaningful glance between Lucille and Anna—and feared, for a startled instant, that she might actually be about to faint, her face changed so distressingly. She did not; she recovered herself with an effort palpable to Paul—and to Anna, too, he thought—for he saw Anna's eyes on her with a somewhat puzzled and disturbed expression. But from this point on her animation seemed to him as artificial as that of a marionette which bobs and grimaces when its strings are pulled. It was so clear to him that she was utterly absorbed in her own dark mental turmoil that he felt curiously far away from her, as if she had shut herself off in some unhappy cell and locked the door against him; and he had an absurd impulse to cry out to her, "Come away from that dismal place. Can't you see how warm and friendly and gay we are outside in the sunshine? Why do you stay there alone in the shadows?"

They had just left the table when the telephone rang and Carl, answering, returned to say that the call was for Harvey. Instantly, with an almost certain intuition, Paul felt that he knew what the message was. He did not dare look at Dorothy now. He began to talk rapidly. He never quite knew afterward what he had said; he only knew that he was trying to drown out Harvey's voice from the next room, with an irrational instinct to postpone the shock for her. Then the receiver clicked and Harvey was standing in the doorway, flushed, self-conscious, excited—and Paul realized that the moment from which he could not save his wife had arrived—at the worst possible time, when they were not alone.

"Well, folks," Harvey cried, "I've got news—maybe you'll have to start calling me *Mister* Dixon! Before you stands—ahem!—no less a personage than Carney Company's new sales manager!" He grinned sheepishly. "Corny way to tell it. Truth is I'm embarrassed!"

"Oh, *Harvey!*" shrieked Lucille joyously, and sprang to her feet, throwing her arms around him and kissing him.

As the others rose, Carl clapping him on the shoulder, Anna enthusiastically shaking his hand, Paul's fingers closed for an instant on Dorothy's wrist. He said in an urgent warning whisper, "Watch yourself—steady, for Heaven's sake!" Then he too turned to Harvey, wringing his hand, and was relieved when Dorothy followed him, saying loudly in a queer, metallic tone, "Congratulations to you and Lucille both!"

It was fortunate, Paul thought, that Harvey and Lucille (two of the finest people in the world, he added loyally to himself) were not too perceptive; they did not notice how unnatural she was. Carl and Anna were another proposition; he was very much afraid they did. It was fortunate also that it did not last long. Harvey explained that the representative from the New York branch was flying back tomorrow and wanted to see him at the hotel immediately, tonight.

"Wants to meet you, too, honey," he said, with a look at Lucille that showed he was proud to introduce her to an important person. "And he says he'd like me to arrange to spend a week in New York right away if possible—going over the plant there and learning the setup. I suppose you wouldn't by any chance want to go to New York with me, huh?"

"You just dare try to leave me at home!" Lucille exclaimed happily—and Paul sensed, rather than saw, the tightening of Dorothy's whole body, the clenching of her fists.

But just before the hurried good-bys, Harvey turned to Paul, suddenly sober.

"One thing I'd like to say," he said with a gruff awkwardness. "I'll have a little influence now—and I'm going to be pulling for every bit of advancement I can wangle for you. Not because you're my closest friend—I wouldn't let that sort of thing influence me about my own brother. But because I think in your own quiet way you're just about the best man in the Middleburg office—and nobody but me seems to have quite sense enough to realize it."

Paul, too touched to do more than mumble a "Thanks," felt that surely this remark would soften Dorothy's disappointment. But when, an instant later, her eyes met his, they held such an odd glitter that he could not suppose it had helped, after all.

The instant the door had closed behind the Dixons, she turned to Carl and Anna. Under her make-up her face was a queer putty shade and in one cheek a nerve twitched.

"I'm so sorry," she cried in a high, shrill voice, "but we have to go too, Anna." Her hand went to her head. "I've had this awful headache all day, and I know it's dreadful to eat and run like this, but——"

"I'm sorry too," said Anna. Her eyes were grave and pitying and Paul's burned with humiliation. If Dot didn't have any pride for herself, mightn't she have managed to keep up a little for his sake? Didn't she have any idea how the way she was acting would make a man feel? Or did she just plain not care? He stammered out some excuse, and was bleakly relieved when, at last, the door closed between them and their hosts and he and Dorothy were outside.

On the drive home neither of them spoke. He drove grimly, his face set straight ahead; she sat huddled in her corner of the car and he thought she was weeping. At the side door of their home he let her out, still silent, and put the car in the garage. Judy's sitter, who lived across the street, was just closing the front door when he came back in the house. Dorothy was pacing up and down the living room; and if she had indeed been weeping in the car, the eyes she turned on him now were dry and hot.

"Well!" she cried. "Say it! Go ahead! Say you think I made a fool of myself!"

"I think," said Paul evenly, "that you acted like an undisciplined child who goes into a tantrum when she doesn't get what she wants."

"Oh, you do?" Her voice was loud and harsh. "What did you expect me to do? Jump for joy?"

"I expected you," he began sharply, "to behave like a rational adult——" and broke off. "No, I didn't. Not any more. I don't seem to know you these days. Dorothy, for the love of Mike, what's wrong? Do you need a psychiatrist? Are you sick?"

"Yes! I'm not crazy, if that's what you mean, but I'm sick all right, good and sick! Sick and tired to the very bottom of me of simpering 'Congratulations, Harvey!' 'Good for you, Lucille!' I want something good and happy for *me,* for *us,* once in awhile! I want——"

"Mommy!" cried a child's voice, breaking in, a puzzled, troubled voice. Judy was standing in the doorway, pajama-clad, her curls rumpled.

"Why, Judy!" Paul went to her quickly; Dorothy stood rigid, hands doubled into fists at her sides. "What are you doing out of bed, Cricket?"

"I heard you and Mommy——" Judy began uncertainly, "Mommy was hollering and——" She stopped, looking from one to the other, her brow drawn.

"Well, Mommy and I shouldn't have talked so loud," Paul said lightly. "Now, come along—I'll carry you upstairs."

When he came back from upstairs, she was standing almost as he had left her, save that her face was buried in her hands. She raised it, and their eyes met; his filled with a deep, cold anger, hers ashamed, but hotly defiant.

"That," he said evenly, "was a nice thing for Judy to hear!"

He saw her wince for an instant; and then, almost as if she physically drew back her hand and flung something away, he saw her throw from her the picture of Judy's troubled small face.

"I don't care!" she cried wildly. "I don't care what she heard!"

Afterward it seemed to Paul that it was at this moment that something broke inside him, too. If she could say that about *Judy*——

"No," he said slowly, "I suppose you don't. You don't care about anything these days, as far as I can see, but your own petty, spiteful jealousy."

"I've got a right to be jealous! Just because you let people walk all over you—just because I'm not like that——"

His whole face had congealed against her. He was looking at her as if she were a stranger, a stranger whom he did not much like. "That," he said, "is absolutely untrue."

"Harvey's done it! They're both getting everything we want! First Anna and Lucille, looking at each other with those smug smiles when the presidency came up—and then Harvey's message and the trip to New York and both of them so important—and Harvey patronizing you and being humbly *grateful*——"

Deep down inside of her something was frightened now; something was warning her to stop. But she could not stop; she had gone too far. It was like trying to check oneself in mid-flight down a steep hill.

"I wish we could move away! I'd rather die than stay here and be humiliated—have those two gloat over us——"

Suddenly one of his hands came down across her mouth.

"All right." The two words came between closed teeth, gritted out. "All right, that tears it! Those two are the best and the most loyal friends we've got. For the last time, Dorothy, will you stop this wicked insanity and get hold of yourself?"

She jerked his hand away.

"For the last time—no! I won't be a hypocrite, I will act like I feel! And—and you keep your hands off me, Paul Fuller. If you think you can manhandle me——"

"That's a red herring! I'm not manhandling you. But of course you aren't even honest any more. Well, Dorothy, you've talked a lot about *your* breaking point—now I've hit mine. I'm done. I'm walking out."

She stared at him, unbelieving, her chest rising and falling stormily.

"Walking out—where?"

"To the hotel. Unless or until you come to your senses."

He wouldn't do it, of course. He couldn't do it. That would be—why, that would be *leaving* her! How dared he threaten her with that?

"Go ahead!" she shouted. "If that's the way you feel about it— go now, right now!"

Then her heart turned over. For he was doing just that. At the door he turned. "Fix up something for Judy—that I have to be away on business or something—till we can think of a better story. We owe her that much—after all she's been put through."

Crumpled up in a chair, incredulous, she heard him go upstairs;

heard him as he moved around the room, doubtless putting things in a suitcase; heard him come down the steps again. Now he'd stop . . . He wouldn't go past the door, he wouldn't! But he did not even pause, and a second later the front door opened—and closed. . . . Cowering there while her world disintegrated around her, Dorothy burst into terrified sobs. . . .

Grampa and Carl found out how matters were three days later when Judy came into the drugstore with a list of things her mother wanted.

"Headache powders—sedative—digestive pills—eyedrops . . . Is your mother sick, honey?" Carl asked, concerned.

"I s'pose so," said Judy with a sigh. "She cries a lot and I guess something hurts. Daddy's staying at the hotel. On business, Mommy said, and she don't know when he'll be back."

Grampa and Carl, over her head, exchanged worried glances. And Judy added, with another and even deeper sigh, "It's lonesome, with Daddy gone and Mommy crying."

The only thing that Grampa (hovering near, overflowing with helpless sympathy while Carl busied himself with the list) could think of that might help was to offer her an ice-cream cone. She accepted the gift with a brightening face, but as she finished it her eyes chanced to fall on the music boxes on the other side of the store and her mouth drooped again.

"Ours is broken," she remarked sadly.

"Already? If Paul got a bad one we'll give him another——" Grampa began, but Judy shook her head.

"It wasn't bad. Mommy broke it. She didn't like to hear it so she grabbed for it and it broke and won't play any more."

She scrambled down from the stool, clutching the package Carl had brought her.

"Well, good-by, and thank you for the cone," she said politely, and took a matter-of-fact departure, apparently unaware of the shock she had administered.

Carl told Anna about it that night in the privacy of their room.

"Oh *no!*" said Anna in consternation. "It can't be that bad!"

"I'm afraid it is, though." Carl's tone was sober. "And after all, it shouldn't surprise us—after what we both saw the other night.

It was clear enough how Dorothy was feeling—and what it was doing to Paul."

Quite early the next morning Anna rang the bell of Dorothy's house. There was a piece of news which she had been delegated to give her friend two days later. But lying awake the night before, deeply distressed over the word Carl had brought her, she had fully made up her mind that she would not wait till the appointed time.

Dorothy opened the door; and caught thus unaware, with no make-up on and no time to prepare her expression, she looked so ill and unhappy that Anna was shocked at the devastation these few days had worked. She seemed already to have lost flesh, and her heavily shadowed eyes were red-rimmed.

"Oh!" It was an involuntary cry of dismay when she saw her visitor, a cry which came before she could stop it. The next instant, with an effort, she had gathered herself together. "Come in, Anna—you'll have to excuse the way I look—and the house——"

Indeed, the usually bright and immaculate living room was dusty, and had a neglected air; last night's paper was still on the floor, and the day before yesterday's faded flowers had not been thrown out.

"Sit down," Dorothy began nervously. "I—I haven't been feeling very well lately—my head——"

"The same kind of headache you had at my house?" Anna asked gravely.

Their eyes met; Dorothy sat down abruptly.

"You know, don't you?" she said bitterly. "I suppose it's all over town by now. Paul was so furious over my getting upset—and showing it at—at your house that he—he——"

She had laced her fingers tightly together, but even that did not stop their trembling. She sat looking down at them a moment, unable to go on. Then she raised her eyes and stiffened her voice.

"He's—left me. He went to the hotel that night. I—I haven't heard a word from him since."

"Dear, I don't think it's all over town," Anna said gently. "Judy let it out to Carl and Grampa. And I don't think he's left you, either. I think—honestly—that he's just walked off for a while because he'd had all he could take."

"And so had I!" cried Dorothy passionately. "Did you ever think of *that*? For years we've been working hard—and we never seem to be able to get anyplace——"

"What place do you want to get, Dorothy?"

"Oh, you're only pretending to misunderstand!" Dorothy cried wildly. "You know perfectly well what I mean! All I'm trying to say is that I'm getting sick and tired of marking time while everyone else gets the breaks! Paul deserved that promotion as much as Harvey—but does he get it? No! It's Harvey, always Harvey! And look at me! I've been working like a dog for years around that Club—but when the honors are handed out do I ever get any? No, Lucille'll get the presidency, just like Harvey got——"

"Dorothy!" Anna's voice broke with a sharp urgency into the torrent of words. "Please listen to me! You've got too much sense to behave like this! You're too fine a person! For pity's sake, can't you see what you're doing? Wrecking your own health and happiness—estranging your husband—spoiling your child's life—all because of this crazy jealousy——"

"Crazy jealousy!" Dorothy cried furiously. "It is not! I—I've got a *right* to feel this way! What am I supposed to do, anyway? Bury my head in the sand like an ostrich?"

"No! You're supposed to face facts! And you can start by facing the one I came here this morning to give you. The nominating committee chose *you* as president, Dorothy—you, not Lucille! And it was Lucille who pushed it—Lucille who worked for it—Lucille who was two-thirds responsible for it!"

"Me? Lucille? Oh *no*—oh *no*——"

The face she turned toward her friend wore the blank, shocked look of one who sees all her carefully built up defenses and self-justifications suddenly crumble. "I—I didn't know. I—I—— *Oh!*" she cried, and then abandoning the effort at self-control, buried her face in her hands and wept bitterly.

Anna knelt beside her, holding her while the great, shattering sobs tore at her till finally they died into chokes and gasps. Then she rose quietly and went to the bathroom, bringing back a wet washcloth and hand towel; and Dorothy bathed her swollen eyes and sat up at last.

"I—I'm—sorry," she faltered. "Putting you through a scene like this. It's just that——"

"I know," said Anna quickly.

Dorothy shook her head. "No, you don't. You couldn't—not even you. It's been such a nightmare since Paul left—— Oh, Anna! Did you ever know you were wrong, all wrong, and yet just couldn't admit it, not even to yourself?"

"Why, of course," said Anna cheerfully. "Everybody has."

"Everybody hasn't been the fool I've been, though. I'm so ashamed—so hideously ashamed! All the nasty things I've been feeling and saying about Lucille——" She began to cry again, helplessly. "And I've lost Paul, I've lost my husband! What shall I do, what shall I do?"

Anna, aching with sympathy, tried to keep her voice matter-of-fact. "Why, what any sensible woman who's seen how foolish she's been would do! Stop crying and go right to that telephone and call Paul up!"

"But—but——" She gulped the sobs back; Anna saw with fresh pity how painfully she was struggling for control. And after a moment, gasping between the words, twisting her wet handkerchief between her fingers, she spoke again.

"How do I know I won't behave the same way again? And how can I call him back unless I'm sure? Oh, *now* I feel like I'd crawl on my knees from here to town to get him back! *Now* I feel like I'd gladly get down and shine Lucille's boots! But I've been sorry and ashamed before! I've asked Paul to forgive me before! And then those terrible feelings of jealousy come back—and it's like I was a different person. I just want to hit out and *hurt* something." She bit down fiercely on her lip to steady it. She said despairingly, "You see, I don't seem to have any confidence in my own strength or will power any more!"

"Oh!" Anna looked at her for a moment in thoughtful silence. Then she said slowly, "Well, Dot, truly there isn't but one answer I can make to that. If your own strength isn't enough, why not try God's?"

Dorothy's white face looked at her blankly; Dorothy's hands made a hopeless little gesture.

"I don't know how! I simply don't know how to take even the first step!"

"Well, if that's what worrying you"—Anna smiled at her—"you don't have to, Dot. God has already taken it."

"I don't even know what you mean," said Dorothy despairingly.

"You would—if you'd read the New Testament. He took it for the whole world when He sent Jesus. And He keeps taking it, over and over. Dot, listen! You *want* to be different, don't you? You *want* to stop tormenting yourself and poisoning your life with jealousy, don't you?"

Dorothy's mouth twisted in a sort of grimace of pain. "What else have I just been saying? What do you *suppose*—when I've nearly smashed everything?"

"Then," said Anna quietly, "can't you see that the very fact that you're so dissatisfied with yourself means you're hearing the voice God put inside you to warn you and help you? It means, in a way, that you're hearing God's own message to you."

"I never thought of it like that—as God . . ." The tones trailed off in a kind of wonder. She pushed the damp, heavy hair back from her forehead. She said bewilderedly, "I guess I never thought about any of it at all. It seems so stupid, doesn't it?"

She was talking more to herself than to anyone else; and Anna waited, watching her with kind, keen eyes.

"Anna!" She looked up suddenly. "Suppose you were me—and had made the mess of things I have. Oh, I know, you never could—but just suppose you had! What would"—her voice broke, but she steadied it and went on—"what would be the very first thing you'd do—to try to be different? To try to make sure you'd be a good wife and a good mother, and that you'd never any more——" She stopped, one hand going to her throat.

"Get down on my knees, of course, Dot," Anna answered gently. "And ask for forgiveness. I have to do it, being me, you know. Often and often."

"Do you? No, I didn't know. And then you—feel better? Feel forgiven?"

"Yes. Because when Jesus died for me He bought that forgiveness. I've only to ask for it. Oh, Dot, read your Bible and learn all about it! All the strength and help you want is there."

"Would that maybe be—the second thing?" Dorothy whispered. "I mean—what *you'd* do?"

Anna nodded. "Of course. And then—if the jealous feelings do come back, what of it? You'll know right where to go for help to drive them off. And they'll come less and less often, and finally they'll stop. *That's* what using God's strength instead of your own means."

Dorothy had stopped tearing her handkerchief; her hands were clasped now in her lap. Anna saw the fingers tighten as she raised her eyes. Her voice was low and a little husky.

"Pray for forgiveness and help. Learn about Jesus by reading His book. Anna—is there anything else?"

Anna's smile was suddenly bright. "Why, yes. Something that will help you lots in doing both those other things—something I wouldn't, myself, want to even *try* to do without. You can start saying 'Come along' on Sunday morning to Judy, instead of 'Run along!'" She added simply, "I've so often wished you would. You need us and we need you at our church."

Dorothy was silent, looking down now at those clasped hands for so long that Anna felt a little uneasiness stirring in her. But then she lifted her eyes again; and Anna's heart gave a leap, for in their depths she was sure she saw the brightness of a growing hope.

"Anna," she said—and this time her voice was almost steady— "I think—I think now I can telephone Paul." She got to her feet. "Will you stand by me while I dial?" she asked childishly. "I'm just a little bit—afraid."

So Anna stood by her side while she dialed Paul's office with fingers that were only just the least little bit shaky. But when she had reached the number and asked for him, her face fell and she cast a rather piteously disappointed glance at her friend as she made the answers.

"Not in? But I thought he was *always* there at this hour!" . . . "Yes, Miss Anderson, this is Mrs. Fuller. Do you know where he is?" . . . "*What?*" . . . "Are you sure?" Her voice had sprung to sudden startled life. "Yes." . . . "Yes." . . . "I see." . . . "Thank you." . . . "Yes, please do have him call me when he comes in. Good-by."

She hung up the receiver. The face she turned toward Anna wore an expression very like awe, and yet the light Anna had seen just now in her eyes had become a glow.

"He's not in. Oh, Anna! I was sitting there just now—and I was thinking of the road you'd been showing me—and then I thought, 'But if only Paul would travel that road with me, if only we could do it all and learn it all together!' And all the time—— But I haven't told you yet! Guess where he is—guess why he's out! He went to see Pastor Martin!"

"Dorothy! Truly?"

"Truly. Miss Anderson said yes, that he usually *was* there at that hour, but that he'd said this was a very important conference— with Pastor Martin."

Anna, who had never pretended to be anything but sentimental, mopped frankly at eyes that had filled with joyous tears.

"Don't mind *me*," she gulped. "Some people cry when they're miserable, but me, I'm a little bit original, I cry when I feel good!"

"I g-guess—I do—both. Only," Dorothy said all of a sudden, "I haven't got time for any sob fest now. Anna! Do you realize Paul's almost sure to be home this afternoon? And do you see this awful house? And my hair needing washing and setting? And not a decent thing to eat in the place!"

"I'll help you. I'd love to. I'll wash and set your hair. I've always," said Anna happily, "wanted to try doing it in a new way," and looked mildly surprised when Dorothy suddenly dissolved in helpless laughter, the first real laughter for many days. . . .

Judy was waiting at the gate to greet her father when he came home that afternoon. Paul broke into a run when he saw his daughter, and the next instant with an ecstatic whoop she was on him and he was lifting her in his arms. When he put her down, she skipped along beside him, chattering excitedly; and then they were inside the house and she was exhibiting him as triumphantly as if she had, singlehanded, captured the world's greatest prize.

"Mommy!" she shouted. "I got him—he's here!"

It was so little that they had said over the telephone a few hours before, just a few broken phrases: "Paul—oh, darling, please come home, please!" and "I was coming anyway—I was coming today, Dorothy." And there was so much to tell, so much to share. But now, in this first moment, they only clung to each other tightly, silently, knowing more surely than ever before that they belonged to each other. The rest could—would—come later.

Judy had put the music box on an end table. "We'll get it fixed, sweet," her mother had promised her. Now as Dorothy stepped back from that long embrace, she knocked against the little table and the small box fell suddenly to the floor. As it did, the lid flew up, and——

"It's *playing!*" shrieked Judy.

So it was. The sweet, tinkling notes were filling the room as they had on that first evening Paul had brought it home. Dorothy's startled eyes met his surprised ones—and suddenly, then, they were laughing—happy, healing laughter, which bore away on its wings the last bitter memory.

."It knew you liked it again, Mommy!" cried Judy. For back once more in her own safe, happy little world after a mysterious sojourn in another that had been perplexingly dark and strange, she could spin as before the gay fancies of an imaginative child. "*That's* why it unbroke itself!"

Her father's face, stooping over her, looked young again and vivid with laughter. "*How* did it know, baby?"

"Oh, it has ways!" said Judy mysteriously. Everything was all right. They were laughing at her and with her, just as they used to do; before things grew, for that space which already she was beginning to forget, so queerly different.

"It might," she offered, head on one side, "have been the Brownies who fixed it, of course."

But then she had a better idea.

"Maybe it was the angels!" she cried. "When it broke it was playing 'Annie Something' and when it unbroke it began to play the angel's! So it could have been the angels wanting to serenade us again. What do *you* think?"

It was her mother who answered. But though she spoke to Judy, she was looking over Judy's head at Daddy.

"Oh, Judy!" she said with the happiest imaginable little laugh. "Oh, Judy darling—I vote for the angels!"

6. NO EAST OR WEST

*A*T TEN o'clock that summer evening Carl Fisher and his father hung a "Closed" sign on the door of their drugstore, locked it, and settled down to the task of taking inventory of their stock. Carl, standing on a stool, was reading off items to Grampa, who had elected the easier job of entering them in a ledger as his son called them off, when a rather frantic staccato knocking suddenly began on the door. It was accompanied by an agitated feminine voice calling, "Please! Oh, please!"

"Must be an emergency," said Carl, and climbed down as Grampa went hastily to the door. A summons like this after closing hours was not unusual. Sometimes people even got Carl out of bed and back to his store after he had retired. Occasionally the emergencies were real, oftener someone had simply got panicky. Carl and Grampa never knew which it would be, so they never refused.

The two who stood on the threshold now were unmistakably of another race. The girl, young and slender, with enormous dark eyes, had a delicate, ivory-tinted face framed by a cloud of night-black hair, and might almost have been the older sister of the ten-year-old boy at her side had it not been for a quality passionately and unmistakably maternal that surrounded her like an aura. The child himself, stocky and sturdy, was probably normally a rather handsome lad, and almost certainly an alert and intelligent-looking one; but just now he was at a disadvantage. His clothes were torn and dirty, his face was bloody, one purpled eye was practically closed, and he was trying valiantly not to cry, with indifferent success.

"Oh, can you help us?" gasped the girl. "We're new here. I didn't know where to go—and then I saw this sign and the light——"

"Come in, come in. Why, boy, what's happened?" Carl did not wait to have his question answered. Even as he spoke, he was lifting the child to the counter to examine the marred little face more closely. "Grampa, will you get me a damp towel and the kit, please? M-m-m-m! You've got quite a shiner here, haven't you?"

"Is he—is he hurt very bad?" asked the girl tensely.

"Oh no!" said Carl reassuringly. "I've got two boys—I've seen them look worse and they lived through it. His face is bruised and cut and this eye'll turn a lot of pretty colors in the next twenty-four hours, but—— Oh, here you are, Grampa! Now, young man, let's get you fixed up!"

His big hands, almost as deft as those of a surgeon, gently sponged the swollen, bruised face. "We'll put something on these cuts and make a pack for the eye. How did you get these injuries, Son?"

The boy's lips quivered; he was silent. It was the mother who answered, a sudden flame leaping in her soft eyes.

"We've just been here a week. He—he wanted to go to the playground tonight—he'd seen the boys playing ball there evenings and he—he plays very well. And when I came for him, I met him on the way—running home—and he was like this. Some boys had beaten him."

"Oh!" Carl's skillful fingers paused an instant. "It must have been quite a fight."

"It wasn't any fight!" the mother denied hotly. "He told me he had no *chance* to fight! Three bigger boys jumped on him."

Carl frowned. "That's bad. I'm sorry to find we've got boys like that in Middleburg."

The boy spoke for the first time, his voice trembling. "They said—they said I was a dirty foreigner!"

Carl and Grampa exchanged a quick, shocked glance.

"They told him not to come back to that playground any more! They said they'd beat him up even worse if he did! And we're not foreigners," cried his mother passionately. "We're Filipinos by blood. But we're American *citizens*. My husband and I were born here, and Alverus is as American as—as——" She stopped, biting down hard on her lower lip.

"Even if you were foreigners, it wouldn't make it a bit better. It's an outrage!" said Grampa indignantly. "What playground was it—Alverus, did you say, ma'am?"

"Alverus Lamino. And I'm Mrs. Lamino. It was the Central Playground. He—he heard they'd be signing up for baseball teams for a boys' baseball tournament there tonight. He wanted to get on one of the teams——"

"That's why they beat me up. They said they didn't want me coming to their playground or playing on their teams." The child's voice was steadier, in response to the warmth and friendliness that had surrounded him from the moment he had set his foot inside the Fishers' drugstore, but the deep, bewildered hurt in the one good eye that looked up at Carl made him wince. It was terrible, he thought, to see that sort of pain in a child's eyes.

He asked quietly, "Were they all refusing to let you play? Or just these three boys?"

"Well—it was only these three that jumped on me. But—but the others didn't do anything. They just stood around—and some of 'em laughed. There was one kid tried to help me—but they just knocked him outa the way."

Carl, adjusting the eye pack, paused a moment and looked at Mrs. Lamino. "I think maybe, Mrs. Lamino, you'd better report this incident to the police."

She looked alarmed. "Oh, I'm afraid that might only make it worse for Alverus in the end!"

"Somethin' ought to be done," said Grampa decidedly.

"But Mr.——" began the boy, and hesitated, not knowing what name to supply. Carl told him quickly, "Fisher. I'm Carl Fisher. And this is my father. We call him Grampa."

"Oh! That's for Grandfather, isn't it?" For the first time the child smiled. He looked at them trustingly. He had accepted them now as friends. "I was goin' to ask—what made them do that to me? Why do they mind my not lookin' just like them?"

"I don't know why, Alverus." Carl's steady voice was troubled. "I knew there were people like that in the world—but I guess I didn't know there were any in Middleburg." He lifted the boy down from the counter and set him on his feet with a smile. "There you are! Does it feel better?"

The boy gave a shy, grateful nod. His mother was opening her rather shabby bag. She asked a little nervously, "How much do I owe you?"

"Nothing." Carl waved away her protests. "Please! I'd like to show you we aren't all quite such bad neighbors here in Middleburg. Now maybe I'd better drive you home. Where do you live?"

"Oh, don't worry—we've been so much bother!" The girl sounded distressed. "It's only a block and a half—around the corner, really—31 Bayard Street. We'd *rather* walk." She hesitated. "I just don't know how to thank you——" she faltered.

"Don't try. And perhaps you'd better have a doctor look at that face in the morning," he advised. "I'm sure it's all right—but I'd rather a doctor would tell you so too."

He and Grampa shook hands with her, patted the boy on the back, and then as the door closed behind the two, looked at each other soberly.

"I wonder," said Carl, "I wonder if Freddie knows anything about this."

"Freddie? Oh yes—he did say at supper tonight that he was going to sign up for the baseball tournament, didn't he? Well—we'll see."

They worked till midnight and the rest of the family were sound asleep when they got home. So it was not until breakfast that they told the story of their visitors of the night before. The other Fishers reacted instantly, and almost violently, with warm indignation; except Freddie, who threw his father one dismayed look and then sat poking at his food and looking unhappy.

"Freddie," asked Grampa, watching him, "weren't you at the playground last night?"

Freddie drew a long sigh. "Yes, sir."

"Did you see what happened to Alverus?"

Freddie looked unhappier than ever. He mumbled, "Yessir, I saw."

"Well, for the love of Mike!" cried Peter, outraged. "You didn't just stand there and do nothing about it, did you?"

"I *couldn't* do anything about it!" Freddie was almost in tears. "I tried to grab one of 'em, and said, 'Here you, leave him alone' —and they knocked me down——"

"He told us one of the boys tried to take up for him," Carl said quickly. "I'm proud to find it was you, Freddie. Who were the three who jumped him?"

Freddie, whose face had brightened at his father's compliment, instantly looked troubled again. He did not reply; his eyes stayed glued to his plate.

"Did you know them?" Carl asked sharply.

Freddie nodded slowly.

"Then please answer me, Son. I asked you who they were."

"I'd—I'd rather not say."

"But I'm *asking* you to say, Freddie."

Freddie raised his eyes and sent his father a miserable look, full of appeal. "I can't, Pop—I just can't!"

"Why can't you?"

"I—can't—that's all."

All the family were looking at him concernedly now. Carl, puzzled, tried another sort of tactic.

"Tell me what happened."

"Well——" Freddie hesitated, and then plunged in. "This kid, he was there, signin' up with the others to get on a team, and then we all left, and this Alverus started walkin' with some of us. And—and these three fellows, they told him they didn't want him round and he couldn't play on any Middleburg team. And he said he had as much right there as they did. And they said he didn't 'cause he was a dirty foreigner. And then they started beatin' him up." His face puckered as he looked around at his family. "I couldn't stop 'em, honest. It happened so awful quick. And first thing I knew he'd got away from 'em and was runnin' and—and—I ran too. I ran home."

"Nobody blames you for any of that," Carl said gently. "You did just about all you could. Now tell us—who were the boys?"

"I told you," cried Freddie desperately, "I just can't tell on them, Pop, I can't!"

"That," said Carl with a hint of sternness, "is a very mistaken sort of loyalty. These boys did a cruel, cowardly thing and they should not be protected to do it again—surely you can see that, Son?"

"That's not it!" The child had grown white, and suddenly his father realized that he was torn by humiliation at having to admit something he would much have preferred to keep secret. Why, of course, he thought, irritated at his own stupidity! Freddie was frightened. No doubt the other boys had threatened to beat him, too, if he told.

"Well"—he tried to make his voice casual—"we'll drop it now and discuss it again later, maybe."

Freddie dropped his head over his plate once more—but not before Carl had seen the look of mingled shame and relief on his face. "When grownups or children do such a wrong against one of their fellow humans as those boys did last night," he thought sadly, "it harms everyone who has any share in it, even those who merely watch it and are afraid not to be silent."

After Freddie had left for school, still unwontedly sober, Peter lingered to speak to his father.

"Don't blame Freddie too much," he said awkwardly. "I remember—it's tough to be scared of bigger, rougher boys."

"I'm not blaming Freddie, Peter. I remember too, even if it has been longer. But I keep thinking—if Freddie's scared, how do you suppose that poor little tyke I saw last night is feeling?"

"Maybe," suggested Peter, looking worried himself, "you're making too much of it, Dad. They're just kids. They're apt to get over it."

"But will Alverus get over it? A thing like that can leave a scar. And besides," Carl said, frowning, "it's set me to wondering— how often does this sort of thing happen in Middleburg? Those boys, you know, were bound to be reflecting grown-up attitudes. I think the whole business ought to be brought out into the open."

"How?" asked Peter.

Carl shook his head. "I don't know. I'm trying to decide."

At dinner that night he was still abstracted, lost in a brown study, and not, Anna noticed, eating very much. Then suddenly he came alive; for Grampa, that amazing old gentleman, was saying in quite a casual manner, "Went by to see Mrs. Lamino this afternoon."

"You *did?*" cried Carl, dropping his fork. "Did you see the boy? How's his face?"

"I saw him." Grampa's voice was quiet. "His face felt better. It was the inside of his head I was worried about, not the outside."

"He's—taking it pretty hard?" Peter asked.

"Pretty hard, Pete."

"What about his dad?" This was Emily. "Is he as upset as the mother?"

"His dad's dead," Grampa said slowly. "He was killed in the war. Mrs. Lamino said he had a medal—awarded posthumously—for courage above and beyond the call of duty."

There was a stunned silence at the Fisher table. Then Emily, eyes flashing, cried hotly, "I think that's the most frightful thing I ever heard of! Jumping on a boy and even taunting him as a foreigner—and his father was killed in action!"

"No, Emily," said Anna mildly. Every head at the table turned to look at her in surprise. "I mean—that doesn't make it any worse, dear. It makes it pretty ironic, I'll admit that. But if the boy *had* been a foreigner and his father *hadn't* been a soldier, what those boys did to him would have been every bit as bad."

There was a thoughtful little silence for an instant, which Carl broke.

"That's one hundred per cent true! But his father being a soldier *does* give me a handle. And it's a handle I intend to use!"

"What are you going to do?" asked Peter, excited.

"Well, I've been thinking about it all day. And in between times at the store I scribbled out the first draft—just a rough one—of a letter I thought I might send to the *Citizen.* Shall I read it to you?"

The assent was general except for Freddie. All evening he had been restrained and uncertain in his manner. Now he was silent. Carl glanced at him once, sighed, shook his anxiety off, and began to explain.

"I'll start off formally—I'm addressing it to the editor—and then this is what I've jotted down. 'Last Tuesday evening a little Filipino boy was beaten severely by a group of other boys at the Central Playground provided for all our Middleburg children. They didn't want him to play on any of their baseball teams because his skin is darker than theirs and his name sounds odd to them. Somehow they seem to have acquired the idea that to be different from them is to be inferior to them. One wonders where they got it. Can it be that their parents have not taught them that the color of a man's skin has nothing at all to do with his worth as a human being? Have they never told them that especially in America, which is made of all races, people should be free of this stupid and cruel prejudice? Have they never talked to them about the meaning of the Golden Rule, and of friendliness and brotherhood on a world-wide scale? Perhaps these parents need to make some of these things clear to their sons, and to show them that in our country, that great melting pot of the earth, our differences, like the various reinforcements of a mighty building, are what make our strength as a great nation under God.'"

He stopped. "That's all I've written. But I'll add that I hope the youngsters who jumped on the little stranger will seek him out and beg his pardon and make friends, and learn how much better Christian love can make a fellow feel than hate. And somewhere in there, when I copy it, I'll tell the story of his father."

"You know, Carl," Grampa said reflectively, "I b'lieve I'd leave that out just now. It's a handle like you said, but the point you want to make is the one Anna made—that it's un-American, unbrotherly, unkind, and un-Christian to dislike or mistreat somebody just because his race is different. And if you put in that part about his father, why, it'll weaken that point, make it seem as if what you're really saying is that it was wrong of them to beat him because, actually, he wasn't a foreigner at all, that in fact his father was a brave American soldier."

"Grampa's right," Emily declared. "You can save his father for a sort of clinching point, a last trump, if you need one later, Dad."

"You're probably right," Carl said slowly. "Well, outside of that—do all of you think I should send this letter?"

They all said they did, speaking with their usual heartiness and enthusiasm; all, that is, except Freddie.

"What about you, Freddie?" asked his father, deliberately addressing his younger son directly. "Do you have any objection to my sending this letter?"

Freddie gulped once, shook his head, said indistinctly, "'Sall right," and relapsed again into silence. Later, when he had gone upstairs, Anna remarked worriedly, "Maybe I'd better go with him——" But Carl put his hand on her arm as she rose.

"I wouldn't, honey," he advised. "I rather feel this is one thing Freddie wants to work out by himself."

"Don't worry about him—he's already on the right track," Grampa said confidently. And Anna, knowing the special bond between the little boy and his grandfather, settled back in her seat, looking relieved; Grampa was seldom wrong about Freddie.

Carl typed his letter that night and dropped it in the *Citizen* box the next morning on his way to the office. Apparently it received prompt attention, for in the middle of the afternoon Joe Turner, associate editor, columnist, and star reporter of the paper, dropped into the drugstore to see him.

"Hi, Carl!" he said, speaking with a sort of wary cordiality. He was a big, powerful-looking fellow who had once been a fine athlete. Now indolence and too many cocktails had thickened his splendid body, and already, at barely forty, one saw the start of flabby jowls blurring the outline of his formerly clean-cut face. Only a few days earlier, as it happened, a friend of Joe's had been talking to Carl about him, less in a spirit of criticism than of concern.

"Don't quite know what's happened to old Joe," he'd observed regretfully. "You know, some years ago his column and some of his articles were attracting a good deal of attention. Used to get reprinted in the Chicago newspapers and even in some of the eastern papers. But lately——" He'd shrugged. "He just seems to have lost ambition or interest or something. Jogs along, that's about all."

"He used to be quite active at our church, too," Carl had answered thoughtfully. "But for the past few years he's dropped out entirely—seems to be going with a different crowd."

"Yeah—too bad—it's not really the right crowd for Joe," the friend had said. "I don't know, Carl—I'm not too good a church member myself—but it seems to me that when Joe lost his religion he lost his vision."

Carl was remembering all this now as he greeted Joe with his usual warm, quiet friendliness. Joe pulled from his pocket a letter which Carl recognized as his own and sat down at the soda fountain. "Came to talk to you about this, Carl."

"Good. Let me fix you a drink while we chat. What'll it be?" . . . "Chocolate soda—fine! Now, is there anything you don't understand about that letter, Joe?"

"Well," Joe answered deprecatingly, "we get so many letters—a lot of 'em from crackpots. But you're a solid citizen, and I thought I'd better look into this—see just what's behind it. You know—well, what your angle is in wanting it printed."

Carl smiled. He said pleasantly, "I haven't got any angle. Doubt if I know what an angle is, in that sense. And there's nothing behind it. It means exactly what it says."

"I see." Joe put his drink down. "Well, frankly, Carl, a bunch of kids scrapping doesn't seem like anything to be getting in a lather about to me."

Carl put both hands on the counter and leaned forward. He was deeply serious now. "It isn't just a bunch of kids scrapping. There's something more than that. These children are only imitating adult attitudes. And I find those attitudes frightening, Joe."

"Now, now—kids are always beating each other up, aren't they? If it isn't about one thing, it's about another."

Carl shook his head. "A fair fight is one thing. Three boys jumping on one is another. Would you have liked it if it had been your boy the others lit into like that?"

Joe grinned. "I'm glad to say that Bill can take care of himself."

"But suppose he couldn't——" Carl stopped. "We've gotten off the point. I don't think gangster tactics need encouraging—at any age—but what's concerning me now is the reason *why* they jumped on this child. As I said in that letter—it was nothing more than that his skin was darker and his name had a foreign sound. Now, Joe, children aren't born with prejudices like that. They acquire them. From their parents or some other grownup. And those unreasoning hatreds carry over into adult life. That's why I say it frightens me—and that's why I can't see this incident as small, even aside from what it's done to that one boy."

Joe held his grin—but with some effort. "Naturally I don't approve of three kids ganging up on one. I'm proud to know my Bill would never do a thing like that. But I don't see all these social implications you're so wrought up about. And I still think you're making a mountain out of a molehill."

"You might turn that proverb around, too," Carl said dryly. "It's possible to look through the wrong end of the telescope and see mountains as molehills."

"I'll have to tell you something, Carl." Joe was unsmiling now. "You haven't covered the police beat like I have. And this paper of mine serves the whole county, you know. You just know the nice folks you meet in this nice drugstore. If you'd got around as much as I have you'd understand that what you call prejudice has got some foundation in fact. We're getting too many foreigners in our town and county, and it's changing the tone of the whole place. No, old man"—he tried to throw a genial note into his voice —"you're a mighty fine druggist and you stick to that! And if you've just got to have something to worry about—why, there're plenty of really big things, with the world falling to pieces the way it is!"

Carl fought against a feeling of deep discouragement. Were there many in Middleburg, he wondered, as intrenched in this sort of wicked stupidity as Joe apparently was? And what made it the more disheartening was that actually Joe was—or at any rate once had been—intelligent.

"The sort of thing this incident stands for may form one pretty good reason why the world is falling to pieces, if it is," he said quietly. "When boys and men can't get along together, when they put hatred and hostility in the place of friendship and Christian love—well, isn't that the root of a lot of our troubles, national and international?"

Joe's mouth had taken on a stubborn line.

"I still say you don't know how much bother these foreigners cause. I do, and that's why I'm not as tolerant as you are. Why don't they live in their own countries? Sometimes I wish they'd all go straight back where they came from—and stay there."

"If they'd all stayed in their own countries—down through the years—there wouldn't have been any United States of America," Carl remarked, keeping his tone agreeable with a little effort. "All our forefathers were foreigners here, you know."

"Entirely different——" Joe was beginning indignantly when

half a dozen customers, entering all at once, interrupted them. With an air of some relief, Joe got up. His voice became affable once more.

"Well, thanks for the drink. Maybe we'll use your letter. No hard feelings if we don't, I hope. Everybody doesn't see things the same way. And frankly, while all you say listens good, about brotherhood and world friendship and all that, I'm afraid in practice it just doesn't quite work out. But I'll let you hear definitely. Good-by—and just stop fretting about things!"

It was the same old story, Carl thought a little sadly. One heard the excuse on all sides. "Christianity is all very fine, but in business it simply isn't practicable." "Christian brotherhood is a great theory, but it's impossible to apply it." "The Golden Rule—Christian ethics—I believe in them, you understand. But in this sort of world you can't live by them, they aren't practical."

And the people who talked like this really didn't know whether Christianity was practicable or not, because they hadn't tried it.

He told Anna and Grampa about the interview that evening before dinner, pacing back and forth while Freddie sat on the floor oiling his catcher's mitt.

"I wonder," said Anna, "if Joe talks like that at home—saying that he wishes all the foreigners would go back where they came from and stay there—and things like that."

Suddenly then Freddie looked up. "Yes'm," he said soberly. "I guess he does." He sighed. "I got to tell you somethin'. I saw Al Lamino today. And I told him it was my pop had fixed him up, and then I asked him to play catch with me. About that time those three boys who beat him up came. They started pickin' on Al again, and I told 'em I thought they oughta quit it, and if they didn't I'd tell everybody they were the ones who'd beat him up in the first place. And then *they* said they wouldn't stand for squealers, and if I didn't stop buttin' in they'd give me worse'n they gave him. And then they punched us both, just to show us, they said, and ran off, throwin' rocks as they went, and I had a hard time makin' Al play catch with me, 'cause he said he didn't want to get me beat up, too, but finally he did, and say, he pitches swell!"

He paused, apparently for breath, and the three adults exchanged glances of pride and satisfaction over his head.

"I'm glad to hear all this," Carl said simply. "Makes me feel good, Freddie. Makes us all feel good."

"Aw—well—course I don't like the notion o' getting beat up, and it sorta scares me," Freddie admitted, pleased at the praise. "But I kept thinkin' about Al—and finally today I decided I'd better tell you who those kids were." He was looking at Carl now, speaking directly to him. "It was Ray Handy and Eddie Walsh and Bill Turner. But specially Bill. Everybody likes Bill—I used to like him too—and Ray and Eddie, they mostly do what Bill tells 'em to do. And the reason I knew about his dad when Mom said what she did just now—well, it was 'cause that's just what Bill said to Al. He said he wished him and ever'body like him would just go back where they came from and stay there." He stopped again, and eyed his father a little uneasily. "So what you goin' to do about it, Pop?"

"I don't know, Freddie." He smiled at the anxious face. "*We* don't want you beat up either, you know. I'll try to take care of that. But for the rest—I'll have to think about it. Let's see first what they decide to do about my letter."

"Dear," Anna asked him later when they were alone, "do you honestly have the least idea that Joe is going to use that letter?"

"Honestly—no. In fact, he practically said so."

"Maybe we'd better just drop it and try to do all we can for the Laminos ourselves," Anna suggested.

Carl's jaw set. "No. I've still got that handle—that clinching argument, as Emily called it. I'll think out a way to use that, if I must."

Joe telephoned the next morning soon after Carl had reached the drugstore. His voice had a heavy, forced sort of geniality.

"Carl? How are you? Well, I've been talking things over with the editor, and we think maybe it's best not to print your letter. You got it off your chest by writing it—that's the important thing, eh?" He laughed heartily at his own wit. "You write us another sometime—we're always glad to hear from you."

"Thanks, Joe. Glad you said that last, because you're hearing from me as of now. Forget about the letter. I've got a lead on a story I want to give you. A good one, I think."

Joe's words came back over the wire minus some of the heartiness. "Now Carl—is it along the same line as the letter? Because if it is—I hate to say this, but——"

Carl interrupted. "It's not actually anything I want to tell you so much as something I want to show you. I think you'll be interested. And it won't take long. If I could pick you up at the Citizen Building a little after five, I'd have you home in time for your supper."

"I wish," said Joe, a little fretfully, "you'd give me an idea first what it's all about."

"Couldn't do it justice. Spoil it all if I tried. This is something you've got to see for yourself."

There was a slight pause, and then Joe consented grudgingly. "Five-fifteen then—and after making with the mystery like this, it better be good!"

"It will be," Carl assured him. He hung up and turned to Grampa, observing with a grin, "Suspicious of me!"

Grampa grinned back. "And with good reason, I'd say!"

Joe was waiting in front of the newspaper building when Carl drew his car to the curb that afternoon. He got in, with somewhat less agility than he might have had he been thirty pounds lighter, and remarked in a voice whose geniality had worn decidedly thin:

"Well, I'm all suspense! Do you often do things this way?"

"Only when the occasion demands it. Hold your horses, Joe—it's just a couple of people I want you to meet. But there is a story in it."

Joe fidgeted impatiently on his seat. "If you say so I'm ready to believe you think there is. I just don't like going into things blindfold." He paused. "I still got a notion that case you're so worked up about it is mixed up in it."

"We'll be there in five minutes," said Carl. "I can't sing or dance a jig in the car to amuse you—shall I try a story?"

"Better keep still if you don't want me hopping out—the more you talk and evade, the more I feel you're up to something!"

Carl laughed. Then he said seriously, "I give you my word of honor—you're going to be glad. Now—just around the corner."

"Who lives here?" Joe demanded as the car stopped, four minutes later, before the Lamino house.

"I'll introduce you when we get in. Come on!"

Joe stopped. "I've been joking till now—but this time I'm serious. I'm tired of all this hocus-pocus. I want you to brief me as to what all this is about before I go in there."

"Joe," said Carl earnestly, "I'm serious too. I don't blame you for being irritated. But I've got a reason that seems good and justified to me for doing it this way. Now please just come along—for in about two minutes you'll understand the whole business."

Joe came, still reluctant and a trifle surly, and Carl rang the bell. The door opened almost instantly. Mrs. Lamino stood on the threshold; and if she had been lovely the other night when she was under a painful strain, she was lovelier now. She was dressed in white and she looked very young, very exotic, and a little bit frightened. Carl saw admiration replace Joe's surliness.

"Mrs. Lamino, this is Mr. Turner, whom I phoned you about," Carl said cordially. "Mrs. Alverus Lamino."

Mrs. Lamino put out a slim ivory hand, gave them a shy and entirely charming smile, and asked them into the small, neat living room. At the same moment a boy came in from another door, his face still patched with two strips of adhesive, his eye free of the pack but discolored.

"And this," Carl added, "is her son, Alverus Jr."

"Hello——" Joe began, and suddenly stopped. He looked at the dark little face with its purple eye and its two patches and froze.

"Won't you sit down, please?" asked Mrs. Lamino in her soft voice.

"Thank you, but——" Joe's indignant gaze softened a little as it rested on her, then congealed again as he turned it back to Carl. "Is this the boy you wrote about in that letter?" he asked bluntly.

Carl nodded. "This is the one, Joe."

"Mrs. Lamino, I'm sorry—I know this isn't your fault and I don't want to be rude," Joe said angrily. "But I told Mr. Fisher——" He broke off. "I might have known and I suppose I did, really. But I don't appreciate it, Carl, I don't appreciate it one bit!"

"I didn't suppose you would, Joe. But the whole story wasn't in that letter, and when you get it——" He picked up a big framed photograph from the nearby table. "May I, Mrs. Lamino? I asked her to be sure to have this out for me, Joe. She said it was always out, anyway. Will you look at it?"

From a dark, youthful face black eyes laughed into Joe's as Carl held the picture before him. The young man was in uniform and wore a sergeant's stripes. "This, Joe, is a photograph of Mrs. Lamino's husband. As you can see, he was a sergeant in the United States Army."

The boy had moved to his mother's side. The little room was very still. Finally Joe raised his eyes from the pictured face. He asked slowly, "Did you say—*was?*"

"Yes. He was killed. At a place you've written about many a time in your paper. You and I didn't have to fight there—we were too old. And our kids were too young. So boys like this one were doing it for us—and our children. The place where Sergeant Lamino died was in Korea, Joe. The boys named it Heartbreak Ridge."

Joe moistened his lips. He glanced at the child and his mother, still standing silent, and seemed about to speak. Then he shook his head very slightly and closed his mouth again.

"He died in action, sacrificing himself to hold a certain point very nearly singlehanded. And he held it. Long enough for his comrades and fellow Americans—I said *fellow* Americans, Joe— to get through. Mrs. Lamino, may I show Mr. Turner the medal?"

The girl, her big eyes misty, opened the table drawer and took out a long leather box. She snapped it open and handed it to Carl. On the rich velvet lay a medal. Silently Carl passed it on to Joe; and Joe stood looking down on it for close to a full minute before he handed it back, carefully, almost reverently. He said huskily, "The Congressional Medal of Honor!"

Carl nodded. "The highest our country can bestow. So now, Joe, I think you can understand why I was so eager to bring you here tonight. Because you see, after what happened to Alverus the other night Mrs. Lamino has been wondering just what it was her husband died for."

"Oh no!" Joe's broad face was red, he was stammering in his

earnestness. "You mustn't, Mrs. Lamino—the boys didn't *know!*
If they had——" He stopped. "But they will! The whole town will.
I wish Carl had told me earlier——" Suddenly his brow was wrin-
kling as if an unexpected thought had struck him. "Lamino!
Lamino! I've heard that name before. What did your husband do
before he went into the service?"

"He was a professional ball player," said the girl proudly. "A
good one!"

Joe smote his thigh with his big hand. "I knew that name was
familiar! Why, I knew all about him! I was handling sports when
he was playing. Very promising youngster he was. Future big-
league material, we all thought. Pitcher, wasn't he?"

"The best in the world!" cried Alverus, speaking for the first
time.

"Well, this *is* a story!" Joe stopped and shook hands with Mrs.
Lamino and Alverus solemnly. "You must be mighty proud. You've
got a right to be! Sorry I didn't get on to it all as soon as you came
to Middleburg. Now let me see—I didn't realize what this was
going to be and I'll need more time and a cameraman. Like to
get pictures of you both and a full story——" He paused, looking
doubtfully at Alverus. Then his face broke into a friendly grin.
"You're not at your best, Son, but the photographer can touch
up the negatives and nothing will show. And don't you worry.
Poor sportsmanship, several boys jumping on one—and I'm glad
to feel sure my own boy would never do a thing like that. But it
wouldn't have happened if they'd realized, and I promise you
they'll be singing a different tune after my story comes out!"

Carl took with him, as he left, the memory of two faces from
which the fear had gone. And that, he thought, was something;
in fact, it was a great deal. His "clinching argument" had worked.
Yet he was fully aware that Joe, now good-naturedly reproaching
him for "going about the whole business in such a crazy, mysterious way," had seen only a part of what he had hoped the dramatic
little episode would reveal fully.

He wondered, as he started the car, exactly what it all had
meant to Joe. A good story, first, undoubtedly. And doubtless he
had learned something, too; for he was far from stupid. Carl felt
sure that after this he would be more careful to find out whether

seeming "foreigners" really *were* foreigners. He would probably
be willing now to admit that "*some* foreigners make good Americans." Yes, Carl thought, the edge of his prejudice was almost
certainly blunted. But if his basic attitudes had greatly changed
he had not given much indication of it.

Carl sighed deep inside—and steeled himself to try what ad-
ministering a shock might do.

"Joe," he said, "don't you feel any curiosity about who the
boys that jumped on young Alverus were?"

"Hadn't thought about it. Do you know?"

"As it happens—I do." He hesitated, disliking the task. But after
all, Joe had to know sometime—all three sets of parents did, if this
incident was to serve, even in a small measure, as the start of a
different spirit in Middleburg. So he went on; "Ray Handy and
Eddie Walsh——"

"Surely not!" Joe interrupted, startled. "They're pals of Bill's
—nice boys!"

"Ordinarily—yes. They're not only pals of Bill's. He seems to be
their leader—their hero. They were following Bill when they at-
tacked the little Filipino, Joe."

There was an instant's silence, and then Joe turned a dazed
face toward his friend.

"Bill? *My* Bill? There must be some mistake!"

"I wish there were," Carl said sincerely. "But it's true. Freddie
tried to take up for Alverus, and Bill threatened to give Freddie
the same treatment if he told."

"But—I can't take it in! I tell you, it's out of *character!* Doesn't
a man know his own kid? Bill's never been a bully—never picked
on smaller boys—one of the best baby-sitters in the neighborhood."
Joe got out his handkerchief and mopped his forehead with a
distracted gesture. "It's *got* to be a mistake, Carl——"

"I don't doubt in the least that everything you say is true about
Bill," Carl answered unhappily, "*when* it's a question of the people he knows. But this was different. So different that from Bill's
point of view he felt justified. He thought Alverus was a foreigner.
And Bill doesn't like foreigners."

"Bill? Doesn't like foreigners?" Joe shook his head bewilderedly.
"I'm in a nightmare—none of this makes any sense at all! Bill

doesn't know any foreigners, to speak of. At his age where would he get such ideas?"

Carl said gently, "From you, I imagine."

"From——" Joe's voice snapped off short.

"Well—you don't like them either, do you?"

"Carl—for Heaven's sake! Is that the way you think I acted just now at the Laminos? As if I didn't *like* them?"

Carl sighed. "You asked me—so I'll have to tell you. You weren't interested in doing anything at all for Alverus until you found out who his father was. Up to that point, you were all set to fling out in a temper. I had to talk fast to keep you. You just didn't feel it was too important as long as the kid that got beaten up was really a 'foreigner.'"

"Now listen——" said Joe huskily. "I know I did some talking to you the other day about foreigners—and yes, it sure did make a difference to me that this boy's father was a soldier killed in action and a fine American baseball player! But I don't really hate anybody—you ought to know me well enough to know that."

"I do, Joe," Carl said earnestly. "But I wonder if a kid of eleven would know the difference—I mean when you're more or less shooting off your mouth about foreigners—does Bill know it isn't hatred?"

"I've never talked like that to Bill!"

Carl shot a glance at his sick face and had to force himself to go on. "Not *to* him. But in his hearing. Must've. Because Freddie quoted him as saying exactly the same words that *you* said to me—that you wished all these foreigners would go straight back where they came from and stay there. To Bill that makes foreigners enemies whom he's got a right to run off."

Joe did not speak for almost a block this time. Then he said heavily, "Well, whatever made Bill do it—it's knocked the props out from under me, finding out he could."

"You don't need to feel like that!" Carl said quickly. "Bill'll change his ideas when you change yours—I'm sure of that. Because Joe—" he hesitated—"I agree that you don't hate anybody —yet. But there was something behind what you were saying to me the other day that could mighty easy grow into hatred."

Joe looked down at his big hands, knotted together on his knees, and said dully, "You've got a pretty poor opinion of me, haven't you?"

"Great guns, no!" exclaimed Carl, horrified. "Did I sound *that* self-righteous?"

Joe shook his head. "I didn't mean that. You didn't sound at all self-righteous."

"I hope not. Because," said Carl with genuine humility, "I get off the track too often myself to sit in judgment on anybody else. If I didn't know where to go for help—Joe! I wish I knew how to say this right . . . We used to work together at the church—" he hesitated—"before you seemed to lose your faith, Joe——"

"Hold on, hold on, you're going too fast!" Joe protested. "I haven't lost my faith—I've just let other things crowd the church out."

"I'm glad to hear it," said Carl sincerely. "Because that must mean that in your heart you do still believe that Christ came into the world, and lived, and died, for the sake of *all* men. And if you believe this, if you know He's everybody's Savior, then you can't possibly want to see any man of any race or any color or any station in life treated with less than respect."

"I know—all brothers—world friendship—dignity and worth of every human being—sure, I know. Jesus taught that—I admit it. But lately," said Joe flatly, "it's seemed to me that it just wouldn't work."

Carl brought the car to a stop before Joe's house. And now as he turned toward his friend, there was an intensity of feeling in his voice and face that was almost passion.

"It's the only thing in God's world that will work, Joe! It's our only hope. Unless man can keep plugging at it, keep coming nearer to attaining it, the human race is lost and doomed. I never believed anything more heartily in all my life. What have you done with that good keen mind the Lord gave you that you don't see it too? With the handwriting already on the wall!" He stopped suddenly. His tone grew quieter, a little constrained. "Didn't quite mean to mount the rostrum. It happens to be something I feel strongly about. And this thing slipped up on me—I guess, like you hinted, I've been a little cloistered. I hadn't known that race hatred and intolerance and prejudice were showing their ugly heads in Middleburg. When I found out—I had to try to do something. That's the whole explanation of why I took you to the Laminos today."

"I don't suppose this will make much sense to you," Joe said huskily, after an instant's silence, "but what I've been feeling—well, it's that these foreigners, who're coming in pretty fast now were changing the character of the county and of Middleburg. I guess, if you get down to it, I wasn't thinking of it from the Christian viewpoint—or about saving the world—but just about what I felt was best for Middleburg."

Carl smiled. "At thirty-eight you surely haven't got so old and set in your ways that you want things never to change here in Middleburg, have you? Always to stay exactly as they have been? You can't put Middleburg off in a nice quiet backwater and isolate it from the rest of the world. But outside of that—I plain don't believe that's what you think, Joe. You're too smart not to know that the Christian way is the best way—for Middleburg or any other town. No, you'd quit thinking when you came to that conclusion—you were substituting prejudice for thought."

Joe opened the car door. He said dryly, "That's twice you've referred to my brain in rather complimentary terms. I don't mind telling you—just now my own opinion of it isn't too high. Maybe, like you say, I haven't been thinking—but without going any further right now I'll promise you one thing, and that is that I'm going to start thinking—and thinking *hard.*"

Carl's smile was very warm. "Will you let me know the results of that thinking?"

Joe nodded.

"And Joe—" he had shifted his gears now, but held his foot on the clutch—"if you don't mind my saying one more thing—it wouldn't hurt a bit if you mixed a little praying along with the thinking. . . . Good-by."

It was two nights later before Joe kept his promise. He called just at bedtime, while Anna was rolling her hair and Carl was climbing into bed with a book.

"Did I get you out of bed?" he asked.

"Almost. Wouldn't have mattered."

"I felt like it wouldn't. And I didn't want to wait till morning.

I've done the thinking—and the praying, too, Carl. Plus a lot of talking with Mildred and the boy."

"Joe," said Carl, "you can get me out of bed at 2 A.M. to tell me news like that!"

The little laugh that came back over the wires sounded like the old Joe; it had none of that false heartiness, that spurious geniality he had felt in the later Joe.

"Don't carry that too far. I might really do it sometime." Then the tone changed, took on a shade of anxiety. "I hope you won't think too badly of Bill. It wasn't quite his fault, you know. He's all right—he's going along with another way of thinking and doing —a Christian way—we *all* are in this family from here on out."

"I never was worried about Bill, Joe, once *you'd* got straight."

"Then that's all right," said Bill's father. "And now I've just got one more thing to tell you—I've talked to the editor and the owner of the *Citizen,* too. I'm making some more investigations and I'm going to do a series of articles along the line you were discussing— half a dozen at least, maybe more."

When Carl came back into the bedroom, Anna thought his face looked happier and more relaxed than it had since that night Alverus and his mother had first knocked at the drugstore door.

"And what I'm thinking," he said when he had repeated the conversation to her, "what I'm thinking, dear, is that it's going to be a fine thing for Alverus and others like him, and a fine thing for this town, and a fine thing for Joe and Mildred and Bill. But also, it could be that it's going to be a mighty fine thing for something else I'm glad to say Joe isn't even thinking about just now—and that's his career."

In all of which predictions, as it happened, he was to prove a true prophet.

7. A SOCIOLOGICAL STUDY

*T*HE serious, good-looking young man who had been working for the past hour at a table in the Middleburg Public Library, his dark head bent over his notes, suddenly stopped, stacked his papers and put them in his brief case, gathered up the three books he had been consulting, and walked to the library desk. The girl behind the desk smiled at him.

"Were they what you wanted?" she asked with a sort of shy eagerness, gesturing toward the volumes as he put them down.

The young man smiled back at her appreciatively. She was, as he had been noticing now for two weeks, a very pretty girl. Hardly his type, for he liked girls a bit smoother and more sophisticated (or at any rate, that, at this especial stage of his development, was what he supposed he liked) but quite charming, nevertheless, with a beauty that seemed to lie not alone in shining blond hair and candid blue eyes, but even more in a kind of aura she carried of health and joyous vitality.

"They helped a lot," he said. "You've been tremendously good about looking things up for me. I appreciate it no end."

"Well, that's what I'm here for," she answered cheerfully. "Anyway"—a dimple appeared briefly in her cheek—"you're a sort of a novelty. I'm dead-sure nobody ever made a sociological study of Middleburg before. Maybe you'll make us famous."

He shook his head with a grin. "In the first place, Middleburg's name won't be mentioned. I'm just trying to give a picture of a typical American town. In the second place, it's only a Master's thesis—it'll never get published."

"And you selected Middleburg as typical?" she asked interestedly.

"Well—yes. Fairly so, anyway. Don't you agree?"

"I haven't visited enough other places to know, I guess," she said demurely. "Are you going to want anything else? A pamphlet came in today—something about Middleburg's early history."

He shook his head. "Thanks—but I've been reading so much lately I think I need a change." He leaned across the desk and turned on his not inconsiderable charm. "Don't you think I ought to study some Middleburg citizens, too? Would you be willing to help about *that?*"

The dimple barely showed again. "You want me to introduce you to some Middleburg citizens?"

"Well, no," admitted the young man with candor. "I want you to go to dinner with me. I was trying to make a tactful approach."

He had judged her from the first to be a singularly guileless girl. Now, as she laughed, her ingenuous face lit up with an entirely frank pleasure.

"Why, you don't need all that tact," she said gaily. "I'd love to go to dinner with you!"

"That's wonderful of you!" The young man threw a gratitude that was not by any means entirely insincere into his voice. "Can you suggest a place we can get a bang-up meal—since you know the town better than I do?"

She nodded, eyes dancing with a sudden idea. "I certainly can! The best meal in Middleburg. At *our* house. Would that suit you?"

"You're asking me to have dinner at your home? With your family?" he asked, surprised.

"Why—yes. My folks will be glad to meet you." She added, "I've told them about your thesis, you know."

Well, he thought, amused, it was the first time he'd ever asked a girl for a dinner date and had her counter with a suggestion that they spend the evening with her family! But actually it was a piece of luck for him. In fact, it was exactly what he'd been hoping might occur, eventually.

"If you're certain it's all right, there's nothing I'd rather do," he said heartily.

"Oh, I'm certain—Mother's always glad when we bring friends home," she answered confidently. "I'll write our address. Here"— she scribbled it on a slip of paper and shoved it across the desk to him—"and we eat at about six-thirty. My father's name is on the mailbox—it's *Carl* Fisher."

"And yours is Emily—which is a lot prettier name than Miss Fisher. And mine's David—to you. Okay—Emily?"

"Oh, I barely recognize myself as Miss Fisher," she said brightly. "Nobody in this town calls me that."

"Then I won't either," he answered, smiling. "See you tonight— Emily."

But it did occur to him as he drove back to his hotel that for an unsophisticated and naïve lass, she had managed very pleasantly and neatly to divest the privilege of calling her "Emily" of intimacy. Probably quite unconscious on her part, he decided. And in any event it was just as well that she wasn't too impressionable. Because otherwise he might feel a little uncomfortable about giving her the idea that he had any particular personal interest in her. Not that she wasn't attractive. But just that at present what he wanted was not social life for its own sake, but simply a chance to observe at firsthand the personalities, interests, and religion of a family of this community who belonged to the "solid citizen" class, were pillars-of-the-church type, and all that. This, he was certain from a few cautious inquiries, was exactly what the Fishers were; and he was lucky to have access to them through Emily.

And of course, he assured a slightly qualmish conscience that at this point seemed to be obtruding with the suggestion that putting people under a microscope was not a very good way to repay kindness, his study would be a scientific one, purely objective, made without prejudice or ill will. Moreover, as he had told Emily, it would not be circulated. In fact, it would never be read by anybody save the few men who would examine and pass on it at his university. So actually this faintly guilty feeling of his was foolishness.

As he came in his room at the hotel, the telephone was ringing.

He answered it, fully expecting to hear Emily's voice explaining apologetically that it didn't suit her mother for him to come to-night, and was relieved to discover that it was his own mother calling him from Chicago. He was only mildly surprised at this, though he had supposed her to be in Miami; he had stopped being surprised at any sudden flitting of hers a long time ago.

"Davey—darling!" Her light, tinkling tones floated over the wires. "I know you're gasping with amazement! I suddenly got just frightfully bored in Miami—and about that time in came an invitation to a house party here—so I flew in this morning!"

"Just like that, eh?" said David, laughing. "Good for you! But won't you get just frightfully bored in Chicago, too?" His voice held the tolerant, rather affectionate amusement which repre-sented the attitude he had adopted toward her years ago; perhaps because the alternative might have been criticism.

"No, because you're coming to see me—aren't you?" she coaxed. "This is a lovely home—right on the lake—and the other guests are awfully amusing, truly—and all just crazy to meet you. Of course, I've told them how handsome you are."

"Then I'd better stay away and preserve their illusions," said her son cheerfully.

"No, Davey, honestly—you will, won't you? Don't say no!"

David grinned. "No," he said.

"Oh, Davey!" she wailed reproachfully. "That's not funny!"

"I'm not trying to be funny, lady. You know perfectly well that I'm here to finish up this thesis."

"You don't expect me to take *that* seriously, do you? The whole idea was absolutely absurd, anyway! I can understand your want-ing a little time to catch your breath after getting out of the Army —but for pity's sake why a thesis in *sociology?* About a dull little midwestern city where I'm sure you only meet very dull people! Why, why?"

"Probably because I'm peculiar," said David, beginning to be a trifle bored. "But honestly I'm not coming just now, Mother."

There was a pause. Then she asked crossly, "Well, what are you doing outside of that silly thesis? You don't study and write *all* day, do you?"

"Pretty much, till now. Tonight I've got a dinner invitation."
She snorted. "I've got dozens of dinner invitations for you!"

"Not like this one. This dinner is laboratory work."

"I don't know what you're talking about," she said fretfully.

She very seldom did, thought David. He replied reasonably,
"It's just that they're going to be part of my thesis, Mother. My
hosts, I mean. Now I've got to dress. Call me some other time.
And have fun. 'Bye."

He put the phone back in place with a slight, unconscious grimace. He had been only ten when his father, a distinguished college professor, had died; and a child of that age takes his parents
for granted without analyzing them. But somewhere in the early
teens David, who remembered his father and was more deeply
influenced by that memory than he knew, had begun to wonder
why the brilliant man had ever married a woman whose interests
were so entirely trivial. Youth and beauty, he supposed—for a
man like Dr. Wainwright would certainly not have been influenced by her comfortable income—and the glamour that surrounded those qualities. Yes, that must be the explanation—and,
he had early decided, that was one mistake he, David, would
never make. Any girl he married would have to be interested in the
things *he* was interested in.

He knotted his dark red tie, recalling this decision, and told
his personable reflection in the mirror that this was the reason
why this really lovely child, Emily Fisher, could never seriously
tempt him. Her beliefs and her attitudes were sure to be highly
conventional. He wanted somebody who could think daringly. He
might have had a difficult time explaining just what he meant by
thinking daringly—but at any rate he was practically certain that
Emily didn't do it.

His father, now—he had been one of the daring thinkers, undoubtedly. David had been about seventeen when he had run
across some notes Dr. Wainwright had jotted down. "I am assur-
edly not an atheist," he had written. "That seems to me a stupid
position. For the universe exists, and who am I to say that it does
not possess a Creator? On the other hand, it is equally stupid to
assume that there is one. For all I know, it may all be the result of

blind chance. So what I say is—I do not know. In other words, I am an agnostic, and this appears to me to be the only position an intelligent man can take."

Reading it, David had instantly agreed, and had as promptly made that attitude his own.

Well, there at least was one point to be considered when he was —as at times he had been—a little inclined to blame his mother for his somewhat neglected childhood. (Not that she hadn't always been quite fond of him—but she was restless and away much of the time, and a great deal of his boyhood had been spent in boarding schools and camps.) She had never smothered him with maternal attention, and since she had left him free to develop along his own lines, he had never had any stale intellectual concepts or outworn religious ideas foisted off on him. Driving through Middleburg's streets in the spring dusk, he told himself once more that he was, at any rate, grateful to her for this much.

It was exactly six-thirty when he parked his car in front of the Fisher house. He was interested to note, walking up the daffodil-bordered path, that it looked almost exactly as he had pictured it; a spreading, comfortable dwelling of quite unoriginal architecture set in a pretty yard. Emily opened the door even before he rang the bell—she had on a blue dress and she was bright-eyed and prettily flushed. All her family were gathered in the living room and she introduced them to him with an air of pride in them that gave him, for an instant, a curious feeling somewhere in his chest, for which he could not account. This—the thought ran through his mind quite involuntarily—was the way some families felt about each other. Then, almost defiantly, he threw the idea away, reminding himself that close family life was "stifling."

Shaking hands with each, smiling his charming smile, he was also studying them attentively. He would, of course, have indignantly denied that already he was fitting them neatly into certain pre-determined pigeonholes; he was, he would have said, merely tentatively classifying them, in a general sort of way. Grampa, for instance—a slender old fellow with deep-set eyes who occasionally dropped his *Gs*—rather the cracker-box philosopher type in a somewhat different setting, he judged. An unusual warmth of personality, David conceded—but then this was a characteristic in greater or lesser degree of all the family. Carl was big and dark, blunt-featured and quiet, a typical, moderately successful, small-city businessman with (no doubt) the typically restricted interests of his group—yet he, too, when he smiled surprised you by the way the heavy face lit up with genuine friendliness. Anna, his wife, had evidently just come in from the kitchen, for she wore a fluffy apron and had a smudge of flour on one cheek—which the others did not fail to cheerfully point out to her; she was slender and blond, still pretty, and David, bowing his dark head deferentially over her hand, was telling himself that she was practically sure to be a nice and attractive specimen of the standard, devoted "Mom," her main interest her family and house, and her next, doubtless, her church. The two boys, Peter, about seventeen, and Freddie, ten, were of course a bit young to place. Probably they also fitted without mental protest into the pattern of that particular stratum of Middleburg society to which they belonged —the "good church people."

Anna smilingly excused herself in a moment to see about the dinner. She refused to let Emily help her, at which Emily grinned.

"All in honor of you," she assured David. "She doesn't usually let me off—but tonight I'm supposed to entertain you."

"Would he be any less entertained if we let him sit down?" Grampa suggested. "This is the chair we call our company chair, Mr. Wainwright."

"Then I'll sit somewhere else," said David. "Because I don't want to be company. I also don't want to be called Mr. Wainwright. David, please—all of you."

They liked that; he could see that they did. There was the same unaffected pleasure in every face; it seemed to say, "We're glad you're friendly."

"Well then—David," said Carl Fisher with the smile that changed his dark face, "Emily tells us you're doing some research about our town. A thesis, isn't it?"

"Yes, sir. And my mother thinks I'm crazy to be doing it." He added, "She may be right."

"Oh, not everybody who does research is necessarily crazy," Carl said with a twinkle.

"I'm sure some are not." David smiled at him. "But my case

is a little different. You see, I'm going to be a lawyer. In fact, I have my law degree and hope to start practice somewhere or other in a few months. My mother doesn't see why a lawyer wants a Master's degree in sociology."

"Well, why do you?" Peter asked curiously.

"Long story. I majored in sociology at college—got interested, and did some graduate work—finally qualified for my Master's in it, except that I didn't write my thesis. About that time I decided to take law, so I let the Master's go. Just after I got my law degree, the Army got *me*. And when I got out—well, I'd been in the hospital awhile and I wasn't keen at all to start practice right away, and at the same time I didn't want to loaf. I just wanted to do something that interested me and yet didn't put me under strain or pressure for a while. So I decided I'd write that thesis and get my degree."

They were very much interested; they asked him why he'd chosen Middleburg, and he described the series of chance occurrences which had turned him in its direction; and they said they were complimented that he thought them worth writing about and they surely wanted to read his thesis when it was done.

"Oh no, you don't," David answered, looking embarrassed. "Nothing is so dull as a thesis—nobody reads them except the fellows who write them and the fellows who have to correct them."

"Were you wounded?" demanded Freddie. "Is that why you was in the hospital?"

David nodded and changed the subject. "You said you were on the high school baseball team, didn't you, Peter? I used to play shortstop on our team."

Both boys were looking at him with deep respect—a soldier who had been wounded. Carl choked off Freddie's questions as to where and when and how, and Peter said eagerly, "I'd sure like to pitch a few with you—bet you could show me some new curves!"

"You're more likely to show *me* some new ones—been quite a while since I played."

"I c'n play baseball," Freddie stated positively. He had stationed himself by the guest's chair and was gazing at him with approval. "I c'n play chopsticks, too—but that's on the piano, of course."

"Now, Freddie . . ." remarked his father warningly.

"I remember—he's Em'ly's comp'my," said Freddie resignedly. "Well, then, David, Em'ly can play too. Real good."

They all laughed and Emily groaned, "The worst thing that can happen to a girl is to have a small brother."

"Won't you play something for me since he's told on you?" David begged.

"Chopin—you're best on Chopin," said her father proudly.

"I'm really not best on anything—I'm very mediocre—and I'm sure I'd get along better if my loving family didn't build me up so much," Emily said ruefully. But David saw that the dimple was flashing again. "Tell you what—I'll play something we can all sing —that's more fun."

They argued then, in hearty and friendly fashion, about what song to sing. Peter asked if everybody didn't know "Swanee River Stomp," and answered himself, "Sure they do—go ahead, Emily." But it appeared that this masterpiece was unknown to all but Peter. Freddie's offering of "The Muffin Man" was received with marked lack of enthusiasm. Grampa and Carl both had several suggestions at which the others hooted amiably. Finally they decided that one song they all knew, including David, was "Let Me Call You Sweetheart"—though Peter jeered, "That sappy old thing!" He sang it with the rest, however, quite lustily. David had heard better singing, but not more enthusiastic; even in this short time it seemed to him that he could discern that this family brought a lot of vitality into everything they did.

A clapping from the doorway at the close told them of Anna's presence.

"Now if he's done calling her sweetheart and seeing the love light shining and all the rest, dinner's ready!" she announced.

David was prepared for a "blessing" at the table before eating; but he was a little surprised when the family all joined hands as they bowed their heads. Emily's firm, warm little hand clasped his on one side; and Grampa's on the other felt sinewy and friendly. It was a good dinner. Emily had not misled him about that. There was a sort of herb and mushroom sauce for the beautifully cooked roast which, David thought, would have done credit to a French chef—and he told Anna so.

"It's an old family recipe," she said, pleased. And Carl remarked proudly that his wife had a recipe drawer as packed as his prescription drawer at the drugstore was.

"I think I like Anna's recipes better'n your prescriptions, though, Son," drawled Grampa. They all laughed appreciatively and David seized the opportunity to inquire, with that charmingly deferential air of his:

"You're both in the drug business, aren't you? I wonder—what led you to choose it?"

Carl considered. "That's never an easy question to answer, is it? I helped my father summers—just like Peter helps us. And I suppose I liked it. So when I went to college I took my degree in pharmacy."

"I think what he wants to know," observed Grampa shrewdly, "is *why* you liked it, Carl."

Carl laughed. "Well, why does he like law and sociology?" He seemed to be hunting a moment for words. "For one thing—you're nearly always with people. I like people. In this job you get to know them—sometimes you even get a chance to help them a little bit."

David did not believe in "helping" people, save in material ways. Food, shelter, a job—yes, surely. But spiritual help—what is sometimes called "moral support" (and this, he took it, was the sort of "help" to which Carl Fisher referred) no. He had never had any himself, even from the father whose memory he so much admired, and he held the firm opinion that such help only weakened the recipients of it. Everybody should stand on his own two feet and work out his own destiny. He asked politely, "Help them—how?"

Carl looked a little embarrassed. He explained apologetically, "In a town this size a druggist is almost like a doctor. People come to him with their aches and pains—pretty often they come in an emergency when they haven't been able to reach a doctor. But just like a doctor, he has to try to keep them from getting nervous and scared about themselves—or maybe it's about someone they're fond of—as well as help out with whatever ails their bodies. Then, too"—he hesitated a second—"well, if they come too often with this

complaint or that and keep telling you, 'My doctor can't seem to
find the trouble,' why, then, you get to know that their real illness
is in their minds or hearts, that they're worried and unhappy."

"And in that case—you give them advice about their—er—personal problems?" David kept his voice carefully sympathetic.

The big man chuckled. "Dispense advice with pills? I don't think
I do too much of that."

"What then? I'm interested, sir—that's why I ask."

Carl looked at him with a suddenly sharpened glance for an
instant. He answered gently, "I point out where they *can* go for
help, that's all. I tell them I happen to know from my own personal
experience that the help's there for them, sure—and that it'll solve
their problems." He added simply, "It's downright amazing how
often that's all they seem to need, too."

He's talking about God, thought David, embarrassed. And then,
oddly, he was embarrassed because he had been embarrassed; for
he saw that no one else at all seemed so, that apparently they felt
Carl's remarks were both natural and sensible. He was hoping no
one had noticed his own disconcerted expression when Grampa
spoke.

"There's times, too," he remarked reflectively, "when what folks
seem to need mostly is just to talk." He smiled. "That's where I
come in, 'cause I let Carl and the clerks do the scurrying around
these days. Privilege of age. So I usually have time to listen."

"You sure were listenin' today," Peter observed in amiable de-
rision. "Old Mrs. Hornsby was talkin' your arm off, nearly. Was
it her neuritis or her nephew this time?"

"Don't matter," his grandfather answered mildly. "Both are
kinda chronic with her. Point is—she's lonesome and probably considerable of a bore to most folks, and she went out feelin' a lot
better just because somebody was interested."

David struggled with an unfamiliar idea almost with exasperation: was it reasonable that a man of average intelligence should
seem to consider that the opportunity to console windy old bores
nobody else wanted to put up with was one of the *advantages*
of his business? He gave it up and asked Peter:

"And what are you going to be?"

"Oh, I don't know." Peter sent his father a half-shy glance and then looked down at his plate self-consciously. "Guess I'll end up at the drugstore too."

"So you'll all be in Middleburg together," David said, looking round the circle.

"Oh, we don't know about that," Anna answered pleasantly. "Emily could marry a man who lives almost anywhere. And Freddie—I think just now *he's* planning to be a big-league baseball player."

David thought, "It's dollars to doughnuts all the same that Emily marries a Middleburg lad and that Freddie too eventually goes in the drugstore! Every one of them's going to stay right in this nice little beaten track, I'll bet." But aloud he only said, "Got to be mighty good if you're ever a big-league player, Freddie."

Freddie answered placidly, with no false modesty at all, "I'm already mighty good." And the discussion dissolved in general laughter.

Carl helped Anna change the plates and bring in the dessert, and during the process Grampa inquired, "What church do you attend, David?"

"Why——" David hesitated, and decided against a direct answer. "I'm glad you mentioned that. I haven't been to any—here—yet. I was just wondering if I could dare ask to go with all of you to your church next Sunday."

The look Emily sent him then was so suddenly, unexpectedly radiant with pleasure that it took him aback. He was glad that Carl and Anna came in at that moment with the dessert—slices of pie that were so light and so melting that Pete was not far off when he announced after the first bite, "Dreamy!"

They lingered over this, talking pleasantly at random; but finally Anna took the plates away and Carl looked at Freddie and said, "Time for our devotions now, Son."

"Devotions?" David was betrayed into surprise as Freddie, seeming to understand what his father had meant, fetched a Bible and placed it in front of Grampa. "Oh! You mean family prayers?"

"Don't you have 'em in your family?" inquired Freddie innocently.

David remembered his childhood meals; first with nurses and governesses, then at schools and camps. He shook his head.

"How funny!" Freddie commented wonderingly, and Grampa said, "Why, a good many people don't, Freddie," quite uncritically. He smiled at David. "It means a lot to us. But——" And he paused, looking at Emily.

"He means, David," Emily said quickly, "that we don't want to force anything on you. If you'd rather not stay——"

"Oh no," David answered. "No, really—I'd like to."

Some slight sense of strain that he had felt in the older members of the group immediately after Freddie's question disappeared instantly. They relaxed, evidently pleased and relieved by his answer. And David found himself waiting curiously for the small ceremony which "meant a lot" to the Fishers.

"We take turns leading—it's my turn tonight," Grampa explained as he opened the Bible. He settled his spectacles firmly on his nose.

"I'm reading tonight," he began, "from the tenth chapter of St. John. Jesus says, 'I am the door.' To know exactly what He meant by that, you have to understand that He was talking about the way the sheep get in and out of the sheepfold by a door. He was saying that He was not only the Good Shepherd of the sheep—and we're the sheep, you know—but their Door, too. 'By me if any man enter in, he shall be saved, and shall go in and out, and find pasture.' He liked to talk in pictures like that, and it makes it plainer. He's telling us He is our Door, our Door to happiness and peace and a good life here, and life everlasting in the next world. 'I am come that they might have life, and that they might have *it* more abundantly,' He says. 'The good shepherd giveth his life for the sheep.'"

It struck David suddenly, as he looked at them over his glasses, that Grampa's face was oddly beautiful in a strange way that had nothing to do with physical beauty. And he wondered confusedly why it faintly irritated him that an ordinary old codger who'd lived the ordinary life of a druggist in an ordinary small city should look like a great man. Surely he could have no right to, thought the young man.

"It's true," said the ordinary old codger reflectively, "that the Cross is at the heart of our Christian faith, and it's true that the Master made how well a person stands sufferin' a sort of a test. In Matthew 20 He asks His disciples, 'Are ye able to drink of the cup that I shall drink of?' But don't forget about His coming to make life more abundant, too! Don't forget how He loved flowers and birds and children! I tell you what—I'm as sure as that I'm sittin' right here that for Jesus, no matter how hard or sad things got, joy was finally always the strongest, and that's the way it'll be in the end for every Christian, because he's got something no trouble can shake. That's why the Christian's life is never drab or limited, and don't let anybody make you think anything else, ever."

(David was wondering uneasily, "Has he sensed the way I feel about all this? Is he talking at me?" The idea was an uncomfortable one, and he resented it.)

"The Christian's life is a great adventure," said Grampa earnestly. "And because he's got a great big purpose and motive in livin', and because he tries to do everything to the glory of God, everything's got a meanin'—even the dull things, so they aren't dull any more."

David was conscious of a rising hostility. The old fellow was spinning fairy tales! The religious person's life *was* narrow. Because he simply made up his mind something was true and then shut the door. . . . Somewhere within him a voice asked mockingly, "And haven't you simply made up your mind it *isn't* true and shut the door?" He answered it indignantly, "I'm an agnostic—like my father!"

When he came back, Grampa was saying, "And because the Christian knows Jesus died for his sins, he also knows that he can get divine forgiveness for them all, and he never needs to be afraid. Not of anything in life, and not even of death."

He closed the Bible and said, "Let us pray."

David moved restlessly. After all this must he sit through a long, windy prayer? But the family only repeated softly together, "Let us give thanks unto the Lord, for He is good and His mercy endureth forever."

They raised their heads. "That's all," Emily said, smiling at him.

Something lingered on her face—on all their faces; a kind of after-glow of mellow serenity. It disturbed him and roused again that half-uneasy antagonism he hardly understood. Probably, he told himself, it was because it was irritating to see people so *unrealistic*.

They drifted into the pleasant living room—Anna again refusing help—and Carl and Pete and Emily and David played scrabble. When the game was over—interrupted by hearty arguments over words and frequent consultations of the dictionary—they sang two more songs, Emily again at the piano. And after this the family, on one pretext or another, melted tactfully out of sight (except Freddie, who knew the melting process meant bed for him, and had obviously to be manipulated into it) and left Emily and David alone.

"How about a ride in the moonlight?" David suggested. So Emily put on a bright red flannel coat and called up the steps to her mother that they'd be gone for about an hour.

And David forgot, as they rode, that he was engaged in socio-logical research and talked as any young man is likely to talk when he is with a pretty girl; that is to say he bragged ever so little, by implication, at least, telling her of the great eastern university he had attended, of the trips he had taken (though he did not speak of a certain Korean trip), of the great family mansion, "closed mostly now except for a caretaker," and generally leaving an impression, as if he tossed it off carelessly, of some wealth and glamour. But also he told her far more than he realized of how lonely his childhood and boyhood had been; and it was this, he would have been surprised to know, which made the deepest im-pression on her. So that her eyes, if he could have seen and read their expression, would have surprised him by being soft with sym-pathy rather than wide with impressed admiration.

They said good-by on the Fisher porch, and he asked her how soon he could see her again. She answered him with the complete absence of coquetry he had noticed before: "How soon do you want to see me again?" And he replied promptly, "Tomorrow night."

She shook her head. "That's my choir-practice night. We don't get through till nine-thirty."

"Well—couldn't I call for you at your church? And we could get a late supper—or just take another ride?"

She considered this and nodded. "That would be nice," she said with frank pleasure. "And if we aren't through—just sit down in the back of the church and wait."

He was still holding her hand; and her face, upturned to his in the moonlight, was so pretty that he bent impulsively toward it. But she stepped back so quickly and smoothly that it hardly seemed a rebuff, so that he laughed, a trifle ruefully.

"You must have had an awful lot of practice at that sort of dodging to do it so well!" he said. "Do you always? You needn't answer that if you don't want to!"

"For fear of incriminating myself?" Her little gurgle of laughter was delightful. "I don't need the Fifth Amendment in this case. Believe it or not—I always do."

"One of these ice maidens, huh?"

She answered a bit heatedly, "That's a theory I've heard advanced before—and I don't mind telling you that it always makes me just thoroughly good and mad! Oh well, let's don't get started on *that* argument—to be truthful it's one I've gotten a little bored with. Now let me tell you where our church is and how to find me there . . ."

David thought it over, driving back to the hotel, with a certain sense of triumph—so much for Grampa's claims about religion and the full life. A girl who wouldn't permit a simple good-night kiss in this day and time! Not that he, David, wasn't a pretty thoroughly moral guy himself. (Though not, of course, because he was repressed, but because he was fastidious.) But this wasn't even a matter of morals. The girl was inhibited and that was that.

Oh well, it was actually better that she didn't want things to get even a little bit sentimental. He didn't either, really. He'd yielded to a sudden impulse, and he'd see to it that it didn't happen again.

Before he went to sleep that night, he made a few notes.

"This middle-class, small-city, family group, typically American," he wrote, "has all the virtues and the limitations of their class. They possess good enough minds and sturdy bodies. They are kind, loyal, devoted to one another, and have a hearty sense of humor and enjoyment of life. But they accept implicitly and, one must add, unthinkingly all the dogmas of revealed religion. And this narrows their horizons, closes many avenues of thought to them, leads them to repress, for the sake of their rigid religious morality, many natural impulses, and forces the impartial observer to admit that however great the appeal of their friendly charm, intellectually speaking they lead an extremely limited life."

It was slightly disconcerting to the impartial observer, however, to realize, just before he drifted off to sleep later on, that he had been dreamily considering not the Fishers' intellectual poverty, but the way Emily looked when she smiled and the sudden sweet gravity that sometimes came into her eyes.

By the end of a week he was an accepted friend in the Fisher family circle. During the following weeks he met many of their own friends. He walked and talked and rode and went to movies with Emily; he pitched ball with Peter and Freddie; he looked with respect at Grampa's stamp collection. Also he helped Anna with the dishes and came to know Fisher's Drugstore well; ate other meals with them; was present at other "devotions"; and went to church with them each Sunday. Finally he had to admit to himself, with some reluctance, that by now he had certainly gathered enough material to complete the last, the "human interest" section of his thesis.

Because he liked them, because they were his friends, these Fishers, he sat down to the task with a sense of shrinking. He had to remind himself again that it was all impersonal and objective and that they would never see it. (Though how hard it was to be impersonal when he kept seeing, behind the words he put down, Emily with her arms full of spring blossoms; Emily racing him to the corner, bright hair blown; Emily laughing across a table at him!)

"You must not," he admonished himself sharply, "let any personal preferences prejudice you in this sort of job—any more than you'd allow a personal dislike to do so!"

That steadied him. And once he had got well into his task, he was helped by a certain quality he did not quite know he possessed; a kind of mental stubbornness which made him cling persistently to any idea he had once fully formed, and which had kept

him from essentially altering his first impressions of the Fishers
in spite of his growing fondness for them. . . . Three days after
he had begun to write, he finished the last line at midnight.

He had worked at it very intensively, staying up late nights, and
as he stacked the sheets together in a neat pile, he wondered if
this was the reason he felt so tired and dispirited. Now he must
get it copied and on its way to the university—and more important
still get it off his mind. He'd take it in the morning to the public
stenographer, whose office was just off the hotel lobby—Agnes
Hobbs—and offer to pay her extra for a rush job.

He was waiting for Miss Hobbs when she came in; for some
reason he had not slept very well, and the plump, plain girl's
obvious interest in him and her candid remark, "You've been rushing Emily Fisher, haven't you?" irritated him. That was one
trouble with these smaller communities—everybody knew your
business!

"You understand, Miss Hobbs," he said a little sharply, "that this
material is strictly confidential. It's a sort of—er—treatise"—he felt
himself floundering and flushing—"quite, quite, impersonal—but
not to be discussed anywhere or with anybody."

Agnes nodded. "I can't wait to read it," she said cheerfully.

He stared at her gloomily, feeling a definite sense of unease. "I
don't think it will appeal to you," he said abruptly. "It's rather
dull. And remember, two carbons—and it's confidential."

He took Emily home from choir practice again that evening, but
she wouldn't linger on the way or let him come in.

"You've worked nights finishing that thesis instead of sleeping,"
she said positively. "You're tired. We'll celebrate tomorrow night—
when you've had a good night's sleep."

"I'll take you out to dinner—we'll drive to that little inn three
miles on the highway—you know, the one where the red rambler
roses look in the window at you while you eat," he told her. Just
for one instant he lifted the hand he held to his cheek, then
dropped it quickly. This was no time to be breaking the resolve
he had kept so well, the resolve to yield to no sentimental impulses—not now, when his stay in Middleburg was nearly at an
end.

Emily must have been thinking of that end too. For she said slowly, "I—I guess it will be a farewell dinner, almost, won't it? I mean—there's nothing to keep you here much longer, is there?"

Was there something a little wistful in her face and voice? David looked away hastily. "Mother's after me to take a trip with her. But I suppose I really ought to decide where I want to locate pretty soon—where the best chance is, I mean, and settle there."

"You'll probably want to be in a big city," she said.

"I honestly just don't know. . . . Shall I come by for you about six?"

Maybe he had imagined the wistfulness. (Maybe he'd wanted to!) For now her voice was quite cheerful when she answered. Six would be fine, she said, and it would be fun, and he must be sure to get a long night's sleep tonight, and 'bye now, till tomorrow. . . . He wondered why he still felt so deeply depressed as he turned away.

He did not go to the library the next day, which was a little unusual, and as he rang the Fisher bell at sunset, it suddenly seemed to him that he had not seen Emily for a long time. His anticipation was so keen that he was definitely disappointed when Anna, instead of her daughter, opened the door.

"Hello, Mrs. Fisher—is Emily——" he began eagerly, and stopped abruptly. For Anna had stepped outside, partially closing the door behind her, and stood there, seemingly barring his way inside. "What's the matter?" he asked quickly, and realized that his heart had begun to pound in a heavy, frightened manner.

Anna looked ready to cry. "Oh, David! I wish I knew! Emily——"

He stammered over a growing dread, "Is she sick?"

"No—no! She—she—oh, *dear!* David, the fact is she doesn't want to see you. She asked me to tell you to—to please go home."

His face looked so blank and stricken that she put a hand on his arm impulsively.

"I feel awful about it! But she wouldn't explain—she said she couldn't tell anybody. She said I was just to tell you that she never wanted to see you again. Oh, David, haven't you any *idea?*"

He had an idea, an idea so intolerable that he instantly rejected it. "No!" His voice was unnaturally loud and sharp. "But I'm going to find out! She's *got* to see me—I won't leave till she does!"

Emily's mother shook her head; she looked deeply distressed. "I'm afraid she won't. She's awfully upset——"

But just at that instant, from behind the half-open door, a stony young voice spoke. "I'll see him, Mother. Come in, David."

"Oh, darling, I knew you would!" cried Anna, relieved. "And whatever it is, David can explain, I know. Take him in the den——"

David did not see Anna go as she went. He saw nothing but Emily's rigid, slender back while he followed her into her father's small study till she closed the door and turned to face him.

"You've been crying!" he said huskily, awed. And suddenly he was angry at a world in which anything or anybody had made Emily weep.

She waved the speech aside. She said with a strange, quiet dignity, "Sit down, David. I think maybe I owe you an apology. I shouldn't have done what I did today. Agnes Hobbs telephoned me at noon."

It was what he had been most afraid of since the first second Anna had spoken; but it hit him like an unexpected blow, nevertheless, and the shock and dismay of it took his breath.

"She said—she said she thought there was a part of your thesis I ought to read. Because she was sure it was about us—about me and my family. I—at first I said no, I'd wait till you showed it to us. And she said she thought I'd better come now." Her voice was losing its chill calm, was trembling a little. She bit down hard on her lower lip for an instant. "I didn't know why she put it like that—but I never dreamed of its being something you wouldn't want me to see . . . I—thought you were my—our—friend—and I was excited and proud . . . And all of a sudden I just couldn't wait! So I told her I'd run over at my lunch hour. And I did. And I read the last part."

David found that his throat had closed and he could not speak.

"You know the one I mean," said Emily. "The part where I'm called *A* and my mother is *B* and my father is *C* and my grandfather——"

He found his voice, a hoarse and almost unrecognizable voice.

"Emily, please! The spirit in which I wrote that thesis was——"

"No! I won't listen!" The tone had flamed into passion now. "I thought at first I'd never see you again—and I didn't change my mind to listen to any excuses! What can you possibly say that would matter now? I've *read* it! No, it's you who're going to listen!"

"*Emily*——"

"Hush!" she said fiercely. "We took you into this home for the friend you pretended to be, David Wainwright! And all the time you were only here to twist everything we are and everything we try to be into something else—something false—and—and absurd——"

"No—no! It was a study—a scientific *study*——"

"Well, that makes everything just fine!" she cried with a sarcasm so savage that deep inside him something groaned, "Have I done this to her? Was it I who turned her sweetness into this bitterness?"

". . . In that case," the young, hard voice with the pain only a little way beneath the hardness went on, "let me quote to you some of the words you said and some of the ideas I gleaned from this scientific study of yours! We have good minds—thank you for that! —but we are citizens of a small community and our mental horizons match our town. Our religion is unquestioning and therefore unintelligent, and you find our faith in our legendary God and our reactionary creed quite pathetic. It sadly limits our thinking, of course——"

He tried once more, "You don't understand——"

But she swept on. "Well, how could I, with my limited mind? Surely you remember what you said about A—that's me! She lives surrounded by books, but she only likes the ones which conform to her notions of sweetness and light and don't offend her rigid morality! She's got inhibitions, poor girl—is that because I don't kiss all the boys I date, David?—and a very narrow range of interests, of course—and her only real goal is to get married——"

"You've *got* to listen——" he groaned.

"Not till I'm done! My mother—B—now she's really a sad case! Because she has charm and good judgment in some ways, and might have been a leader in a larger circle. But all this she's sacrificed, because she accepts the old-fashioned idea that being a wife and a mother comes first, and so she's sunk herself in her home and her family—oh, she does some church work and club work, but her world is a very small one! And my father——"

He did not even try to interrupt now; it was no use.

"My father, *C*, is in a rut, and he'll stay there all his life because he likes it, he *wants* to be in a rut—isn't it dumb of him? He has no ambition and never even tries to climb any higher in the world —and as a result he probably has not had a really original idea in years. He is kind—every now and then, David, you toss us a pale little bouquet like that in your kindly condescension!—and has a pitiful, fuzzy desire to 'help' people—which only weakens them and gets him shamefully imposed on. You don't blame him too much for all this, I sort of gathered, because he took the attitudes straight from *D*—his own father, my grandfather. Now *he—D—*is quite a character! Fancies he's leading a full, rich life if he lets neurotic bores talk him to death! The rest of the family greatly admire and look up to this funny old fellow—who's a kind of self-appointed philosopher, pretty likable but also pretty laughable. They think he's the last authority on things in general—but actually his views are as limited and as conventional and as downright mistaken as the views of all the rest of them! My brothers don't get so much space, do they? But it's easy to see you think they're doomed because already they've begun to conform to the pattern—the small-town religious pattern——"

"Are you through?" he asked in a choked voice. "Are you nearly through, Emily?"

"Yes." She brushed one hand suddenly across her eyes in an exhausted little gesture and her voice dropped to a drained weariness. "Almost. It's really our religion that you don't like, isn't it, David? That's mainly why you've decided that we're stupid and narrow and provincial, isn't it? And that's what I don't understand! Because you must know how many of the best and greatest minds on earth, ever since Jesus was born, have been proud and happy to devote all their powers to *Him*. Do you know anything about Martin Luther? Not even you would say that *he* just dumbly and unquestioningly took as true everything he was told, without ever thinking—or examining his beliefs—or proving them—would you? Well, we aren't great saints or geniuses—we're just ordinary folks— but we *do* think about our religion, and we *do* study our Bible, and we've proved the truth of what we believe in the best way anybody can prove it—we've tried it, and it *works*."

She stopped. "But it's no use," she said. "I don't know why I keep talking. You won't understand. Because you're so *prejudiced*—because you've shut your mind so *tight*——"

He gave a little start; he said in honest bewilderment, "*Me* prejudiced? Me—shut my mind?" And even in his acute misery he was thinking that this could not possibly be true—why, he'd used those very words about *them!* And yet—he'd made a terrible mistake somewhere. So he stopped protesting—and stared at her in an anguished uncertainty.

"Emily——" he asked, and his voice caught, "—do you—do you hate me?"

"Does it matter? But I don't. Maybe I did—at first. Because after all when you've thought somebody was your—good friend—why, it isn't very nice to find out that all you've been to him was a sort of human guinea pig. But I don't hate you. I think maybe I'm sorry for you. Because you're so wrong—so lost . . . Oh, David, please go away now!"

"There's something I've got to tell you first," he said. "It's something I didn't put in that thesis—I didn't have sense enough to know it. I've just found it out—but it must have been true almost from the first. It's only that I love you, Emily—that all the time I was writing that I was falling deeper and deeper in love with you."

For a long moment there was silence in the little room. Emily turned away suddenly and went to the window, her back to him. And he asked despairingly, "Doesn't it mean anything at all to you?"

She faced him then; her eyes were very bright and deeply sad. "Yesterday—it would have meant everything. Today—I don't even believe it. Maybe you feel something—but it isn't love—not what I mean by love. How could you love me when you don't really even *like* me? We don't fit. We don't fit—in *any* way." She suddenly buried her face in her hands. Her voice came to him muffled. "Oh, please go—please, please go! And don't—ever—come—back!"

He did not see any of the family as he left. He must have driven to the hotel, for he found himself walking in its door, but he could never afterward remember how he got there. The clerk hailed him as he passed the desk and called to him that there was a package for him. His thesis, he thought dully. Upstairs he opened it and found that Agnes had returned it without copying, as he had expected. She had written a stiff little note saying that under all the circumstances she was sure he would not want her to do it, and she preferred not to, herself. . . . David flung the manuscript violently in one corner of the room.

Then he sat down on the edge of the bed, facing the window, and wondered what to do. Outside the light had turned violet, and through this sweet-scented evening he should be riding right now with Emily—to the little inn where red roses would nod at them while they ate. And it seemed to him in that moment that this last month was the first time in all his life when he had not been lonely.

Well, it was gone now—his place in Emily's heart, his place in that warm family circle. He had thrown it all away. And with the realization a wrenching pain assailed him, a pain of grief and loss and bitter regret. And it was then that, unsummoned, there rose before his mind's eye the picture of a face; an old face, sensitive and intelligent, a face which he had once thought (almost resentfully) was beautiful in its own way; the face of Grampa Fisher.

He knew now, in a flash of illumination, what made it beautiful; it was its vast kindness, its tenderness for all mankind. And David forgot that he did not approve of spiritual help, or of "talking over" one's troubles. He only knew that of a sudden he wanted, urgently and desperately wanted, to talk to Grampa Fisher.

He might still be at the drugstore—there was just a chance. David dialed the number with unsteady fingers and went weak with relief when Grampa's own voice answered.

"It's David, sir——" The tones broke with their earnestness. "Can I see you? Alone? I—it's awfully important—to me——"

There was just an instant before the quiet, warm voice came back, when he sensed the other's surprise. Then Grampa was asking him where he was, was saying matter-of-factly that he'd be along as soon as he'd phoned Anna he'd be a mite late; and David stammered out his thanks and hung up.

For one instant after he heard the knock on the door and opened it, he was frightened. Even as he invited Grampa in, he was wondering helplessly what to say, how to explain.

"Maybe I shouldn't have bothered you——" he faltered. He sat down suddenly and put his head in his hands. "I don't know where to begin!" he admitted huskily.

Grampa sat down opposite him. His voice was steady and serene and somehow vastly comforting in its matter-of-factness. "Why, just begin with whatever comes into your mind first!" he said encouragingly. "And keep on till you feel like stopping. I expect that way you'll find you'll get it said—whatever it is you want to say."

And so David began to talk; haltingly at first, searching for words, finally pouring them out with complete un-self-consciousness; and curiously enough he found that what he was telling of first were his childhood, his parents, and his home.

". . . And it's queer, sir—I've always tremendously admired my father's memory—I still do, in a way. But somehow while I've been saying all this, he looks a little different to me. He looks cold, I guess—brilliant but cold, like sun on ice. I—I seem to know now—from knowing all of you, I guess—that there was something he didn't have. I suspect he was unhappy and lonesome. Because I don't think he loved anybody much. Like me—till now."

He ran his hand through his black hair in a confused way. "Always in my mind Mother's been the frivolous one, and I've often thought she must have been a terrible disappointment to him. But I don't know—maybe he failed her first. Because she *is* warmhearted in her own flighty way—and maybe he chilled her. Maybe if he had been different she would have been too. I guess if my mother has been a social snob my father must've been an intellectual snob. And me—perhaps I've been both."

His voice cracked on the last sentence; Grampa waited in silence while he struggled for composure. But still David felt in that silence the steady kindness of his gaze, almost as if it were a warming light that shone on him; and after an instant he began to talk again.

He told now about his college days, and how he had become a member of a small group who thought of themselves as so modern and so advanced intellectually that they had scornfully discarded most of the heritage of the past, under the conviction that actually nothing very worth while *could* have been said or written until they came along to say and write it.

"And of course the Bible went with all the rest. It was dated, too." He paused. He said, slowly and painfully, "I called all this thinking things out—but I didn't really think anything out. Emily was right about that. I see it now. I just fell in with a current of ideas that appealed to me as popular and successful—talk about blind, unthinking acceptance!" He drew one hand across his forehead, and Grampa saw that it came away wet. "Everything she said—Emily—everything—was true."

He got up and walked to the corner where he had flung the thesis; he separated the last pages and brought them back to Grampa. "I thought I'd never look at this again—but I want you to read this part."

Grampa adjusted his spectacles in the familiar gesture, and after one grave look at the young man took the sheets and read them, slowly and carefully. Then he handed them back. His face was quite unchanged. Almost for the first time since David had begun to talk, he spoke, and there was not the faintest trace of resentment in his voice. He asked mildly, "Why did you want me to read that, Son?"

"Because Emily read it. I'd given it to Agnes Hobbs to copy. And Agnes showed it to Emily. And Emily never wants to see me again," said the young man bleakly. "She doesn't hate me." He swallowed. "She's sorry for me. Because I'm so wrong—and lost—she says."

"And what Emily does—and says—makes a lot of difference to you, does it?" Grampa asked gently.

David raised miserable eyes and spoke with a stark sincerity. "All the difference between living and dying."

"There's somethin' else I've got to ask you," said Grampa quietly.

"And it's important—so stop and think. What is it at this minute that you're wantin' most? Is it to get back in Emily's good graces? Or is it maybe—to save your soul alive?"

David stared at him. In his confused mind the words said themselves over and over bewilderingly: "to save your soul alive, to save your soul alive . . ." And then, strangely, they had become other words, words he had often heard but never bothered to understand. "For what shall it profit a man, if he shall gain the whole world, and lose his own soul?" He knew what it meant now, he understood; there was nothing a man could give in exchange for his soul.

"We don't fit," he heard Emily's voice saying. He had wanted to cry out in protest against those words this afternoon, but now he understood this, too. And he saw, in that bright, painful light which seemed to be shining in all the dark hidden corners of his mind that everything he had loved most in her, everything which had made him so happy with the Fishers, sprang from just the one big thing which they had and he lacked; sprang from that sure belief, that certain faith, which was the mainspring of their beings and the impregnable center of their lives.

He looked at Grampa with eyes from which the confusion and the painful bewilderment had begun to clear. He said humbly, "I want most what all of you have got. I want most to save my soul."

The Sundays he'd sat beside them in church; the evenings he'd been at their table listening with almost hostile reluctance to their family devotions; the times when he'd waited in the back of the half-darkened church for Emily choir nights and heard her fresh voice sing, "Oh Love that wilt not let me go!"; wonderingly now, almost incredulously, as the barriers he had built crashed down, he realized that while he had been hardening and fortifying himself against it all it had been stealing into his heart. He had thought he was holding aloof, preserving his careful skepticism—and yet, slow step by step, he had been drawn nearer to that ineffably beautiful and tender figure they had constantly held up for him to see, the figure of Jesus Christ.

He hardly realized that he had not spoken all this aloud. He said, as if Grampa would understand, "I don't know why I didn't realize—why I didn't see——"

And Grampa nodded. "It's somethin' you don't see till you have a personal experience," he answered. "Like nobody can explain what love is to a fellow who's never loved."

They were silent a moment. Grampa was smiling. "And now I don't need to do any talkin', do I?" he said. "I don't have to go tellin' you what to do. You know—don't you?"

Yes, he knew. He had learned it in those weeks when he had thought his mind was closed to it. To ask God's forgiveness in the name of that Christ who had died to make his pardon sure; to start all new, in the love of God and the knowledge that Christ was his Savior; to try from henceforth to walk in his Master's steps.

He looked at Grampa, and because old habits of thought are hard to break, a pang of doubt assailed him and he asked anxiously, "And are you sure it will work—for me, as it has for you?"

"Sure?" echoed Grampa. "There's nothing in the world I'm more certain of, Son—why, I'm surer than sure!"

David drew a long, shaky breath; and suddenly and wonderfully he too was sure—surer than sure.

Grampa, watching him, saw it come to him, as he had seen it come to others. And as always the joy of it set his heart to singing. But he did not believe in laboring a point. And the sooner the boy was left alone now to make his own peace with his God, the better. So he said simply, "I'll be gettin' on home," and rose.

David came to his feet too. "Emily——" he began huskily—and stopped, his eyes pleading.

"Oh, Emily," said Emily's grandfather. "I'll have a long talk and sorta explain things to Emily this very night. 'Course it may take a while for her to see it—and might be you'd have to be patient and work for it and wait some——"

"For all the rest of my life, if it takes that long!" cried the young man—and could say no more for the moment.

"Well now, I don't set myself up to be a prophet—never did," said Grampa. "But I don't much think it'll take long—no, I think it'll all work out a little sooner than *that*."

He took with him, when he left, the memory of the boy's face, lit with trembling hope. . . . And even though he had said he did not claim gifts of prophecy, Grampa found that he was indulging in a few visions of the future as he drove homeward. There was one which especially pleased him; rather a sentimental picture it was, befitting the sentimental old fellow Grampa admitted himself to be. But he felt that it was both true and not far distant, and he smiled as he surveyed it.

What he saw was the pleasant living room of the Fishers, with all the family gathered there. David and Emily sat side by side on the sofa—the girl beaming proudly, the boy shy but radiant. And the Fishers, all attentive interest, waited; waited for David to begin to read to them his brand-new version of the last section of his thesis, the "human interest" section.

8. AN ANNIVERSARY GIFT

*H*E WAS young, not quite eighteen. His face still held the soft curves of childhood in spite of his big frame and broad shoulders, and his hair, blond and curly, had that springiness and shine found only in very youthful hair. The elderly woman in the photographer's studio who moved forward to greet him looked at him with the hint of admiring, maternal tenderness which he was likely to evoke in women of middle age or past.

"Is it ready?" he asked eagerly. "I mean—the miniature. I'm Eddie Parker——"

"Oh, I remember you," she assured him, smiling. "And it's ready. It came out beautifully, too."

She took a package from the shelf behind her and unwrapped the tissue paper around it. "See? The new one looks pretty different from the old one, doesn't it?"

The two pictures lay side by side on the counter, one a faded, dog-eared cabinet photograph obviously of 1935 vintage, the other an oval miniature, fresh and delicately tinted. The boy looked up from an intent study of the latter with a pleased expression.

"It sure *is* different. I think they'll like it, don't you? It's my mother and father, you know." He added unnecessarily, "On their wedding day." For obviously the girl in misty white and the proud and solemn young man in a tuxedo of somewhat old-fashioned cut were bride and groom. "It'll be their twentieth wedding anniversary pretty soon."

"And this is your anniversary present to them?" The boy nodded proudly. "I *know* they'll like it." She peered through her glasses at the delicate face of the bride. "You're blond and blue-eyed like her, aren't you? And your dad is dark. They were a good-looking couple."

"I guess they still are," said the boy a bit absent-mindedly. "They aren't terribly old—thirty-eight and forty. Well——" He pulled out his wallet and carefully counted bills and change. "This is right, isn't it? Including the frame. Leaves me seventy-five cents to run the rest of the week." He sounded entirely cheerful about his bankrupt condition. "But it's worth it."

The clerk laughed. "I'm sixty-three—I agree on both points . . . that's not terribly old, and it is worth it. And I'll just bet," she added sentimentally, "that they're an awfully happy couple. Sure to be when their son is this fond of them."

"Why—yes, of course," said the boy awkwardly. Just for an instant then an odd expression flashed over his face, a look almost of faint trouble. "Well—thank you. Good-by."

The clerk, repeating her usual stereotyped, "Come in and see us again," found herself unreasonably depressed by a feeling that some of the glow had left his face as he strode away.

As for Eddie, he was annoyed with himself for what he sensed had seemed like just a shade of hesitation in his agreement. Of course Mother and Dad were happy. They always had been. It was only—well, Mother hadn't been exactly like herself for a long time now because it appeared that she simply couldn't get used to living in Middleburg. Until a little over a year ago they'd lived in New York City with Mother's parents, and Mother missed them a lot. On the other hand, Eddie couldn't help thinking, Dad had lived away from *his* folks for nearly nineteen years. But then, a person had to learn to when he was grown, didn't he? He himself would be going to college in two weeks, and he'd miss his family, but he'd be all right.

For Dad and for Eddie, of course, there was nothing strange or homesick about coming to Middleburg. Dad had been a Middleburg boy—he'd lived there all his life until, as a young man, he'd made a trip East and fallen in love with Mother and been persuaded to take a job in Granddaddy Woodville's big wholesale business. Sometimes Eddie, as he grew older, had wondered a little if Dad had really wanted to do it. Grandfather Parker owned a lumberyard and factory, and Eddie had gathered that until that trip East Dad had always expected to go in with his father some-day, and eventually to manage the company himself. Maybe the change had been a disappointment for both of them in a way, thought Eddie. It had often seemed to him lately that when Dad spoke of Middleburg it was likely to be with a touch of wistfulness. And he'd insisted on bringing Eddie back to Middleburg to see the older Parkers every summer since Eddie was four.

He'd had to insist—a little, anyway. Because Mother didn't care for Middleburg. After Eddie was eight, she hadn't always even come with them. She never actually opposed their coming, not strenuously at least. But she was continually turning up with plans for the seashore or the mountains, which she'd propose in a bright, tactful tone; and when Dad would answer rather sharply (as he did sometimes), "I'm going to see my parents once a year, and I'm going to give them that much chance to know their grandson!"—occasionally adding, "He *is* their grandson, too, you know!"—she'd droop a little and look plaintive.

But for Eddie no other place could have been as much fun as Middleburg. From the first time he came, he'd loved the spreading, roomy house, with its wide porches, so different from the tall, narrow house in which they lived with Granddaddy Woodville and Nana in New York City. And he'd loved the tree-shaded yard where he played with other boys and romped with the dog. In New York he had to go to a playground or a park, and the dog must be taken out sedately at stated intervals on a leash. He felt freer and easier in Middleburg than he did anywhere else in the world, somehow. He felt as if nearly everybody in town was his friend. He always had.

So for Eddie everything about the move to Middleburg had been good except the reason why it had been made. Grandmother Parker had died quite suddenly; and as if there just wasn't too much left to hold him here after that, Grandfather had slipped away and joined her six months later. He had left his business to Dad, of course, since Dad, like Eddie himself and his mother, was an only child; Mother hadn't wanted but one, she'd always said. And it was then that Dad had decided he wouldn't sell the lumberyard, he'd live in Middleburg and run it himself.

Eddie guessed he'd never forget the commotion that had followed that decision! The dismay, the tears, the pleas from Mother and Nana; the bribes of a better position and a bigger salary from Granddaddy. Oh sure, they'd tried to keep it from Eddie, but there was too much of it, they couldn't. Dad had held out, though; that had surprised Eddie a little, he didn't know just why. And Mother had given in, and that had surprised him too. Only maybe she hadn't, really, deep down inside of her, for there was no getting around the fact that she'd been homesick ever since. She spent about half her time, it seemed to Eddie, writing long, tear-stained letters to Nana, who wrote back every day.

Nor had it helped, Eddie supposed regretfully, that he himself had opposed her lately in certain plans on which her heart had been set. First she'd wanted to take him to New York for the entire summer, except for two weeks when he and she and Granddad and Nana would go to the seashore. And Eddie couldn't, he just couldn't. He'd tried to explain it to her as reasonably as possible; he'd been selected from the high school baseball team to play this summer on the Middleburg junior baseball team, and there was a schedule of games with towns of three other nearby counties. "Don't you see, it's a big honor?" he'd told her anxiously. "I'm *lucky*. And everybody says Middleburg has a better chance at the pennant than ever before. I *can't* leave!"

But she hadn't seen it, and he couldn't make her. She'd finally even got a little sarcastic, which wasn't like her at all. "I'd *supposed*," she'd said with a heavy, ironic emphasis on the word, "that you were planning to be a doctor, not a professional baseball player!" And she'd gone off to New York by herself for the month of July, looking hurt and forlorn—and had come back less reconciled to Middleburg than ever, apparently.

The other point of contention had been going on, more or less, ever since last Christmas until just lately. Mother and Nana and Granddad had had it all planned that Eddie was to go to college in New York and live with them. Mother had been quite radiant about it; she'd visit him often, she'd said, and of course Dad would come too, when he could. It had really been tough to smash that dream, but as it happened all of this was precisely what Eddie did *not* want. For one thing, all his classmates were going to college much nearer home, and he wanted to be with them. But more important was a reason he simply didn't have the heart to give Mother; he didn't want to live with Nana and Granddad, he wanted to live in a dormitory and be one of the fellows. He loved his grandparents, but now that he'd been away from them he'd begun to realize how much they'd both coddled and dominated him. He was half ashamed of feeling that way—but he'd grown past either coddling or domination. He just couldn't go back to being their little boy again, that was the sum of it. And without quite saying so to himself, he knew that they'd still treat him like one—because they'd never yet quit treating Mother like a little girl.

So at last it had reached the place where Eddie was saying, "If I have to go East to college I won't go at all—I'll stay here and work with Dad." And he'd won there, too, finally.

Dad himself had taken no part in either of these controversies. He'd merely said that he felt that Eddie was old enough now to have a voice in his own plans and his own future. But Eddie had been almost certain Dad agreed with him and was keeping still just out of loyalty to Mother. The trouble was that Mother was also pretty certain of the same thing, and she didn't consider his keeping still loyalty. The only thing she would have considered loyalty was his taking *her* side. . . .

It was at this point in his musings, when he was almost home, that Eddie became uncomfortably aware of something: he had never before, he realized, looked at the entire picture quite this clearly. Seventeen is of necessity a somewhat self-centered age. Absorbed in his own activities, he had been vaguely aware of the situation in his home in general, and aware, more acutely, of individual instances as they arose; but he had never, as it were, backed off and tried to look at the whole canvas until today. Now that he had, he couldn't say he felt good about it. *Were* his mother and father happy together? At just this moment he wasn't sure that he could give as positive a "Yes" to that question as he would have liked.

It was half past five when he reached home, and the car was not in the yard. That meant that Mother had already gone to pick Dad up at the office—a job that usually fell to Eddie. Glad of a chance to get in without having to dodge any possible questions about his package, Eddie went quickly upstairs. He unwrapped the pictures, put the old one back in its accustomed place on the storeroom shelf, and took the miniature to his own room. As he stood it on his desk and stepped back a pace to study it again, the two faces seemed to be looking at him with so much happiness and pride that he felt a sudden surge of optimism. He'd been crazy, he decided relievedly. Everybody had their ups and downs, he guessed—but they *loved* each other, his mother and dad, so of course everything would be all right. Since he was at an age when spirits rise rapidly, he felt quite reassured and cheerful again as he nibbled thoughtfully at a knuckle and tried to compose a fitting sentiment to inscribe on the very ornate and lavishly decorated anniversary card he had bought yesterday. Finally he wrote carefully in his best hand, "Here's looking forward to your golden one. With love, from Eddie," and was surveying it and feeling quite pleased with himself when he heard the downstairs door open, and in the next instant, before he could call a greeting, his mother's voice floated clearly up to him. Immediately Eddie's heart gave a dismayed lurch somewhere inside his breast, for it was a voice choked with tears and close to hysteria. Clearly something was very wrong.

"I can't stand it any longer!" cried the overwrought voice. "For a whole year I've tried! I've given in on *every*thing—coming here in the first place, and going home this summer without Eddie, and his college—*every*thing! And there's no sense to it, you could sell that lumberyard tomorrow, and Dad says your job is still waiting, a better one. We could all be happy again!"

Eddie, who had come to his feet involuntarily, stood with his hands clenched. He oughtn't to listen—he ought to call to them that he was there—and he hated listening, he hated knowing. If that's the way things were, he wished he needn't find it out! But somehow he couldn't utter a word, he couldn't move; he could only stand there with those knotted fists and that sick lump inside him, while the voices, so well known and yet sounding so different, battered at his shrinking ears.

"Elise, will you try just once to see my point of view?" That was his father now, those hard, almost hating tones, they were *Dad's*. "You've never seen anybody's but your parents' and your own—which are one. But everybody has a point of view, you know, even *me!*"

The bitter sarcasm in the last pronoun seemed not to register with her—or else she chose to ignore it. She cried, "I know your point of view! I've sacrificed myself and my parents to it for a year!"

"You don't know it because you've never bothered to try to understand it." The voice was level, steely, almost uninflected. "You talk about sacrifice—your sacrifice of a year . . . Well, until we came to Middleburg my whole life had been a sacrifice for nearly nineteen years—nineteen years, Elise."

Almost without realizing it Eddie had moved toward the door. He stood there now, leaning against the wall, white and nauseated. He heard his mother say in a dazed sort of way, "*What?* What do you *mean?*"

"The queerest thing of all," said his father, still in that odd, flat voice, "is that you really don't know! Nothing could make you seem as far away from me as that—that you thought I was satisfied, that you still think I ought to be, that you never cared enough to know how it was for me! Maybe it's partly my fault. Maybe when we got engaged, and your parents couldn't bear to part with you, and your mother wept for weeks, and your dad offered me a cushy job in his own organization—maybe right then if I'd said 'No' and taken you somewhere away from them, and gotten a job of my own, and made a home that was *ours*—well, maybe you'd have grown up. Spoiled girls do grow up sometimes. But I yielded, and I worked in a place where older and better men than I rightfully resented me because I'd been given a position I hadn't earned, and we lived in your folks' home, and even the boy and you were more theirs than mine, and now—now that the chance has come and that I finally summoned the pitiful courage to break away and take it—well, I guess it's too late . . . A child of eighteen can grow up, maybe even a child of twenty-eight—but a little girl of thirty-eight——"

"No—hush! You're cruel—cruel and hateful and not even honest!" There was furious anger in the cry—but oh, there was pain and bewilderment, too . . . Couldn't his father hear it? "All this terrible picture of your bitter sacrifice—you've built it up since you decided you wanted to come here! It isn't true, it isn't true! We were *happy*—and Mother and Dad adored you! To talk as if all these years you'd been miserable, and as if you'd been neglected and downtrodden and your interests never considered—oh, it's a wicked, wicked lie!"

"Is it?" His father's voice was very tired now, tired and drained. "But I don't think I said that I was miserable every moment, or that your parents weren't—in their own way—good to me. I was trying to say something else—that until this past year I've never, since we married, felt like a real man, doing a real job, and on the way to being of some small but real consequence in a community. And I can't leave it. I can't go back to being your father's son-in-law and nothing else."

She burst into passionate sobs. It must, thought Eddie dully, be a weapon of last resort which she had used effectively often in the past—but it wouldn't work now, and why didn't she see that? Her words came through the sobs, choked and incoherent. "And it means—nothing—nothing—you don't care—not even a little—that I'm miserable?"

There was no rustle of movement. His father had not gone to her or put his arms around her. What was he doing? Just standing there and watching those sobs tear her apart? Then, almost a minute later, he spoke.

"No, Elise," he said sadly. "I honestly don't think I do care. Maybe it's partly because I'm so tired of it all. But I think it's more because I've realized that you are never going to be able to bear living away from your parents, and that you will never be happy except in just one spot in the world. You came here determined to find no charm and no grace in the situation, and of course you haven't. You've sulked and pouted and refused every friendly advance—you've wept and moped and felt sorry for yourself for more than a year. I don't think either of us can take it any longer.

If you can hold out for a few weeks longer till Eddie has got off
to college—well, I guess then you'd better go back to your mother
and father."

"You want a divorce? Are you saying, Phil—that you want a
divorce?"

Eddie sat down on the edge of his bed with his head in his
hands. Everything his father had said was appallingly true, in a
way—but it wasn't all Mother's fault that she'd been spoiled and
babied by everybody all her life—yes, by Dad, too, till just lately
. . . He hadn't even tried to make her different, and now he was
angry at her for not being different . . . He'd given her tenderness and petting, always, and now it seemed all of a sudden he
had no tenderness left . . . And couldn't he hear in her voice what
Eddie could hear, the shock and the terror?

He was answering harshly, "I have no use for a divorce. It is
inconceivable that I would want to marry again. But if *you* want
one, I won't oppose it."

In the tiny silence that followed, Eddie fancied he heard her
breath catch convulsively. Then her voice came, high and wild.

"Yes, I want one! I hate you! I want to be free of you—I'll be
glad, glad, glad to get away from you! And I warn you—I warn
you—you aren't going to take Eddie away from me! I mean to have
him Christmases and summers and spring vacations——"

"You're screaming—do you want the neighbors to hear? And
must we quarrel over the custody of a boy of nearly eighteen? I
don't even want to take Eddie away from you—but on the other
hand, I don't intend to let you take him away from me, either.
Or even to keep him with you for all of his vacations."

"We'll see!" His mother's voice was dangerously out of control
now. "Daddy'll have something to say about that—Daddy'll do
something——"

"I don't doubt he'll try, Elise. As I've hinted before, none of you
has ever felt that the boy belonged to but one side of the family.
But even your father may not be successful in *that.*" (And if
Mother's voice was out of control, Daddy's was made of splintered
glass, with cutting, hurting edges.)

"Oh!" cried his mother in a kind of strangled gasp. "*Oh——*"
And she must have turned then and fled, for Eddie heard her

flying feet on the stairs, and the rush of them past his door, and then heard her own door slam. The next instant, like an echo, the front door slammed too. Daddy had gone out somewhere.

And suddenly at that all the whirling, conflicting emotions of these last few moments—all the shame and the grief and the half-frightened sense that his life was tottering on its very foundations—merged for Eddie into a flame of white-hot anger. Let them make a mess of their own lives if they liked—they wouldn't be allowed to make a mess of his! Quarreling over which of them would have him the most! Well, he didn't want either of them! He said it over and over to himself, shaking—he could do without *either* of them. He'd run away, he'd get a job somewhere; he was big and strong, he could earn a living, he wouldn't take their money to go to college——

It was at this point that his eyes fell on the miniature. His hand went out with a sudden savage impulse to hurl it against the wall and smash its tinted ivory; but the two young faces, shy and proud and radiant, seemed to look back at him so trustingly that his arm dropped. He stood there staring at it an instant, his lip quivering. Then, with a fierce little gesture he swept card and miniature together into a desk drawer, flung paper on top of them, almost as if he were burying something, and closed the drawer. After this he pulled his suitcase from under the bed, opened his bureau drawer, and began to toss shirts and socks and underwear in the case.

He was in the midst of this packing operation when a voice outside, evidently from the back yard, called, "Yoo-hoo! Eddie!" Eddie hesitated, half inclined to pretend he was not at home. But if the voice kept on calling it would doubtless bring Mother out of her room, even though her windows opened on the front lawn. So after an irresolute second he went to his own window and looked down into the cheerful face of Peter Fisher, his best friend in Middleburg.

"Hey!" said Peter. "Was just passing by and thought I'd stop and see if you were here. All ready for the big event?"

Eddie leaned against the window frame. "What big event?" he asked sullenly.

"What——" Peter broke off, staring. His candid face expressed an amazement that bordered on shock. "Oh well," he decided charitably, "maybe you've just waked up from a nap or something and aren't quite all here yet. The championship game tomorrow, just in case it's slipped your mind—in which Mr. Eddie Parker is the white hope of Middleburg."

"Oh—that. Well, they'll have to put somebody in my place, Pete. I won't be here."

This time Peter's mouth dropped open and stayed that way for a full second. "You won't—— Say, Eddie, can I come up?"

Eddie nodded. "Come in the back door. And be quiet on the stairs—my mother"—he swallowed a little on the word—"she's resting."

A moment later Peter stood in the doorway. He had been, by his own standards at least, as quiet as a mouse on the stairway. (Not that Elise would have heard him if he had clattered up in sabots. In the next room she lay rigid on her bed, and the only thing she could hear was Phil's voice cruelly calling her "a little girl of thirty-eight," or worse still, saying with a dreadful sadness, as if something were dead, "No, honestly, I don't care.")

Peter's eyes rested solicitously on his friend's face, and a worried look came over his own . . . Something was wrong with old Eddie, sure, for now that you saw him close he looked sicker'n a pup. But before he could make the concerned inquiry that was on the tip of his tongue, he caught sight of the half-packed suitcase on the bed.

"You're not packing for college two weeks ahead of time, are you?" he asked, surprised.

"I'm not going to college," Eddie answered shortly. "I'm just gettin' out, that's all."

"You're just—*what?*"

"Getting out. Leaving. Vamoosing."

"That's what I *thought* you said. Only it doesn't make any sense." Peter surveyed him in deep bewilderment. "Where? Why?"

"What's it matter where?" Eddie said recklessly. "Anywhere. I'll hitchhike along and pick up a job. Maybe I can join the Navy."

Peter's expression had now become that of a rational man suddenly confronted with a lunatic—a lunatic, to make matters worse, in the person of a familiar companion whom he had hitherto considered perfectly sane. He spoke to the point quite simply from the depths of a profound perplexity. "Have you gone off your nut?"

Eddie sat down abruptly on the edge of the bed.

"I might as well tell you, Pete. Everybody'll know it pretty soon. My mother and father are getting a divorce."

"No!" said Peter involuntarily.

Eddie sent him a bleak glance, and was silent.

"Are you sure? I mean," faltered Peter, "it might be just a little fuss or something——"

"You think I'd say a thing like that about my own folks if I wasn't sure? I *heard* them. They didn't know I was here. Or maybe," he added bitterly, "they just forgot all about me. Anyway —my door was open and they were right at the foot of the steps and—— Oh, never mind the rest. I'm sure, that's all! They're only waiting till I've gone off to college. Well"—Peter heard his teeth slide together for an instant—"they needn't!"

Pete felt in distress that he had been flung into a situation with which he felt quite inadequate to cope, yet about which something certainly ought to be done.

"But, Eddie—well, you know how sorry I am and all that— b-but," he stammered, "I still don't think you oughta run away. Your mother and father—even if they *don't* agree with each other —they'll feel awful about you doing that——"

But here he stopped, for Eddie's suddenly tightened lips showed him that any appeal on the score of his parents' feelings was worse than useless at this moment. It was then, with a sensa- tion of relief, that Peter remembered the game; maybe he could work it with the game.

"What about the game?" he demanded, trying to sound indig- nant. "Just running out on that, huh? You know good and well that without you in there pitching it's going to be a slaughter."

"Spike Jackson can take my place——"

"And lose the game for us, as you know. This is for the *cham- pionship*," Peter pleaded. "What'll the fellows think when I have to tell 'em you've walked off only one day before?"

A line had come between Eddie's eyes. He was wavering, Peter thought exultantly—and pressed his advantage eagerly.

"My little brother Freddie—why, you're his hero! He worships you, honest, and a lot of other kids his age round here feel the same. Your leaving like this is goin' to seem like high treason to Freddie and his friends. You'll be letting down the team, and letting down the town, and letting down all those little guys like Freddie who think you're tops. A man," said Peter, trying to sound very wise and adult, "a man's got no right letting his personal troubles interfere with his—er—public duties! Where'd the world be if everybody acted like that?"

Eddie pushed his thick blond hair back from his forehead. He said slowly, "I reckon you're right, at that." He added, looking at his friend with an expression in his blue eyes which made Peter feel slightly sick with sympathy, "Only thing is—it'll mean staying here tonight—having dinner with 'em. I—I didn't want to see them any more."

Peter swallowed a lump in his throat, and Eddie stood up, closed his suitcase, lifted it down from the bed, and kicked it underneath. "I won't unpack this," he said. "I'll be leaving right after the game."

"Well, you got to stay a little longer than that." Peter spoke quickly, thinking hard. "Because I want you to have dinner with us after. Freddie'll be crazy to talk it over and all."

After an instant's hesitation Eddie nodded. "Okay. Better anyway, I guess. If my folks think I've gone to bed, they won't start looking for me till morning."

Peter felt quite weak with relief; that gave him about thirty hours to plan something. "Bring your baseball suit over to my house and we'll get ready there and go together. Then your clean clothes'll be there when we come back. My family are all going——"

He could have kicked himself for a clumsy fool when Eddie said drearily, "My father was going. I guess he'll forget about it—now."

There was a little silence. Then Peter said awkwardly, "Well—I'll be toddlin' off. See you tomorrow. 'Bye."

Peter was unwontedly quiet at dinner that night. Afterward he waited restlessly till Freddie had been sent upstairs to bed and Emily had gone out with her fiance, David. Carl and Anna and Grampa were in the living room. He came in, sat down opposite his father, and announced, "I've got to talk to all of you. It's something—well, it was a confidence and in a way I feel bad—but I can't let him—and I got to get help——" Here he paused, feeling with some reason that he had not been very clear or coherent.

"How," suggested Grampa, "about beginnin' at the beginnin', Son?"

So Peter told them the whole story. "And the most I could get him to promise," he concluded, "was that he'd stay through the game, and then have dinner with us afterward. But we ought to try and stop him from running off, don't you think?"

The three older people looked at each other. "We'll have to do that," Carl said. "But I hope we can do it by persuasion. I wouldn't like to go to his parents about it."

"I sure hope not!" Peter looked worried. "He'd be awful mad at me about that."

"One of us had better talk to him tomorrow night," Anna said, and added indignantly, "The poor boy—how *can* mothers and fathers?"

"I'll tell you what," Grampa remarked thoughtfully, "I'd like for us to choose our text for family devotions real careful. Because there isn't but one answer for Eddie. He's feelin' all hurt and outraged and angry—like his folks have done him a wrong——"

"And he's right!" cried Anna. "They have!"

"I know. But all the same, he's got to forgive 'em, Anna. That's all that'll save him from gettin' all warped and twisted out of shape."

"Dad's right," said Carl. "That's his only solution."

"He's got a sort of special admiration for you, Pop," Peter remarked. "You won't mind, will you?" he added a little anxiously. "I mean—talking to him."

Carl sighed—a very small sigh. He never felt equal to jobs like this, but he never dodged them when it seemed to him that they were especially his. This one clearly was, so he answered, "No, Pete—I'll make a chance. Drive him home after dinner or something."

At the Parker home that night dinner had been an almost silent meal. The game was not mentioned. Elise and Phil had clearly forgotten it, and Eddie took a certain bitter satisfaction in not reminding them.

The next morning Elise did not get up for breakfast. She said she had a sick headache, and stayed in her room with the shades drawn. Eddie and his father got their own breakfasts, and neither talked. When, just before he left the house, Phil said abruptly, "Please tell your mother I won't be home for lunch," and hurried off with the barest hasty "Good-by," Eddie realized how much he had been hoping that his father might remember. Well, he told himself, the Fishers would be there to cheer him on—that was enough. But he knew deep within him that it was not enough, and that he felt both betrayed and forsaken.

Well, he couldn't hang around this mausoleum all morning, that was a cinch! He'd go to a movie—do something to pass the time till he could buy himself a lunch and go by the Fishers' for Pete. So he scrawled a note and fastened it to his mother's door with a pin. "Dad won't be home for lunch. Neither will I. Also not to dinner. Having dinner with the Fishers. Eddie."

Then he put his baseball outfit in a small suitcase and left the house. . . .

Peter had fretted a good deal for fear Eddie's mental distress would hurt his game. But whether his pain and anger served as some sort of spur; or whether it was for the simpler reason that they found relief in the vigorous exercise, and that the healthy young mind and body of the boy seized eagerly on this outlet for the destructive emotions to which he was so wholly unaccustomed, which he knew so little how to handle; or whether it was just chance and luck—for these causes or some other, the fact was that Eddie Parker, the star of the Middleburg junior baseball team, had never shone so brightly. He played a superb game, and Middleburg won the pennant 6–4 largely because of this in a contest that left the enthusiastic fans limp and hoarse.

So when Peter and Eddie reached the Fisher home, a little later than the others, they received the tumultuous welcome due victorious heroes. Particularly from Freddie.

"Oh boy!" he cried ecstatically. "What a game! Were you steamin' 'em in today, Eddie—wow!"

Eddie, feeling tired and let down now that it was over, managed a small smile.

"And when you threw that ball to second for the double play——" Words failed Freddie at this point; there were none magnificent enough.

"Hey now! What about a little family loyalty?" kidded Peter. "Didn't the throw from first to second help a little bit?"

"Oh sure, sure, Pete, you did swell! But Eddie—Eddie, *he* set up the double play!"

Peter laughed. "I'm deposed," he said cheerfully. "We'll get outa these smelly uniforms, Mom—and by then I sure hope you and Emily have a big supper ready!"

Eddie realized suddenly that he too was hungry, and that it was good and comforting to be here with these friendly people.

The talk at the table mostly concerned the details of the game. All of the Fishers, except perhaps Anna, were avid baseball fans, and the game was thoroughly rehashed, to Freddie's intense delight. Several amusing things that had occurred during the afternoon were related, and greeted with laughter. And in the midst of it all, Eddie had for one instant a sudden flashing vision of his parents, sitting silently at home over their dreary meal; or if they did speak, speaking words that were sharp and hurting. Surprisingly then, something ached in his chest; it was a stab of painful pity, which almost immediately he indignantly repelled . . . If they were miserable whose fault was it? Their own!

After the dessert Carl cleared a space in front of him, and as Freddie brought the Bible and a small book of devotions to his father, a quiet fell on the Fishers. Eddie waited respectfully; he had been here to meals often enough by now to know this custom of theirs, and he liked it.

"I'm going to read two verses from Ephesians tonight," Carl began in his deep, pleasant voice. "They're favorites of Grampa's, and he selected them. They are from Chapter 4, verses 31 and 2. 'Let all bitterness, and wrath, and anger, and clamour, and evil speaking, be put away from you, with all malice. And be ye kind one to another, tenderhearted, forgiving one another, even as God for Christ's sake hath forgiven you.' " He closed the Bible and looked at them. "That makes it clear, as the Bible does in so many places, that God wants us to forgive others even as He, for Christ's sake, forgives us, doesn't it? I've known a few men who went through months, years, or even a lifetime, cherishing resentment for a wrong; and whether it was real or fancied, the result was the same—they were bitter, unhappy people. For that's what it does to a man—it darkens his whole spirit. I came across a practical suggestion the other day for helping the person who's finding forgiveness difficult. It was this; that whenever he said the Lord's Prayer he'd try for a while to stop a moment after he reached that phrase that goes 'And forgive us our trespasses, as we forgive those who trespass against us,' and think—and say—to himself, 'That means that what I'm really asking is, 'Forgive me as I forgive John Smith'—or whatever the name of the man against whom he feels so bitterly is. A man can't realize that," said Carl simply, "and not have it sink down into his heart and soul that he's got no right at all to ask or expect forgiveness through Jesus Christ for *himself* as long as he refuses to forgive others. The old Hebrew law had it, you know, that a man must forgive his brother seven times. I guess they felt like that was being pretty patient, don't you? But then along came Jesus and said no, not seven but seventy times seven."

Carl closed the Bible and opened the booklet. "And now two sentences from this little book. 'And when we forgive, let us remember that to forgive is to forget—even as God, for the Savior's sake, has cast all our sins behind his back and has promised to remember them no more. If we learn to love all those with whom we live, and to cover their faults with the mantle of sweet charity, we shall find love flowing back into our own lives—and we shall be the happier. . . .' Grampa, will you lead our prayer? And then we'll say the Lord's Prayer together."

Eddie had listened half rebelliously as he realized the trend of the devotional. What did the Fishers know about it? Their family life was all right, it was easy for them to have all this sweet charity Carl'd been reading about! They didn't know what it did to you to find out that your mother and father hated each other. Hated each other more than they loved *you*, their child, since even for your sake they wouldn't try to settle their differences and hold your home together! If these Fishers had something like that to forgive, they'd find it wasn't quite as simple as it had all sounded just now.

He hardly heard the few sentences of Grampa's prayer for the churning confusion of his own thoughts. But as, mechanically, he began to repeat the Lord's Prayer with the others, something surprising occurred; he found, when he reached the phrase of which Carl had spoken, that seemingly without intention or volition the words his lips were silently forming were, "Forgive me my trespasses as I forgive Mother and Dad."

And it was at that instant that something happened inside Eddie Parker.

He could not have analyzed it; he hardly understood it; and certainly he had no idea what an important thing it was. He did not say to himself, "I do forgive them." He did not say—or consciously think—"I'm going to stop judging them, I'm just going to love them and do whatever I can to help them." If this was, in effect, what he felt, he yet could not have formulated it. All he knew was that the brief flash of pity he had felt for them during the dinner hour had suddenly expanded into a great ache. Their lives, estranged from each other and poisoned by the hurt and bitterness of that estrangement, with him away at college and his life necessarily increasingly independent of theirs, looked to him in this sudden insight of his so unspeakably arid, so utterly lacking in everything that made the Fisher household warm and rich and happy that his throat tightened with the pity of it and behind his closed lids his eyes stung. Only a few seconds ago he had been so sorry for himself, and so angry with them for the ruin in which they had laid his home and the way they had smashed his pictures of them that there had not been room for any other emotion. Now self-pity and anger alike disappeared, swept away by this tidal wave of aching sympathy. And he forgot to be sorry for himself in a self-forgetfulness so complete that he did not even realize he *had* forgotten.

After dinner he and Emily and Carl and Peter played scrabble, to the accompaniment of much argument between Emily and Peter and frequent frenzied consultings of the dictionary, while

Anna sat near, engaged in the mending and patching which seemed to be perennially necessary for Freddie's garments at this stage of his existence; and Freddie and Grampa worked absorbedly over their beloved stamps. The game had just ended, and Freddie was reluctantly facing the fact that his hour had struck and he must go to bed, when the telephone rang and Emily, who answered it (because it always *might* be David) came back with the word that Eddie's mother wanted to speak to him.

"Eddie!" Elise's voice came over the wire with a tense, held-in note that sounded as if it might at any moment break into tears or hysteria. "*Eddie——*"

"Yes, Mother?"

"Dad and I both felt terrible about the game—why didn't you remind us? Why didn't you, Eddie? Had you rather be with the Fishers? You didn't say a word—and we didn't read the paper today——"

"I'm sorry," said Eddie gently.

"But that isn't why I called you. Your suitcase——" Her voice caught in a strangled sob. "I went in your room just now to get it out—I was thinking about your packing for college and wanted to check on how much it would hold—and it was half packed! I don't under*stand*—and I'm here alone. Dad went back to the office—I'm frightened. . . . Eddie, what does it *mean?*"

"Nothing. Nothing, Mother—now. Don't worry about it. I'll come straight home. Soon's I can get there."

Peter went upstairs with him to get his uniform. "Eddie . . ." he began hesitatingly—and paused. "I hope you won't be mad about this . . . Dad wants to drive you home and talk to you a little—and I'd like to explain to you first. I told them what you told me—not Freddie and Emily, of course, but the others. I—I just *had* to," he finished, his brown eyes apprehensive.

"You mean on account of me planning to run away?"

Peter nodded rather unhappily.

"I see how you felt," Eddie said after a moment's silence. "I'm not mad, Pete. Now I got to hurry."

Carl, waiting in the car which he had brought up under the porte-cochere, was trying to formulate to himself the best way, in the short time he had, to approach things with Eddie. But as a matter of fact, he did not need an approach. It was Eddie who made it.

"I know what you want to talk to me about, sir," he said quietly, as soon as he was in the car. "Pete explained."

"He said he would. I can't tell you, Eddie, how sorry I am about it all. But it wasn't exactly your parents' troubles I wanted to discuss with you—but your own reaction to them—this business of leaving home."

"Yes," said Eddie slowly. "That's what I was planning, but——" He broke off an instant. "Mr. Fisher, did your father have me in his mind when he selected that passage you read tonight?"

"Yes, Eddie. Of course, it was for the rest of us, too—everybody needs it. But it was especially for you. Because, you see, no one of us felt quite wise enough to advise you in his own right. But we knew Who could tell you the right way and the only way to get through this thing without terrible damage to your spirit—and so we brought you *His* message, hoping it might help."

"Yes, sir. Well—it did," Eddie said huskily.

Carl drew a long breath of relief. He answered simply, "I can't possibly tell you how good that makes me feel. Then I can tell Grampa and Anna and Pete that you've given up the idea of walking out on things?"

Eddie nodded. "Guess I'll be sticking round," he said soberly.

"He's grown-up," thought Carl with the little pang of an older man, and a father, that it had had to happen so suddenly and so painfully. "He'll never quite be a kid again." But hard on the heels of this came the feeling that Phil Parker ought to be mighty proud of his boy, if he only knew. And Carl was suddenly determined that he should know, one way or another.

Aloud he said cheerfully, "In that case, you'll be here for the surprise birthday picnic we plan to give for Peter before you two go off to college. I want your help with the guest list."

They were still deep in interested discussion of this and other aspects of the picnic when Carl stopped the car in front of the Parker house.

"Good night, sir," said Eddie, getting out. Carl noted with thankfulness that his voice was steady now. "And—thanks for everything."

They shook hands, and as Carl drove off he was hoping with all his heart that whatever awaited the boy inside that house would not be too hard.

Elise had heard the car and she had the door open by the time he reached the porch. She threw herself on him, clutching him.

"Dad told me at dinner that you won the game for Middleburg—— Oh, Eddie, I'm so jealous of the Fishers!"

He shook her gently. "Don't be like that!"

"And on top of that, finding the suitcase——"

Eddie unfastened her arms and stepped back. He had turned a little white. "I'd better tell you about that. I was going to run away," he said.

"To—run——" She stared at him, eyes wide with shock. "But— *why?*"

"I heard you and Dad yesterday afternoon—when you were talking about a divorce. I—I guess I figured there was no use for me to stay round any more."

Every bit of color had left her face. She sat down limply, as if her legs would not any longer support her. She was panic-stricken, and yet Eddie saw, again with that unfamiliar sensation of pity, the desperate effort she made to rally herself, to dissemble, and to put on a front for him.

"But, darling—you and I would still be together—at least vacations. . . . I—I've tried to fit in to life here—but it just won't work, that's why we're separating . . . Don't you see? It's—it's no use to make a tragedy of it——" Her voice broke. She could not *bear* the way he was looking at her—the steady sadness of his eyes . . . And he looked older, the very planes of his face less soft and immature! It broke her heart, and with a little cry she buried her face in her hands.

"Don't!" he said. "I'm not running off, Mother. I changed my mind. Or maybe something changed it for me. Anyway, I'm not." He bent over her. "I think you ought to get to bed. You're worn out. I'll help you upstairs."

She was too broken to resist. She let him help her up, his hard,

strong young arm around her. At the door of her room he kissed
her cheek, and the little gesture of tenderness almost undid her.
She gave him a choked good night, but as he would have left her
she caught his arm.

"You said—something changed your mind for you . . . Was it
the Fishers, Eddie? You didn't—you didn't talk to them about *us,*
did you?"

He answered a little reluctantly, "I told Pete. Pete told them."

"And they persuaded you not to leave? You wouldn't stay for
me—but you'd stay when they asked you?"

"It wasn't quite like that." He hesitated. "They have family
prayers—devotions, they call it—every night. It was some verses—
Mr. Fisher read them from the Bible—about forgiving each other.
And he talked a little—and read from a book about loving the
best in each other." Gently he disengaged her fingers from his
arm. "I'm awfully tired, Mother. The game was tough—and—
everything. I'll turn in too now, I guess. Good night."

She said again faintly, "Good night." She went in her room and
sat on her bed, thinking blankly, "He forgives us—Eddie forgives
us . . . But what have we ever done to *Eddie* except love him?"

Inside her a voice seemed to jeer cruelly, "But he wants you
to be like the Fishers, he wants the sort of home the Fishers have."
And suddenly she hated the Fishers passionately.

It was ten minutes later before she heard Phil come in. Eddie's
light was still on, and she heard Phil knock at his door and speak.

"Eddie, Son"—his voice was husky and unsteady—"I forgot your
game. I forgot it until it was over—and I heard people talking
about it, saying you won it. I'm—sorry. I wish you'd reminded me
this morning."

There was a brief silence. Then Eddie said awkwardly, "I wish
so too. But you'll have lots of other chances to see me play."

Phil's voice came again, constrainedly, "I felt pretty proud when
I heard folks talking——" And—after a slight pause—Eddie's, grateful and a little embarrassed, "Well—thanks, Dad."

She heard their good nights then, heard Eddie's door close
again. As Phil went slowly toward his room, she called him softly.
She was still sitting on the edge of her bed in the dark when his

tall figure appeared in her doorway, the light behind outlining it.

"Phil," she whispered, "I don't want Eddie to hear, but I had to tell you. He—heard us yesterday—he was going to run away from home . . . No, wait! You won't need to talk to him—he isn't going to now."

"He heard us—yesterday?" His breath drew in sharply. "That's —appalling." He added, his voice low and bitter, "No wonder he wanted to run away—I don't see why he changed his mind."

"Only because of the Fishers!" She felt her voice rising in jealous anger and brought it down again. "They said something—he'd told Pete. Anyway, it's the Fishers whom we've got to thank that our son didn't try to run away from us!"

"Then," he said in a hard, level tone, "I do thank them," and turned and left.

It was late the next afternoon that Elise, answering the door-bell, found Mrs. Carl Fisher on her threshold.

Anna, who had promised to solicit funds for the Red Cross, had been somewhat dismayed, a few days earlier, to discover the Park-ers on her list.

"Mrs. Parker's such a peculiar woman," she'd said rather nerv-ously to Carl. "She's lived in Middleburg a year, and nobody really knows her. She won't join anything—she won't accept invitations —she hasn't returned a single call. And often as Eddie's been here, she's never once invited Peter to a meal with them." She sighed, "It's nearly always the wives I see on these Red Cross visits, and I dread asking her for anything."

The slight trepidation with which Anna approached the task had not been relieved by what she had learned later about the situation in the Parker household. Still—there their names were, on her list; and she had put them off till the last and wanted to finish today. So she'd forced herself to ring the Parker bell, and now she produced her best smile as she said, "Good afternoon." Mrs. Parker's greeting in reply was so icily unpromising that she decided she had better explain in a hurry that it was not a social call.

"I'm soliciting contributions for the Red Cross," she said pleas-antly, "and your name is on my list."

"Oh!" Elise stepped back. "Will you come in?" she asked, not very graciously. "I suppose Phil will want to give what he did last fall—he's not here, but I could look at the checkbook and see——"

"Thank you." Anna followed the reluctant hostess in and sank down in the chair to which she was perfunctorily waved. "I've been at this job all day and it's really good to get off my feet," she explained with a disarming friendliness.

Elise, who had drawn a big desk checkbook from the table drawer and was bending over it, did not reply. After a moment she said coldly, "He gave fifty dollars last year—right after we first came here. I guess he'll want to give the same this time."

"Oh, thank you—that's very generous!" Anna got out her book and began to enter the amount.

"Of course," said Elise deliberately, "I myself won't be in Middleburg much longer." Suddenly her eyes blazed. "*As you know!* As you know very well, Mrs. Fisher—since my son seems to have discussed *his* family's private affairs with *your* family last night!"

"Oh, but he didn't!" Anna exclaimed at the sudden attack.

"No? Apparently it was solely through your influence that he did not run away from us! It seems that he got some sort of nice little sermon at your house about *forgiving* us——"

Anna's eyes on the hostile face were honestly perplexed. "And that makes you angry?" she asked wonderingly, and saw the blood rise to the mother's cheeks. "We are very fond of Eddie. We didn't want to see him do something he was sure to regret later. Something that would hurt you badly."

Elise's lip was quivering now. "I know you think I'm horrible —and ungrateful—I can see just how I sounded to you—but can't *you* see how that makes me feel, can't you? My own child—my *only* child——"

Suddenly then, to Anna's horrified pity, her whole face seemed to crumple and break up; as if the chill resentment it had worn were only a defensive mask, and behind that mask was just raw pain. "He's all I've got—and it's with you he shares his triumphs and his problems—not with me, not with me!"

"But that was because——" Troubled, Anna left the sentence hanging in air. And Elise finished it bitterly.

"Because I *am* his problem, you mean. Do you suppose that keeps it from hurting? Eddie doesn't understand—nobody does except my parents. You are sitting there right now thinking what a terrible woman I am——"

"No," said Anna indignantly, "I'm doing nothing of the sort!"

"Aren't you?" She spoke the two words with a doubtful, rather pathetic eagerness. "I've been so miserable—so lost and homesick. I'd never been away from my people before, and all my friends are back East—and Phil didn't *need* to come here—he had a good job with Daddy. In a way it wasn't even fair, because that was a sort of unspoken agreement when we married—that we'd always live at home with my parents . . . And I'm wretched away from them—and now Phil says he never *liked* living with them and never *liked* working for Daddy——" She stopped. "I'm—sorry," she said in a low, ashamed tone. "I accuse Eddie of discussing my private affairs, and here I pour them all out on you—after starting off by being so abominably rude to you——"

"I'm glad for you to talk if it helps," Anna said gently.

"Then you see?" Elise's eyes clung to hers, demanding, pleading for reassurance and support. "You see how it is?"

"Yes. I think I see." And indeed she did see. A woman, she thought pityingly, faced at thirty-eight with the necessity to make the adjustments to maturity that most girls begin to make at eighteen; and a man who had not been able, perhaps partly because he was fighting to overcome the weakness that had made him yield to her years ago, to be patient or to help her.

"Oh, that helps!" cried Elise. "To feel you approve——"

Anna shook her head. "No. I didn't say that. I don't."

"You—don't?"

"No. Because to me marriage is sacred and binding, you see. It's been a lifetime career for me. A very great happiness—but a responsibility, too. A responsibility to my husband and to my children."

"But doesn't that responsibility work both ways?"

"Yes, it does." She smiled. "Don't think I'm saying Carl and I haven't had any adjustments to make! Everybody has. But if there are love and respect on both sides, and a willingness to meet each other halfway, things usually have a way of working out."

"Your 'if' is a very big one," said Elise bitterly. "Anyway—they haven't worked out for us. And I've tried, I've really tried."

Anna studied her, wondering how far she dared to go. "Have you? You say you've been so lonely—but there are lots of us here who would have loved to be friends with you—who've tried to be —and you, well, you didn't seem to want us."

"I know—I——" A painful flush stained her face to the hairline; she dropped her eyes. Then she raised them again. "I see that— now," she said honestly.

Anna leaned forward timidly but eagerly. "Perhaps I'm being awfully presumptuous—but if you do, it isn't too late, maybe! If you'd try to learn to live away from your parents and to like Middleburg—and ask your husband to try to be patient and help you in learning—mightn't it work? We do love Eddie," she ended a little incoherently, "and Carl knows and likes your husband, and —and I think you and I could be friends——"

She stopped, afraid that she had intruded, afraid that the other must be angry. But it is difficult to be angry with one who, without arrogance or airs of superiority, just humbly and wholeheartedly wishes you well; and this was the spirit that shone unmistakably in Anna's face and sounded in her voice. So the eyes that met hers held no anger; only pain and uncertainty.

"I'm—sorry," Elise said with difficulty. "It *is* too late, I'm afraid. But—thank you." She tried to shape her unsteady lips to a smile. "At least I begin to understand why Eddie feels as he does about you."

"I think I see Eddie coming now," Anna remarked, looking out the window. She got up. "I wish you weren't so sure it's too late," she said wistfully. "You might like us here in Middleburg if you'd give us a chance. I know we'd like you."

Such a sense of loss and regret swept Elise then as she looked into the friendly, sympathetic face and remembered all the useless loneliness of this past year, with so much warm companionship so near, that she could not answer. She put her small, cold, trembling hand into Anna's outstretched one and felt a firm clasp.

"If you ever feel that you'd like to see me again—will you telephone me?" asked Anna. "I'll be glad to come."

Elise nodded. Her lips formed the word "Good-by" as their hands fell apart. And then Eddie was with them, greeting Anna with pleased surprise.

"Still Red-Cross-ing?" he asked. "You must be tired." He turned to his mother. "She's been at it off and on for nearly a week."

"I've enjoyed it," said Anna serenely. "Folks respond so generously. And then"—she smiled at Elise—"I get to know such nice people!"

"Eddie, why don't you drive her home?" Elise said quickly. "I won't need the car to get Dad—he said someone else—someone he had an appointment with—was driving him home."

The glance Anna sent her was filled with such a quick, appreciative understanding that it seemed to Elise as if the other must have guessed why she made the suggestion; guessed that just for an instant, seeing the way Eddie's face had brightened when he came in, she had had a stab of bitter maternal jealousy again—and was determined that she would not permit it to stay in her heart.

Eddie, who had agreed to the proposition with delighted alacrity, flung back over his shoulder, "I may stay and talk with Pete about somethin' for a while. Be back in time for dinner."

When the door had closed behind them, Elise moved to the window, and standing hidden herself by the curtains, watched them wistfully as they went down the walk, Eddie laughing at something Anna had said. And suddenly Elise thought oddly, in words that she had not even known she remembered, "Her children arise up, and call her blessed; her husband *also*, and he praiseth her."

As they reached the car, in the very act of climbing in, Anna paused an instant and glanced back. With wonder Elise saw that she looked distressed, and indeed, almost as if she were hesitating whether or not to run back to the house. Then Eddie said something and she climbed in. And Elise found herself saying out loud, in an incredulous, awe-stricken sort of way, "She's thinking that she hates to leave me here, forlorn and unhappy—she *cares*, she really *cares* about how I feel!" And the idea that someone could care that much about another person not a member of his family or a close friend, about a stranger in fact, was so new to her that it was as if a door had opened on another kind of landscape. Were there people like that, really, not saints or preachers or missionaries, but just ordinary people, who actually cared so strongly as this about other people?

Slowly she went upstairs. At the open door of Eddie's room she paused. Soon he would be gone. And she would be off to New York to live with her parents. That sense of the ending of things, which is one of the most poignant emotions that humanity feels, was strong on her as she moved into the room and began to hang up his clothes, flung about with his usual abandon. There would be so little ever any more that she could do for him! His desk drawers were open too. As she began to close them, she saw that one of them had some crumpled papers thrown in, helter-skelter, in a disorderly manner. She lifted them out, meaning to smooth and lay them back flat and straight—and it was at this instant that she saw the anniversary card.

The brightly colored letters stared up at her. "Happy Anniversary!" And underneath in Eddie's bold black scrawl the message which he had been at such creative pains to compose: "Here's looking forward to your golden one. Love, Eddie."

Her throat closed. She put out a shaking hand and picked the gaudy card up. Then it dropped from fingers gone suddenly limp. For underneath it lay his gift to them, the miniature. She stood there looking down at it, and felt the pain rising up in her, spreading over her, till she seemed to be made of nothing but this vast and aching sensation of irremediable loss. And she dropped on her knees there by the open drawer, her outstretched arms resting on it, her head bent over them, and sobbed as she had never sobbed before in her life, with great, wrenching gasps that seemed to tear her throat in pieces. . . .

"Elise!" said a shocked voice. "*Elise*——"

She had not heard him come. But there he was as she raised her devastated face, bending over her, his own face working. "Elise——" he said again hoarsely. "What *is* it?"

She could not speak yet. But she picked up the card from the floor, and she took the miniature from the desk, and she handed them both to him. Then she stumbled to her feet and buried her face in her hands, fighting for control. When she took them down, he was still standing there, his head bent over the boyish message and the picture.

"Phil——" she said in a choked uncertain voice. "Phil——"

He raised his head then. He looked at her but she felt he did not see her. His eyes were dazed and stricken.

"I—give—up," he said slowly. "If you'll forget all I said, Elise— if you'll drop the divorce—I'll sell the business here and we'll go back to New York. I can't do this to Eddie."

She heard her own voice coming as if from far off. "I can't— make you live with me again—when you don't love me any more——"

He was seeing her now; noting, a bit wonderingly, that in these few days she had grown thinner, and that her face was drawn and devastated by weeping.

"Poor little Elise!" he said.

There was deep sadness in his voice, and a sort of weary resignation. The unwelcome feeling came to her suddenly that it was as if he were no longer rebelling against and resenting his conviction that she would always be a little girl (A little girl of thirty-eight now . . . But someday a little girl of fifty? A little girl—she shivered—of sixty?)—that he was facing and accepting it.

"Poor child!" he said again, and this time he spoke with a sort of exhausted tenderness. "If I gave you that idea—I'm sorry. Because it isn't true. Perhaps sometimes I've almost wished it were true. But it isn't. I do love you. That was something that was settled for me a long time ago, and there's nothing I can do about it."

The first feeling Elise had was a surge of exultant relief, as the thought came, "We can go back home—I've won! We can go back to Mother and Daddy and all be happy again!" But this was followed almost immediately by a strange, an almost poisonous depression, which seemed to spread through every fiber of her. She stared at him helplessly, bewildered at her own suffering in this moment of triumph; not realizing that growing pains which have been long delayed can be painful. She clung to the back of Eddie's desk chair as if it were holding her up; seeing the soft, responsibility-free security of life with her parents slip away from her, and terrified at its going—yet hearing over and over, like an echo, Anna Fisher's warm voice saying, "To me marriage has been a lifetime career," and knowing above all that for her the moment of choice had irrevocably arrived.

"Well, dear?" Phil said wearily.

He was waiting for her answer, but he was sure he knew what it would be; this was clear to her. And then suddenly something else was clear, too—that now, at last, he looked like a defeated man, his shoulders sagging, his eyes dull and patient.

She did not in the least perceive how new a thing it was that she should thus see and interpret what *he* was feeling; she, who had been conditioned from babyhood to consider her own feelings of primary importance and to expect that all those around her would so consider! She was hardly even aware that since last night she had experienced what was, perhaps, the first keen suffering for someone else's sake—first Eddie, now Phil—that she had ever felt. She only knew that suddenly she could not bear that look on her husband's face, and that in this moment nothing mattered but to wipe it off.

She threw herself at him, and her arms went tightly, almost convulsively, around his neck.

"No!" she sobbed. "No, Phil, no! No, darling! We aren't going back. We're going to stay here—we're going to live here!"

She heard his breath draw in; he held her off, looking down at her incredulously, sure he could not have heard aright. So she said it again, more fully.

"We're going to stay in Middleburg—I'm going to join the Middleburg Woman's Club, and we'll go to the Fishers' church, and we'll ask folks in to dinner . . ."

But still he could hardly believe; still he was afraid to trust a happiness he had given up any hope of ever possessing.

"I don't understand," he said, dazed. "Are you sure? Are you *sure?*"

There was pain on the face she raised to his; the pain of renunciation, for in that moment she put the childhood to which she had clung so long behind her. But there was joy, too; the joy which comes with the conquest of love over self, and with the dawning realization that adulthood brings responsibility (that was what Anna Fisher had called it) but also a richness of fulfillment immaturity cannot know.

"I'm sure. Phil, Phil, if I try very hard to grow up and to be the kind of wife and mother Anna Fisher is—and even yet we might have another baby, mightn't we?—will *you* try, too? Try to help me and to be patient with me when I'm slow about learning, or when I backslide?"

He believed her then. She saw the belief break like a light over his face. And in the instant before he caught her close she thought that never before, not even when they were young and tumultuously in love, had he looked at her quite like this—as if he were seeing a kind of lovely miracle.

He put his cheek on her wet cheek, and his voice came, all broken with tenderness. "I don't want you to be like Anna Fisher! I don't want you to be like anybody but yourself. The self I've always known was the real you . . . Oh, Elise, Elise!"

And it was so that Eddie found them when he came in five minutes later, still in each other's arms like reunited lovers; wanting, both at once, to tell him about it, wanting to assure him that his anniversary gift was the most meaningful one he could possibly have chosen. . . .

"All this love stuff!" He felt compelled to scoff affectionately, finally, in order to assert his young masculine superiority to such sentimental scenes. "At your advanced age—here I come in and catch you acting like a couple in a movie clinch!"

But his eyes were shining and he kept breaking into grins. "One thing," he conceded, "you do look more like you look in the miniature now!"

"The idea!" his mother exclaimed indignantly. "I'm very pretty in that miniature, if I do say it, as I shouldn't! And now my hair is messed and my eyes are red and——"

"So they are, now I look closer," her husband agreed. "How about slicking up and we'll all go out to dinner somewhere?"

From her room, as she bathed her flushed face and got out her prettiest dress, Elise could hear their voices. They were talking about the game—the great game, which Eddie had won. Eddie was eagerly and earnestly detailing every play, and Phil was interrupting to ask questions.

She stood still a moment, listening and smiling to herself. She was thinking of Eddie's anniversary gift; and she was thinking, too, that someday she must tell Phil of that other and bigger gift for which they had to thank their son; that gift which, she had begun (as yet a bit dimly but with a promise of future brightness) to perceive, was drawn from so deep and sure a Source, the same Source from which sprang the Fishers' strength and serenity; the gift of Eddie's forgiveness.

9. FEATHERS OVER THE TOWN

*T*ED DARLING:
                                    Saturday, October 31, 1954.

I've just done something rather peculiar. I've only this minute finished a letter telling you of various events of the week—such as the wedding Emily and Aunt Anna and Uncle Carl and I went to, for instance, at which I kept thinking that maybe Pastor Martin would be performing the same ceremony for you and me next fall!—and how much I miss you, and things like that. Nothing peculiar in that, you say. Right, mister! The peculiar part is that now I'm writing another I don't intend to mail.

There's a reason, of course. I've been thinking a lot these past few days of a certain promise we made each other before you sailed—the promise, I mean, that we would tell each other *every*-thing. I remember exactly what you said:

"You see, Harriet, if I get the idea that you are shielding me, not telling me any news but good news, I'll be worried no matter how cheerful your letters seem. But if I know that you're keeping me fully informed, then at least I won't fret unless there really is something to fret over!"

I felt the same way and said so. It was an agreement. But now I'm wondering. Germany is an awfully long way off, darling, and you're not exactly as happy as a lark in the Army anyway, and you don't need to add bother about me to restlessness and lonesomeness. Yet—I did promise. So this double-letter arrangement is my compromise. I'm going to tell you every bit of this unpleasantness in which I'm involved just now, right up to today. But then I'm going to put the letter away for a few days. I'll add to it from time to time as things work themselves out—because they *have* to work out, one way or another, very soon—and then I'll send the entire, completed account to you. So, Ted dear, when you read this somewhat ominous beginning, just tell yourself, "Whatever it was, it's all over now." Of course it may not be over in exactly the fashion I'd best like it to be. But honestly, honestly, there is not one single thing about it all for which my conscience hurts me. And so I think that I can promise you that even if the story doesn't quite have a happy ending I'll be able after a little while to put the humiliation and the feeling of terrible injustice behind me and forget it—almost. I believe I have enough sense and enough religion to do that.

So with this lengthy preface, I'll begin! I'll have to tell about things in my own way, but then you know me pretty well by now and know about what to expect from me, don't you?

And one thing I think you know about me, Ted, is how happy, except for missing you, I've been here in Middleburg till this happened. I thought it was the friendliest town on earth—no, I take that thought back! I'm not going to make it past tense. I still think so, and I won't let this one unhappy thing cloud my picture. And of course there isn't any cloud to fight off about this home or the Fishers. I wrote you two months ago when Uncle Carl got me this job that I was the luckiest girl in the world, alone as I am just now, to be living with them—and I've felt that way more and more every day since then. It's such a happy home! There's so much discipline and yet so much freedom—so much respect for each other and yet so much informality—so much gay companionship and so much deep, unsentimental affection—and underneath it all, and running through it all, and I guess *making* it all, actually, is their faith, their warm, vital faith, which is not only a Sunday matter but a practical reality every hour of every day.

Well! I stopped because perhaps that's off the track. But I don't think it is, exactly, for living with them has done something to me, Ted, and it's one reason I know I won't let this business break my heart, no matter how it works out. If this was a digression, it's over now!

I haven't written you much about my boss, Mr. Rockford Steele (whom everybody but me seems to call Rocky!) except that I liked him. But he's very much a part of what's coming next, so maybe I'd better describe him a little bit. He is about thirty-five —which doesn't seem *awfully* young to me, but is considered very young indeed for the position of a junior executive in Middleburg's newest and fastest growing business, the Middleburg Plastics Corporation! He makes a big salary and he has a beautiful home and two cars and membership in the town's swank country club. He also has a pretty wife and he's quite good-looking himself. He's very considerate and kind. He drives himself hard and he expects a good deal of the people around him, but to me it's interesting to work for somebody who's crazy about his job and right up on his toes about it. So I really haven't minded the extra hours—especially as he always pays generously for them. I've met his wife, of course—Peggy Steele. She breezes in and out of the office fairly often. I like her, too. She's sweet. They haven't any children and I was awfully glad when he told me, last week, that they have an application in with the welfare folks to adopt a baby and hope to get one in a few months. Because it has seemed to me, sometimes, that Mrs. Steele was a little bit restless. I suppose a woman who hasn't any special interest in civic or church work and who has two maids and no children might get bored. I've also found myself thinking, once or twice, that both Mr. and Mrs. Steele were a little too smart and nice for the—well, maybe the word I want is *light-weight*—crowd they run around with socially.

And, darling, if you're thinking here, "Now I'm *sure* she's digressing," why, you're wrong. This is very much to the point, as you'll see later.

Now here, although it's going to seem quite irrelevant, it's time for me to speak of Jane Clark. After that I promise I'll begin to draw the various threads together.

Jane is a few years older than Emily and me. She lives with her widowed mother in a cute little house right across the street. She's not engaged or married—I expect she'd like to be. (Miaow!) She's friendly and neighborly, always running in and out, and her mother is the same way. Jane's always seemed to me to be a good-natured sort of girl, a little bit flighty and awfully talkative— they're on our telephone line and Grampa gets terribly frustrated sometimes when he has to wait half an hour to get the line—but kindhearted and sociable. She loves to read very romantic stories about poor girls who marry rich young men, getting them away from all the spiteful rich girls. She sleeps in the front bedroom of their house, and Emily and I have a front room, too, so we can't help seeing that her light burns late nearly every night. Em asked her about it once.

"I'm curious, Jane," she said jokingly. "Are you studying some deep book or something, burning the midnight oil every night?"

And Jane answered, "Mercy, no, it's just that I adore reading," and began to tell us the plots of some of the stories.

So now, Ted, if you're still with me by this time, I'll get to what happened on Wednesday night.

I'd planned to go to a movie that night with Grampa, but I had to telephone him late in the afternoon and break the date. Because Mr. Steele called me in just an hour before quitting time and told me, looking as if something or somebody had just hit him hard in the stomach, that an important report which we had thought wasn't due till next week would have to be in the next *day*— Thursday.

"We've got hours of work on it still," he groaned. "And to spring it on me like this at four-thirty in the afternoon! There's nothing for it but to work late. I hope it doesn't put you out too much, Miss Richards."

Of course, I said that was all right. I went back in my little cubbyhole and phoned Grampa and sent word to Aunt Anna I wouldn't be home for dinner, and assured Grampa I had my key and they could lock the front door. As I hung the receiver up, the buzzer sounded from Mr. Steele's office and I went back. He looked quite harried. He said he'd been trying off and on for twenty minutes to get his wife and she was out—and would I please keep calling her at intervals and give her the news, and also would I order sandwiches and coffee for him and me? And just about that time in she came with one of her friends I'd never met—a Mrs. Elliot.

She introduced me right away—she's awfully nice about that, she never acts like the secretary is a piece of office furniture.

"Rocky's just had her two months and already she's indispensable," she said gaily to her friend. "The best he's ever had, he says."

I was blushing in, I suppose, a very pleased sort of way when this Mrs. Elliot drawled, "Oh, but much, much too pretty, Peggy dear!" Then she looked mischievously at our startled faces and laughed. "I mean, of course—the pretty ones always get married!"

I said hastily to Mr. Steele, "I'd better order the sandwiches," and was just about to tell the ladies good-by when Mrs. Steele exclaimed, "Sandwiches! Oh, Rocky, don't tell me that means you're working late tonight!"

"I'm afraid that's just what it does mean, sugar," said Mr. Steele crisply. "I've been trying to phone you. And every minute counts, so if you and Janice will excuse me now and run along——"

"But, Rocky!" She was almost in tears. "It's your birthday. Had you forgotten? And—I hadn't told you—it was going to be a surprise—but all the gang are coming over for a party tonight, with presents and everything—and it's too late to call it off——"

"My sainted aunt—I *had* forgotten!" groaned Mr. Steele.

With a stammered good-by that nobody heard I escaped, but even with the door closed I could hear him explaining about the report and how there simply wasn't anything he could do now— and I could tell that she was trying awfully hard to be a good sport but was terrifically upset and disappointed. Finally he told her he'd do his level best to get home before the party was over, and she said that would be fine—still sounding as if she wanted to cry. I felt awfully sorry for both of them about it.

Really though, there never was a chance for him. The sandwiches came, and we didn't even stop work while we ate them. At about nine-thirty he asked me to get him the factory performance reports from the file. And I told him the factory never had sent them over, as far as I knew. He ran his hands through his hair in a distracted way and said he had to have them, and there was nothing for us to do but to drive to the factory and finish the whole job there.

Well, the factory plant is nearly two miles out on the highway! But I phoned the night watchman—the one inside, not the one at the gate—to open up the office where the files stay for us, and we gathered up all our material and took off.

And at twelve-thirty I typed the last words of that report, stating that the assembly departments' output "showed an increase of 26.2 over the preceding six months," and Mr. Steele heaved a weary sigh and remarked that that finished it and he hoped he hadn't half killed me.

"Oh, I can take it!" I said. "But I'm thinking about your birthday party. No chance to make it now, I'm afraid."

He gave a guilty start—he'd forgotten all about it. "Oh-oh, am I in the doghouse now!" he said ruefully. "I'd better phone her." But the phone was dead; the switchboard was off. There were two other phones in the building communicating directly with out-side—but they were in the rooms where the night crew was work-ing and, as he said, "You couldn't hear yourself think there." So he decided he'd just better go straight home. Only it wasn't quite "straight." Because he had to stop for gas. And of course he had to take me home. So it was nearly one when he finally drew the car to the curb before the Fishers'.

I remember that I noticed the light was on in Jane's room, and that the red and gold maples were lovely in its glow. As I stepped out—I was on the side of the car toward Jane's house—I discovered that my foot had gone to sleep. My ankle turned as soon as my shoe touched the ground, and if Mr. Steele hadn't been right there, having politely come round the car to open the door for me, I'd have fallen. Mr. Steele laughed about my being asleep "on my feet," and since I'd wrenched my ankle a little and it kept still turning, he took my arm rather closely and helped me up the path. Then I couldn't find the key and kept groping around in my bag, and we joked about that a little—we were so tired I think we were a bit lightheaded by now. He said he'd always told Peggy that finding anything in a woman's handbag was a job for an archaeol-ogist. When I finally did find it, I dropped it; and he didn't have a match or a flashlight, so we had to grope on the porch floor in the dark for it. It all sounds so trivial, and it was—but the total result, if anybody had been watching (which was something that never entered my head at the time) was to make it appear as if we'd lingered there on that darkened veranda.

The next morning when Mr. Steele called me in to dictate to me he was awfully appreciative about the wonderful help I'd been and what a fine spirit I'd showed, and so forth. And then he re-marked, in an offhand sort of way, "The crowd were just taking off when I got home last night. I came in for a lot of ribbing."

"Why?" I asked, surprised.

And he answered carelessly, "Oh, just that soon after we went to the factory plant Peg tried to phone me. At the town office, of course. When there wasn't any answer, she told all the crowd I must be on my way home. So of course when I didn't get there, they were kidding her—and me, after I arrived—about where I was, with some remarks from Janice concerning my pretty secre-tary."

I didn't enjoy this one bit and I guess he saw I didn't. Because he laughed and said, "Why, you're not going to take that seriously, are you? It was just a joke."

I still didn't think it was a very funny joke, but I managed a weak little smile and we dropped the subject.

And this, Ted darling, was Thursday. That night I turned in early, and last night, Friday, Grampa and I filled our delayed date for the movie. When we got back and I went up to the room Emily and I share, I found her propped up in bed reading. We chatted while I got ready for bed, and then she said suddenly, "Harrie, I'm a coward. There's something I ought to tell you—and I don't want to. I've been putting it off ever since I got home this afternoon."

Naturally I looked at her blankly, and she looked back at me unhappily. "You've got the right to know," she said. "So I guess the only way to do it is just to plunge in. Here goes!"

What had happened was this: Agnes Hobbs, who is a public stenographer here, had come by the library at noon and asked Emily to have lunch with her because she had something very important to say to her. So they went out together for a sandwich, and when they were at the table, Agnes announced, in a very portentous voice, that there was an ugly story going around which she felt she must bring to Emily.

"About me?" Em asked, puzzled, and Agnes said oh no—that it was not about Emily. "It's about your cousin Harriet and her boss."

Emily said she didn't even catch the significance of that at first because the whole idea was so fantastic. She just stared at her and replied, "Harriet gets along very well with her boss—what on earth do you mean?" For at the moment she jumped to the conclusion that Agnes was telling her I was going to be fired.

So then Agnes gave this pitying smile. "I'll say she gets along well with him!" she said. "That's the point. Everyone is saying that they're having an affair."

Emily told me she was so completely flabbergasted that all she could do was splutter that this was the silliest lie she'd ever heard in her life and that nobody with one grain of sense could possibly believe it. That offended Agnes, who remarked stiffly, "I don't say I have absolute proof that would stand up in a court of law! But it's good enough for all practical purposes. I happen to *know* that Rocky missed his own birthday party Wednesday night because he was out in the country somewhere with Harriet. And I also happen to know from an *eyewitness* that he brought Harriet home at 3 A.M. so drunk she couldn't stand up and they stayed a long time on the front porch, which was pitch-black dark!"

It was all such a tissue of falsehood that Emily hardly knew where to begin denying; but she told Agnes that in the first place we weren't out in the country at all, that we were working late on an important report—and here Agnes interrupted. With a superior air she said, "I realize you want to stand up for your cousin—but I know from one of the guests at that party that Peggy Steele tried to telephone Rocky's office at ten—and he *wasn't there.* And they stopped for gas at my own cousin's filling station out on the highway away after midnight."

Emily said that she kept her temper with a big effort because she didn't think losing it would help me. She explained to Agnes just what had happened; how we'd had to finish our job at the factory; and then she told her that she knew positively that I'd never touched a drop of liquor in my entire life, and that outside of that she roomed with me and would certainly have known if I'd come home drunk, and that also it hadn't been 3 A.M. but a little before one.

And it didn't do a bit of good. That's what amazed Emily, and that's what amazes me. Do people *like* to believe the worst? Agnes just shook her head and said in an incredulous way, "Maybe so.

But I must tell you I think you're wasting your breath denying it, Emily. I think you'd be better occupied trying to improve the girl's morals than defending her."

So then Emily got up; she told me she still didn't lose her temper. She just said with all the dignity she could muster that she really couldn't sit there and listen to such slander any longer. And then she added, "And I must say, Agnes, that I'm terrifically disappointed in you, and much more concerned about *your* morals, repeating these cruel lies, than I am about Harrie's. My advice to you is to go straight home and get down on your knees and do some good, hard praying about it all."

With that she walked out, leaving Agnes spluttering, "Well, I never—of all things," and such phrases.

Ted, dear Ted, I won't even try to tell you, for I'm sure you must know, how stunned I was, and still am. I feel as if I were walking around in a bad dream. I just can't take it in that anybody could really believe such things about me, or that the story could spread so fast on such flimsy evidence. Of course, I was able to tell Emily immediately that the only person who could possibly have been the "eyewitness" Agnes mentioned was Jane Clark; and I told her why I knew this must be true and just what had actually happened. We agreed that when Jane saw me stumble and watched Mr. Steele helping me up the path, she jumped to the conclusion that I was drunk. Heaven knows what she thought— and said—we were doing those few moments on the darkened porch; I'd rather not speculate. And when Jane's talk got tied up to the gossip Peggy Steele's friends were doing and Agnes' cousin added *his* bit, I guess the case looked airtight.

At first Emily was all for barging right over to Jane's this morning and having it out with her. But I vetoed that, because I thought that Jane would simply take exactly the same attitude Agnes had and it wouldn't do any good. So finally Emily said that maybe there hadn't been as much talk as Agnes had implied, and that perhaps the best thing was just to ignore it and let it die down. Neither of us said, but I'm sure both of us were thinking, that the trouble was that maybe it wasn't *going* to die down all that easy. I asked her not to tell Aunt Anna and Uncle Carl and Grampa for a few days till we saw how things were developing—and at last

she agreed, but a little bit reluctantly. If it keeps on, they'll have
to know—but just now I'm so raw and sore about it all I'd like to
have a little while to get hold of myself and be sure I can discuss it
calmly with them.

I'm so confused, Ted! Why should Jane and Agnes want to do
me an injury? I thought they *liked* me. And I never did them any
harm. I'm really in a daze over it. I've been thinking that perhaps
the best thing to do is just to go back to Chicago—and ask for my
old job or get another one—and live in Mrs. Ware's rooming house
again. For one thing it doesn't seem quite fair to the Fishers for
this scandal to be connected with their home, and for another I—
well, to tell the truth I'm not sure that I can *take* it. If I did do that,
I suppose Agnes and Jane would say that Mr. Steele had set me up
in a love nest there, and every time he left town they'd claim he
was visiting me.

Oh, I'm sorry, darling! I shouldn't have written that last. The
one thing I can't let myself do is to get bitter. I guess before the rest
of the family come in (they've gone to see the high school football
game because Pete's on the team) I'd better follow the parting
advice that Emily gave Agnes! Good-by, and all my love. Harriet.

. . . This is Tuesday night, Ted dear, and I've just had a talk
with all the family—except Pete and Freddie. I came home from
work pretty downhearted this afternoon, after two days at the office that have been, I might as well admit, tough to take. You see,
by noon Monday I was pretty sure my "affair" with the boss was
being discussed there—and by today I was certain. I can feel it in
the looks that follow me, some disapproving, some curious, maybe
one or two a little envious—I can sense it in the way the whispering
stops as soon as I come in the restroom, where the other girls are—
and worst of all, I'm afraid I can tell it from the attitude of two or
three of the boys I've turned down for dates. Don't get hot, darling,
nobody's insulted me! It's just a subtle familiarity: "Hi, baby!"
. . . "Been having a big time lately, beautiful?"—that sort of thing.

And that's why I told Aunt Anna and Uncle Carl and Grampa
about it tonight.

I've tried to tell you how they are, Ted. They get worried and
distressed, of course, just like other folks, but underneath I always

seem to feel a deep-down serenity, and that's the way it was this time. They were shocked and indignant, but they stayed calm and levelheaded. The one thing that seemed to really upset them all was when I said I thought maybe if there was going to be a scandal about me I shouldn't stay here. They all jumped on me then! They wanted to know what kind of people I thought they *were*, and I had to promise I'd never mention *that* again.

"And anyway," said Aunt Anna, "it would be running away, Harrie. You can't do that—you're not guilty."

"That's just the point!" I said. "I don't like defending myself for something wrong I didn't do!"

Uncle Carl looked at me with that nice slow smile of his and remarked, "It's a lot happier situation than defending yourself for something wrong you *did* do, my dear!"

And Aunt Anna said, "That's right, Harriet. Nobody can really put you in the wrong when you're not in the wrong, don't you see?"

When I came to think it over, that was rather comforting.

Emily told them then that she'd wanted to go to see Jane right away and explain, but that I hadn't felt it would do any good because I'd been sure she'd react just like Agnes, with incredulity.

"We might wait a little while, at any rate," Uncle Carl said. "Because it is true that sometimes the more you protest against gossip the faster it grows."

"Got to talk to her sometime," Grampa remarked quietly. "For *Jane's* sake."

I guess I was a little overwrought. I said very promptly that I wasn't interested in doing anything for Jane's sake, that she had done her best to injure me, and I couldn't forgive her and didn't think she deserved forgiveness. "Do you, Grampa, really?" I demanded. "Do you think she deserves it?"

I guess nobody has a smile like Grampa's. It's the *warmest* smile I've ever seen. He smiled at me like that now.

"Well, do you know," he answered, "I'm just mighty glad I don't have to decide that question. That's something I can safely leave to the Lord. My instructions are pretty clear, and they don't say anything about deserving—they just say I'm to keep on forgiving." Then he added mildly, "I don't think Jane or Agnes either

just exactly planned on doin' you an injury. They got a little excitement outa believin' the worst and they couldn't resist the temptation to pass on some spicy gossip and they just didn't stop to
think, or maybe wouldn't let themselves think, of the harm it
would do."

I muttered something about the result being the same, and
Grampa agreed with me. That, he said, with much simplicity, was
precisely why they ought to be told how much harm they had
done.

"You're right, Grampa," Emily declared gravely. "And I intend
to do it, too, sooner or later."

"Once," I said despondently, "I read a little incident about a
woman who told her pastor she'd been guilty of unkind gossip
and wanted to make amends. She asked him how to do it, and he
took her to the church tower and there he ripped open a feather
pillow and the feathers flew out and drifted in every direction.
Then he asked her if she could gather up every feather and put it
back and she said, surprised, that of course she couldn't. And he
told her that it was just as impossible to recall all the slanderous
gossip she'd said."

Grampa's eyes twinkled at me. "Well now," he said, "that's a
pretty doleful little story, ain't it? The feathers wouldn't drift
around over the city forever—they'd scatter and disappear someday! Still, it's a mighty true story, one way. Tell you what—it's a
good one for Emmy here to remember to tell Agnes and Jane—
yes, it's a fine one for that—but not such a good one for *you* to be
mullin' over right now, picturin' that silly gossip goin' on and on
and on, like feathers drifting till doomsday."

I don't know quite why, Ted, but that made me laugh. And they
all laughed with me. And somehow I feel better now. In spite of
the fact that I still dread waking up and going to the office in the
morning, there's a sort of pleasant glow that lingers and makes
the sick, scared feeling easier to take. So good night, dear, and
love, from—Harriet.

                                                    Friday Evening.
. . . I wanted to write you last night, Ted dearest, but I was
tired—and excited, too, I guess—and I decided to be sensible and

wait. Now I'm glad I did, because—— But I'll tell you that when I get to it. You said once that I had a tidy mind—I think you were teasing me, weren't you?—but anyway I like to take things up in the order in which they come.

So back to Wednesday at the office—on which day nothing happened except more of the same thing, and which was therefore pretty rugged. When I got home Emily showed me a very brief and stiff note of apology from Agnes; it really said nothing except that she was sorry Em felt she'd "slandered" me, and she begged her pardon. I couldn't quite see why Emily was so pleased over it, but she said she knew Agnes, and from her it meant a lot and indicated she'd go further later on. It seemed to cheer Emily; I can't say it greatly cheered me. And now for Thursday, for that was the day things broke wide open.

I came in Mr. Steele's office bringing some letters he'd dictated for him to sign and found him talking on the telephone. I started to leave, but he motioned me to sit down, and went on talking. He was saying very apologetically,

"I'm just as sorry as you are, Peggy, but we've been asked for a supplementary report and we've got to get it out." . . . "Yes, yes, I know—I wish the powers that be wouldn't spring these things so suddenly, but they do, and *they* call the turns, not me, and that's that. I wish you'd try to understand." . . . "Well, for Pete's sake, darling—*I* don't care what you do with the tickets. Can't *you* decide that? Give 'em away—take Janice—anything! All I'm telling you is I can't possibly use mine tonight." . . . "Peggy, listen carefully, will you? I know we finished *that* report—this is a supplementary one—additional data—look up 'supplementary' in the dictionary, honey." . . . "I'm sorry—didn't mean to sound cross—I just want you to understand. I don't work till midnight for fun, you know." . . . "What? Honestly, Peg." . . . "Oh, all right, all right. Glad you do see it. That's a good girl. Good-by."

But he hadn't sounded as if he thought she was a good girl; he'd sounded what my mother used to call "outdone" with her. And he turned to me now looking bothered.

"I wonder if Peg's not very well," he remarked abruptly. "Maybe I ought to try to get her to a doctor. It isn't like her to get upset over little adjustments in the schedule. Well, Miss Richards, I suppose you gathered I'm going to have to ask you to work late again tonight."

My heart had sunk clear down into the soles of my shoes. He didn't seem to know what was wrong with his wife, but I was terribly afraid *I* did. I didn't know what to say, and so I just sat there, staring down at my hands and saying nothing.

He was looking at me, a little surprised. "I'm awfully sorry," he said. "I promise I'll make it up to you somehow. And I really think this is the last for a while."

"It—it isn't *that!*" I blurted out. "I mean—it isn't that I mind working—it's just——" Then I bogged down.

He was watching me keenly now. "Well—just *what?*" he asked.

I could feel the embarrassed red creeping right up to my hairline. I said miserably, "I hate to tell you—but I'm afraid the last time I stayed started some unpleasant gossip. About you and me."

He stared at me a minute and then he laughed. "Oh, that's absurd! Where ever did you get such a notion?"

He didn't believe it; he thought my imagination was working overtime; or maybe he thought—well, I don't know *what* he thought, but I had to show him I wasn't a silly, hypersensitive creature. So I told him the whole story.

His face changed, got hard and grim as he listened. "Oh, for the love of Mike!" he said in a sort of furious disgust, and he stood up and ran his fingers through his hair in a quick, irritated gesture.

I got up too. "So—so maybe," I faltered, "it would be best if—if you got somebody else to stay tonight——"

"This is preposterous!" he said angrily. "I'll do nothing of the sort. I'll put a stop to this idiotic talk right now——"

"But how?" I asked, trying to reason with him because he was honestly in such a rage, Ted, that I could tell he wasn't seeing the thing straight. "It isn't so easy." And I thought about the feathers. "Even the office force has been whispering," I went on, because I thought he might as well know that, too.

He was looking dangerous by now. "Which ones? Their names, please," he demanded ominously.

That scared me. "Please, Mr. Steele," I begged. "At least half a dozen. You can't pitch into all of them. In fact, you can't afford even to notice it. It would just make matters worse. They certainly won't talk any more kindly about us because they're angry with me for getting them into trouble, and with you for having them up on the carpet."

He stood there glowering at me in an uncertain sort of way. "I guess you're right," he said finally, in a frustrated growl. "But if you knew how I hate to feel helpless——"

I did know. He's a man of action. But there are some things you can't just charge head on, and I said so; then I came back to my point. "So—if you'll ask someone else to work tonight——"

"Now look here!" He came around the desk to where I stood. He sounded very impatient. "We certainly don't need to dignify such asinine foolishness by giving in to it! Nobody else will do—you know that. Just forget all about this."

"But Mr. Steele," I began desperately, "your wife——"

"My wife?" he cried in a kind of outraged roar that frightened the socks off me, honestly, Ted. "You're not insinuating that *Peggy* would listen for a second to such nonsense——"

I folded up. I just wilted. I stammered, "You *said* she was up-set——" and turned to run for cover, he seemed so *furious*.

Then suddenly his face softened and he caught my arm and brought me round facing him. He put his hands on my shoulders. He said quite gently, "I didn't mean to bellow at you, poor child. But leave my wife out of it, will you? She isn't like that. She hasn't heard anything, and if she had she wouldn't care, she'd laugh it off. We'll keep our chins up, and we'll carry out our plans for the evening and that's that."

"Oh, I *beg* your pardon!" simpered a voice from the door in a sort of horrible, phony embarrassment.

The file clerk, Gladys, was standing there with a sheaf of papers in her hand. You see, Ted, the door to my office was standing open—it's a sort of small anteroom to Mr. Steele's, really, and Gladys had come through there. Gladys knows perfectly well she isn't supposed to approach his office that way unless I'm there and admit her. I couldn't help thinking she was trying to catch us out. And Mr. Steele, in his anger, said just the wrong thing. "What are you doing, coming through that way?"

"The door was open." And now instead of a phony embarrassment there was an equally phony meekness and apology in Gladys' tone. "I'm terribly sorry—maybe I'd better close it—I'll leave this stuff on your desk, Miss Richards——" And she fled, shutting the door behind her before either of us could say anything else.

"I'm going to fire that malicious little busybody this minute!" Mr. Steele raged, and started after her, but this time it was *I* who stopped *him.*

"You can't!" I cried, stamping my foot with nervous irritation. "Use your head! It would just make matters ten times worse!"

Afterward I was appalled that I'd spoken to my boss like that. But it worked. He stood there breathing hard and looking more frustrated than ever, and after a minute he said dejectedly, "I guess you're right." Then he squared his shoulders and his mouth took on a stubborn line. "But I still say we're not giving in to this lunacy! You can go now, but I'll be expecting you to work tonight."

I didn't feel up to arguing. I just left, glad to escape. I felt absolutely sick.

After lunch Gladys tiptoed in, pretending to glance fearfully at Mr. Steele's door, and told me she was sorry she'd butted in "at the wrong time." Of course, I tried then to explain to her, and I must admit it was a horrible experience. She just wouldn't listen. She kept interrupting to tell me that I needn't bother about *her,* that she understood perfectly, that he was an awfully good-looking guy and she was certain she'd do the same in my place . . . And oh, for Heaven's sake, honey child, don't think I'd got to make excuses or explanations to *her,* she'd never liked Peggy Steele, and for her part she wished me luck . . . and I got sort of desperate, as if I were trying to fight my way past cobwebs, strangling cobwebs I just couldn't break through. She was simply *closed* to anything except what she'd made up her mind to believe, and I didn't get anywhere, not anywhere.

So all afternoon, although I worked like fury trying not to think, I kept feeling sicker and sicker. A little before five-thirty Mr. Steele came in. I could tell he was trying to sound casual and as if nothing had happened.

"I've got a dinner conference—one I can't break," he said. "I'll be back at seven. It gives you time to go home for your dinner if you like. The office'll pay taxi fare." Then he added, rather warningly, it seemed to me, "Please be back promptly at seven—there's at least four hours' work," and breezed out as if he felt everything was settled.

But it wasn't. Because no matter how hard he protested that his wife wasn't upset, I knew—call it feminine intuition if you like, but I absolutely knew—that she *was*. That drawling Janice Elliot, with her hints about pretty secretaries, was certain to have retailed all the gossip to her. And anyway I felt very deeply that the group the Steeles ran round with just wasn't like Pastor Martin's flock, who are the Fishers' best friends. If Aunt Anna thought she *saw* Uncle Carl making love to somebody else, I'm perfectly sure it would be her own eyes she'd disbelieve in, and not him! But what was unthinkable to her wouldn't be unthinkable to Peggy Steele, especially when Janice Elliot was probably egging her on.

So I sat there and pondered for quite a while after Mr. Steele was gone. I didn't want to be a quitter, and I remembered what Aunt Anna'd said, and I didn't want, either, to let them all put me in the wrong, or seem to, when I *wasn't*. But at the same time I couldn't, I really couldn't, bear the idea that I was, however innocently, causing any trouble between a man and his wife. And at last I wrote a letter:

"Dear Mr. Steele:

"With real regret I tender you my resignation, effective immediately. You have been a most kind and considerate chief, and I am extremely sorry to desert you at a busy time. But as I see it, I have no choice. My presence in your office is just going to keep alive and feed these cruel, fantastic slanders, and there is nothing sensible for me to do but to leave. It's so unfair that it shakes my faith in human nature, but I don't see how I can get around facts or avoid the conclusion and the decision at which I have arrived. Please, therefore, do not expect me back any more. With best wishes, Harriet Richards."

I propped the envelope on his desk where he'd be sure to see it, and then I got my personal stuff out of my desk and left. My stomach felt all hollow.

When I got home, nobody was there but Emily.

"Oh, hello!" she said. "Everybody's left us—they've all gone to the Jonsons'—even Freddie—for supper and to see the movies of their summer's trip."

I accused her of having stayed away just to keep me from coming home to an empty house, but she insisted cheerfully that she hadn't much wanted to go anyway. Aunt Anna had left a nice little dinner—which Em ate and I merely fooled round with—and as we were washing the dishes I looked at the clock and thought, "Mr. Steele is just about getting my note now!" After dinner when we were back in the living room, Emily remarked quietly, "All right, Harrie—you might as well tell me and get it off your chest. Something else happened today, didn't it?" So I told her all I've just written you, Ted, about the day and what I'd done at the close of it.

She sat still a minute, frowning. "Well, that settles it," she said then, getting up. "I had something rather nice to tell you—but I'll make it short now. Agnes came by today. She was really penitent this time. So we went out to lunch again and I told her all about you. I told her just what sort of girl you are, and about your parents' deaths, and about Ted, and—everything. By that time she was crying into her soup. She isn't a mean girl, truly, Harrie. She wants to come to see you and ask you to forgive her—and she—well, she's going to pick up all the feathers she can. . . . Now I'll be off."

"Off—where?" I asked, my mind still on Agnes.

"Why, to see Jane, of course," Emily answered a little grimly. "Now that it's come to your resigning, she's got to be told."

This time I didn't protest. I let her go.

I was nervously trying to read the newspaper, and in reality doing nothing except wondering what was happening across the street, when the doorbell rang. I opened it, and immediately got a shock—there was Mr. Steele on the threshold! What's more, he stepped right inside without even waiting for me to ask him, looking big and angry and downright dangerous.

"Now look here!" he began, flourishing my letter under my nose. "This won't do! You've got to come back! For one thing, I can't spare you at this especial time. And for another, if you run out now it'll just convince everybody that there's truth in that gossip."

I stood looking at him miserably; after the way he'd bellowed at me when I'd tried to suggest earlier that Mrs. Steele might be upset, I didn't dare tell him that it wasn't "everybody" I was worrying about at this moment so much as just his own little Peggy! And he said, a little less violently, "I've brought a brief case along with everything we'll need, and if you feel it's unwise to work at the office tonight, we'll just get in the car and drive to my house—and do the job in my own living room with my own wife sitting there! But as for this resignation"—he flipped it contemptuously on the table—"I'm not accepting it, that's all."

He's such a positive character—please don't you be *quite* that positive, Ted, because people like that intimidate me! (That's about two thirds a joke, but not quite three thirds one!) But all the same I wasn't enough intimidated to walk into Mrs. Steele's house with him and have him blandly announce I'd come to spend the evening! And I was trying to find a tactful way of saying this, and not succeeding, and getting interrupted and shouted down, when the bell rang again.

And if, darling, the sight of Mr. Steele at my door had been a shock, I'll just ask you to try to fancy what the sight of *Mrs.* Steele, face white and eyes blazing, occupying the same position, did to me! I was, in fact, so completely taken aback that all I could do was to gasp, "Oh, Mrs. Steele!" And at nearly the same instant Mr. Steele, from just behind me, said in an amazed tone, "Why, Peggy—what brings you here?"

She stepped inside. She shut the door and stood with her back to it, as if she were facing enemies. Her eyes were still shooting sparks, and she snapped out each word. "More to the point—what brought *you* here?"

He just stood there and stared at her. If I'd been married to him I wouldn't have liked to have him looking at me like that—with that incredulous scorn. And I saw her sort of wilt and sag under it, and then call her anger back to help her.

"After you said you were working late *again*—Janice said if she were me she'd investigate, and——"

"*Janice?* What's *she* got to do with it?" he shouted, but she had the bit in her mouth now, Peggy had, and she galloped on.

"So I drove to the office, to see if you really were working—you weren't there last time you told me you would be, remember!— and I was just parking when I saw your car pulling away. And I followed it—and as soon as it stopped here I looked at the mail-box, and sure enough there was the Fishers' name. I just *happen* to know the Fishers are all out tonight—I met that Mrs. Jonson in the super market this morning and she was buying a lot of stuff because they were coming to dinner tonight—'the whole fam-ily,' she said—and so——"

He grabbed her by the shoulders; he almost shook her. "Will you stop? How on earth can a man be so wrong about the woman he's been married to ten years? Just today I was assuring Miss Richards, and believing every word I said, that *my* wife would never listen to or credit any gossip or slander about me! Have you gone absolutely crazy, Peggy?"

It was so plain that he was speaking with a furious sincerity that actually I believe the first pang of uncertainty, the first sus-picion that she'd made an idiot of herself, hit her at that moment. But I suppose it was just a suspicion, and she was still angry and jealous; and then, too, maybe she couldn't bear being put in that position. Anyway, she seemed to waver just one instant and then jerked herself away.

"You brought her home drunk the other night—and stayed on a pitch-dark porch with her for ages! Janice heard it practically at firsthand. You're certainly expecting a lot of faith if you think I ought to just smirk and be pleased about *that!* And you're not at your office now, you've come here to spend the evening with her——"

But about this time I decided I'd been a patient Griselda long enough, and I entered the scene.

"Mrs. Steele!" I raised my voice to get her attention and she spun around and looked at me. "You're talking about me as if I weren't here, but I am here and I can speak for myself! What's more I intend to! I was *not* drunk! I've never in my life so much as tasted a cocktail—and I wonder if you can say the same! I'd worked very hard with your husband till quite late, getting that report out, and coming home my foot went to sleep in the car. So when I got out, I stumbled—and that wrenched my ankle a little—it's weak anyway on account of an old sprain—and Mr. Steele took my arm and helped me up the walk. Then it took us a few minutes to get in because I couldn't find the key—and that's the whole terrible story!"

From this you can infer, Ted, and you'll be right, that I'd worked up a bit of fighting spirit; as Grampa says "got my dander up." I had the lady's entire attention, that was certain. Her eyes, so it seemed to me, lost a lot of their fire and began to look scared. But still she couldn't give in.

"How do I know that's true?" she said rather wildly. "And even if it is—partly—Janice says *all* our friends think there's something awfully phony about this working-late business, and you and Rocky alone night after night——"

"Alone?" I broke in, astonished. (Mr. Steele was trying to speak, but I beat him to it!) "In that office building where there are always other people working late, too? At the factory where there's an all-night shift?"

"What about here—tonight?" she cried. But it was a last-ditch stand. I saw it, and Mr. Steele saw it.

"It appears, Peggy, that you actually prefer to believe the worst," he said—and I simply can't tell you how coldly angry he sounded. Every word was congealing as it came out, like an icicle. "We shall have to disappoint you. If you want an excuse for a divorce, you'll have to hunt another one—there just isn't any co-respondent. Will you read this note, please?" As he spoke he handed her my letter of resignation, which she glanced at in a dazed, frantic sort of way. "Miss Richards was resigning, as you can see, because of all this rotten talk. I came here primarily to tell her she couldn't. It's news to me that the family aren't here. I didn't intend to stay, anyway." He added bitterly, "I had just suggested that we go over and work at my house tonight—since she felt she couldn't come back to the office . . . Naïve of me, wasn't it? But I had all these funny idealistic ideas about **my wife and my marriage, you see."**

Suddenly then I was sorry for her. She looked so stricken and so lost. She caught desperately at the one thing left she could think of, evidently; she managed to stammer, her breath coming in ragged gasps, "If—if there's nothing in it—why *should* she resign?"

It was at this exact moment that the door opened and Emily and Jane Clark walked in. It was quite some evening, Ted! Mr. Steele didn't immediately see them because his back was to the door. So he made his next remark after they were inside—and they heard it.

"That's not a very intelligent question," he said in that same chill, dispassionate voice. "Naturally it's because the whole thing is so fantastically untrue, built out of nothing whatsoever, that she feels she can't take the lies and slander any longer. Also because it has now spread to the office—some of the people there being, I'm sorry to say, as evil-minded and wickedly malicious as the cruel woman who started this rumor on no more grounds than a foot that went to sleep!"

You'll have to admit that this remark was pretty much of an earful for Jane to get. And, as it developed later, she was already almost at the breaking point. So now she just burst frankly into noisy sobs, crying like a kid cries.

"Oh, oh!" she gulped between the sobs. "I'm not that bad—I'm not that awful—I'm not! Oh, I just can't *stand* it—I feel so perfectly *terrible*——"

Mr. Steele had turned quickly and we all stood there just sort of frozen for a second. You know, Ted, I really do have to hand it to my cousin Emily. I mean she's got all kinds of poise. She said, as coolly and pleasantly as if things were quite normal, "It's Mr. and Mrs. Steele, isn't it? I've met you at the library, but you probably don't remember me. I'm Emily Fisher. And this is my friend, Jane Clark, who's feeling very bad just now because——"

"Jane Clark?" It was Peggy Steele who broke in. "But she's the one who said she saw——" And then she clapped one hand to her mouth and stared at Jane in a horrified kind of manner. I suppose it was just as well for Jane that she was too busy mopping her eyes to see that look, and even better that she didn't catch the really poisonous glare that Mr. Steele sent her before he turned and spoke to Emily.

"Miss Fisher," he said, all formal and a little pompous, "I'm exceedingly sorry to bring this disagreeable scene into your home. I suppose you're wondering what it's all about——"

"Why, no," Emily contradicted a trifle apologetically, in her nice, quiet voice, "I know what it's about. Though of course I didn't expect to see you and Mrs. Steele here. Jane wanted me to bring her over to see Harrie so she could——"

"So I could ask her to please forgive me, boo-hoo-hoo!" wept Jane. (That's honestly the only way I can describe how she said it, even if those boo-hoos do look funny, Ted. They sounded funny, too, and I'll just let you imagine the others and leave them out.) "Oh, I could positively kill myself! Oh, Mrs. Steele, you're not here because you *believed* any of it, are you? I didn't more than half believe it myself, even when I was telling it. I realize that now! It was just an exciting story, and it seemed like it *might* be true, and I guess I got a little kick out of telling it and seeing folks look surprised and shocked. And—and—how could I guess that it would grow and spread like—like ten forest fires?"

Then she said some other things that were almost lost in sobs, so that only words here and there came out, ". . . already—feeling bad—and when Emily said . . . And now that I see——"

And after this she sank down on the sofa and devoted herself seriously to crying and doing nothing else.

Peggy Steele knew now how it had all happened, of course; knew beyond any further doubt. And she stood there looking so forlorn, so really *devastated,* that you might have thought the discovery that her husband had not been untrue to her, after all, was bad news. But of course I knew it wasn't that. It was partly, I'm sure, that she was so hideously ashamed that she could hardly stand herself; and partly that she must have felt that this time she'd really lost him, and lost him in an even more painful way than to another woman.

She said in a husky little whisper, "You'll never—forgive me, will you, Rocky? You couldn't, of course. I don't blame you—I don't——"

Then she stopped talking and started sort of blindly toward the door. Mr. Steele caught her by the arm. It seemed to me—I was watching anxiously because I was praying he wouldn't be stuffy and unforgiving—that his face had softened, but his voice was still stern.

"*My* forgiveness, Peggy?" he said. "It's Miss Richards' forgiveness you should ask first of all!"

"Oh, no!" I cried, in a real agony of pity for her humiliation. "Don't make her do that, please——"

She pulled her arm away from his hand and faced me with a strange, broken kind of dignity,

"Nobody needs to *make* me," she said clearly. "I do ask your forgiveness, Miss Richards—very humbly. And I wouldn't wonder or blame you if you refused it. So now if you'll excuse me——"

But thank goodness, Mr. Steele caught her again, this time with a different sort of grasp. "Peggy——" he began, and then he looked at us as if he wished we were somewhere else and said desperately to Emily, "Please—is there somewhere I can be alone with her? For just five minutes?" And Emily, without a word, crossed the room and opened the door to Uncle Carl's little den.

Well, Ted, I spent that next half hour while they were talking it all out, I suppose, in the den trying to stanch the buckets of tears Jane kept shedding, and insisting over and over that I *did* forgive her, and no, that I *wouldn't* hate her all the rest of my life. She was fairly wallowing in remorse, poor old Jane! I guess the fact is that anybody as fond of melodrama as Jane would want to make the most of a scene of remorse, too, even if it was sincere— and I do truly believe it was. But you'll have to admit that it was a rather queer twist, for it to work out that I was comforting *her* for the harm *she'd* done *me*.

When the door to the den opened, she took a hurried leave; I think she was a little afraid of Mr. Steele. Peggy Steele looked to me rather like a soldier who has come through a severe battle with some painful wounds but is happy to find himself still alive. She tried to smile at me, and though her lip was unsteady, she managed it pretty well.

"I'm going to tear up this resignation," she said, and proceeded to do so before I could say either yes or no. "And—and shall we all three go to our house now so you and Rocky can finish that report?"

"Why don't they work in Dad's den?" suggested Emily. "And maybe you'll visit with me awhile, Mrs. Steele."

Peggy looked almost pathetically grateful at that; as if she hadn't really expected that anybody in this family would want to visit with her. And I went upstairs and got my portable and we went into the den, Mr. Steele and I, to work. Which, by the way, we somehow managed to do quite effectively—though I'm sure I don't know how, after such a hectic hour.

We heard the family come in at about nine, and we could hear Freddie chattering to Peggy Steele before they sent him upstairs to bed. At ten-thirty we came out, having got done in considerably less time than we'd dare hope, and Peggy was still there, and she and the Fishers were all sitting round and talking like old friends. I introduced Mr. Steele to the others, and then he and Peggy left. It seemed to me, for a moment, as if there were something Peggy wanted to say after she'd finished her shy good-bys. But after a moment of hesitation she just added, "Thank you," and nothing more.

And now for the something else I spoke about, the something that happened today. She came in the office this afternoon. She came right into my cubbyhole (I could see the heads craning after her, but I cared less somehow), and when I told her Mr. Steele was out, she said, "I know he is. I came to see you."

That made me a little nervous, because I had a shrinking from discussing what had happened with her. But she only sat on the edge of my desk, refusing a chair, and swinging her slim, pretty legs. And all she said, a little bit timidly, was, "Rocky told you we were adopting a baby, didn't he?"

I replied that he had, yes; and she went on after a minute. "It seems as if our wait is nearly over—we applied almost a year ago. Now we've been told we'll be able to get him next week."

I told her I thought that was grand, and I meant it, too.

"Yes. But—but—a baby needs a very special kind of atmosphere in his home, don't you think?" she asked anxiously.

I didn't know exactly what she meant. And she explained, "It's the atmosphere I felt last night in the Fishers' home—that hour and a half I spent with them while you and Rocky were working." She said it very seriously, almost solemnly, as if it were awfully important; and of course, then I did know what she meant, and I nodded and said yes, I understood.

She began to twist her fingers together a little nervously.

"Well—I've been thinking that maybe if I'd friends like them that —that things might've been different." Her eyes met mine bravely.

She said earnestly, "Please don't think I'm trying to dodge my responsibility! I didn't *need* to choose that crowd for my best friends, and I didn't *need* to let myself be so influenced by their—their"—she hunted for a phrase, and found it—"their cheap cynicism. But that's all over now. And what I've been thinking—and it seemed to me maybe you could help me—is that if there were an older woman, somebody like Mrs. Fisher, who'd be willing to be my friend——" She stopped. She smiled at me appealingly. "Oh, I'm not saying it right! I—I do want her friendship especially. She's made such a wonderful job of being a wife and mother . . . But I—*we,* Rocky and I—we'd like to know *all* of you better! Would you come to our home sometimes? And—and let us come to see you?"

I had to blink hard. It was all I could do to keep from boo-hooing like Jane, I was just that much touched. And I stammered out, "Why, of course—we'd be glad and *happy.*" Then I worked up a pretty good grin. "But I'd better warn you that as soon as I retail this talk to Aunt Anna she'll call you up and want to put your baby on the Cradle Roll of our Sunday School and invite you and your husband to the church supper next week!"

As a joke it fell flat, but as a statement of fact—which it actually was—it went over big. "Oh," said that chic young matron and leader of the smart set in Middleburg, Mrs. Rockford Steele, wife of our rising young executive, "oh," said she, (and her eyes were shining like stars, positively, Ted, I'm not exaggerating) "do you think she will? Do you honestly think she will? Oh, that would be wonderful!"

Well, well. God really *does* work in a mysterious way, His wonders to perform, doesn't He, darling?

So I guess this is a good stopping place for my long story, and it had better be, 'cause it's very late. And after all, it's a happy ending, isn't it? Oh yes, I know, there are some feathers still floating around. Jane won't be able to recall them as fast as she scattered them. For quite a while yet, I'm sure, they'll brush against my cheek from time to time. I don't know how long it will take for the wind of truth to blow them all away, and I'll probably get a bit upset about them occasionally. Also it may be I've got a scar or two from the whole episode, along with a few lost illusions.

But perhaps it's that tidy mind of mine again that wants to put some entries in the credit column to match these debits, Ted. And there *are* some credits, when I think it all over. Things are going to be different, and better, much better, for the Steeles—that's a big credit. And as for me, it's true I do know a little more than I did before about the darker side of even fairly decent human nature, and I don't like knowing it; but maybe that also means I know more about my own darker possibilities, too, and where to keep a guard. Because, while I never did what Jane did, I *can* look back and remember unkind gossip I've repeated, and that's a sin I don't believe I'll ever allow myself to fall into again.

Even the lost illusions, the finding out that a good many people seem to rather enjoy thinking the worst of other people, might have its compensations. I'm a little vague about this, but what I *think* I'm trying to say is that the best way to feel about folks is the way Grampa feels; he doesn't have "illusions," he has a realistic understanding of human nature at its best and worst, but along with this understanding goes a persistent love for it. He *loves* people; and he doesn't sit in judgment on them, he's sorry for them when they're wrong, and he'd like to help them if he could, but whether he can or can't, he goes on feeling kindly toward them.

And one thing I must never forget, one thing you must never let me forget, Ted, is that this love of people of his springs from and is a part of, his love for his Lord.

The scars? Oh, they're already healing! There won't be one left when you come home, I promise.

So good night (though it's almost good morning) and here goes all my love, flying across the Atlantic to you. Your Harriet.

10. THE FIRST GRANDCHILD TO MARRY

*T*HE wedding rehearsal was over, and the wedding party had separated with gay good-bys, and significant allusions to the "*next* time we meet." Now, at home in the family living room, the bride sank down in a big chair, kicked off her high-heeled shoes, and remarked pensively:

"It was a fine wedding rehearsal—don't you all think so? With just one small and unimportant lack—the groom wasn't there."

"Now, Harriet!" protested her cousin, Peter Fisher. "You would go and make a bitter remark like that just when I was thinking I'd done so well pinch-hitting for him that you probably hadn't missed him at all!"

Harriet Richards laughed. "You were wonderful, Pete. And it will come in very handy for you, no doubt, someday—knowing the ropes ahead of time. But the point is what about Ted? His wedding isn't in the dim and misty future—it's tomorrow. He's the one who needs the practice."

"But Pete's best man. And now with all this wide experience he can coach Ted," said Peter's pretty sister, Emily.

"What you've got to think about, my dear," advised the bride's uncle, Carl, "is that the fact that Ted's staying on his job one day longer gives him just that extra day for his honeymoon."

"Oh, of course it couldn't be helped," the bride conceded. "He hasn't been on this job long enough to ask for a lot of time off, not even when it's a matter of getting married . . . What time is it, somebody?"

It was her aunt, Anna Fisher, who answered. "Ten-thirty on the dot. Now relax, honey—plane's not due till after midnight. Couldn't you manage to take a little nap?"

"A *nap?* Before Ted comes?" asked Ted's bride in incredulous tones, as if she really weren't sure she'd heard such an outlandish suggestion correctly.

Anna smiled at her. "Yes, yes, I know, I'm getting old, but——" She stopped. "There's the telephone!"

"At ten-thirty? It must be from Ted——" Harriet had sprung to her feet and was across the room and speaking into the mouth-piece almost before anyone else had had time to make a move. "This is she—yes, this is Harriet Richards." . . . "Yes—go ahead!"

The others, listening with the inevitable slight anxiety which a late message produces, especially when an airplane trip is in-volved for a relative or close friend, noted with relief as she slowly returned to them that her face expressed merely disappointment, no darker emotion.

"It's a wire from Ted," she said disconsolately. "There's a storm there, and the planes are grounded. He said the next train would put him here too late to risk—and so he's going to drive all night —and he hopes to be here by seven in the morning." She sent them a glance which unconsciously appealed for reassurance. "I don't feel good about his driving all night alone—and with a storm some-where on the road, maybe."

"The only thing you got to worry about is whether he'll decide it's a good chance to get outa the whole deal and start driving in the opposite direction," said Grampa cheerfully, responding to that appeal in his own manner by making her smile—even if it was a rather small and reluctant smile.

"Ted's a good driver and very careful—he'll be all right," Carl assured her. "Tell you what—you let me put a mild bromide in a glass of hot milk for you and drink it and trot off to bed!"

"It won't help Ted one bit for you to stay awake worrying," Anna seconded. "Goodness, Harrie, he isn't going to take any chances at a time like this—you know that!"

Grampa patted her. "You pray for him real good and hard— that's your best bet for helping him."

Watching her with concerned affection, the little group saw the tension leave her face. Emily caught her arm, laughing.

"I'll put her to bed—I'll be her personal maid tonight! You can be fixing the milk, Mommy—and all the time *I'll* be making her feel very superior by telling her how long David and I have got to wait for *our* wedding!"

The storm must have blown over in the night, or else it did not reach Middleburg. For the next morning was so bright and fresh and clear that Pete woke the girls at six-thirty caroling just outside their door in a voice that made up in volume what it lacked in tone, " 'Tis your wedding morning, shining in the skies!"

Harriet sat up in bed, brown curls rumpled, hugging her knees with her slim arms, and looked at the other bed, where Emily also was just struggling out of the mists of sleep.

"It *is* my wedding morning!" she said in an awed voice. "And Ted may be here in half an hour!"

Emily sat up in bed and gazed at her solemnly. She was thinking that this morning Harriet looked different; not just sweet little Harriet, but someone—well, glamorous and a little mysterious, invested with a sort of strange, misty radiance. Maybe, thought Emily, it's because she's on the threshold of something new and wonderful and perhaps a tiny bit dangerous—and fell to wondering if *she* would look like that too when her day came.

"I guess," Harriet remarked dreamily, "other people *have* gotten married before."

Her cousin's impressed, slightly awed respect dissolved in laughter. "You sound pretty doubtful about it, though! Anyway—*you* haven't. Harrie—we'd better dress—Ted might get here a little early."

Sunlight was streaming through the house as they came downstairs, and the wedding presents and the bright litter of ribbons and wrappings lent everything an excitingly gala air. The girls joined Anna in the kitchen; breakfast was practically ready and it smelled wonderful.

"How long shall we wait for Ted, honey?" she asked, looking at Harriet with a smile that was a caress.

"Oh, not at all—you know how it is when a person is on a cross-country trip—I'm hardly looking for him before eight, really——"

She would, as Anna knew very well, be looking for him, and also listening for him, every minute.

At seven-thirty they decided to go ahead. Harriet, who was having a little difficulty looking easy and relaxed, had picked up the big tray of country ham and eggs and started toward the dining room with it when the doorbell rang.

"Ted!" she shrieked ecstatically—and for one terrifying instant the fate of the Fishers' breakfast hung precariously in the balance. Then she righted herself, regained control of the platter at the exact instant when all seemed lost, set it down on the counter, and with a laughing, radiant glance at the others, flew to the door.

A second later they heard her say, "Oh!" in an oddly deflated tone; and then she rejoined them, carrying a package wrapped in shiny white paper tied with pale-green ribbon. "It's only a wedding present!" she sighed.

"Only!" cried Peter. "That settles it! I'm going to take the one I've got for you right back to the store this morning!"

Harriet sent him a slightly sheepish smile. "I'm terribly grateful —but I thought it was Ted. Well—if he has to be *much* later, I'm sure he'll call."

"He'd *better* turn up," said Peter darkly. "I'm not prepared to carry this stand-in business too far. And by the way—I guess he's bringing the wedding ring. As best man I'm responsible for that, you know."

"Reminds me, Mother"—this was Emily—"I want you to check my maid-of-honor dress this morning sometime. Just to make sure everything's all right."

"We will. And Harriet's wedding dress, too——"

"What about my tux?" demanded Grampa. "I got troubles about that tux. It needed some alterin' and the tailor promised it back yesterday—and it hasn't turned up yet. Are my overalls clean, Anna? I might have to give the bride away in them."

"The more I listen to all of you," observed Anna placidly, "the more I realize how comparatively unimportant Harrie and Ted really are in this ceremony. It's the Fishers who're the central figures, that's plain."

Even with a wedding in the family, Carl and Grampa had to go to the drugstore. For the first two hours they were too busy to check on whether Ted had arrived; in fact, they took it for granted that he had done so. During a short lull at eleven o'clock, Grampa, picking up the newspaper for a glance, had just observed in a pleased tone, "We're on the society page, Carl—nice write-up of the wedding, and a big picture of Harriet," when the phone rang. Carl answered it, and returned two minutes later, with a somewhat worried expression.

"Well," he said slowly, "I just hope there's going to *be* a wedding!"

Grampa looked up quickly. "What? What's wrong?"

"That was Emily—Ted hasn't come yet and there hasn't been any word from him."

"Oh!" The two men exchanged a deeply concerned glance. "An accident, do you suppose?" Grampa asked quietly.

"I'm trying to believe that in that case we'd have heard. Dad, I think I'd better get hold of Chief Baldwin and ask him to check with the highway patrol. And maybe you'd better go on home— you might be some comfort to Harrie. I'm afraid she's upset. I'll put Bob and Smitty in charge here for the rest of the day. And I'll be home for lunch, tell Anna, to stay."

"You'll probably find Ted with us when you get there," said Grampa, trying to feel optimistic.

But Ted had not arrived by lunch, although Anna waited till one o'clock to serve it. Also, the only news they had had was indirect and negative; Chief Baldwin had reported that no accident involving a Theodore Stewart had been reported anywhere on the highway along which he was traveling. Harriet hardly ate at all; she was white now, and her eyes were frightened. The others kept glancing at her anxiously, and lunch, in spite of everybody's best efforts, was tense, with long intervals of silence, which was most unlike the Fishers.

The doorbell kept ringing; and each time there was that start of agonized hope and fear for Harriet, and each time, when it proved to be another present or a congratulatory telegram, there was the corresponding sickening disappointment. Just at the close of lunch Grampa's tuxedo came. At the same moment Emily answered the telephone and turned to report excitedly that Long Distance was calling Miss Harriet Richards.

This time they were all certain it must be from Ted. But it was only a distant friend calling to wish Harriet happiness by word of mouth, and when she turned from the telephone, Harrie was looking a little frantic.

"Something's happened!" she said desperately. "There's no use trying to fool ourselves with soothing bromides any longer—Ted wouldn't *do* this. It's after two—and our wedding is at six——" She stopped, her lips quivering. ·

It was Grampa again who furnished the diversion; deliberately, as they all knew. He had put on his tuxedo coat, and it was obviously three sizes, at least, too large for him.

"Will you all look at this?" he demanded in an outraged splutter. "What on earth did that tailor do to my coat? Or have I shrunk?"

He did indeed, with those sagging shoulders and dangling sleeves, look remarkably like a scarecrow, and they were glad of a chance to laugh. Even Harriet managed a wan smile. Another ring of the doorbell, and the return of the tailor's delivery boy, who had almost instantly discovered his mistake in leaving the wrong box, gave Grampa the chance to say to his granddaughter, "Well, *now*, Harrie, maybe I can do you credit when I give you away," thus expressing his confidence that the ceremony would take place in spite of mysterious delays.

"Usually," Anna said quickly, "no news really does mean good news in a case like this. It's going to be something quite simple when we do hear it, darling—like the car's breaking down in a place where he couldn't send a message or something."

"There isn't such a place on that highway," Harriet answered, looking faintly cheered, nonetheless.

But by three o'clock nothing anybody could suggest was able to cheer her. And for that matter, nobody else felt very cheerful either.

"Let's check the hem of your wedding gown," said Anna, her ordinarily placid face a little drawn. "It won't take more than ten minutes—but it ought to be done."

The dress was spread out on the bed; it looked, Harriet thought, like water with sunlight on it, as it gleamed and shimmered there. She asked, her voice low, "Do you really think I'm going to get to wear it, Aunt Anna?"

Anna said she did—with more heartiness than she felt; and she and Emily slipped the smooth ivory satin over Harriet's brown head expertly and zipped it. Then they surveyed it carefully, decided that it dipped a fraction of an inch just in front (a thing no uninitiated eye could have discerned) and while Emily stood off and directed, Anna took half a dozen small stitches. They had just concluded this operation when the bell rang again, and an instant later from below Carl's voice floated up, clearly enough for all three to hear.

"Why, Chief Baldwin! Come in—any news for us?"

With a wordless gasp, Harriet gathered up her train and fled, Anna and Emily close behind.

Chief Baldwin, who had barely begun to say, "Well, yes——" stopped, startled at the vision in glistening satin and orange blossoms which seemed to be literally hurling itself down the steps toward him—managing, Heaven knew how, not to trip herself up!

"Ted——" she cried. "*Ted*——"

"Why, you poor child!" exclaimed the Chief quickly. "Take it easy—the news is good!"

Harriet sagged, reaching out a hand to the banister, and Emily put a solicitous arm around her. The Chief regarded them sympathetically. "I guess you've been a pretty worried bunch. Well, he's okay and he ought to be here before five."

"Oh!" breathed Harriet, weak with relief. "*Oh!*" Then she rallied to inquire, "But where—on—earth—has he been?"

The Chief grinned broadly. "In jail."

"In jail!" It was practically a stunned chorus from Anna, Emily, Harriet, Grampa, Carl, and Peter, all at once.

The Chief chuckled, rather pleased with the sensation he had caused.

"It's quite a story! Seems he tried to save time last night by taking a short cut. That was a mistake—he lost his way, the road got bad, it was raining torrents, and finally his car got stuck in the mud. It was then four o'clock and still, he said, black as pitch. He decided that all he could do was to nap and wait for daylight to try to get away. Now here's the funny part—he was pretty tired, I guess, and the rain that didn't hit us kept on comin', and when he woke up, blest if it wasn't nearly nine o'clock."

"But—*jail?*" cried Harriet.

"I'm comin' to that." The Chief was not to be cheated of his tale. "Well, the car had sunk so deep in the mud he saw he'd have to have it hauled out. There wasn't any house near, but after walkin' a mile, he said, he came to a farmhouse. There wasn't any telephone but they gave him some breakfast and hitched up their mule, and what with the farmer and the mule and your lad, they got it out. By the time he got back to the highway it was noon. For quite a stretch along there the telephone wires were down, and he kept stopping, trying to find a place to telephone. Finally about one, he got past the damaged area. Well, by then, of course, I'd contacted the highway patrol. But their dispatcher got a little mixed and gave out a pickup order instead of a tracer. So when Ted stopped in this last place he got arrested."

"But when he explained——"

"Well, now—it's a little hard to explain to those boys. They get a lot o' explanations, you know, that aren't what you'd call exactly straight. They said all they could do was take him in as ordered, and he'd have to do the explainin' to somebody else."

"They wouldn't even let him *telephone* me?" asked Harriet between relief and indignation.

"They just aren't supposed to," said the Chief, a little apologetically. "All those arrangements have to be made by somebody higher up—at the jail. And what with the storm and the officers who were usually at the jail being off helping—well, there was considerable delay, and Ted's just now gotten hold of me. Of course, I straightened it all out with those other chaps in no time— and Ted asked me to come right over here and explain, said he was so bothered about the time getting scarce that he wouldn't even stop to telephone himself." He smiled at Harriet. "All's well that ends well, young lady—and you mustn't begrudge me the fun I'll have someday tellin' your children how I got their daddy out of jail on his wedding day!"

"Oh, goodness, tell them anything you like—I'm so terribly grateful——" She was crying a little, but her face and the smile she sent him were so radiant that the Chief half expected to see the combination produce a rainbow. "Now please, please, *everybody* keep their fingers crossed! Surely nothing *else* can happen!"

"Nothing will, I'm dead-sure," declared the Chief. "And tell Ted I won't wear my uniform to the wedding—don't want to scare him!"

With which, laughing heartily at his own joke, he said good-by.

The entire atmosphere of the house seemed to have changed. It had become a gay, excited place, filled with running up and down stairs, with activity and laughter and anticipation. Emily produced a brooch of her grandmother's for the "something borrowed" which the bride must wear—"and I do mean borrowed," she warned, "'cause I want it back!" Anna came up with an heirloom lace handkerchief for the "something old" and a dainty silk garter for the "something blue."

"And of course the wedding dress is the something new," said Harriet happily. "You know, honestly I feel like I'd been reprieved from——"

She spoke in a muffled tone for Emily and Anna had just slipped the gown over her head again and the last word was lost somewhere in those shining folds.

"Now sit down," Emily said importantly, "because I'm going to fix your hair—the dress messed it up. And then Mother, at the last, the very last, you help me get the veil and the wreath of orange blossoms on, and——"

At this moment an automobile horn blowing loudly in a series of toots that had a somewhat weird rhythm sounded just outside, and Harriet immediately sprang to her feet.

"That's his special signal—it's *Ted!*" she cried, and had started a wild dash to the door when she was forced to stop by the slim and determined figure of her aunt barring the way with outstretched arms.

"No, Harriet—you can't! You've got on your *wedding* gown——"

Harriet paused irresolutely, and Emily promptly reinforced her mother. "Of course you can't! Why, Harrie, it'd be *awful!* To let him see your wedding gown before you come down the aisle!"

"I s'pose you're right," groaned Harriet. She looked at them hopefully. "Couldn't I take it off and just run downstairs one *minute?*"

They told her firmly that she couldn't possibly, there wasn't time; and besides Ted himself had to get showered and dressed in a terrific hurry; and altogether, it was quite, quite out of the question.

"I'll go down and explain, honey," said Anna comfortingly. "Don't look so disconsolate. Goodness, Ted'll be around all the rest of your life."

When she got downstairs, Ted, unshaven, clothes rumpled and muddy, wearing a grin that was compounded in equal parts of relief, happiness, and sheepishness, was being greeted and teased with enthusiasm. They were crowded round him, wringing his hand, laughing at him, inquiring how he broke out of jail, demanding to know if somebody had sent him a file—and was it in a cake or a meat loaf?—when Anna broke it up.

"For mercy's sake, stop tormenting the boy!"

"Thank you, Aunt Anna!" He returned her kiss. "It may be funny now but it sure wasn't funny then! Where's Harriet?"

"Upstairs," said Anna. "Gracious, Ted, we're glad to——"

"I'm going up to see her——"

"You are *not.*" Anna caught his arm. "She's in her wedding gown —you'll have to wait for the ceremony."

"Oh, see here!" cried the outraged bridegroom. "Can't we forget about that old tradition—under the circumstances?"

"No, we can't!" She added with an evident sincerity that made Carl and Grampa smile, "It would be just terrible, Ted. She's got to—well, to *burst* on you as she comes down the aisle! Haven't you got any romance in your soul?"

"Not a bit," Grampa answered with a grin. "Any man that would sleep like the dead and be late on his own wedding day——"

"Never mind that!" The groom gave them a harassed glare. "You mean I really can't see Harriet?"

"You really can't—till you see her at church. And anyway—you've got to get ready yourself."

"I'll take you up—where's the ring?" asked Peter.

Ted reached in his pocket and his face suddenly went blank. In sympathetic dismay all the other faces went blank with his as he moaned, "Oh *no!* Nothing else could happen—not today!" and felt frantically in one pocket after another. The combined sigh of relief when he pulled a ring box from the fourth one might have been heard in the kitchen.

"I showed this to the police to prove I was really on my way to my wedding," he explained with a weak grin. "I was afraid for a minute I'd left it there." He mopped his brow and let out a long "Whew!"

"You come straight along," said Pete firmly, seizing his arm. "Before you sprain an ankle or have an epileptic fit or maybe even break out in leprosy spots! I don't put *anything* past you today." He was dragging him up the steps as he spoke, and he turned to shout at the others, "And I won't leave him alone even in the shower, I promise you. He'd probably manage to drown or electrocute himself!"

However, when they came down in a surprisingly short time, Ted was not even the worse for wear. In fact, he was very spick-and-span, in his new dress clothes and, Grampa assured him, "a fine-lookin' figure of a bridegroom." He added, "Pete says you didn't have any lunch. Now, I got some milk and crackers out here in the kitchen and you've just barely got time for 'em, so come along."

"They'll taste good," said Ted gratefully. "You look mighty distinguished, sir."

"Rather thought I did, myself," Grampa agreed with no false modesty. "Sorry your folks couldn't come, Ted."

"I'm sorry too. But Dad still can't get around with that broken hip—though we're sure now he'll be all right. And Connie, my stepmother—she's a fine girl and would like to come but she can't very well leave him with my little sisters under the circumstances—they're only three and five. We're planning to spend a day with them on our wedding trip."

"Well, that's fine," said Grampa, who approved of families sticking close together.

But Ted suddenly was not listening. He was looking at Grampa earnestly.

"Do you remember, sir, whether you were—well, scared—just before your wedding?"

Grampa laughed. "Do you think I wouldn't remember that no

matter how long ago it had been, Son? Yes, I was scared—are
you?"

"A little. Or—maybe it's not scared, exactly—maybe it's just—
shaky." The clear young eyes met Grampa's, a little shadow of misgiving in their depths. "All of a sudden it seems to me like I need
to grow up in an awful big hurry—and I wonder if I can. I'm going
to be a family man—responsible for someone else's happiness—and
I do want so much to make Harriet happy, but——" He paused. He
said soberly, "One of my best friends married before I went overseas. And I just heard the other day—his marriage has smashed.
His wife was discontented, they said, and homesick—well, I guess
nobody thinks that'll happen to him, but—it just makes you study
a little."

Grampa put his slender, strong, veined old hand on the young
man's arm. "It won't happen to you and Harriet, Ted," he said
quietly. "I don't know your friend and his wife—but I'll guarantee
they didn't have what you and Harriet have got, or things
couldn't've gone like that. I'll guarantee that they didn't have that
priceless ingredient you two have—a strong common faith. That's
what's going to make it certain that you and Harriet will weather
any storms that come."

"You truly believe that, sir?"

"With all my heart," said Grampa earnestly. "Because it means
your love for each other is backed up by all sorts of other things—
like kindness and patience and wanting what's worth while in life
instead of cheap pleasures or just money, and like knowing where
to go for help when problems come. The problems will come, you
can be sure of that, and just romance—well, it isn't enough to solve
them and get you over the humps, Son. That's why a lot of mar-
riages don't work out well—the bride and groom think all they
need to live happily ever after is bein' romantic about each other!
But people who've got what you and Harrie've got, whose religion
and church mean to them what yours mean to you—why, you've
nothin' in the world to worry about. Life may get hard, but it'll
always be rewarding—and love for each other is rooted in love for
your Lord, so it can't fail you——"

He stopped, watching the young face a little anxiously. How
hard it was to say effectively these things one felt and meant so

deeply! He wished humbly that he had at his command words that would be flaming and convincing. He said, "You and Harrie'll be all right, you'll be fine," and hoped fervently that Ted understood what he could not fully express.

"Dad! Ted!" Anna was standing in the door. She was dressed for the wedding, and she looked flushed and pretty. "Time to go!"

Grampa looked at Ted. "Ready?" he asked, smiling.

Ted's answering smile was a little shy, but the look of slight strain had left his face. "Why, yes, sir"—he summoned up a somewhat wavering grin—"I think I just might be able to go through with it now—if the bride's still willing. And—thank you, sir."

Anna and Carl and Freddie sat together on the side reserved for the relatives of the bride; the rest of the Fishers were all in the wedding. Someone sang; the organ played softly for a while; and then there was a pause—and the familiar notes of the wedding march began.

"It's always a thrill, no matter how often you hear it," thought Anna. "And it's always oddly moving, too. Because it represents one of those great human dramas, like birth, like death, which can never grow stale or dull." Now the ushers were marching up the aisle—there came David! What a handsome boy he was—he and Emily would be marrying next. . . . Anna sternly repressed a very small maternal pang. . . . And here were the bridesmaids! So young, grave with a sense of the importance of the occasion of which they were a part, yet all starry-eyed with excitement, the pretty things. Emily, as maid of honor, would come last—just before the bride. . . . Oh, there she was! Bless her! Emily's mother felt a glow of pride in her first-born. Not just in her beauty—though today, with the candlelight falling on her fair hair, she was very lovely—but because she was candid and honest and sweet and wholesome. . . .

Then Anna forgot David and the bridesmaids and even her own Emily; for the sudden, dramatic clarion notes which meant the bride had entered the sanctuary were sounding. And something stirred in the roots of Anna's hair and ran down her back-bone. Dear Harriet—she was coming now, on Grampa's arm. And Ted had emerged from the small room behind the pulpit with Pete. Now his head had lifted, his eager, steadfast gaze was on his bride, and she was answering that look with one of utter trust. It was the complete dedication on both the young faces that brought this lump into your throat, Anna thought suddenly. Youth, almost inevitably, is self-centered to a certain extent—it hasn't learned to spend itself for others, it is too intensely concerned with its own affairs. But here, now, she was watching the very hour, the very moment, when for both of these young people, this boy and girl, still in their early twenties, somebody else had begun to matter more to them than they mattered to themselves.

The bride had reached the altar; Emily was holding the bridal bouquet; the music was playing very softly now, and the Pastor's warm, friendly voice rose above it as he stood a little above and before Ted and Harriet, his quiet, kind eyes looking down on them affectionately.

"'And both Jesus was called, and his disciples, to the marriage,'" he said. "That is from the gospel of St. John, Chapter 2, verse 2. You know the story of the wedding feast at Cana—and perhaps you have thought sometimes wistfully as you made out the guest list for your own wedding how fortunate that young couple were to be able to have the Savior as a guest at theirs. But, dear friends, you also may invite Him to your marriage—and it is an invitation which He never refuses. Be sure, too, that wherever and whenever He has been invited, all down through all the years since God sent Him to the world, invited not just as a wedding guest but as a permanent partner forever after in the marriage, it has always been the same—He has always, always come to bless. His forgiving and cleansing Presence has thereafter brightened every joy, hallowed every sorrow, been a lamp unto the feet and a light unto the pathway, filled that home with a happiness not at the mercy of circumstance, with a serenity too deep to be disturbed. And so, at this hour, when you, Harriet, and you, Ted, pledge your lives to one another, I pray that you will also pledge them anew to Him, and that He will, by your permanent invitation, abide in your home as long as you live, until you shall one day join Him in His."

He raised his head a little, clasping his Bible, and closed his eyes. A long bar of gold fell across his face from one of the stained-glass windows. He prayed, "Even so, come Lord Jesus. Be

Thou their guest, their guardian friend, their only Lord and Savior. Amen."

He opened his eyes, smiled down at them with tenderness, and began, "Dearly Beloved . . ."

Harriet had not wanted a big wedding reception. "Just a supper at your house, Aunt Anna, with only the family before we leave," she'd begged. So that, of course, was the way it was. The only exception was David—on the ground that he was so very near to being "family." Anna had somehow found time, during that confused day, to fill the house with flowers. Devoted friends and neighbors had insisted on serving the wedding dinner, keeping themselves unobtrusively in the background. The bride and groom sat side by side at the head of the table; they were neither eating nor talking much. Their happiness wrapped them like an invisible garment, setting them apart. They did not withdraw themselves, their responses were warm and quick, but just for this moment they were aware of the others mostly as a sort of beloved background.

The self-appointed waitresses had taken away the sliced turkey and ham, the cranberries and the tiny peas, the avocado salad and homemade rolls; and now, smiling, they brought in a three-tiered wedding cake, decorated in flowers and wedding bells, and placed it before Harriet and Ted.

Carl stood up, rapping with his fork for attention.

"And now—if our bride and groom can slide down the rainbow, to wax poetic, from the edge of that rosy cloud where they are so obviously perching and join us poor earth-bound mortals—why, I think," said he with a grin, "it's time to cut the wedding cake!"

They looked at him with smiles that were polite and a little vague, as if they weren't quite sure what he'd said, but knew it had been intended to be amusing and wanted to respond properly. Then they stood up, Ted picked up the knife, placed it in Harriet's right hand, put his own over it, and together they cut the first slice.

Grampa, sitting at the bride's right hand, found that he was exercising that ability which grows keener as one grows older, to vividly recreate the past. He never had, and did not now, in the ordinary acceptance of that phrase "live in the past." His interest in the present was too intense for that, and his share in it still demanded all his powers. But lately he had been aware that time had telescoped rather oddly for him; so that he seemed, in a sense, to be "living" in three eras, past, present, and future.

Well, this was the first of the grandchildren to marry, and an old gentleman was entitled to be a little sentimental on such an occasion, he thought! This year, too, if Mary had been here, they would have celebrated their golden wedding. His heart would hold the anniversary, just as it still held, every day, the memory of her. Held it happily. For when she left him, he had been able to tell himself, and to make it hold (not that it did not take a certain amount of resolution at times—but in that resolution he had never faltered) that after his forty years with her he would be a pretty ungrateful specimen and untrue to the faith they had both cherished if he could not wait patiently and cheerfully, watching her children and his, for the few years that were left until he would join her.

It had been a very long time ago that he and she had been where these youngsters, Harriet and Ted, were tonight; but Grampa thought, half amused at himself, here he was feeling just like the old folks at whom he had politely wondered when he was young, the ones who kept shaking their heads and saying in a bewildered way, "Seems like it was just yesterday!" The time did indeed appear very short. Smiling a little (and not knowing that he smiled) Grampa realized, too, that as he turned his gaze back over those years, something had happened to them; as if he somehow saw them from a different angle. He had always known that even when life was hard and sad it was a gift of infinite value; but tonight, from this distance, there was more than that . . . It was that in a curious manner the dark spots now looked to him as good as the bright ones, because the whole had blended to form a pattern that would have been less beautiful had it been all one shade. You couldn't consider them separately any more, these dark areas, but only as parts of the entire picture.

He remembered the death of their first baby—and Mary, just nineteen, clinging to him and sobbing. . . . And yet, finally they had found that nothing had ever before made them so aware of the reality of a spiritual world and the actuality of the soul's immortality as this grief which was so bitter at the time, so hard to take. Moreover, this keener awareness they had given later to their other children; so in a way, Grampa reflected, you might say that the spirit of that first, dearly loved baby had lived on in the home which for a few short months he had blessed with his laughter, deeply influencing for great good the lives of the brother and the two sisters who had never seen him. Could he have done more with his life, small Stephen, if he had lived to be old, even?

And there was the time when the business into which Grampa had sunk his whole capital had been on the brink of failure, and in despair he had told Mary that perhaps she had better take the children and go back to her parents, since he was apparently unable to support her and them. He'd thought he'd known his girl after ten years of marriage—but he had learned things about her then that had given all of his life a richer color forever after; about her courage, about her loyalty, above all about how deep ran the current of her serenity, fed by what an inexhaustible spring!

The panorama kept unfolding . . . So many ups and downs, he thought—small ones to laugh at later, like some of the vicissitudes of the children's adolescence, and big ones, which seemed near for a space to breaking their hearts, like the sudden death of Harriet's sweet mother; but all combining now to form that clearly perceived whole which had been joyous and adventurous. For now that the pattern of his life was so nearly complete, Grampa felt, with humility, that it was a good pattern. Good in spite of many human errors and the need to seek forgiveness often, because running through it all like a bright scarlet thread, binding it together, giving it purpose and meaning and motive and a constant sense of the importance and zestfulness of living, was their love and their faith, his and Mary's—their love for each other and for God, their faith in Him and in His Son, Jesus Christ.

And in this faith they had raised their children; and the children, in their turn, had passed it to *their* children; and now in his inner vision, Grampa saw the torch still being handed on. Tonight it was these beloved two who received it into their strong young hands; and Grampa felt a perfect confidence that they too would pass it down the line with light undimmed. . . .

There was a little touch on his arm. The bride was looking at him, leaning toward him. Her eyes (Mary's eyes, he had often thought, gold-brown and deeply intuitive) were on his face with a grave, intent sweetness.

"Grampa darling," she asked gently, "what are you dreaming about?"

Grampa patted the slender hand. Even more vividly than before, time did that trick of merging for him. All that had gone before for him lived on in him, he was made of it; yet he was also vitally a part of this moment itself and it was part of him; and at the same instant his whole being reached forward eagerly in anticipation to something splendid, the greatest and richest experience of all, still ahead.

"Why, about the past, I reckon, Harrie," he said. "And even more about the present. And most of all about the future."

She did not quite know what he meant; how could she, he thought? But she smiled at him with much affection and a little bewilderment, and Grampa smiled back. He was filled with tenderness for her and for them all; filled, and fulfilled, and deeply content.